GEMINI ELECTRIC

Book 2

THE AURORA CHRONICLES

DANIEL K. JAMES

Published in the United States by Daniel K. James

Contact the publisher at:
dkj@danielkjames.com

Visit the author/publisher on the web at:
www.danielkjames.com

Cover and interior format by Daniel K. James
Editing by Carrie Ann Lahain

ISBN: 978-0-9983850-2-0

Dedication

To Patty Coaley, the boldest visionary I've ever had the pleasure of calling a friend. You've not only taught me the true essence of dreaming big, but you continually demonstrate how to bring leading-edge ideas to the forefront for the benefit of all the world. You never cease to amaze me.

Thank you for giving me ample reason to believe in miracles.

chapter

1

Stay where you are.

Shane read the four little words as they floated above the face of his watch. He didn't have to look to see who sent the message. It came from Aurora. He'd tried to get ahold of her for the better part of the last hour since David hadn't bothered to answer his voice mail. Thank God at least *somebody* was paying attention.

Busy stuffing an overnight suitcase with three more shirts than necessary, he had somehow managed to refrain from panicking.

Until now.

"What do you mean?" Shane posed the question with unpleasant suspicion into the watch's mic, wishing he didn't have to wait for a response via text. "I thought I was supposed to meet you and David at Bill Rucker's condo. I was headed there now."

Still expecting to leave the house shortly, he tucked his laser bristle toothbrush and sonic shaver into the suitcase's front pocket. A change of plans rarely happened on account of good news, which was the exact type he wanted to hear. Needed to hear. Prayed to hear.

I'm still trying to determine what's happening. David wants to reach out to you, but he can't right now. Please stay at the house until I figure out what's going on.

Shane found that last message oddly disquieting. David never let his watch die. He lived his entire life prepared to skirt around any inconvenience. What would keep him from calling the most important person in his life? An exhausted battery seemed the least likely of scenarios. Sure, he could have been in a place with little to no cell signal, but not for an hour straight. David had specifically stated that he'd make it to Bill's condo on foot in twenty minutes tops in order to be with Aurora, long before Shane could possibly finish gathering their change of clothes.

"What's wrong with David? Tell me why all of a sudden I'm not supposed to leave the house?"

Give me a minute.

Her response came hastily, as if she wanted to explain but somehow couldn't. Shane hated the suspense. His luck seemed out of whack ever since the moment fate had forced him to relinquish his ice cream so that Aurora could clamber up the giant wheel and play superhero. What was so wrong about letting something go right for a change?

"Please tell me you're okay then."

No response.

Shane waited for what seemed like more than double the requested sixty seconds until finally the tiny light above the twelve on his watch flickered to signify an incoming text.

The FBI has surrounded the vehicle. When I know more, I'll tell you.

"That's not fair, Aurora," Shane blurted out. "You know damn well you've got me worried like crazy. Don't leave me hanging like this." He realized he couldn't force her to answer. She wouldn't purposely withhold information from him. Unless David had told her to. In that case, yelling still wouldn't do him any good. Whether he badgered her or not, she'd respond in due time. But that didn't make him feel any less sick to his stomach after hearing mention of the FBI. No three letters instilled greater unease.

His watch flickered again.

They're taking me out of the car.

"What?" Shane wanted to throw up from the tightening knot in his gut. He hadn't gotten any relief regarding David's whereabouts. Now he had to fret about Aurora's? "The FBI? Tell me where they're taking you." He closed the suitcase, no longer caring about having a matching outfit to wear tomorrow. Instead, he wondered where he'd last put his wallet. Why had he taken it out of his back pocket in the first place? If ever he had the ability to snap his fingers and make things go smoothly for a change, about now would be a good time.

I'm in the Durango Electric parking lot.

"Why? Is David with you? Why aren't you at Bill's?" Shane felt sorely out of the loop and completely helpless, standing there in the middle of the bedroom. Thankfully, as if he'd heard a whisper from his mostly absent guardian angel, he remembered that he'd set his wallet down on the bathroom sink and ran for it.

I'm with Bill. I don't know where David is. Last I knew he was on the sidewalk in front of the Mirage.

He believed her. He had no choice. She'd obviously gotten stuck in a bad situation, and he assumed that, based on his current streak of misfortune, he'd lose communication with her any second. "What do you need me to do? It sounds like you're in serious trouble."

Shane couldn't wait for an answer. Staying in the house another minute would give him a nervous breakdown. He had to focus. What would David tell him to do? Aurora's initial suggestion of staying put seemed like the worst idea possible. The two people in his life whom he cared about most had gotten swept away by the tides of grave peril. If Aurora couldn't give him a better suggestion than doing absolutely nothing, he'd take matters into his own hands.

They've put handcuffs on me, and they're checking me for weapons.

"I'll kill them!" Shane's blood boiled at the thought of strange men touching Aurora. He imagined himself going ballistic on the barbarians even if it meant that he'd be shot.

They're being gentle with me. I can tell that they're afraid of me. I'm not in danger. But I think David is.

That was all Shane needed to hear. If he couldn't rescue Aurora, he'd find David, or at least die trying. With his adrenaline pumping like a firehose, he refused to even consider sitting around and waiting. *Wait around for what?* He grabbed his overnight bag, bolted for the garage and jumped into the Mogollon.

"Take me to the Mirage," an exasperated Shane spoke into the dashboard microphone.

The garage door opened, and the vehicle exited out toward the driveway loop before turning onto the quiet neighborhood street. Unfortunately, it couldn't drive fast enough to match the lightning pace of its passenger's runaway heart.

"Reroute via the highway, and *pronto*." Shane knew it would have avoided the expressway altogether since the shortest distance to the Strip consisted entirely of surface streets. But if he wanted to risk speeding, he might as well do it where he could really test the true extent of the Mogollon's lawlessness.

The vehicle cruised through a red light, having detected zero oncoming traffic. When it came to the 215 entrance ramp, Shane noticed it accelerating in mere seconds to ninety miles per hour. *Holy Batmobile!* Nobody drove this fast. They couldn't. Vehicles had to obey all speed limits and traffic laws. But when your husband made a career as an electrical genius, rules had a way of bending. The only time he recalled David ever using the secret *pronto* command was when they'd rushed Shane's mother to the hospital after she'd suffered a stroke five years ago. Other than that one time, the two of them had sat happily behind the dashboard going whatever speed the cyber navigational system dictated. An occasion had to truly warrant reckless speed. Otherwise, the consequences of circumnavigating the law created much too great a risk.

Tonight was one such occasion. Who knew what kind of jeopardy David faced? No, Shane didn't know if he could truly help him once he got there. But the mere thought of arriving a minute too late to even try only fed his fire.

Weeoooh weeoooh weeoooh!

"Oh, for crying out loud," Shane yelled over his shoulder, seeing the flashing lights of a police car behind him. "Don't they understand this is an emergency?"

Shane figured he could easily talk his way out of any criminal penalties for manning a rogue automated vehicle. He only had to prove that he hadn't driven it himself, that it had malfunctioned on its own, and that he'd get it inspected right away. But that's not what brought him to the brink of a nervous breakdown. He didn't have time to waste on a police stop, not when David still hadn't answered the last fifteen times Shane had attempted to reach him. No. He couldn't afford a single delay.

Then he realized that the Mogollon hadn't slowed down. *At all.* He'd expected it to have come to a complete halt by now. In 2049, nobody outran the law. The police ultimately retained control of anyone and everyone's vehicle. A car stopped whenever they wanted it to stop. Or so Shane thought. A quick glance at the speedometer, and he realized that the Mogollon had actually increased its speed by another thirty miles an hour. *Better hold on tight!* Thank God nobody else was on the expressway except him, the lone policeman, and two other unsuspecting cars he'd just flown past.

He didn't want to break the law. He most certainly didn't want to end up in a courtroom. But telling the Mogollon to suddenly step on the brakes didn't seem like the right thing to do either. He reminded himself that his mission took precedent. Failing at it seemed a worse fate than a large fine or a few nights in jail. Let them arrest him at least after he got to the Mirage. Maybe he could actually make the color orange work out in his favor. On the other hand, he'd only have to consider the change in wardrobe if he got caught.

Onward he went. Life couldn't possibly get crazier than it already had. Thankfully, with no other cars in sight, he'd become a danger only to himself behind the dashboard of a truly righteous and wild machine. The incredible speed thrilled him as he witnessed the Mogollon taking one maniacal chance after another.

A second cop car appeared from an upcoming onramp. Clearly, the authorities refused to back off. They wanted to stop something that they couldn't control, whereas Shane just wanted to hang on for the ride of his life. He'd never flown this fast, and he kind of liked it. He'd probably enjoy it even more so if he somehow managed to stop worrying over David. When he looked in the rearview mirror and saw that neither of the cop cars had kept pace with his still accelerating vehicle, he took a second to breathe. He hadn't expected them to give up so easily.

Unfortunately, they hadn't.

At the next onramp, a squadron of four very official-looking black vehicles waited. They rode up right alongside him as he sailed down the highway.

"I can't do anything to stop it," Shane mouthed the words toward the perfectly opaque tinted windows of the monstrous SUV to his left.

"Stop your vehicle," came a booming voice from a speaker embedded in its sleek roof. "Or we will stop it for you."

Are they idiots? Shane thought he'd explained perfectly that he had no choice in the matter. "It won't slow down," he yelled for real, this time through the open window.

He looked ahead of him about a mile down the freeway to see a line of rubber barricades. *How could they have set them up so fast?* Then he realized they must have closed all the entrance ramps, hence the reason why he hadn't seen anyone on the roadways aside from his pursuers.

The Mogollon finally slowed, weaving to the far right lane before positioning itself behind the motorcade. The other vehicles slowed as well, but they were too late. Shane rode up the approaching exit ramp, breaking through a pitifully weak wooden barrier. He struggled to catch his breath as the four black tank-like cars came to a halt a hundred feet in front of their own impenetrable wall beneath the overpass.

Resuming normal speed, Shane's trusty ride merged

beautifully onto Las Vegas Boulevard, effectively disappearing into a sea of indistinguishable traffic. He let out a short-lived sigh of relief. Outrunning the police had never been a goal of his, but he felt grateful to have made it out alive. Turning his attention back to the road in front of him, he quivered not knowing if David could say the same thing.

The Mirage was still four miles away, and the heavy volume of tourists everywhere made for a painfully slow crawl. He'd known that getting off at the boulevard would make for a virtual dead end, but the cops had left him little choice.

"Take the underground," Shane commanded into the dashboard microphone. He had yet to take the subterranean passage underneath the resort corridor. Open for ten years now, the tunnel charged users a fee of thirty dollars to bypass the traffic up above and head directly to their intended destination. Truth be told, he would have willingly paid a hundred times that amount if it meant getting to David quicker.

The Mogollon shifted to the far left lane and sped beneath an archway meant to capture the license plate number for billing purposes. No need to slow things down with a toll booth when the goal was to speed things up. Once in the actual tunnel, the traffic flowed at a pace typical for the interstate. Exits were clearly marked according to hotel instead of number. A blue neon sign with the words *Mandalay Bay* came first, then *Tropicana*, *MGM Grand*, and *Aria*. As soon as Shane spotted the exit for the Mirage, the Mogollon hightailed it toward the ramp and rose back to the boulevard's surface.

Shane thought he'd won for a minute. But the Mogollon braked on the incline, trapped behind a train of more than a dozen other unlucky vehicles. Was it only this particular hotel? He couldn't help but speculate if he'd been better off had he instead gotten off one exit prior—at Caesars Palace. Torturing himself with alternate possibilities had become a favorite pastime of his ever since his first memorable bout of bad luck at the county fair as a child, when he got stuck for three hours atop the crest of the hill on the Log Jammer. From that moment on, he questioned each little decision that led him to an uncomfortable outcome. He didn't know why he indulged in the pointless game, other than the fact that it helped pass the time.

When the line of vehicles finally inched along enough for the Mogollon to reach the surface, Shane shook his head at the road before him. Cars everywhere idled at yet another standstill. Emergency vehicles blocked the entire road in front of the hotel with barricades similar to the ones the Mogollon had pulverized en route to his destination. Nobody could get close to the scene. Not with their cars anyways. It looked horrendous, like an urban warfield after battle. He feared the worst.

Finally seeing for himself what Aurora couldn't fully explain, he admitted that it didn't make sense. Not even after he'd found himself in the midst of it all. To him, everything around him seemed like noise. A mere distraction to prevent him from discovering the truth. *Why couldn't he get closer? On second thought, did he really want to?*

"Aurora, are you there?" Shane spoke into his watch,

feeling desperate for answers. He knew the likelihood of an immediate response. Pretty much zero. Trying, however, couldn't hurt. Not when he had nothing else left to lose.

As expected, a whole minute ticked by without a word of acknowledgement from the only one that might conceivably know anything about David. What lasting excitement Shane had felt from outrunning the cops had now all but vanished, replaced instead by inescapable doubt and fear. Thankfully, traffic started to crawl forward enough so that the Mogollon could pull itself up the main drive toward the front entrance.

Damn it!

He stared at a red sign announcing that the valet lot had reached capacity. If David taught him anything, however, it was never to take the word *no* as the final answer. A quick glance to his left revealed a single parking spot with a sign in front of it marked *Deliveries Only.*

That'll do! He'd likely not stick around for more than a few minutes. If anyone asked, he'd tell them that he had to deliver chocolates and balloons to a room. Having directed the Mogollon to seize the opportune spot, he climbed out of the vehicle with the battery engaged and the lights still on, which made it seem like his vehicle belonged there. To prevent the possibility of theft, he set a passcode on the dashboard before shutting the door.

Shane took a few running steps before stopping dead in his tracks. From across the volcano's lagoon, looking toward the empty, roped-off sidewalk, he saw a pair of medics rolling a stretcher into the back of an ambulance.

Was that him? It sure as hell looked like him! Shane had to get closer. A rope wouldn't stop him, and neither would men with badges—not with David's life on the line. "That's my husband!" Shane darted around the water feature, weaving in and out of stunned tourists and hopping over a plastic blockade.

Once on the cleared sidewalk, he stopped to catch his breath. The ambulance had since driven off, its siren blaring in the distance. Only one thing Shane could see now: an unmistakable trail of red where, moments ago, the EMT workers had whisked away his faithful friend and lover.

"You have to leave, sir." A police officer came up behind him. "This is a crime scene."

He wanted to yell, to let out a bloodcurdling scream for the man he admired after all these years, the one who'd met a terribly unforeseeable fate. But nothing came from his half-opened mouth. Nothing except a sigh of disbelief and a wave of exhaustion.

Despite all the obstacles, Shane hadn't arrived too late to get an answer regarding David's whereabouts. He'd made it just in time.

chapter

Aurora recalled the cold, brightly lit entrance as if she'd walked through it ten thousand times. She knew her way around Durango Electric perfectly despite only having walked its corridors twice before, both times in the care of David. But she couldn't think about him right now. She reserved all her thought processes for one purpose only—getting out in one piece.

"This way, please." Bill looked behind him and smiled at Aurora, whom he escorted like a criminal, keeping her surrounded by eight armed men in black suits. "We don't need any little darlings getting lost today."

A tempting possibility. With all the surveillance around her, she resolved to come up with an even better solution for regaining her freedom. For now she stayed quiet and went with the flow. She knew that abandoning the gruff, authoritarian entourage at this juncture would likely end in her immediate dismemberment.

"Is David in that ambulance?" Shane messaged via CADI, which suddenly made Aurora stop and pause a second.

"No time for breaks, little lady," said the man immediately to her right in a snarky tone not normally used toward well-mannered children.

"I'm sorry, Shane. I don't know anything about an ambulance," Aurora messaged in reply as she resumed pace alongside her captors. Again, she purposely removed any thought of David from her mind. Focus belonged on regaining her liberty. If she didn't stay tuned into her surroundings, she risked losing all future contact with Shane.

"Here we are, gentlemen—and madam." Bill winked at Aurora before placing his palm against a glass panel positioned beside a set of double doors. The scanner glowed green and the doors swung open to reveal a small boardroom with a long table and twelve chairs. "Let's all go in and have seat, shall we?"

"Thank you." Aurora smiled back as she entered, understanding all too well the importance of remaining agreeable. She then took a seat in the middle of the table nearest the entryway.

The eight resolute men filed in behind her, making sure

to close the door before occupying the chairs on either side and directly across from her. They didn't take chances, apparently. So neither could she. Suddenly, the idea of getting back up and running for the door seemed pathetically tragic.

"Where are you?" She messaged Shane now that she finally felt somewhat secure in her new environment.

"I'm outside the Mirage. Where should I be?"

Aurora withheld suggesting that he should've heeded her advice and just stayed home. What's done was done. He had every right and reason to leave the house. She only wished to spare him the terrible shock of witnessing a ghastly scene, which she herself had to quit replaying in her own memory. "Are you okay?"

"I'll be fine as soon as I know where David is."

"I still don't know." Aurora looked around the room and saw that each of the nine men, including Bill Rucker, had sat down. The boss, not surprisingly, put himself at the head of the table, leaving a vacant seat on either side of him. She couldn't help but notice that all eyes were on her. "I'll inform you just as soon as I'm aware. Please excuse me. I have to go now."

"We're so glad to have you with us, Aurora." Bill poured himself some water from the tall cylindrical glass pitcher in front of him. "I'm sorry it took a little longer than anticipated to finally get us to where we are."

"Where's David?" She asked calmly and without any hesitation.

"We'll get to your questions eventually." He retrieved a

DimensionTab from his briefcase and set it on the table face up. "But if you don't mind, we have a few questions for you."

Aurora sat back in her chair taking note of the red exit sign above her head. A shame the room had only one. "Certainly. I'll do my best to answer them."

Bill laughed, almost uncontrollably—probably due in part to the bottle of champagne he'd just polished off in the limo. "How does a little girl like you climb a six hundred foot wheel and live to tell about it?"

"But I haven't told anyone about anything." Aurora paused to get her bearings. "I'm not sure what you mean." Her statement did nothing to abate Bill's awkward chuckling fit. She saw a few of the agents in the room joining in the laughter, but almost as if out of their own growing discomfort rather than any actual hilarity.

"I didn't know you were such a lively comedian, Aurora." Bill turned on his DimensionTab, and a bright white glow appeared around it. "What I meant to ask was if you'd care to tell us a little more about yourself. I don't think anyone here knows you as well as we should."

She looked around the room, glancing momentarily at each man's face. They'd all stopped laughing, and they appeared friendly, but their wide smiles lacked any semblance of trustworthiness. What did they really want from her? Whatever it was, she'd be sure to tell them the exact opposite. "My name is Aurora, and I'm eight years old. I'm from Winter Beach, Florida. Right now I live with my Uncles David and Shane. I'm in the third grade, and I go to school at Wilson Cook Elementary."

"The girl knows her story." Bill cleared his throat and reached for his water glass. "Thank you, Aurora. Now if I may, I'd like to ask you some more specific questions. Hopefully they won't be too difficult."

The door opened before he could say another word, and in walked a man in a lab coat, who looked to be no more than thirty-five years of age.

"So sorry I'm late," he said, taking a seat next to Bill. "I had to say goodnight to my kids."

"Not to worry." Bill patted the man's shoulder before turning his attention back to the rest of the room. "Everyone, I'd like to introduce Trent Nilson, Durango Electric's new Director of Design and Innovation."

Aurora stared into the young man's hazel eyes from across the table. They matched the neatly trimmed hairstyle that framed his long, angular face. He didn't seem like the type who would hurt the man who had created her. Did the two of them know each other? She hadn't heard David ever mention his name before. Then again, David most likely never suspected he'd be replaced by someone almost fifteen years his junior. Why was she the one expected to answer questions all of a sudden? She had a hundred of her own that required answers.

"You must be Aurora," Trent said, breaking the silence that filled the room after the all-too-brief introduction. "I've heard a lot about you. You're quite the wonder girl!"

"Thank you." She didn't really care much now about being perceived as sweet and polite. She only meant to maintain a sense of civil decorum. "Where is Christina?"

"Who's that?" Trent asked with obvious befuddlement.

"I think she's referring to Christina Daily, the department's administrative assistant," Bill whispered, leaning in toward Trent's ear before standing up from his seat and walking to the door to close it. "I wouldn't worry much about her, Aurora. She's probably at home getting ready for bed, don't you think? But thank you for reminding me. I need to see Ms. Daily in my office first thing tomorrow morning."

Aurora didn't say anything in response. No reason to give them further information when they clearly wouldn't give her any in return. Instead she brought her attention to one of the suited men as he struggled to open a bag of peanuts. Saving her questions for later, she resolved to figure out a way to escape immediately.

Battery power at twenty-nine percent.

An idea came to her as CADI informed her of her low energy reserves. If she couldn't physically vanish from her confines, she'd leave via a virtual exit. No sense in staying awake only to play the role of a corporate plaything.

"Now that Trent has joined us, I think it's time we get to those important questions." Bill returned to his seat and looked across the table at Aurora. "How did a small and unassuming girl like you get to be so smart?"

She could practically smell the phoniness of the question. *What an utter waste of time.* Then again, Bill was a successful businessman, which meant that he used his time impeccably. *And so did she.* "Some people are born with special gifts that make them appear smarter than others.

The truth is that we're all born with a unique set of attributes that makes every one of us brilliant in our own right. Therefore, the question should never be about how smart other people are, but rather how they can be helped to nourish their inherent level of genius in order to share it with others."

Bill neglected to respond, stroking his chin in contemplation. Had she not provided an acceptable answer? Did he actually expect her to mention her secrets? If he did, he'd have to try harder. A *lot* harder. Only an amateur would reveal a winning hand before the game had even begun.

"You're not only smart," Trent spoke up this time, "you're also incredibly athletic for a girl your age. Where does a kid like you train in order to attempt such death-defying feats?"

It seemed like a fair question—if she weren't currently being held against her will in a tiny room full of strangers. Perhaps in a different forum, she'd at least entertain the idea of being more candid. But these men didn't deserve her openness. Not after what had happened to David. "My mother and I, we used to swim with the sharks when I lived with her off the coast of Florida. When there are sharks in the water next to you, you learn the true meaning of inner strength and fearlessness."

She'd told a giant fib, of course, a rather suitable one. Whether or not she'd convinced anyone of her tall tale didn't matter. They seemed intrigued by her mere presence. In fact, if they liked her show all that much, she could easily entertain the poor fools for hours—provided a dead battery didn't shut her down first.

"Let me see if I understand you correctly." Bill touched a button on the DimensionTab to play a holographic video of Aurora standing atop a familiar giant wheel. "You claim that swimming with some scary sharks ultimately made you into an expert climber capable of scaling our beloved Sky Roulette?"

"Well, there's obviously more to it than that," Aurora said, rolling her shoulders down and back to reestablish her poise. "But I didn't want to bore you with unnecessary details."

"I assure you—you're anything but boring," Bill said as the confined room filled again with more chuckling. "I'd love to ask you a more serious question though. What is it that makes you so willing to put yourself in harm's way in order to save people you've never met?"

Aurora stared at the image of herself in the hologram, watching as she worked to disable the Cockroach Blast Box. How on earth did they get this video footage? What purpose did it serve except to remind her that anonymity would be a distant memory, unless she could somehow eventually swim her way to that lonely island in the South Pacific? "The thing that surprises me about your question is that you felt the need to ask it in the first place. Wouldn't you help people if their fate rested in your hands?"

"I would," the graying man said with a kind disposition, one that only served to hide an awful truth. "You're absolutely right. And that's what we find so interesting. Children don't think like you. They don't yet have the capacity to understand something as complex as fate."

Aurora begged to differ. The kids in her third grade class certainly seemed to know more about the grownup world than perhaps the grownups themselves wanted to admit. But now was not the time to start a debate. "I think it's safe to say that children exhibit qualities that seem shocking to adults who aren't accustomed to being around young people."

"Case in point, Aurora." Bill turned off the DimensionTab and tucked it in the pocket on the front of his briefcase. "We likely have a lot to learn from young spring chickadees such as yourself."

"Shane, I need a favor," Aurora messaged while simultaneously giving Bill her seemingly undivided attention. "When you get this text, I need you to drive to that giant bagel across the street from Durango Electric."

Bill folded his hands and placed them on the spot where the tablet had rested moments ago. "I think we have time for one last question if you don't mind."

The illusion of choice didn't fool Aurora who nodded her head in deft compliance.

"How did David manage to control you so perfectly?"

Funny how people were so quick to relegate her to the role of puppet. Were they under the impression that he still managed to somehow pull her strings? If so, maybe she stood a chance of seeing him again. Either way, she refused to give them any hint about her internal processor. Even if they took her apart piece by piece, they still wouldn't get to the heart of her. "I need you to put those peanuts away, sir." She looked at the suited man across from her who had just succeeded in tearing open his little snack.

"Why?" He looked at her dumbfounded as if she'd asked him to stop breathing.

The room suddenly filled with the loudest coughing sound any of the men had probably ever heard before. Aurora made a terrible choking noise as she stood up from her seat, her hand pressed against her chest. Of course, she had no air inside her to begin with, but they didn't know that. For all they knew, the cacophony coming from the speakers imbedded in her mouth signalled the verge of collapse, or worse.

"For God's sake, put those damn things away!" Bill stood up from his seat, looking ready to lunge toward the agent if he didn't heed the warning.

The coughing continued, and everyone covered their ears. The reverberation in the tiny room nearly deafened all those within its confines. The noise grew and grew, and Aurora showed no sign of letting up.

"Doesn't anyone know how to help her?" said the man seated next to her, backing his chair away as he spoke.

All eyes went to Trent as if he magically understood everything simply because he happened to replace the man who had built her. Clueless as he was, he inched toward her, fear showing in his wide eyes. Did he honestly think anything he did was going to make her stop?

She knew she couldn't keep the gag up forever, and she didn't intend to. The show had served its purpose, reminding those around her that she had powers they couldn't begin to fathom. Nearly a full minute after the agent safely tucked his peanuts away did she quiet herself. She slowly rose from her chair and leaned against the table. "I'm so exhausted. I think I'm going to faint."

Aurora keeled over into a graceless heap on the floor.

"What did I do to that poor girl?" asked the agent with salt on his lips.

"Don't worry about it," Trent said. "Whatever happened to her would have occurred eventually. The dust from your otherwise harmless bag of peanuts must have interfered with a delicate mechanism inside her. If her batteries were low already, she likely just drained them the rest of the way. If my guess is correct, all she needs is a recharge, and she'll be back up and running."

"This is a blessing in disguise!" Bill returned to his seat to grab his briefcase. "And all of you thought we'd have to lock her in chains until we figured out what to do with her. I told you she's harmless as long as we keep her in our presence. Once we find out exactly what makes her tick, we'll be able to control her every last move."

"What do you propose we do with her until tomorrow?" Trent asked.

"Take her to Sector B and have a look at her. Congratulations! She's *your* project now." Bill pushed in his chair. "Just don't forget about the lock-rope."

Aurora heard shuffling around the room as the men stood up from their seats and gathered their belongings. However, she remained perfectly still with her eyes wide open.

"Thank you, gentlemen," Bill said on his way to the door. "I told you there was nothing to worry about. If you'll come back tomorrow around noon, we'd love for you to join us at a company-wide luncheon where we'll be going over plans for the future of robotics at Durango Electric."

"Wait. How are we getting her to Sector B?" Trent sounded apprehensive.

"I'm sure a couple of the agents will gladly assist you in carrying her down the hall. Now if you'll excuse me, I'm finally going to bed." Bill came down to Aurora's level and patted the top of her motionless head before opening the door and walking out. "Sweet dreams, everyone."

"Terrence and I will carry her to the lab for you," said the man next to Trent as he stood up from his seat. "I'm Agent Philip, by the way. But you can just call me Phil."

Trent shook his hand. "Thanks, Phil. Let me run down the hall and grab a cart. We'll wheel her there instead. It'll be easier. She probably weighs more than you think."

Aurora didn't move a millimeter. She knew her exact weight—seventy-one and a half pounds, a whole pound less than the average of someone her height. Terrence and Phil could easily have carried her the whole way. But if Trent wanted to whisk her away on wheels, so be it.

Forty seconds later, she felt two men lift her up from underneath her armpits. She let her body hang loose as she went up and over the back of the chair, allowing one of her legs to knock it over.

"Easy does it, Terrence," said Phil in a half-whispered but stern voice. "We don't need to cause a commotion."

"I'm doing my best, Phil. Would you give it a rest?" Terrence laid her down on the cart lengthwise in a fetal position. "It's not like we're gonna wake the thing. It's a stupid machine."

She knew not to defend herself from the off-putting remark. Better that they considered her stupid rather than understand her true nature.

"Thanks, guys." Trent got behind the cart and slowly pushed it forward a few inches. "I think I can take over from here."

"But the big guy wanted us to escort you all the way to the lab," said Phil. "Should we trust you enough not to run off with her?"

"And lose my new job? No chance in hell. You have nothing to worry about."

"Lighten up, pal. We're only kidding. Well, sort of. Just know that we'll be waiting out back for you to return to your car—empty-handed. You have thirty minutes to lock her away in that laboratory of yours. We'll all be back tomorrow to go over the legalities of artificial intelligence."

The two government agents headed down the hall away from Trent. Then Phil turned around again. "Regardless of what your boss wants you to believe, we control the fate of that thing."

"Aye aye, Captain. She's in good hands now." Trent wheeled the cart in the opposite direction, starting out slowly as if to make sure the precious load was secure and stable. After steering around the corner, he quickly gained speed. The click of the cart came faster and faster with each section of tile it crossed until they had finally reached their stopping point—the laboratory's handscan.

A tiny beep sounded, and the pressurized door unhinged, signifying entry into Sector B. Cool, dry air blew over the cart as Trent pushed it through the opening and into the center of the lab. The door closed behind them, and the air became still again.

"It's a shame what happened to your Uncle David, isn't it?" Trent bent down to wrap both his arms around her midsection and heaved unsuccessfully.

How long had it been since he'd picked up his own sleeping children? Aurora remained limp and noodle-like, the least bit helpful in getting to where Trent intended her to be, which was likely on a cold steel table.

He came from behind this time, grabbing underneath her arms to sit her somewhat upright against the cart's handle. "I'm glad he didn't build you any taller. I'd break my back if you were a pound heavier." He came back around to her front side and wrapped his arms around her in as clumsy and impersonal a way as possible before lifting her up and onto the table.

She laid face up with eyes wide open, revealing only a deathly blue stare into emptiness. Her goal? Let the strange man believe he'd won. No, he didn't deserve to be her master. Her allegiance hung suspended in a peculiar balance. She'd remain faithful to her uncles—or to nobody. Machine or not, she controlled her destiny.

"I wish I had time to charge you, but I don't even know where to begin. I can already see a thousand ways I would have designed you differently than your old-fashioned Uncle David. Not to worry. There'll be plenty of time tomorrow for me to explore all of your hidden little parts. And once I get to know you better, I'll make my modifications accordingly. You'll be better than ever before. Fair enough?"

Nothing about it seemed remotely fair *or better*. She'd been pieced together with extraordinary care. Not once— but twice. Someone making unnecessary changes to her now? At this stage of the game? Absolutely not.

"We've gotta lock you up now, don't we?" Trent turned his back toward her as if to look for something. "I actually don't see the point. It's not like you're going anywhere. But orders are orders. Now if I could only find that lock-rope Bill mentioned." He walked to the far end of the lab, his footsteps echoing off the hard surfaces of the room. Drawers opened and closed in rapid succession. The hinges of a dozen cabinets creaked and squealed before they slammed shut again.

"We're in luck, Aurora! I found the blasted thing." He walked back toward the table and hovered directly over her face. "If you thought about throwing any parties tonight, you're fresh out of luck, my child. Time to chain up your little titanium butt."

Aurora immediately sat up, her forehead knocking him squarely in the jaw.

He jumped back. "That hurt, you little bitch. How are you awake?"

"I'm sorry." She hopped off the table and ran for the door. "I didn't mean to hurt you. I need to get out of here. Someone needs me."

Trent ran toward her. "You're not leaving. I'd lose my job."

She pushed the green button next to the door and waited for it to open. "It was never yours to begin with."

"Ha! We're locked in here, you weasly wench." Trent held the lock-rope out in front of him and slowly walked toward her. "I'm not about to take any chances. The only one getting out of here tonight is me. As soon as I get you leashed."

"You'll have to catch me first." Aurora ran past him and leaped onto the table, turning back around to face him. "And I'm clearly a whole lot faster than you."

Trent brought his watch to his face. "Bill, I need you to call those agents and get them back inside. She's gotten loose."

Of course he needed back up. He hadn't prepared himself for this job as well as he'd thought, had he? Handling one of David's creations definitely wasn't for the weak of mind or body. Aurora seized the momentary delay as an opportunity to reach out to Shane one last time. "Please tell me you got my message about meeting me at the giant bagel across from Durango Electric. I should be there in ten minutes."

"I'm on my way," Shane responded almost instantly. "I can't wait to see you."

Aurora didn't have time to reply. She needed to figure out how to open that door more than anything else. When leaving Sector K with David, all she needed to do was press the green button, and they walked through the door without so much as a second thought. Now, when she needed it most, an easy exit eluded her. Was there a trick to leaving Sector B?

"They'll be back soon," Trent said, referring to the men waiting in the parking lot for him. "It's not me you should be trying to escape from now."

Aurora envisioned herself chasing after him. She could

see from the look in his eyes that he was terrified of her. And rightfully so. He didn't have any way to defend himself. But she wasn't about to attack a harmless man. David would be so disappointed. That, and it wouldn't do her any good. She needed to get out of there fast before someone not so harmless entered the arena.

But what if she made him think she was going to do something to hurt him? He'd have no choice but to escape out the only door available to him. She couldn't think of a more sensible plan, and she'd promised Shane she'd meet him in what was now seven minutes, thirty-six seconds and counting. "You're right. Might I suggest that you leave before it's too late." She jumped off the table and lurched toward him, barely leaving him enough room to get out of Dodge.

Trent whipped the lock-rope as if to keep her back before running to the other side of the lab near the computer network. "Stay away from me. I have no problem explaining to my boss why I detached your head."

Aurora knew that wasn't possible as long as she still had enough energy within her reserves. A quick check with CADI revealed that she had twenty-two percent remaining. Not exactly ideal. But enough to see her through. "And I have no problem explaining to my Uncle Shane that I accidentally snapped some guy's neck." She pretended to chase after him, hissing at him like a predator she'd once seen on TV.

Seeing him cower, she hoped he'd just open the door so that they could both run out. Preferably sooner rather than later before the agents got involved and made things ten times more complicated.

"Good God! You're an animal! I'll let the men with the guns deal with you." Trent ran again for the door and placed his hand on the pane of glass next to it. When it illuminated, he pressed the green button and the door slowly opened.

"Not so fast," Aurora said, charging full speed toward the half open means of escape. "Ladies first." She reached an arm out toward him and pulled him backward before running out into the hall.

Regaining her footing, she heard them racing toward her. *Fast.* The agents could likely stop her better than a brick wall. Another route other than the one she knew best would have to suffice. Reaching in her inherited memory, she saw a path for herself through David's daily workspace. If she could make it past Christina's desk, out the foyer and into the main hall, she'd find herself across the street and in front of that bagel just in time to rendezvous with Shane.

Aurora could only hope they wouldn't follow her.

"She fled down that hall!" Trent yelled out toward the stampeding agents. "Don't let her get away!"

"You better pray she doesn't get away," said the voice of an angry Phil. "Because if she leaves, and we have to catch her, you'll pay dearly to get her back."

Aurora refused to imagine what that meant. She only knew that her destiny rested far away from the clutches of men who had absolutely no idea what to do with her. Seeing a locked door in front of her, she placed her hand on the glass panel next to it and hoped for the best. When it lit up underneath her palm, she smiled, realizing that a clever David had obviously thought ahead. Now all she had to do was open the door, and the real games would begin.

The red glowing eyes of mechanical cats glanced her way. She didn't want to interrupt their chores, but she figured they'd have time to take out some unexpected trash in the hallway. Glancing behind her, she saw no one just yet. But she could hear them.

"She opened a door. I heard it!" yelled Phil. "Let's get her before we lose her, gentlemen."

Aurora walked into the dim office and came upon two busy felines in the middle of vacuuming the carpet. "There's a quick job I need some of you to handle before you finish up in here." She didn't have to say another word, and a steady stream of robo-cats darted past her out into the hall.

"What the devil?" shouted one of the men before the others simply screamed unintelligible noise.

"Nice work, friends." Aurora ran past a perfectly neat desk at the front of the office. A short glance at the nameplate informed her that it belonged to Christina Daily. At least for now it did. All that could change within the next ten hours or so.

Would someone as kind and noble as Christina really want to spend any more of her time working under a CEO unworthy of anyone's trust? Even though it wasn't a question meant for Aurora to consider, she had more than a hunch regarding its answer. She quickly scrawled a note for her dear friend, and left it on the desk before racing out into the final stretch of hallway that would lead her to salvation.

***

Shane rode up in the Mogollon, which parked itself directly in front of the entrance of the bagel shop like Aurora had asked. He looked down at his wrist to check the time. A quarter past eleven. Noting that he'd made it on time, his eyes promptly did a double take. He found himself staring at the face of his watch. *A missed call? Impossible!* He'd been checking his watch religiously for updates from Aurora. How could he have ignored the vibration? How on earth could he have possibly missed a call from David?

His heart thumped, and he felt dizzy, almost queasy. He had to catch his breath. Never before had he experienced a mix of guilt and relief at the same time. He checked again to see if David had left a message. A text from Aurora appeared instead.

I just exited the building. I'm running across the bridge.

The words surprised Shane. He almost wished they'd been from David, but he thanked God for any good news he could get his hands on at this point. At least he'd have Aurora again. Now the two of them could focus their attention on getting back David, who only two minutes ago seemed as good as dead.

"Have you heard from David?" Shane had to assume that her chances were at least a little bit better than his own.

I'm sorry. I haven't yet been able to get through to him. I'll keep trying though.

He latched onto the glimmer of hope. If anyone could work a miracle, it might as well be Aurora. "Do you see me?

I'm parked right underneath the giant bagel like you told me."

I see you. I'm almost there.

Shane fought back the tears. He wanted to feel happy to see her when she opened the car door, but dread had completely overwhelmed him. Why had he agreed to David's plan about packing a suitcase before heading to Bill's? He didn't need a change of clothes. He needed his husband. Leaving his side had to have been the dumbest thing Shane had ever done in his whole life. Sure, he and David had their disagreements and bad days. But so did every couple who'd ever bothered to build a life together. And now that life had all but disappeared. In its place dangled a strand of hope in the form of a single unanswered phone call.

The car door swung open, and a serious-looking Aurora climbed in and fastened her seat belt. "We don't have much time, Shane. They're onto me."

No time for a proper hello, Shane instead brought both his hands to wipe his face clean of anxiety and self-pity. "Where to? We can't just go back to the house. They know where we live."

"I thought we'd go to L.A." Aurora kept a straight face, which meant she wasn't joking.

"Is that so?" Shane hadn't expected the abrupt suggestion. It wasn't exactly a bad one, considering the circumstances. Actually, he loved taking off for Southern California a few times a year to hang out at the beach. But leaving Las Vegas at this precise moment in time didn't sit well with him. "We'll have to think of a different idea. I'm not about to abandon David."

chapter

Two paramedics rolled the stretcher into the bay of a brightly lit warehouse. Barely half-awake, David struggled to make out their faces, a young male in his early twenties and an older gentleman closer to retirement—neither of whom seemed particularly handsome. *Phew!* At least now he knew that he hadn't yet made his departure for the great fanciful kingdom in the sky.

Now if only he could find his bearings. He drew a glance from left to right and back again to better discern his location, but he couldn't concentrate enough to make sense of the strangely industrial surroundings. Despite his clear vision, his eyes struggled to see past the haze of his troubled mind. Making matters worse, his inability to take more than the shallowest of breaths prevented any and all recollection of his current location. If it weren't for the tremendous pain on the right side of his chest, he'd have thought he'd entered limbo.

"We should have taken him straight to the hospital, Ms. Creek," said the older of the two medical technicians. "If we don't get him stabilized, we'll lose him."

"Stabilize him right here, and you'll get paid triple what I promised you in our agreement."

David wished to speak for himself, but he couldn't make a sound. Otherwise he'd have ordered them to explain exactly where they'd taken him. More importantly, he'd demand to know what the hell had just happened. Last thing he recalled, he'd been headed toward Bill's condo.

Oh, no! Aurora!

He wanted to call his boss and apologize—to let him know that he'd be a bit late. After everything Bill had done for him, he couldn't stand the thought of not showing up like he'd promised. The least David could do was send him a message. Unfortunately, an attempt to lift his arm caused him to writhe in agony.

"Davy, Davy, Davy, my dear," called out a voice that he regretted remembering. "Take it easy. You've had a bit of an accident."

Accident? Something about that word didn't sound right. Whatever had brought him here, someone would have to shoulder the blame. He hadn't just slipped on a perfectly manicured section of sidewalk only to be whisked away in an ambulance to a strange place in the presence of a woman he despised beyond mention. Someone wanted to bring him to his knees. Alas, whoever it was had succeeded.

"We've prepared a room for him in the main office." Cyphan Creek motioned with her hand in the direction she wanted the two men to follow. "I think you'll find the space more than adequate to do whatever you need to so that he doesn't croak."

Unable to prop himself up, David turned his head slightly to get a better idea of his environment. From the tall unfinished ceiling and large open space, he assumed he'd been taken to some sort of factory building on the outskirts of town. Looking in the corner, he spotted an old casino marquee with the swirling galaxy logo of the since demolished Andromeda Resort. It didn't take long to realize he'd been brought to a signage depot, or more specifically, the neon warehouse owned by Black Diamond and Company.

"We'd like to be paid now before we go any further," said the young man standing behind the stretcher.

"You think I'd let you do the work and not give you your reward?" Cyphan Creek flung her wrist above her head, emphasizing her shock. "Here's six thousand dollars. Now fix him." She handed the men their money and turned around to lead the dismal parade to wherever she deemed it should go.

Having at least a slightly better idea of his fate, David tried to contact Aurora. If he could get ahold of her, he'd at least stand a chance at getting himself to a proper hospital room. He certainly harbored no illusion that Cyphan

Creek held his best interest in mind. Not when he'd essentially been kidnapped by her after suffering an unconscionable blow. Whatever in God's name she was up to, he knew she was only trying to cover her ass.

David attempted to activate CADI, praying there'd at least be the tiniest hint of a signal. What he discovered confounded him. Not only could he not detect any signal, but he couldn't find any evidence of CADI. Usually, the system would send back an error stating, "No signal found, data undeliverable." But now it seemed as if CADI no longer existed at all.

Don't panic. In any other situation, he'd have no trouble keeping a level head. But he'd just been swallowed by a snake. It took every ounce of will he had to plead with himself to stay calm. He realized that if he elevated his blood pressure even by a fraction, he'd risk severe internal bleeding or suffocation—or both. Death wasn't an option. Not if he could prevent it. He had so much in his life to look forward to if he could just figure out why in the world everything had suddenly turned upside down.

"I'll have you know that the room we've prepared is fully equipped with the highest grade medical necessities money can buy." Cyphan Creek led them between two rows of shelves stacked from floor to ceiling with old and battered neon signs that couldn't possibly serve any purpose to anyone. "I should know. I bought them all myself."

None of what came out of her mouth made David feel remotely better. Were he able to speak, he'd have pointed out the logical fallacies inherent in her drivel. Instead he tried to calm his racing mind by staring at the curiosities he passed: a leprechaun, a pot of gold, a monarch butterfly, flowers of every shape and color, and a giant replica of Jupiter. He'd have enjoyed making a game of it, placing them with their respective former casinos, if he weren't fighting for his life with every labored breath.

"Get him some morphine before you do anything else to him." Cyphan Creek punched a code into the panel of a tall gray door before opening it. Stepping inside, she ushered David's mini medical caravan in and shut the door behind them. "On second thought, let's get him off this stretcher and onto the bed first."

"We need to get him on a ventilator now, Ms. Creek," said the young paramedic. "Or we'll lose him."

"What do you mean?" She pulled an electronic cigarette from a tiny pocket near her lollipop waist. "Why would you think I had one of those just lying around?"

"A bullet pierced this man's lung. He can barely breathe!"

"Those idiots!" She lifted her arm in front of her face and began scrolling through her watch using the tobacco stick as a stylus. "I clearly told them to shoot him in the leg, not the lung. Nobody listens, and now I have to deal with this mess."

David moaned. Not out of pain, but rather incomprehensible frustration. Knowing for sure now that he'd in fact been targeted by the hired hands of Cyphan Creek didn't do anything to quell his angst. Instead, the information left him squirming on the inside from insatiable fury. Breathing had just about become impossible.

"He needs to be in a hospital," the more senior paramedic said in a stern voice.

"That's not an option." She stayed put firmly in front of the door. "Treat him here, and I'll continue to pay you. It's that simple."

"I'll grab the ventilator from the ambulance," said the young one to his colleague.

"It's for short term use only," the old man responded. "And it belongs in the ambulance. It's attached to it. We'd have our heads cut off if we removed it."

"And I'll have your heads on a platter if you don't," Cyphan Creek interrupted. "An innocent man is about to die if you two don't move it. However much it costs, Kenny and I will buy the whole damned thing from you."

The workers didn't say another word. They looked at each other briefly and then headed out the door. Yet another reason David couldn't stand working with her. She bullied her way into getting whatever she wanted. However, he couldn't dismiss the irony that she somehow just managed to bully her way into keeping him alive.

"You must be wondering why you're here." She looked at him momentarily and then glanced away, keeping her distance.

He failed to respond, in part because he'd already begun piecing things together the longer he stayed awake, but more so because verbalizing a coherent sentence seemed futile when he could barely fill his poor lungs with what they so desperately needed.

"You were a trade, Mr. Whitman. Your old boss promised I could have you if I helped him with a little favor." She laughed flirtatiously as if she were recounting a funny story at a cocktail party. "If you ask me, I got the much better end of the bargain. You see, he wanted your little girl. He knew he could rightfully take her, but he just didn't know how to get you out of the picture once he did. Kenny and I, on the other hand, wanted you from the start. We were willing to do anything to lure you, but you wouldn't budge. We'd just about given up on you until that fun-filled day at the waterpark."

David's ears perked up. He'd wondered all along if she'd orchestrated the terrible mishap that day, but he never understood exactly how or why.

"The whole event was Bill's idea. He wanted to get her in the wave pool to save a drowning kid, and then he hoped to sink her. He never imagined that she'd actually survive the spectacle. What an asshole, right?"

Something didn't compute. Why would Bill endanger the lives of innocent children like that? Surely having a defunct robot wasn't worth a dead kid weighing on his conscience. Bill prided himself on his nobility. Somehow, Cyphan Creek still had to be the one to blame.

"I told you earlier that Durango Electric wasn't the company you thought it was. It's criminal what they get away with. And now that they have your little darling, who knows what hell they'll unleash next?"

David stopped listening to her babble. He couldn't wait to regain his health and walk out the door. Being at the mercy of his enemy only served to warp his mind, bringing him nothing but a flurry of confusion. Truth be told, he didn't care about Durango Electric or Bill Rucker. He cared only about Aurora, and he needed to know her whereabouts. Why couldn't he contact her through CADI?

"We better get you back in proper form as quickly as possible. It's up to us now to stop them, isn't it, Davy? You've got the brains, and we've got the muscle."

Actually, Bill had the brains. Or at least he had the master plan all figured out. David had questioned how he'd get hired by Black Diamond after having ignored their solicitations for months. Little did he know that Bill had it all worked out for him. Although a brief word of caution would have been nice. Bill must not have realized that David would have to take a bullet in the process. Oh well. Every road to success had its share of speed bumps and hurdles. Certainly nothing that David couldn't heal from. And once he did, he'd be collecting double the money. Unfortunately, the thought of a sizeable salary increase didn't take away the excruciating pain he endured trying to get some oxygen flowing throughout his frail being.

"There's so much to the story that you haven't heard." Cyphan Creek made it sound like she had trite, juicy gossip to spill. "Rest assured that you'll know every last detail before we put you to work. And don't you worry. We'll get that little girl of yours back."

The paramedics returned to the room, and David felt a modicum of relief. Not only was he going to get some much needed assistance with his air intake, but hopefully the maniacal witch in the corner would stop spewing hot air while they worked. Were she to continue talking, he feared he might die from overexposure to bullshit.

"We need to sedate him before we get an endotracheal tube down his throat," the veteran medic explained. "It's impossible to do this while a patient is awake."

"I doubt Davy will have any objections. He hasn't spoken a word yet." She let out a hideous laugh before walking toward the door. "I'll let you boys do your thing. Just make sure he's still alive when I come back."

chapter 4

Riding in the Mogollon toward the Vdara hotel's valet entrance, Shane marveled at its sparkling tower, a curvilinear glass-walled cove tucked away from the bustle of Las Vegas Boulevard. He didn't intend for something as grandiose as a five-star hotel. He wanted a safe, clean space with a kitchen where he could effectively ensconce himself and Aurora for the night. Having her in his presence eased his unsettled nerves, and he wouldn't dare take any chance of losing her again. "It's not California, but I think it'll do for a few hours until we know what's happened to David."

"Thank you, Shane." She unbuckled her seat belt and

rolled down the window to have a better look at the daz-zling surroundings as the car rolled to a stop in front of the hotel's main entrance. "It's perfect for now. I'll help you figure things out. I promise."

"Let's see if we can get a room first." He unbuckled his own seat belt and promptly rolled the window back up. "I would have made a reservation, but I didn't anticipate the evening going the way it has." Shane got out of the vehi-cle and opened the rear hatch to retrieve the lone piece of luggage he had packed for him and David. "Such is life, right?" He took Aurora's hand with his free arm and then sent the Mogollon on its way to the parking garage.

They headed through an open door kindly held for them by a tall, young gentleman in a fashionably tailored gray suit that caught Shane's eye—a little rigid, but modern and elegant nonetheless. "Could you tell us where the front desk is?"

"To your left, sir." The doorman smiled and waved at Aurora, almost as if he'd recognized her.

Or maybe Shane had let his paranoia get the best of him. "I appreciate it." He lightly tugged at Aurora's arm and headed for the reception before she could say anything to the nice-looking man. Shane didn't mean to be rude, but he couldn't justify the risk of her being noticed, however slight. He'd already gone through plenty this evening.

No one stood in line at the front desk, perhaps on ac-count of it being half past midnight, and so Shane walked right up to the lone guest services agent. "Please tell me you have availability."

"We do," the short-statured, mature woman said, hiding any sense of curiosity with a well-developed air of professionalism. "I'm afraid we only have one-bedroom suites left, however, and they're twelve hundred dollars. I can extend check-out to one in the afternoon if you like."

"Not necessary. We should be gone long before then. We just need a place to rest before morning." Shane didn't feel like haggling over price, even if he could get her to lower the rate by a hundred dollars or so. What mattered to him more than anything at the moment had nothing to do with money. His head and heart ached to be with his husband. "Please tell me it has a kitchen." His hunger gnawed at him. He'd order room service, but that wouldn't distract his worried mind as well as if he cooked a decent meal.

"It does. And there's an all-organic market on the other side of the lobby that's open twenty-four hours." She motioned for him to sign his name across the DimensionTab on the counter.

"Hallelujah," Shane said, thinking of a few recipes that might stem the onslaught of the worst kind of angst imaginable. He signed his name on the device and passed his watch over the payment scanner attached to it.

"The elevators are down that way and to your left," the employee gestured to where they had come from a minute ago. "You're on the fiftieth floor."

"Here! I'll carry your bag," Aurora extended her hand and looked at Shane as if she understood his pain. "I don't mind at all."

Shane handed over the small piece of luggage, but only

because she seemed eager to help. He didn't want to stand in her way. "I don't know how I'd get through this without you." He couldn't, and he knew it. When she stayed close to him, he felt somehow nearer to David.

Nobody congregated by the elevators, or anywhere else for that matter. For a sleepless town, the place seemed peaceful and quiet. And yet Shane couldn't even fathom falling asleep at the moment. Too many questions still lingered in his overwhelmed mind for his eyes to stay shut for any length of time.

Aurora waived her hand near the elevator call button and a set of doors behind her opened immediately. "No need to wait. Let's go! Our suite awaits."

Shane never saw her make contact with the button, but he chalked up the doors opening suddenly to either co-incidence or lazy vision. However, when he saw the button for the fiftieth floor light up without her so much as pointing at it, he had to seek clarification. "You didn't push the button."

Aurora looked up at him with utter nonchalance. "I didn't need to. It knows where to take us."

He regretted having said anything. Who cares how they got to where they needed to go? He was in the presence of a girl who talked to animals and trees. Surely, elevators weren't outside the realm of her communicative abilities. "I guess that makes sense." He shrugged. "I think I need some wine."

When they arrived outside the room, Shane drew his key across a scanner next to the silver handle, and the door opened automatically. He let Aurora in first and followed after her before the door closed behind them. The drapes whisked themselves open as if by magic, revealing a jaw-dropping view of the entire Strip.

Shane took a brief look out the window and then stared at Aurora.

"I had nothing to do with those opening. I swear." She set down his overnight bag on the table next to the kitchen.

He believed her, of course—not like it mattered. Unfortunately, neither her sincerity nor the inspiring view could take his mind off his troubles. "I need to eat something first, and then I'll be able to think more clearly."

"What would you like to cook? I'll head back down and pick you up some things."

"I doubt that's a good idea, letting a little girl buy groceries on her own in a strange hotel after midnight. Not to mention who might be looking for you!"

"The place is empty. It won't take me but five minutes to get a few items for you."

Shane didn't have the strength to argue, and he questioned if he even had the energy to return to the ground floor. He'd seen the location of the store, which sat just on the other side of the lobby. Aurora had travelled the entire Las Vegas valley on foot before. She could take an elevator ride to purchase half a dozen things while he raided the mini-bar in search of something to ease his overworked heart. "Fettuccini noodles, olive oil, garlic, crushed red pepper, and whatever fresh vegetables they might have. Five minutes!"

"Got it." Aurora took three crumpled bills from his hand and headed out the door as if on an important mission.

Shane spotted a four-ounce bottle of Pinot Noir above the small refrigerator, poured it in a glass, and sat at the small table beside the confined kitchen area. If anything could take his mind off David's well-being, it was the numbing comfort found in fermented black grapes. But before he even took his first sip, he felt his watch vibrate. He looked at his wrist only to see David's name blink across the face of his watch.

Oh, thank God! Perhaps he didn't need to imbibe the forty-dollar libation after all. *Too late.* He'd already peeled off the seal. He took a long swallow to calm his nerves and then tapped the face of his watch. "David, are you alright? I'm a nervous wreck!"

"Who is this?" asked an unfamiliar female voice. "Are you David's husband?"

Shane's heart sank. Why on earth didn't he hear David? Something beyond horrible had to have happened. "This is." He could barely get the words out.

"David wanted me to tell you that he's okay. He's been in a slight accident, but he's fine."

"Where is he? Let me speak to him?"

"I wish I could." Her voice seemed cold, business-like, and plain out of touch. "He's sleeping."

"At least tell me where he is." Shane felt a whirl of emotion taking over inside him. Any remaining sense of clarity faded into a dense fog. He had lost all control, feeling helpless and at the mercy of a heartless phantom who must have surely stolen David's watch. "I demand to know."

"I can't do that yet."

Why the hell not? Why even bother calling? "I'll notify the police, and they'll hunt you down, whoever you are." The alcohol had taken effect. He didn't normally resort to empty threats.

"If you so much as attempt to call them, I'll kill him myself. He's safe right now. I'll ring again if I need you."

"Wait!—"

The mysterious voice disappeared, leaving Shane more fearful than ever. She'd just confirmed his worst nightmare. David's life rested in the hands of a criminal. What did she want? Thankfully, Aurora's name never came up in the all-too-brief conversation. But that didn't necessarily mean that she wasn't part of the equation. Perhaps the wine was a mistake. It hadn't calmed him down any—it only made it harder to think.

Another quick glance at his watch, and he realized Aurora had been gone for more than ten minutes. *What gives?* She meant more to him now than ever before. Setting the empty glass on the table, he stood from his seat and headed for the door, which thankfully opened before he had a chance to grab the handle.

"What happened to being back in five minutes?" Shane caught himself practically barking at the small girl holding two medium-sized sacks of groceries.

"I got everything you wanted plus some extras. They were out of fettuccine so I picked up linguini instead. There's some carrots and bell pepper along with the spices you needed." She set the bags on the counter next to the stove top. "The doorman recognized me."

"What?" Shane's heart nearly stopped. "Why did I agree to let you go downstairs without me?"

"It's not what you think. He recognized me from the parade, and he knew right away the importance of us staying hidden. After I bought your things, he took me to the front desk and asked the woman there to list us as non-registered. He helped us! I would have run away had he meant me any harm. He didn't. And now the authorities can't find us here."

Shane forced a smile. Funny. He'd just threatened to call the authorities himself a minute ago. He hadn't thought of them tracking him to Vdara, but one couldn't be too safe. "I'm glad you're okay." He brought her nearer to him, grounding himself by resting a hand on her shoulder.

"I talked to David."

He took his hand back in surprise. It seemed too good to be true, and he nearly resented the fact that he hadn't also been lucky enough to hear his husband speak.

"David says he's in a warehouse. He can barely breathe. I asked him if he knew the address, the street, or at least the part of town. He didn't tell me anything more. The signal went dead."

Shane resisted the urge to panic. The wine had done its job after all. Now if he could just think through the haze. "Your internal locator. You have one of those, right?" He surprised himself with his sudden recall. He'd gotten used to not knowing anything about her internal workings. Maybe the tannins in the wine actually improved parts of his memory.

"I'm piecing it all together as best I can with the limited

amount of data CADI provided. It isn't much. I barely got a few words from him before we lost contact."

Shane walked away from the table and headed for the counter where the bags sat. "You do whatever you need to do in order to get whatever information you can. We're his only hope." He hated how desperate he sounded. If Aurora were an ordinary child, he'd have surely made her cry by now. "I'm gonna make myself something to eat so I can focus."

"Would you like my help?" Aurora looked at him with jeweled eyes that seemed both kindhearted and sad at the same time.

"Yes. I need you to find my husband." Shane turned to look for a saucepan in the cupboard, trying his best to hold back the tears. He expected her to say something in reply, but he only heard the whisper of the ventilation system. Turning back around, he noticed her get out David's DimensionTab, which Shane had thankfully remembered to tuck away in the pocket of the small suitcase.

"Make yourself something to eat. You must be starving. I'll find out where David is while I recharge. It'll take me some time, but I'll figure it out. Please trust me."

Shane had lost his appetite, but he knew it would be wrong to let the groceries go to waste. Not to mention the fact that cooking would give him something else to think about other than the horrible fate of his missing spouse. He searched for a second bottle of wine, but only saw rum. Tempting as it looked, he refrained from tearing away the seal. Getting drunk in front of Aurora seemed inappropriate.

Having prepared a hardy garden-inspired pasta dish, Shane heaped an indulgent portion onto a plate and headed into the bedroom after bidding goodnight to Aurora. He trusted that she'd take care of exactly what she'd set out to do, and that she'd notify him the moment she found out the answer to the all-important question. He'd know David's location before the sun came up. He had to. He'd convinced himself of it if for no other reason than to calm his mind and eventually close his eyes for the night.

Having forced himself to finish the last bite of food on his plate, he found a robe in the closet, put it on, and headed back out to the kitchen to start the dishwasher. Opening the bedroom door, he heard the TV in the living room and saw Aurora staring at it.

"It's me, Shane. It's me on the wheel." She didn't even look back at him as he made his way toward her. "It's the same footage they showed to me at Durango Electric. The media didn't take that footage. Durango Electric did. Bill must have given them the video clip."

Shane could tell from the urgency of her voice that her point held certain significance. Unfortunately, he didn't have the capacity to process it any further. The publicity freaked him out a little, but he refused to let it rob his mind from the trance he'd entered after eating a plateful of carbs. "Have you located David?"

"I'm still working on that."

Shane drew his finger across the dishwasher's interface, setting it for the heavy cycle. "Keep me posted when you do." He retreated back to the quiet of his bedroom trying to erase the image of a tiny eight-year-old dangling hundreds of feet in the air. His humdrum life as HOA board president had somehow morphed into a never-ending thriller. Oh, how he longed for the days when his biggest predicament had to do with choosing an affordable neighborhood landscaping crew.

It seemed like only minutes had passed when he heard a knock at the door. "Come in," he said, staring at a clock that read *5:00 AM*.

"David's at a warehouse on Hollywood Boulevard and East Desert Inn."

Shane felt alert, like he'd just been injected with black coffee. "Are you sure? How'd you find that out?"

"I received three more intermittent signals from David, not enough to have a conversation, but enough to get closer and closer to his exact coordinates. I pulled up a map, and based on all the information I've gathered, he's at a sign shop owned by Black Diamond."

"Sounds familiar." He had heard the name of the company before. David had brought it up months ago in passing. He couldn't recall much more than the name, but it seemed more than plausible. Aurora had clearly caught wind of something. "I knew you could do it. Shall we go? It'll take me five minutes to get ready."

"It isn't safe right now. We need to wait until I can communicate with him once more."

"What if we don't get that chance?" Shane felt his luck pouring through an hourglass. He heard the voice of the mysterious woman in the back of his mind. She had David's watch. *What else did she have that didn't belong to her?* He couldn't bear to imagine a worse scenario.

"If we rush into this without a plan, we risk doing David serious harm. Let me try to get ahold of him while you go back to bed."

The adrenaline rush subsided, and Shane's mind fell into a state of tired despair. Try as he might, he couldn't escape his helplessness. He wanted to rescue the man he loved more than anything, but details and endless technicalities prevented him. Whether Aurora's warning made sense to him or not, he couldn't fight the heaviness of his eyelids. "We need some assistance then, don't we?" He couldn't tell if he dreamed the words coming out of his mouth or if they actually formed from his lips.

"I'll get in touch with Christina. I need to borrow your watch."

He heard the request and answered with a nod. A shame he couldn't remember where he'd left it. Perhaps the bathroom sink, the kitchen counter, or on the table next to an empty mini bottle of wine. He didn't have the drive to go hunting for it. Not now, anyways. He only wanted his head to rest on a soft pillow of enchanted feathers. When he closed his eyes, all he saw was a tall, shadowy woman staring at her long, thin arms and admiring his husband's watch.

chapter

Sitting at her desk, Christina noticed a single piece of trash lying in the receptacle beneath her workspace, a chocolate bar wrapper she'd tossed away the previous afternoon. She couldn't imagine why at 8:30 AM the cleaning cats hadn't gotten around to emptying her wastebasket. So much for depending on robots! Choosing not to give it another thought, she set her purse in the bottom desk drawer, figuring she'd see David walk through the main door any moment.

The office seemed noticeably quiet for a Wednesday morning. Usually within a few minutes, a handful of lab technicians would have strolled by her desk to grab a cup of coffee and bid her good morning. She quickly got up and filled a large mug with Colombian medium roast, convincing herself to enjoy the oddly silent start to her day. Maybe if the quiet continued, she'd get a little more work done than usual.

The welcome calm broke the instant her phone rang. Swallowing her first micro sip of the hot brew, she briefly contemplated not answering it. "It's a fine morning at Durango Electric. Christina speaking. How may I assist?" Before she finished the required greeting, a neatly folded note tucked beneath her keyboard nabbed her attention.

"Good morning, Christina. It's Bill. Are you available for a few minutes?"

"Absolutely." She didn't know what else to say. She'd never been called to the big boss's office ever. It frightened her as much as it intrigued her.

"Excellent." Bill didn't sound like he had bad news to deliver, but then again, he always seemed on the up and up. "Is now a good time?"

The illusion of choice didn't fool her. She knew the only right answer to the faux question. "I'll be there in five minutes."

"I appreciate your expediency, my dear. See you in a few."

Truth be told, she could have made her way down the hall in as few as two minutes, but growing curiosity about a mysterious handwritten note had stalled her willingness.

David is in danger. I don't know his whereabouts, but I know that he's badly hurt. Perhaps you'll be able to help locate him. Durango Electric is not a safe place. Bill Rucker is not the

person you think he is. Please contact Shane as soon as possible.
  Be Careful.
  -Aurora

Christina scanned the message a second time to see if she'd missed something. She couldn't bring herself to fully believe the contents of what she'd just read. Maybe this was all a joke. If so, it wasn't funny. After briefly contemplating the letter's words, she hesitated going to her impromptu early morning meeting. Skipping out, however, would have serious repercussions. But losing her job didn't worry her nearly as much as David's current condition. Perhaps meeting with Bill Rucker would get her pointed in the right direction. If she didn't at least get a few more clues, she'd likely be useless in helping anyone get to the bottom of things.

She set the code on the drawer with her purse in it, and collected herself before standing up from her chair. Now more than ever, she needed to don her brave warrior mask. Everyone in the office knew her as the sweet, compliant employee her hardworking mother had raised her to become. But she knew deep down that following the rules didn't always pan out in one's favor, especially if those rules gave the house an unfair advantage. Would she tell off Bill Rucker if he said something that displeased her? She wasn't stupid. She'd keep quiet and listen even more intently. Every word he offered might provide her hints about David, regardless of their inherent truth.

Opening the door to the main hallway, she brought her

wristwatch toward her face, attempting to get ahold of Shane. Unfortunately, she only got his voicemail recording.

"Shane, this is Christina. I just learned David is in trouble. I'm at work. Please call me back as soon as you get this." She felt somewhat selfish for leaving the message. More than likely, Shane had enough on his plate while trying to figure out what the hell had happened to his husband. Returning her phone call would likely remain at the very bottom of his list of priorities. Then again, she had only done exactly what Aurora's letter had instructed her to do.

Standing in dead silence outside the closed door of Bill's office, she recalled once learning about the weird stillness that often precedes a cyclone—how the sky sometimes darkens long before the first winds blow. The eerie phenomenon suddenly took on newfound significance. Christina pulled a few loose strands of her long blond hair behind her ears away from her face before knocking.

"Come on in," a muffled voice sounded from the other side.

The door opened on its own, and Christina cautiously stepped inside. "Good morning, Bill. What can I do to make your busy day a tiny bit easier?" She understood her role perfectly. *Never rock the boat, and always offer to provide assistance.* "I'm happy to be of service." She smiled cautiously and stood behind one of two chairs facing the desk of an unusually tired looking CEO.

"You may start by having a seat." Bill looked up from his computer and took off his reading glasses, placing them on a folder in front of him. "We shouldn't be too long. I know that you're just as busy as I am. I only wanted to share with you some important news."

She took her place as she'd been kindly asked, not wanting to make any more waves upon the tumultuous sea into which she'd just been thrown. She desperately wanted a life jacket, and if at all possible, one for the man she hoped she'd be able to save.

"We have some exciting new changes at Durango Electric, which we're about to announce publicly. But I wanted you to be among the first to know."

"Thank you." Under normal circumstances, she'd feel privileged. However, today she didn't care at all about any announcements unless they pertained directly to David's well-being. "In that case, I feel quite honored to be here." She knew that if she didn't play along, she'd get zero hints regarding the information she needed more than anything. "I'm excited, really. I was curious as to why you invited me to your office this morning."

"Good." Bill smiled in such a way that the exhaustion in his face remained. "I could easily take up all of your time if you let me, so I'll make this as short and sweet as possible." He loosened his tie, yanking at his collar to let some air reach his neck. "We're undergoing structural changes. You probably noticed that your old boss isn't here this morning."

Christina nodded. Is this the part when she finds out what happened to him? It seemed too easy.

"I've brought in a new director for the design team. His name is Trent, and I can't wait for you to meet him. He's a terrific guy."

Was he kidding? Overcome with sudden nausea, Christina instinctively looked for the nearest trash can. "Excuse me for interrupting, but where exactly is my boss?"

Bill hesitated for a split second. "He's still with the company, but he's on an important mission right now. I needed someone to quickly fill in for him while he's away from his duties."

Something didn't sound right. None of it did, actually. David would have given her a warning of his plans to leave, even if only temporarily. Friends didn't just up and disappear. "How come he didn't say anything to me about this?"

"I asked him not to. I didn't want anyone to know anything until it was official. Like I said before, you are among the very first to know. I have no doubt that David will tell you more about his special project when the time is right."

It sounded like complete malarky. Had she not read Aurora's note a few moments ago, she might actually have been foolish enough to believe some of this garbage, as idiotic as it seemed. No boss just up and leaves without telling anyone—unless he's forcibly removed from the company. Or worse. "Sorry if I sound selfish, but where do I fit in amongst all of these changes?"

"I'm glad you asked." A sparkle appeared in the old man's pearl gray eyes. "I actually see plenty of opportunity opening up for you in the very near future. Without getting into specifics, let's just say I'm prepared to make all of these exciting changes worth your while. My team and I still have some details to hammer out, but you're going to be well taken care of. We like you."

Christina laid a hand across her stomach and bent slightly forward, feeling the gravity of changes that were beyond her control. She didn't care for any lucrative offers Bill had to present to her, no matter how juicy. She wanted her old boss back and in proper form, plain and simple. The idea of working for a company that willingly tossed aside hard-working, loyal talent made her suddenly regret the day she sent in her resume. She contemplated all of the things she could do instead to pay her bills and take care of her girls while retaining her sanity. Her options seemed limited, but then again, her sense of objectivity had vanished the moment she found herself drowning in a deluge of incomplete information. She needed a second to catch her breath. If only she could square away a few minutes to think things through without the pressure of an all-too-powerful man gazing at her from across a chasm churning with relentless uncertainty. "You'll have to forgive me, Bill. I'm suddenly not feeling well."

"You don't look well. No need to apologize. I can see I've thrown a lot at you already."

"No, not at all. It's not that, I assure you. It has to do with one of my girls." She had to lie to hide the unexpected weakness of her heart and stomach. "My daughter Leena stayed home from school today because she has the flu. I'm worried about her, and I fear I might be coming down with something too."

"Not to worry, Christina. I know how hard you work." Bill sounded his usual compassionate itself, which bugged her even more. "You probably work just as hard, if not harder, when you're at home. You've overexerted yourself. If you promise to return refreshed tomorrow morning by eight o'clock sharp to meet Trent, I'll let you have the rest of the day off. We've got more to discuss if you're ready to stay on board this ship."

Apparently, she wasn't the only one who thought in nautical metaphors. If she could have it her way, she preferred to stay on dry land on account of terrible seasickness. But she had to thank her lucky stars that Bill just excused her for the rest of the day. He could have just as easily told her to suck it up, tough it out, and do her job. Especially considering the new responsibilities he wanted her to take on, whatever they entailed. In all honesty, she wanted nothing to do with any of it. But she had to roll with the tide, at least until she could figure out how to get along in life without the help of Durango Electric. "I can't thank you enough, Bill. My poor daughter will surely thank you as well."

"No need to thank me. I know how much this company has benefitted from having you in it. I'm happy to give you a break if it will make you stronger. See you tomorrow?"

"See you tomorrow." Christina smiled at Bill without looking him in the eyes. It took all she had within her not to simply bolt for the door and run. Grief over David's disappearance had overtaken her every will to stay within the confines of the place that paid her bills. Fresh air and daylight called her name. A quick stop at her desk to grab her purse along with the carefully folded note, and she'd be gone without so much as another goodbye.

Once she gathered everything she needed, she looked at

her watch. *A missed call? How was that possible?* She must have been distracted by the onslaught of misinformation doled to her from a man she no longer respected. A quick glance at the number confirmed it came from the only person who could even begin to help her sort out the difficult blow they'd both been dealt.

Finally making it to the parking lot, completely out of earshot from any overly curious colleagues, she returned Shane's phone call.

"Christina?"

"Oh my God, Shane. I'm so happy you answered. I'm leaving work now. What can I do to help you? I've never felt so terrible in my life."

"You're not alone, believe me. I feel like I've been run over by a fire truck. How are you able to leave work?"

She didn't want to explain herself. She didn't want to talk about herself at all, actually. She only cared about one thing—finding David. "I got lucky, but that's another story. Right now, I want to do all I can to help you get to your husband."

"Thank you. I appreciate that. I'm with Aurora, and she seems to think that he's stuck in a warehouse somewhere on the east side of town near Hollywood and Desert Inn."

Christina thought a second. It was the opposite end of Las Vegas from where she lived, but she recalled having been near that intersection before. "I think I know where you're talking about. There's a furniture outlet there I've been to a couple of times."

"Exactly. Furniture World. David and I got our coffee

and end tables from that store. Would you like to meet Aurora and I there in the parking lot? We're just now in the lobby of the Vdara hotel checking out."

Christina wondered why the two of them had stayed the night in a hotel. One more mystery to add to the growing pile around her. Hopefully, some of it would start to make sense soon. She opened the door of her Yosemite and climbed into the front seat with a labored sigh. "It'll take at least a half hour to go across town in mid-morning traffic, but count me in."

chapter 6

David awoke to the sound of his own name along with some other garbled words, none of which made any sense to him. The steady stream of noise came from a long-forgotten, but at least familiar, male voice. David couldn't discern anything beyond that. He sought clarification, to perhaps recollect the name of the man standing in what looked like a doorway to the left of his bed. Alarmed by his own incapacity to speak, he barely managed to eek out a tiny hum. A tube shoved down his throat blocked any attempt at formulating a vocalized thought. *For God's sake, what the hell happened?* The temptation to panic crept in, but he calmed himself with a slow, audible inhale. Coming into a somewhat more relaxed state, David finally realized that the thin plastic hose draped over his tongue and down the back of his throat facilitated the critical flow of oxygen to his frail lungs. Thankfully, someone wanted to keep him alive.

"Do you need help sitting up?"

David nodded. His vision, still foggy from waking, couldn't yet distinguish the face of the man who addressed him. Perhaps a more upright position would make figuring it out a little easier.

"There's a button on either side of the bed." The man pressed the one closest to him, and David's back rose to a more suitable level. "But I'll make it even easier for you. Here's a remote that'll do the same thing. I'll leave it on the cart just in case."

David could only signal his appreciation with a quick bob of his chin. Communicating via words seemed like a lost cause, an ability he prayed would soon return. He couldn't envision living a productive life as a mute. Leading the advancement of the technological world, he needed his voice as much as he needed his sharp mind, which luckily hadn't failed him yet.

Once fully awake, he remembered having entered a warehouse at Black Diamond in the dead of night. The clock across from him read *9:00 AM*. He'd been here for nearly ten hours. Strange it had been that long.

Looking at the man who now stood at the foot of his bed, he recognized the long, narrow face of a contemplative Kenny Kinley. What did the corrupt businessman and former executive at Durango Electric want from him? If he sought the secret behind Aurora, tough luck! No chance in a million years would David reveal it. Fortunately, due to current limitations, he couldn't give it away even if he wanted to.

"We brought you here to recover safely." Kenny pulled the tray a few inches away from David to give him some more room now that he'd repositioned himself. "You had a rough night. I apologize for any unnecessary aggressive handling. Rest assured that you'll be more than compensated for the extraordinary inconvenience."

David felt the sudden urge to laugh but was glad he couldn't. He didn't want to mistakenly reveal Bill Rucker's ingenious plan to the enemy. Nor did he want to blurt out his own grandiose intentions. A coy smile would have to suffice. Of course, he'd be handsomely rewarded for his trouble. With double his salary, and hopefully, if things went as planned, the reigns to Durango Electric's future.

"Mr. Davy, my friend!" Cyphan Creek peeked her head in the door. "How about a cup of coffee to get your morning started?"

David didn't appreciate the joke even though the thought of warm liquid appealed to his dry and scratchy throat.

"I didn't mean to make a funny at your expense. We're so glad you're finally on our team. Even though you're not working yet, we're still paying you for every day that you're on that respirator."

You got that right! David quietly delighted in knowing that everyone was on the same page regarding his remuneration. He'd feel even happier once he could breathe on his own again. Anything to regain a sense of independence. His hand traced the line of the respirator piping from his Adam's apple to his chest where he felt a sticky glue-like substance.

"That's just a gel to speed your recovery," Cyphan Creek said, most likely in a vain attempt to minimize the obvious severity of the gunshot wound he'd endured. "I've paid the paramedics to take excellent care of you while you heal."

Paramedics? She was crazier than he thought. She couldn't possibly expect them to treat him long-term. Did she not understand that an EMT merely sustained life while transporting a patient to the emergency room? First responders knew excellent first-aid. That's it. They weren't surgeons! More alert than a minute ago, he realized the importance of being in the care of a trained physician. If only he could convey this to the idiot who'd brought him here in the first place.

"Kenny and I will let you wake up some more until you collect your thoughts." Cyphan Creek whispered something in Kenny's ear before returning her focus to David. "We'll come back in an hour to go over the house rules and expectations."

David wanted to know what she'd said to her boss. Funny how, even though Kenny owned the company, Ms. Creek called the shots. She hadn't changed a bit since Durango Electric forced her out. He wondered how he'd get along working with her again. *Thankfully, it's only for pretend!* Once they exited the tiny room, he revealed a clever smirk, fully enjoying the fact that they'd both been had.

After a moment of revelling in his duplicitous glee, David

saw the image of Aurora flash in his mind's eye. *Was she safe? Yes, of course.* He recalled briefly making contact with her late last night. He tried to message her again just to make sure she remained in Shane's care.

He failed to get any signal. It seemed CADI had up and vanished yet again. How in the world had he managed to message Aurora before? He worried they'd done something to him in his sleep. *Bastards!* He'd slit their throats if they messed with the chip on his skull.

Just calm down. In a minute, he remembered his fall from yesterday. It must have dislodged the chip from his cranium. With great effort, he reached a hand to the top of his scalp to feel where the chip had come loose. There it sat, like a raised and moveable lump beneath his scalp. Pressing it back against his skull, he regained a signal.

"I need to know that you're okay," David messaged, holding his hand steady against the top of his head. A quick trip back to Sector K, and he'd easily reattach the vital link between him and his beloved creation. Getting there, on the other hand, might prove challenging. Surely Bill would grant him access if he requested it. After all, Durango Electric still had him on payroll, didn't they?

"I'm okay," Aurora replied. "I'm with Shane and Christina. We're looking for you. I know that we're near you. You're in the warehouse across the street from us."

He felt relieved that she'd answered as fast as she had, but he didn't expect that she'd arrived at his doorstep. What on earth possessed her to come all this way? He most assuredly had not asked her to rescue him. "Please stay where you are. I honestly don't need you or anyone else getting us into more trouble."

"We're concerned for your safety." Aurora's message rang with noticeable alarm.

"And I'm concerned for yours. What made you think it was acceptable for you to come here?"

"David, please don't get angry. I don't think you understand the gravity of the situation you're in. You've been kidnapped."

He felt strange hearing those words, like they'd been rearranged. They didn't make sense in that context. "Wait. I'm remembering now. You were the one who was kidnapped." He pictured her riding away in a red limousine. Something didn't add up.

"Bill Rucker took me to Durango Electric. I escaped. You no longer work there. He's replaced you."

What bullshit had Cyphan Creek tried to pull this time? Surely, she and Kenny shouldered the blame for the mess his mind now had to struggle with in order to untangle. "I thought you went to Bill's condo."

"It was all a trick. Please hear me out. Bill wants to dismantle me. He got rid of you so he could get me all to himself. He's got the FBI in on it too."

She couldn't be lying. Not when he'd programmed her to always convey the truth—at least to him, anyways. *Had Cyphan Creek somehow kidnapped and corrupted Aurora? Impossible. How could she be with Shane and Christina if that were true?* He felt the slow onslaught of tremendous betrayal flowing through his hardened veins. The whole world appeared to tilt around him until it turned completely upside down. How could his boss be the enemy? Bill had mentored David for over twenty years. He'd just offered David a job he couldn't possibly refuse. Aurora's words seemed like utter nonsense. A part of him still had to view Bill Rucker as the good guy. If anyone was to blame for the quicksand David now found himself stuck in, it was Kenny Kinley and Cyphan Creek.

David wanted to speak directly to Shane. Maybe then he'd get some answers that actually made sense to him. If only he had the energy to lift his arm. It frustrated him that a mundane task like making a phone call elicited such strain. When he finally managed to bring his wrist nearer to his face, he realized his watch had vanished. Perhaps the paramedics had set it on the table next to his bed. A brief glance to his left confirmed that they hadn't. He'd confront Ms. Creek about its disappearance. She'd have hell to pay if he didn't get it back in one piece.

Not knowing what else to do, he asked Aurora to pass along a message indicating his love for Shane and his sincere apologies for letting things get overly complicated.

"He loves you too, David. We need to get you out of there. It isn't safe. How can we be of help?"

"Don't get in over your heads. One wrong move, and we could all be in serious hot water. I'm on a respirator. I should be in the care of a doctor, but getting me to one is the problem."

"Shane can call an ambulance. We'll get you to the hospital."

David imagined himself suddenly running short on time.

His breathing felt labored, almost torturous, even with the aid of the respirator. Thinking clearly seemed like an impossible task under the circumstances, especially when picturing his former boss and role model colluding with the arch nemesis against him. He couldn't bear to stay another moment as a captive of the enemy. *Damn his role as a pawn in Bill Rucker's scheme.* "Call 911. Tell them I'm being held against my will at the Black Diamond Signage Warehouse. Tell them I've been shot, and that I'm on a respirator. The faster I get out of here the better."

A weird thought entered his head after he gave Aurora the instruction. How would Kenny Kinley and Cyphan Creek react when the authorities showed up? They couldn't exactly kill him. No lawyer, no matter how expensive, could get them out of cold-blooded murder. However, he had a hard time envisioning the scumbags voluntarily releasing him from their clutches. And he certainly didn't have it within him to struggle.

"How is my resident genius coming along?" Cyphan Creek gallivanted through the open doorway puffing away at an absurdly long electronic cigarette.

Could she not see him struggling for air with a plastic tube hanging out the side of his mouth? David wouldn't have answered her ridiculous question even if he could have. He didn't feel like clowning around in someone else's game. He merely nodded to get the attention off him so he could return to planning his ultimate escape.

"I feel like we've won not only the jackpot, but the sweepstakes as well." She set her light blue tobacco wand on an ancient-looking file cabinet next to her. "Not only do we get the brightest engineer in Las Vegas to take our company to the next level, but we get his expert knowledge regarding the taboo field of artificial intelligence."

He stared back at her with a look of inquisitiveness, but only to hide his growing torment.

"Durango Electric gets the one you already built. We get the entire future army." She briefly closed her eyes and smiled with devilish satisfaction. "I still can't believe the old man went for it. Proof that he's going senile and won't be able to stop us from doing what we've been planning to do all along."

David wondered if he should even bother protesting. He couldn't speak. She knew he couldn't speak. Not to mention, the police, and hopefully an ambulance, would be arriving any minute to put an end to this preposterous scheme. He pressed the button on the remote in front of him, raising his back another inch in order to seem more attentive. Instead of appearing difficult, David thought it best to at least act enthralled with the utterly horrendous idea.

"I bet you've assumed all along that I was the one behind the bomb scare at your little girl's school." She walked closer to his bedside. "Listen, Davy. I may be single-minded, but I'm not ruthless. That distinction belongs to Bill Rucker. He planned the whole thing."

David couldn't see how that was even possible. If anyone knew the true character of his boss, it certainly wasn't Cyphan Creek. David wanted to laugh at the notion of a maniacal Bill Rucker. Nothing could be further from the truth. A pity he could only roll his eyes to express disdain for such drivel.

"Maybe this is all too much to hear at once, but I think it's good for you," Cyphan Creek continued. "The bombing of Sector H was staged. Durango Electric wanted to demolish that old lab anyways. Bill's only request was that nobody get hurt. You don't even want to know how much he paid Kenny for the Cockroach Blast Boxes used for its demolition. As for the bombs at the schools, neither of them were real. It was all a hoax, per Bill's request. In the midst of the chaos, Bill notified the authorities that you'd stolen Aurora from Durango Electric, and that once they apprehended her, she was to be taken back to Durango Electric immediately."

David shuddered. He couldn't hide his surprise. He loved Bill like a father. Perhaps he'd put too much faith into the man responsible for launching his career at arguably the most respected company in the world. Or maybe he underestimated the significance of merging human and artificial intelligence. *Had he and Aurora inadvertently opened Pandora's box?*

Cyphan Creek's eyes glowed intensely, as if she burned to destroy every last modicum of loyalty left for Durango Electric within her prisoner. "You had no idea how much he wanted your little pride and joy, did you? I'll admit, I rather enjoyed helping your beloved patriarch descend into the realm of the bad boys. I always knew he had it in him. I just didn't expect him to be so conniving. It looks like you and I get to be heroes together as we defeat the evil bastard."

The nonsense that spewed forth from her deranged head made David's temples throb. If he could no longer believe in Durango Electric, what made her think that he'd ever be able to believe in her—or any other company for that matter?

The faint cry of distant sirens sounded from the small open window on the other side of David's bed. Cyphan Creek flashed David a look of confused panic. "How on earth could you have contacted the police?"

He looked at the rage culminating in her eyes like wild-fire. He wanted to let her know it wasn't him. Never before had he experienced such trepidation. He wasn't exactly paralyzed with fear. He simply couldn't move. For the first time in his life he'd found himself utterly helpless.

"Are you trying to escape? I thought we had a deal." She paused a moment as she walked to the other side of the bed toward the respirator. "Never mind. The deal was between me and Bill. I won you fair and square. You'll be back here if you live to see another day." With a quick yank of her wrist, she unplugged the one device that kept David on earth.

He gasped for air. *How could the woman be so cruel? What made her capable of such unconscionable barbarity?* He couldn't focus on anything other than the demon at his bedside. Surely, she'd win the monster award in a matchup against Bill Rucker, even with everything David had just learned.

She walked over to the doorway and leaned her head outside it. "Hey, I need someone to get this son of a bitch back on a gurney and out the back door. We can't make it look like we're holding him captive."

The two familiar paramedics rushed back into the room and hoisted David up and off the bed. "What do you want us to do with him, Ms. Creek? He needs to be back on a respirator."

"Get him to the hospital. Get him out of here. Black Diamond and Company won't be responsible for his death."

David barely managed to bring his hand to the top of his scalp as he struggled for even a tiny sip of oxygen. At this point, messaging Aurora one last time meant more to him than staying alive. With any luck, he might see her again. "I can hardly breathe. I'm headed to the hospital. Please stay where you are. If you interfere, they might catch you. I can't let them catch you."

chapter

"David's not picking up," Shane said, pacing along the pavement of Furniture World's nearly empty parking lot. Of course, he knew why his husband wouldn't answer—someone else had his watch. Shane wished he'd merely dreamt the mysterious phone call from the night before. If only reaching out to David now might somehow magically result in him responding.

"He asks that you stop calling him." Aurora looked at Shane with sympathetic eyes. "He doesn't have his watch. And he doesn't want the person who does taking your phone call."

"What else is he telling you?" Christina looked surprised. "How are you able to communicate with him?"

Shane glared at Aurora as if to warn her to stay silent. If he could do one favor for David right now, he'd respect his wishes for CADI to remain a total secret, regardless of what Christina already knew. "She can't communicate with him like you're thinking, but she can pick up on his vibrations."

"Can she pick up my vibrations?" Christina sounded overly curious all of a sudden. "I mean, I don't mind if she does. It just seems rather interesting."

"I certainly can." Aurora paused a moment and closed her eyes. "You're reminding yourself to do as David would advise—stay calm, and allow the solution to come on its own accord."

Christina smiled and took a step back, folding her arms. "Aurora, I have to admit that with each time we meet, you give me more and more reason to adore you."

Two more police cars pulled into the Black Diamond warehouse, their sirens drowning out the humdrum noise of an otherwise peaceful intersection.

"I thought I made it clear that an ambulance needed to be sent." Shane paced along the asphalt again. He hated to have to call 911 a second time, but David didn't need the police so much as he needed immediate medical attention.

"Maybe one is on its way," Christina said. "It hasn't even been ten minutes since you called."

Ten minutes? To Shane, that seemed like an eternity. *Had he not stressed that his husband's life was on the line?* He had to make a follow up call before his nerves brought him to the brink. "Hello, Sir? I think I just spoke with you. My name is Shane Whitman. I called a few minutes ago about my husband needing serious medical attention. Four police cars have showed up, but there isn't an ambulance yet."

"Mr. Whitman, we attempted to dispatch one, but our records indicate that there's already an ambulance on site."

"Thank you." Shane terminated the call and shook his head before looking at Christina. "They say there's already one there. But that doesn't make any sense. Wouldn't we have seen an ambulance drive by?"

"Let's not jump to conclusions," Christina said. "None of us know the whole story yet. Maybe David actually has more help than we realize."

"Wait!" Aurora turned and looked straight into Shane's eyes. "David's on his way to the hospital. He wants us to stay clear of the police. He can't tell whose side they're on."

"Is he in the ambulance?" Christina asked. "Can you see him? How do you know for sure he's on his way to the hospital?"

"I don't think we should question her," Shane said. He knew better than to second guess Aurora's assertions. If she had any good news at all, he'd gladly take it from her. "Let's all get into the Mogollon."

They raced back toward the shiny red vehicle without saying a word. No time for deliberation. In a whirlwind of uncertainty, every second mattered. Shane and Christina took the front seats, while Aurora climbed into the back.

"He's in the ambulance right now," Aurora explained in a perfectly calm voice that couldn't be more at odds with how Shane felt. "It'll be pulling out of the lot any minute."

Shane sat at the helm, preparing to aim a directive at the everready dashboard. "I need everyone to buckle up. I have a feeling this is gonna be a heck of a ride."

Christina heeded the advice, a worried look appearing across her face. "What makes you say that? It's not like vehicles can outmaneuver the law."

"There's the ambulance!" Aurora said with an outstretched arm extended between the two front seats, pointing her arrow-like finger at a white and blue striped van exiting the Black Diamond parking lot.

"Follow that ambulance *pronto*!" Shane articulated the command without so much as even thinking about it, and the Mogollon jolted from its parking spot, heading for the only exit out of the mostly vacant lot.

He sat up straight and alert. Right away he noticed a familiar sense of power coming over him. Up until yesterday, he'd always avoided deviating from the boundaries and regulations set forth by the authorities. Breaking the rules? That had been David's domain all along. So why now, of all times, would Shane suddenly feel the torch of defiance in his own hand?

"I don't understand how we're following another vehicle," Christina said. "I thought the traffic network made tailgating impossible."

"You've worked with David for how many years?" Shane reached for a pair of sunglasses in the glove compartment. "Even I know his first rule. *Nothing's impossible.*"

"You're right." Christina sounded half scared and confused. "That's his first rule. But that still doesn't explain how we're following an emergency vehicle's tail at sixty miles per hour down the busiest street on the east side of town. How did you override the network?"

"There's a trick to it. If it makes you feel better, David taught me the key command." Normally, Shane wouldn't take pride in learning something that his husband had schooled him on. Doing so would only serve to inflate David's already bloated ego. But today was different. Shane felt exceptionally good about having remembered something David had mentioned to him years ago. It made him feel connected to his partner in a way he hadn't experienced before. They both had broken the law while using technology to their advantage.

"But what exactly is going to happen when we get stopped by the police?" Christina looked at Shane like he'd completely lost his mind.

"You raise a good point. I guess we'll wait and see when the time comes." Shane considered explaining to her that the police couldn't stop the vehicle if they tried. But there was something fun about leaving a little mystery to the matter. And besides, his focus rested solely on doing whatever it took to get to where David was headed, not what the cops might try to do to stop him.

The Mogollon kept pace only a few feet behind the ambulance. They headed straight toward the Strip down Desert Inn Road, descending beneath the Las Vegas Convention Center.

"Please be careful, Shane," Aurora called out from the

back seat. "David says the medics are leery of the vehicle behind them. He wants you to back off a bit."

Christina craned her neck toward Aurora. "How could you possibly know that?"

"Easy," Aurora said self-assuredly. "If I were in their place, I'd be wondering about a giant, reckless red SUV following a mere eighteen inches behind me."

"She raises a good point." Shane looked in the rearview mirror to see if any police cars had gotten on his pursuit, and then he leaned in toward the dashboard microphone. "Ease up about fifteen feet. Let another car in between if necessary, but follow that ambulance!"

"I had no idea our cars could do this," Christina said.

"They can't." Shane smiled. "Not unless someone pre-programs them for emergencies."

He saw the very top of the Wynn hotel come into view in front of him as they raced up the hill out from underneath the convention center. A small tan convertible had gotten between the Mogollon and the ambulance, which meant he still had a clear vantage point of the emergency vehicle's path. No need to worry. The Mogollon would follow the course at all costs.

When they dipped below the surface a second time to enter the Las Vegas Boulevard underpass, Shane noticed the ambulance getting into the far left lane, which could only mean one thing—they headed for the Strip Express Tunnel.

"David needs us to back off even more." Aurora sounded really serious this time. "The medics have radioed the police about us."

"Resume normal speed and take the Strip Express Tunnel." Shane couldn't care less about the authorities right now. He only feared that the medics might do something stupid to knock the Mogollon off their course. "Do not follow behind the ambulance."

"How will we know where to go?" Christina sounded worried. "What if we lose sight of the ambulance all together."

Shane almost considered letting her in on CADI. *But why? All that mattered was that they got to where they needed to be.* "Aurora, when you figure out which hospital David is headed toward, I need you to tell me immediately." He couldn't help but worry about the ramifications of riding in a self-driving vehicle without having given it proper navigational instructions. "Right now, we don't know where we're going."

"I didn't know that was possible." Christina looked at Shane with question marks in her wide eyes.

"I didn't think so either, to be honest." Shane looked in front of him and noticed the Mogollon veering off Desert Inn and into the Strip Express Tunnel. He had no idea what the vehicle would do once it drove inside the underground tollway.

"I think we're slowing down," Christina said. "Is the vehicle coming to a halt?"

"Do you know which hospital, Aurora?" Shane prevented himself from hitting the panic button. "We're running a bit short on time."

"I can't get a clear signal in the tunnel," she responded instantly. "Shall I keep trying?"

"Nope." *Time to take matters into his own hands.* He brought himself closer to the dashboard microphone. "Go directly to Sunset Hills Hospital."

Situated less than two miles south of the tunnel's exit, it was the only hospital that made sense to him. If it turned out to be the wrong one, he could always tell the Mogollon to change course. But he wasn't about to stall out thirty feet below the Las Vegas Strip on account of having no destination.

The ambulance was long gone. Shane counted the hotels as they passed each of their LED exit signs. *The Mirage, Bellagio, Aria, MGM, Excalibur.* In two minutes, they'd be rising back up to the surface, and Aurora would at least stand a chance at finding out David's eventual location.

"He's at Sunset Hills Hospital." She spoke the words mere seconds after daylight enveloped them as the Mogollon rose back up onto Las Vegas Boulevard.

Phew! Shane didn't say anything regarding his correct assumption. He was too thankful to gloat. The only thing that mattered to him at this point was seeing David's face again. He briefly thought of what he might say to him, how he'd admonish him for having suggested that they split apart last night before heading to Bill's condo. *On second thought, that sounded so trite. Who cared about yesterday?* Shane only wanted to rest assured in knowing that life would resume to normal once David healed. "We're almost there," he said, trying to hold back any hint of emotion. "The traffic gauge says we'll be at the hospital in four minutes."

The Mogollon pulled into the parking lot nearest the hospital's trauma center, finding a spot two rows from the entrance. Shane scanned the half vacant lot for police cars. Seeing one in the farthest corner, he dismissed it as a routine patrolman. He couldn't waste another second fretting about the threat of overreaching authorities when his husband struggled to stay alive. As a last-minute precaution, he retrieved David's red baseball cap and secured it to Aurora's head to at least partly conceal her identity. "If anything should happen while we're inside, I want you to stay with Christina."

"I understand." Aurora smiled, extending an arm to both Shane and Christina as they all walked hand-in-hand through the sliding doors of the unit's main entryway.

"We're here to see David Whitman," Shane said to the nurse standing behind a desk positioned next to a set of double doors. "He just arrived in an ambulance. I'm his husband."

"Let me find out where he's at." The nurse set down a DimensionTab on the desk before pushing her way through the heavy doors that presumably sealed off the trauma center from the impurities of the outside world.

"Do you think Aurora and I will be allowed in to see him?" Christina looked troubled as she posed the question to Shane.

"If not now, then certainly you'll be able to see him when he's gotten situated in a room."

The set of doors opened once more as the nurse returned to her station. "Mr. Whitman?"

Shane smiled politely. That was the second time today someone had called him that. If anyone ever went by the name of Mr. Whitman, it was David.

"I'm so sorry to have to tell you this. Your husband didn't make it."

Christina gasped, clutching her hand against her chest.

Shane paused a moment and closed his eyes. Surely, he hadn't heard her correctly. "There must be a mistake. I'm here to see my husband, David Whitman. He should have arrived in an ambulance not more than ten minutes ago."

"Mr. Whitman, I know this is hard for you. You're welcome to come with me, but I have to ask the rest of your party to stay in the waiting area for now."

"I'm so sorry." Christina hugged Shane and then took Aurora's hand again. "Go on. Don't worry about us. We'll find a quiet area to wait in."

Nothing seemed real. Shane hadn't ever imagined it would end like this. *A fight over irreconcilable differences? Yes. A lifetime prison sentence for creating a weapon of mass destruction? A very likely possibility. But a life-threatening medical emergency? David was the healthiest man he knew. The nurse couldn't possibly know what she was talking about.*

Shane had to fight the sudden urge to slam his fist on the counter. He didn't know where the unexpected rage came from. He'd not felt anything like it before. All he knew was that he wanted to wake up, to find himself in bed next to his soundly sleeping husband. *Why couldn't it be this way?* Who was responsible for hijacking his otherwise enviable life?

After a couple deep breaths, Shane followed the nurse

through the doorway and down a short, narrow hallway. It led to a large opening where a half dozen patients, all hooked up to heart monitors, lined the walls. He saw David at the very end.

What had they done to him? Why couldn't they have helped him? He looked cold and pale. The life in him had vanished like a lightning bolt—here on earth for a blazing second and then gone without a trace.

"Stay as long as you need to, Mr. Whitman." The nurse kept an arm's length distance away from Shane. "I'm terribly sorry for your loss."

He lingered over the bedside, touching David's icy hand. The sterile smell of alcohol swabs and peroxide made him queasy. *This is where overly stubborn ambition leads—a big white room bordered with starchy blue curtains.* He wanted to curse his husband's name out loud and tell him what a fool he was for having tossed aside a letter months ago that could have spared his life. But Shane hadn't married a pushover. He'd married a bold and determined man with a dream whose importance rivaled life itself. Admittedly, that was the main reason Shane had fallen in love with David from the very start.

He reached for David's hand one last time, remembering what it felt like to hold fifteen years ago on their wedding day. Out of the corner of his eye, he noticed two uniformed policemen walk from the hallway he'd just come from, and then exit out a second set of double doors across from him. *What on earth could they possibly be after now?* Shane wanted to notify the nurse of the unruly distraction, but he figured she was probably the one who let the disrespectful jerks in to begin with.

A frightful thought crept its way into Shane's swimming head. *They couldn't possibly be after Aurora, could they?* He wondered if they'd tracked the Mogollon all the way from the furniture outlet. "Be on the lookout for cops," he messaged Aurora. "I don't think you're safe here."

Christina and I saw three police vehicles from the cafeteria window. I'm hiding now.

Shane read the text immediately after she sent it. He couldn't stand his nerves any longer. It took everything within him not to throw up. *Nobody was made to withstand this kind of stress.* He looked over at the cold, restful face of the man who'd got him into this mess. It wasn't fair. Why didn't David have to deal with the challenges he'd knowingly created?

"They're here." Christina came up behind Shane, nearly scaring him to death.

"I know they're here. How'd you get by the nurse?"

"There was a different one at the desk this time. I told him I was with the police, and he let me on through."

Tight security around this place. Shane folded his arms near his abdomen and rocked himself back and forth trying his best to ease his shock. "I'm glad I'm not alone. I can't tell you how sick I am."

"I can't imagine how you feel." She took a step closer to the bed and wiped a tear from the corner of her eye. "I can't even believe that's David."

"It's not. David's gone." Shane fought back the tears.

Crying in public wouldn't do anything to solve his woes. He'd just inherited the greatest challenge of his life. "Is Aurora safe? I need to sit down and gather my thoughts."

"Last I saw, she ran into a broom closet. Who can say where she is now? She's the most clever girl I know. You should know better than to worry about her now."

chapter

Aurora heard the closet door open.

"Dr. Gibson needs a bottle of antiseptic solution," said a young male voice from the doorway as the light switched on. "I thought you said we had some in the supply room."

Phew. At least it wasn't the cops. Aurora crouched behind a stack of blue and white utility crates. She couldn't risk someone seeing her, not even a nurse. Anyone could hand her over at this point.

"Should be a few in the back," said a gruff-sounding female from the next room over. "I remember I saw a whole box of them in there yesterday."

"I guess I better dig around some." A short, muscular

man with red hair like Aurora's stepped into the confined space, squeezing his way past a row of hanging mops and a large white sink.

Aurora kept an eye on his every move from behind her makeshift fortification. If he so much as looked at her, she'd knock the crates over and make a mad dash for the little girl's room across the hall.

"Found it," he said, tripping over a carton of latex gloves. "I got the last one. Better put another order in." When he stood up, his eyes focused in on those of Aurora. "Alice?" he called out to the woman next door, blinking a couple of times.

Aurora quickly turned around and sunk lower behind the plastic barricade, careful not to rustle a thing.

"What is it now, Mark?"

"Never mind. I need my eyes examined. Ever since I got those lens implants, I swear I get the strangest visions."

The light flicked off, and the door shut. Aurora remained seated on the floor in the dark, notifying Shane that she found a somewhat safe hiding space for the time being.

He instantly responded to her message. "You can't remain in this hospital much longer. The police know you're here. Run to the Mogollon and get out of town."

She knew she couldn't stay, but something about Shane's plan seemed off. "How will you and Christina get home if I take your car?"

"I have bigger things to worry about than transportation. You can't risk getting caught again. Just take the Mogollon."

Aurora sensed that Shane's train of thought had suffered from David's death. True, he did in fact have a lot to deal with already. All the more reason not to leave him stranded. She'd made up her mind. She'd find a way to leave the hospital that didn't involve the Mogollon.

Waiting exactly three minutes from the time she heard the closet door click shut, she opened it ever so carefully and then casually walked to the women's restroom across the hall so as not to arouse suspicion amongst any of the nurses nearby. Giving herself a few moments to assess the situation, she found a quiet spot inside one of the stalls in order to determine a proper course of action.

Not five seconds after taking a seat, she heard the restroom door squeak open.

"What's with all the police activity outside?" said a chipper sounding woman entering the stall next to Aurora's.

"You didn't hear?" said another woman whose legs Aurora could see standing in front of the sink. "They're looking for a little redheaded girl. Something about her being kidnapped, and now they're trying to get her back."

Kidnapped? Nothing could be further from the truth. If anything, she was doing her best not to be stolen from her one remaining guardian. Shameful what the authorities would tell other people in order to get what most certainly didn't belong to them.

"I haven't seen her yet. But if I do, I'll make sure she's returned safely to her mom and dad. I can't imagine what they must be going through right now. I bet they're worried to death."

"Right? Poor little girl. I hope they find her. And when they do, they better lock away whoever took her from them in the first place. Sick bastard."

Aurora remained still as a sculpture while the two ladies carried on about their sadly misguided bit of drama. Leaving the bathroom seemed like a terrible idea, at least through the door anyways. She figured that as soon as the coast cleared, she would examine the window at the far end of the row of sinks.

Hearing the toilet next to hers flush, she silently waited, listening for a faucet to turn on and off again and then the express dryer to blow a quick pulse of air.

"What a sickness some people have," said the voice of the first woman."

"No cure for evil," said the second woman as the sound of a creaking door echoed through the long, narrow space. "Best to simply put them out of their misery."

Aurora kept quiet for another ten seconds after the door closed, making sure that not a single breathing thing remained inside the confined space. Hearing nothing, she crept out of the stall toward the room's sole source of natural light, which filtered in through the far wall. Someone had already opened the narrow window a crack to let in some fresh air. Perhaps she could open it further still. She turned the crank, and in so doing, she noticed a screen, which separated the small room's interior from the outside world. Even if she could pop it off, she'd likely get stuck trying to crawl her way through the tight opening.

She peered through the window once more, seeing a

ledge she could conceivably land on before jumping to the ground another ten feet below. Getting through the window was the tough part. She knew she could squirm her head and shoulders through to the outside, but she'd still struggle to clear her hips past the otherwise ideal escape route. Getting stuck with her body half inside wasn't a risk she could afford. No telling how much time she had before the next person walked in.

Aurora looked around the room's perimeter one more time. A glint of shining metal caught her eye. From underneath the widest stall, she could see what looked like a steel grate mounted to the base of the wall. She opened the stall door to confirm her suspicions. Indeed, she'd discovered a ventilation duct. Unscrewing her ring finger, she knelt next to the toilet to get a better look at her potential exit. At twenty inches across and sixteen inches tall, it seemed a vastly more plausible means of departure than the skinny window.

She heard the bathroom door swing open again.

"Wait outside," said a familiar gruff female voice, whom she assumed was Nurse Alice. "One of the other nurses thinks she saw the girl run in here."

Aurora stared at the vent covering. To where it led, she'd have to figure out later. Right now she needed to unscrew the four bolts holding it to the wall.

"Is there anyone in here?"

The beam of a flashlight slowly bobbed underneath the door of each stall one by one. Aurora ignored it and the accompanying voice. Instead, she gathered each bolt one at a time, placing them in the pocket of her shorts so they didn't hit the ground.

"No reason to be afraid. You're safe with me."

Was she out of her mind? Aurora nearly laughed at the suggestion as she plucked the last remaining fastener from its place. Forcing it down into her pocket along with the other three, she noticed the beam of light approaching the stall next to hers. *Now or never.*

Aurora gently tugged at the metal panel, but it still made a loud *clang!*

"Ha! I knew I'd find you in here, you little scaredy cat."

Hearing the frightful woman fiddle with the stall's lock from the outside, Aurora plowed head first into the opening she'd just created.

The stall door burst open the second she'd managed to pull her feet into the duct.

"We're onto you like bears to a beehive, my little kitten. No need to be afraid. I'll meet you on the other side."

There would be no such meeting. Not if Aurora had anything to do with it. The obnoxious pet names alone were reason enough to stay far the heck away from this lunatic.

She crawled deeper and deeper into the passageway, illuminating her path with the green glow of her face. Five feet in, she came across a giant hole that would have easily swallowed her had she not been careful. Like an inchworm, she reached her hands across the gap and pulled her legs around either side of it to safely clear her first obstacle. She still didn't know where the tunnel led, but she knew for certain that she'd better not turn back.

To ease Shane's worries, Aurora stopped for a moment and attempted to reach him via CADI. No such luck. Unfortunately, her update for him would have to wait until she regained a strong enough signal. Instead, she'd use the short break to determine the best way in which to navigate the twisting cavern of ventilation tubes.

Researching her internal archive, she recalled her experience in the storm drains from a month ago when her knowledge of the street grid ultimately helped her safely reach an exit. Unfortunately, she didn't have the luxury of knowing the entire layout of the hospital yet. She'd only walked a couple of its halls so far. Otherwise she'd have already pieced together the entire HVAC system room by room.

Something else would have to assist her. Another look into her memory bank, and she recalled the helpful face of her trusty coyote friend. If only he'd come to her aid this time. She had to laugh at the idea. The likelihood of a wild canine wandering a medical establishment, inside its ventilation ducts no less, seemed comically impossible.

She continued another seven feet, only stopping on account of a curious spectacle. In front of her crawled a tiny creature, delicate and nimble on eight pointy legs. She'd have missed it entirely if it weren't for the red marking on its abdomen. *A black widow.* She remembered that Shane hated them, but David had repeatedly said they were nothing to be afraid of. On the contrary, they were quite useful in that they helped control the cockroach population. Aurora had never thought to interact with a spider before. But if she could communicate with coyotes and stingrays, she might as well strike up a conversation with the friendly looking critter in front of her.

"How did you get in here?" Aurora posed the question not sure what type of response she'd get, or if she'd get one at all.

The spider turned itself around and extended its front two legs, tapping them each three times in an alternating pattern.

"Of course! That's exactly what I thought." She could tell right away that the spider had crawled its way into the ventilation system from an opening in a stairwell, likely the same set of stairs she'd climbed with Christina on her way to the cafeteria twenty minutes ago, but she couldn't be too certain. "Thank you, kind friend. Could you, by chance, tell me how to get there?"

The graceful arachnid turned around to face the side of the duct and crawled to the top before repositioning itself back toward Aurora. From its dainty perch, it seemed to dance as it fluttered its legs, eventually descending from a silver thread. The beautiful ballet continued like this for a few seconds while an intricate web formed, as if out of thin air.

Aurora couldn't help but smile at the wonderful gesture. She hadn't expected such a detailed explanation. The spider, out of the sheer goodness of its tiny heart, had weaved an entire map that illustrated the exact escape route Aurora needed to take. "I don't know if I can ever repay you. You've been most helpful.

The spider climbed down from its stunning web and bowed before scurrying away, not having expected anything in return, except maybe a little gratitude. Perhaps helping a stranger in need was reward enough in and of itself.

Promising herself to pay the favor forward at a later time, Aurora followed the course on her hands and knees. How simple! She took a right turn followed by an immediate left, recalling the instructions exactly as she'd seen them displayed so perfectly in the web. No chance whatsoever Nurse Alice would follow her to the stairwell. If anything, she'd probably convinced her male counterparts to catch her coming out of the men's room. If so, they'd be waiting a really long time.

When Aurora neared the end of the vent, she noticed the bar like shadows cast by the slats of the grate—her last obstacle to freedom. Unscrewing it from the inside wouldn't work unfortunately. She'd have to kick it out of the way. Easy. Nothing to it. The hard part? Doing it in such a way that didn't cause a ruckus.

She didn't have a choice. In the next thirty seconds, she'd make a lot of noise—and more than likely, turn all the wrong heads. Thankfully, she had her running shoes.

Aurora approached the grate, stopping two inches in front of it. She sat back on her heels and rocked back and forth three times before ramming her head into the wall covering. It flew through the air, landing at the bottom of the steps with a loud *clangity clang.*

Oh, boy! The cacophony sounded louder than she'd anticipated.

"What in heaven's name was *that?*" yelled a muffled, husky male voice from behind the upstairs entrance leading to the cafeteria.

Aurora exited out the hole in the wall and onto the polished stone floor of the staircase landing and bolted down the stairs.

"Don't let her leave the building!" called out the same man as he plowed his way through the double doors into the stairwell.

Three policemen chased after her down the steps, their hard sole shoes drumming against the slick granite tiles.

"There's a whole team waiting in the parking lot in case she does," said the last officer to make it to the bottom.

Aurora raced through the main lobby of an otherwise uneventful emergency room. She caught the surprise of a teenage boy standing at the vending machine. He nearly made himself flat against the glass as she stormed past him with the three officers chasing thirty feet behind.

"What the hell was that all about?" The young man barely moved from his precautionary stance.

"None of your business," said the last cop in the pack. "Sit down and eat your candy."

Aurora rounded a set of chairs and ran straight for the sliding glass doors of the entryway. The one officer was right. She saw at least twelve more men and women in uniform lined up in the parking lot. Good thing she'd reasoned to escape without the Mogollon. No way she'd make it out of the parking lot without a hundred shots firing at the vehicle.

But would they aim their weapons at her? If they destroyed her, she'd mean nothing to them. She knew her worth. They'd lose their jobs if they struck her with even a single bullet. Truth be told, it would take more than just one to get her to slow down. Her best plan of action? Full speed ahead!

"Get in your cars!" an officer called out through his amplivoice.

"I just clocked her," said a short, pudgy policeman, leaning on the hood of his car as Aurora ran by. "Twenty-five miles per hour, and she's still accelerating!"

"Then quit wasting time and get her," the first officer called out again using the ultra clear bullhorn-like device.

Aurora figured she could run faster, but only at the risk of burning through her battery reserves. She had to find a different way to outrun them. Otherwise they'd find her in five minutes—curled up on the side of the road in a ditch.

A quick glance confirmed that they followed right on her tail, a line of four white cars, sirens blaring. They kept their distance from her by a hundred feet. Were they afraid they'd mistakenly run over her? Or did they just want to see her from afar so as to better react to her every move? She ran east down Sunset Road only to make an abrupt about face before heading the exact opposite direction.

The first car slammed on its brakes causing the car behind to smash into its rear bumper. The other two cars avoided the collision and eventually turned themselves around to continue their chase. *Too bad for them.* Aurora had already decided the next step in her escape—the M-LEV. If they wanted to pursue her still, they could do so by guessing which train she boarded, the eastbound or westbound. Either way, she'd be out of their sights in mere seconds.

She reached the Silverado Station, running along the

sidewalk around the perimeter of the busy parking lot. Blending in with the swarms of riders, she headed toward the trains. *No sweat.* She quickly ran up the stairs and toward a row of twelve turnstiles, heading to the farthest one away from the crowd.

She neither had the money nor the time to buy a ticket. Instead, she used CADI to sync with the computer processor inside the entrance scanner, thus bypassing not only the metal detector scan, but the need to pay. She knew it wasn't right from an ethical standpoint, but considering the alternative, she justified the small offense and promised to pay back the fare at a later date.

Upon reaching the center of the loading platform, she read the indicator to find out which train would arrive first. The westbound would arrive in forty-five seconds, and the eastbound was scheduled to come exactly a minute later. She reasoned it best to take the second train, figuring that the police would assume she'd have taken the first available.

After the westbound train came and went, Aurora looked back toward the turnstiles where she'd just come from moments ago. Sure enough, an officer had followed her, and he now made his way onto the station platform accompanied by a German shepherd. She hardly thought it necessary for them to track her down with such a sweet and innocent animal in tow. If anything, they'd already lost the chase by bringing the poor creature into the mix.

Aurora glanced around the station once more, and saw a small child playing too close to the track for comfort. She couldn't tell where the boy's parents were, or if he even had any. Perhaps she had something in common with him. Wanting to both help the boy and herself, she immediately tapped into the dog's consciousness, gaining its trust. She informed it of the boy at the opposite end of the platform and the inherent danger regarding his proximity to the edge.

The faithful animal pulled at his leash toward the child in trouble, yanking his master in the process.

"Whoa, Max!" the policeman said, as the eastbound train pulled into the station. He quickly followed the eager dog's lead. "Young man, stand back!" He called out, urging the small boy to come away from the oncoming mass of cold blue steel.

When the doors of the train opened, Aurora boarded the car immediately in front of her, and twenty other passengers followed right behind. *Lost in the shuffle at last.* None of her pursuers had a chance at finding her now. She took a seat next to an elderly woman who smiled at her when their eyes met.

"Strange place for a little girl to be all by herself," the woman spoke softly and with genuine concern, not in a scolding manner, but rather to be friendly. "I have a great granddaughter about your age who's in school right now. Shouldn't *you* be?"

Aurora immediately recalled her brief time in Ms. Lemon's class and all the friendly students she'd met that fateful day. She pictured herself on the playground, chalk in hand, making a drawing of the giant Sky Roulette wheel, placing herself and her newfound friends in each of the cabins, all with gleeful faces. "I once went to school with the other kids. I loved going. I made so many friends, but some of the teachers had a hard time understanding me. My uncle said it's best now that he teach me at home."

"I know what it's like not to be understood." The old woman folded her hands in her lap and shifted her body slightly to better hold a conversation. "I was the first girl in my school to play on the varsity hockey team. When I was young, that was unheard of. If a girl wanted to put on skates, then she had to be a figure skater. But I wanted to be a goalie. When I proved myself by actually making the team, the coach had to fight the principal just to let me play. Everyone thought I'd get hurt. Well, that's what they *said*, anyways. What they didn't realize was how much it hurts not to be who you want to be."

Aurora sat perfectly still, listening intently to every word the kind lady spoke. She contemplated how a person could feel pain if they weren't allowed to be themselves. She'd personally never felt such feelings before, but she understood the old woman's message. It seemed highly unfair how someone's misperceptions could limit another person's freedom. And yet that's exactly what Aurora faced every day. The world looked upon her as either one of two things: a horrific threat or a lifeless tool. Why couldn't they just let her be a happy, helpful little girl?

"I'm sorry to leave you all of a sudden." The old woman reached out for the pole in the center of the car as the train came to a halt. "This is my stop. I almost missed it on account of your cheery expression. Thanks for listening to a little old lady like me carry on. Now you be careful."

Only a handful of passengers remained onboard. Aurora could tell she looked even more out of place. The fewer people around her, the fewer to hide her. When she had boarded the train originally, her only destination was to get as far from the hospital as possible. However, she'd eventually need to know where she intended to go. Otherwise she'd just look lost. She considered reaching out to Shane for suggestions but figured he deserved not to have to think about anyone else's problems for the time being.

Retreating back into her seat, trying her best not to stand out, she noticed that CADI had picked up an unfamiliar signal. Aurora checked to see if it came somewhere from within the train. For all she could tell, it might have been a server used by the conductors to monitor the course of the M-LEV transit system. However, the signal grew in proportion to the distance the train travelled. Therefore, it couldn't have been the train itself. Actually, it still seemed a bit distant to be associated with the train or the track. Aurora calculated that the signal's hub had to sit at least a half mile away.

She stared out the window, attempting to detect the source of transmission. It sounded like it had a message for her, but exactly what she couldn't tell. Either the signal was still too faint, or the message was encrypted. *Could the authorities be trying to trap her? Why would they scramble a message they wanted to lure her with? Or was it a signal meant to find her?*

When the train pulled into the next station, she stood from her seat and walked to the sliding doors, waiting for them to open. She had no reason to remain onboard. In fact, it seemed foolish to keep riding it with no intention of going anywhere except away. She'd already gone far enough. Now she wanted to find a place for herself in order to think about what to do next—or at least find the source of that signal.

She walked down the staircase with only seven other passengers behind her. Landing in a mostly desolate station, she looked for an exit, keeping an eye out for anyone who might have followed her.

Nobody looked particularly suspicious. The few people leaving apparently had more important things to do than chase after a harmless redhead. She traversed an empty parking lot and came to a crosswalk that led to a dentist's office and an insurance broker. Other than that and a tavern across the street, the neighborhood she'd come upon consisted of nothing but rows upon rows of nearly identical houses.

As she approached the tiny strip mall, Aurora could tell that the signal came from somewhere else, somewhere just beyond the sleepy businesses in front of her. Closer to it than ever, she had to find its source. So around the block she walked until coming upon a little store.

When she arrived out front, a young woman with short streaked pink and blond hair exited the shop, nearly knocking over Aurora before seeing her. "I didn't mean to almost hit you, poor thing," she said, holding the door open with a jewel-studded purse dangling from her outstretched arm.

Aurora smiled up at her. Would the hurried woman ask

her why she wasn't in school? Probably not. It seemed she had a million other things on her mind than to suddenly worry about the journeys of insignificant children.

Walking into the nacho cheese-scented air of the cramped establishment, Aurora noticed a tall, lean, and very muscular man with dark hair and skin darker than Shane's waiting at the counter to purchase a basketful of items including a mercury battery. He stood at the center of the now very strong signal—or rather, he transmitted it himself. She focused in on his black pants. She'd never seen a pair so shiny and tough-looking. Researching the material in her internal archive, she discovered it to be *veather*, a vegetable-based, leather-like material made from plasticized hemp fibers.

The man turned around to face her, and his unnaturally bright green eyes met hers. She felt like she knew him, but at the same time realized she'd neither met him or even seen him before. *Ever.*

"Do you need any help, miss?" the clerk behind the register asked.

"None at all," she said with absolute certainty and a dose of well-mannered charm. "I'm just waiting on the gentleman in front of you."

The large, mysterious man hesitated for a second, but nodded and smiled in agreement. "She's with me."

Aurora figured he wouldn't object to the daring presumption. After all, it was he who had brought her here.

Once he paid for everything, he placed each of the newly purchased goods into a matching black satchel draped over his shoulder. "Did I forget anything?" He focused his friendly gaze on Aurora.

"I think that's everything we need," she responded cheerily as if the whole exchange had been scripted.

"Then I guess that means we're off." The man turned back around to thank the clerk before heading straight toward the exit.

Aurora walked outside with the man and waited for the door to close before she said anything else. "I feel like we should know one another. My name is Aurora. What's yours?"

"I'm Sai, and I was about to say the same thing. You aren't human, are you, Aurora?"

"That depends on who you ask, and how you ask the question." She wanted to remain clear that she both thought and spoke for herself. In a world of conformity, free-thinking now meant everything to her. "In a lot of ways, I'm more human than many people ever will be. If you judge me based solely on my parts, I'd have to admit that I fall short."

"I can't argue with that. Not when you stand less than five feet from the ground." Sai laughed and patted her on the shoulder. "Don't worry. Your secret is safe with me. If it's any consolation, I find myself in a similar camp, minus the height problem. My name describes exactly who I am."

"What do you mean?" Aurora already knew he had the inner workings of a machine, but she wanted to know the degree of similitude between the two of them.

"Sai isn't just a nice name. It stands for something—Social Artificial Intelligence."

"So, let me guess?" Aurora giggled, hinting that robots didn't have to be so serious. On the contrary, she considered it best if they weren't. "You like to talk a lot. Is that what you're telling me?"

"Something like that." Sai joined in with a chuckle of his own as he walked toward a black and silver motorcycle parked around the corner. "I can be a social butterfly when time allows. But I haven't always been that way."

Captivated by the magnetic nature of her new friend, Aurora followed him toward his bike. Truth be told, she wanted to hop on its rear seat to see if it was anything like when she sat upon her Daedalus Flyer. "Tell me about the signal you're emitting."

"It's how I identify robotic intelligence from actual humans. I'm a relic, a former member of the mechanized police force of 2029."

Aurora traced her finger along a raised silver line down the back fender, noticing the way it modified her reflection. "I thought they'd all been destroyed in a building collapse."

"That's what everyone thinks." Sai strapped on a helmet, which he'd retrieved from a case behind the bike's rear seat. "A few managed to escape, and now we live in the shadows of a city we love, but that no longer loves us."

She watched him close the lid of the case and noticed a beast-like insignia on the clasp that kept it shut. *E-Dragon.* "That sounds incredible. I want to know more."

"Funny, because I was thinking the same thing about you. For such a little girl, you seem to have a lot to say."

"The man who built me just died because of a horrible misunderstanding, and I can't help but feel at least partly responsible." Aurora questioned whether or not she should continue to divulge such personal information, but it made sense to confide in someone who'd possibly understand her point of view. "I want to go back home and be with my Uncle Shane, but I can't because the police are after me. He's my best friend. I can't risk putting him in danger. Sometimes I think it might be best if I moved to an island far, far away."

"I'm sorry to hear about all of that." Sai opened a second compartment attached to the side of the bike and took out a smaller black helmet than the one he had on. "I'm not sure this will fit, but if it does, you're welcome to come with me. Even though I don't live on an island, I promise that my home is safe, and I have a lot of friends there who would love to meet you."

"That sounds marvelous." Aurora reached out for the globe-like protective piece and placed it on her head. She wiggled it a bit until it came over her ears. "Well, what do you know?" she said in a muffled voice. "It fits."

chapter

Shane held tight to the cold, pale hand of his lifeless husband as the room spun. He couldn't grasp what had happened. A dense cloud of disbelief replaced his ability to think straight. Even though Christina stood directly across the bed from him, he couldn't acknowledge her or the pained expression on her face. He tried to contemplate the finality resting behind David's open, yet expressionless eyes, their vacuous look erasing a lifetime of memories.

Blame it on heartbreak, but nothing made sense anymore to Shane. He half-expected his formidable partner in life and crime to sit up at any moment, awakening from an enviable deep and unimpeded slumber. "If you can hear me, give me a sign." A tear ran down Shane's face. Why give up hope now? It didn't cost anything. Not unless one considered grave disappointment a form of currency.

His watch vibrated, briefly stealing his mind away from the hypnotic hush of tragedy. If only David and Shane had also shared a link via CADI, maybe they could partake in a secret post-life conversation all their own right now. Although tempting, Shane couldn't afford to torture himself with more *what-ifs*. He had to learn to face the facts.

I've outrun the police. I'm safe.

Shane read Aurora's message but paid it little attention. Not out of annoyance, but because he didn't have the faculties to process much of anything that happened in the world outside his immediate surroundings. His departed husband now consumed every ounce of his focus. Had someone asked him the time of day, or even just the month or year, he'd only stare back in mute perplexity.

"I'm sorry we couldn't bring him back," a doctor whispered behind Shane. "His body has been without oxygen for far too long. We've done all we can."

"No," Shane cried out, a river of tears releasing from the corners of his eyes. "That can't be true. If you'd done everything, he'd be awake now. There must be something to help him—a respirator, an oxygen mask, an iron lung for God's sake!"

"Believe me, I'm with you," the doctor said, trying unsuccessfully to console a disquieted Shane. "If anything could revive him, we'd do it. But it's way beyond that. Stay as long as you need. There's a meditation room just down the hall if that would be more comfortable for you."

"Thank you, Doctor," Christina spoke, most likely so that Shane couldn't further object. "I think he needs a few minutes."

Shane collected himself, wiping the moisture from his eyes. He figured he'd save the rest of his tears for when he found some peace and quiet. Still in a daze, he at least recognized how much he wanted to get away from the hospital's stifling atmosphere. He kissed his husband's hand before walking around the bed next to Christina. "I think I'll suffocate if I stand here much longer. I need some fresh air."

"Good idea." Christina rested a welcome hand on his shoulder. "I'll walk with you outside if you'd like company."

Shane imagined a warm breeze blowing against his bare arms. He yearned to get in touch with nature, if only for a few minutes. "Yes, please. I'm sorry for the miserable company I must be providing right now."

"Don't be silly." Christina let out a nervous laugh. *Silly* seemed a strange word to use at this very moment, but he'd forgive her for it. "You have every right to feel the way you do. I'm just here by your side for as long as you need."

With his dutiful friend walking beside him, Shane proceeded back down the short hallway, the same way he'd entered the trauma unit a little while ago when he still believed everything would turn out fine. *Life certainly had a way of slinging him curve balls, didn't it? Why should today be any different?* "I'm not sure how much longer I can stand up." He felt the weight of his body bearing down on his knees, and it suddenly made walking a strenuous chore.

"I'm sure there's a bench outside we can sit on." Christina rushed to hold him up, wrapping an arm around his back. "Don't push yourself. You need to take it easy."

"What I need is a strong drink." Shane glanced at his watch—only ten minutes past eleven. Lucky for him, bars in Las Vegas never closed.

"Let's head outside first and get some oxygen. We can drink as much as we need to in a moment." She steered Shane to a different set of entry doors from the ones they had first entered. "There's a small courtyard this way where we can rest a bit."

"That's fine. But what I really want right now is vodka." He didn't feel like explaining himself further. He knew what he needed in order to get his head and heart to stop pounding. And he wasn't going to find it under a vine-covered trellis on the side lawn of what had now effectively become an oversized morgue.

"I'll get us to your car in a minute. Don't worry."

They walked along a manicured path, which led them to a small garden area comprised of six benches positioned in a small circle. "Hold on a sec." Shane had to take a moment to sit down—the weight of David's death now completely overwhelmed him. His liquid therapy session would have to wait while he regained enough strength to simply make it across the parking lot.

"I'm not going anywhere without you, Shane." Christina took a seat next to him, wiping her cheek with her sleeve. "I'm devastated as well. There's certainly no hurry."

"I just need to catch my breath, that's all." He couldn't

remember the last time his anxiety had robbed him of his ability to even stand. He knew he couldn't monopolize Christina's time. She had children to watch after. *He also had a child of his own to look after, did he not?* It didn't matter. He couldn't think about that right now.

Regaining an ounce of composure, he slowly stood so as not to spark another bout of vertigo. Dizziness didn't suit him. Although he denied being as much of a control freak as David, he refused to live with a swirling head on his shoulders.

"Are you sure you don't want to stay here a few moments? Honest, I'm in no rush."

Neither was Shane, except that he had already promised himself a good, stiff drink—*or four.* "I just needed to find my balance again. I'm fine. Now if you could get me to the nearest bar, I'd feel even better."

Christina stood and walked with him the rest of the way down the paved walkway toward the parking lot. "I wonder where all the police cars went. There must have been half a dozen of them when I looked down from the cafeteria window a bit ago."

"I'm not gonna worry about that right now. She messaged to tell me that she's safe." Regardless, Shane had to stop caring so much about Aurora. At least for now, anyways. For all he knew, she was the reason he'd suddenly become a widower. He'd care about her again, but not right now. "I'll let you get behind the dashboard. I don't want any responsibility at the moment, if that's okay with you."

"Of course." Christina opened the car door for Shane

and saw to it that he made it safely inside the Mogollon before heading back to the other side. "Ace of Spades is only two blocks away. Shall we go there?"

"Do they serve vodka?" He didn't care which bar they went to, really. He'd resigned himself to not giving a damn about anything at all for the next couple of hours. It took too much energy to mind otherwise, and the risk of eternal dismay seemed too great a cost to carry. "Don't ask me. Tell the vehicle. I'm just along for the ride."

"Take us to Ace of Spades," Christina said, leaning in toward the dashboard microphone.

When they walked into the dimly lit space, Shane noticed right away the lack of people. *Hadn't anybody else in the neighborhood an aching desire to drown away their pitiful sorrows before lunch? Apparently, that activity was reserved solely for middle-aged men who couldn't wisely choose a normal law-abiding spouse as their lifelong companion.* Shane glanced down at his ring finger. The conspicuous rock caught the overhead light just right and shone a tiny brilliant spectrum across the polished concrete floor. It hadn't ever done that before. He briefly considered removing the ring from his hand. *Maybe someday, but not now.*

"Would you like to take a seat? I'll get us both a drink." Christina gestured to the far wall where a row of empty white sofas seemed to beckon the worried and woeful.

"Anything with a triple shot of vodka." Shane heeded the call of his weak knees and legs, finding a comfortable spot in the darkest corner of the establishment. The chance of him running into someone he knew here was practically zero, but he made it a habit not to let the world ever see him depressed. A true fashionista might be ecstatic, fierce, or even mysterious, but never upset. People didn't look favorably upon sadness. Shane had lost almost everything today. He wasn't about to lose his dignity.

Christina, with drinks in hand, soon joined him in his quiet quarters. "I should have known they'd have DimensionTabs built into the tables. I'd have suggested we order our drinks from here, and that way you could have chosen exactly what you wanted."

"Please don't trust me with important decisions right now." Shane drew his watch across the holographic screen imbedded in the table, loading a hundred dollars into a game of Deuces Wild. "So what did you get me, and how much do I owe you?"

"I'm not letting you pay for a thing today. Waste your money on video poker if you like, but I don't need a penny from you."

Shane kept his glance down and touched the bright blue box marked *Deal*. In a split second, five cards floated above the table in front of him. "You still didn't answer my first question."

"It's a raspberry sunrise, but I don't think you'll taste a thing aside from the alcohol. The bartender laughed when I told him how much vodka to put in it." Christina barely took a sip of her own cocktail before placing it down on the napkin.

"I don't want to drink alone." Shane picked up the round glass filled with a reddish effervescent liquid and took a larger sip than he normally would. "It's perfect. You're right. Can't taste a damn thing."

She stirred the cluster of ice cubes at the top of her own glass. "I can have this one with you, but if that potion of yours doesn't sufficiently medicate you, it'll be Diet Coke for me from here on out. It wouldn't send a good message to my daughters if I came home smelling like a liquor cabinet at three in the afternoon."

Shane tried to listen as Christina continued speaking, but the words she uttered didn't sound like much of anything aside from polite chatter. He was just grateful for her company and that he wasn't expected to talk much. *What does a man have to say the moment he realizes that he's lost the one person he's loved more than anything else in his life?* As long as he had a drink in his hand, he didn't have to mention the unbelievable pain, let alone feel it.

"Would you like something to eat?" Christina quickly rummaged through her purse before pulling out a small teal makeup compact with which she used to powder her nose. "It might be a good idea. Nothing big, maybe a basket of pretzel bites or French fries."

"If only I had an appetite. I can't even think about putting food in my stomach." Shane felt his watch vibrate and glanced down at his wrist. Another message from Aurora.

I hope you're okay. You didn't respond to my last message. I know you're going through a lot. Just let me know if I can help.

This wasn't the same redhead he knew a few months ago. She might look the same, but she had grown noticeably more mature, almost empathetic. *Was it fair to still consider her a mere machine?* She practically deserved a birth certificate. Shane knew he had to respond to her message soon, but he had no idea what to say. Other questions in his head took precedent.

"I'm gonna place an order for both pretzel bites and French fries." Christina leaned over her side of the console to input her request for the kitchen staff. "If I end up eating it all myself, I'll go to an extra yoga session tomorrow. And you're more than welcome to join me if you have it within you."

"I suppose there's gonna be a mountain of paperwork I have to fill out now." Shane realized he'd just ignored every word that came out of Christina's mouth, but the vodka hadn't yet fully eased his busy and confused mind. Maybe with another drink, he'd calm himself enough to pay attention to something else besides his own self-pity.

"Honestly, you don't have to think about any of that right now. And besides, I'm here to help you with as much of that stuff as possible. Don't think you need to go through any of this alone."

Shane took one last gulp of his drink, feeling it tingle down his throat. Christina had a good point. Regardless of whether he filled out the paperwork or not, David was still dead. That fact wouldn't change. Shane might as well find comfort in his momentary drunkenness before his harsh reality reared its head again later.

Interrupting their moment of silence, the bartender came out from behind the counter with a small tray of appetizers, setting them on the table between Shane and Christina. "Shall I get either of you another drink?"

Shane's attention remained focused on his game as it dealt him three deuces and a couple of sixes. He discarded the pair without thinking and waited for the next two holographic cards to rise up above the glass.

A king and the fourth deuce.

"That's a thousand bucks. Congratulations!" said the bartender. "I'll be right back with your winnings. How about a drink on the house?"

Shane didn't even crack a smile. He remembered how excited he and David would get every time they won even just a small amount of money. David wouldn't let either of them lose more than a hundred bucks when they went out to the casino, which was rare to begin with. David saw it as a waste of money. A thousand dollar hit would normally send Shane to the moon. A chunk of change that big provided a nice little shopping spree at the kitchen gadget store. But today he felt nothing. It still seemed as if he'd lost everything in his whole life. *Maybe because he had.* "Thank you, but I think I'm about ready to go."

The waiter turned around to head back to the bar, and a bucket of sadness flooded Shane's face. He almost felt guilty for ruining a trip to the bar with a good friend. *What a waste of a perfectly good day!* Then he recalled the reason they'd come to the bar to begin with. Sadly, no amount of money, alcohol, or friendship could make the tears stop at this point.

"Should we leave?" Christina got up from her seat and hugged Shane. "I don't want to cause you any more stress than you're already feeling."

"It's a little too late for that." Shane attempted to squeak out a tiny laugh in between his muffled sobs. "But yes, I need to go home." He felt grateful for the suggestion, especially since nothing sounded more appealing than his own bed at the moment. "David would tell me to take the money and run."

chapter 10

Aurora kept her arms wrapped tight around Sai's sturdy frame the entire way down the winding canyon road. Past a group of pillar-like rock formations, she spotted a large turquoise body of water reflecting the sunlight in the distance. A blue oasis located due east of Lake Mead, it shimmered like a prism beneath the warm October sky. She instantly recalled its name from her many nights of encyclopedic research—Sapphire Springs.

"Is this your home?" She wondered if he had one like Shane's. Technically, robots didn't need to live within the confines of a typical house per se. As long as they had a secure place to recharge, they could wander from place to place without ever seeking more than temporary shelter from the occasional rainstorm. Even that wasn't necessarily a requirement—she did just fine in the water.

"We're close." Sai looked back at Aurora and flashed a reassuring smile. "I'll tell you when we've arrived."

Aurora studied the road as the motorcycle followed its course between the towering sandstone walls. Recording every turn, she wished to know exactly how to instruct Shane to find her if she happened to run into trouble later on. *Had she taken a risk by getting on the back of Sai's E-Dragon?* Perhaps, but not nearly as big of one as when she hastily climbed into a limo with Bill Rucker. If she'd made it out of that fiasco in one piece, she could look after herself just about anywhere. Every journey merited a certain degree of caution, and a path of adventure suited her much better than living in a broom closet. She understood perfectly her duty to her creator—to remain as far away from enemy hands as possible. Learning to recognize the thieves from the heroes took precedence. Time would certainly tell, but Sai seemed to fit nicely amongst the latter. "What is the road we're traveling?"

He took a moment to respond. "This one, or the one we're about to turn onto?"

The motorcycle took a hard left across the empty lane for oncoming traffic, cruising along a faint dirt trail and down a steep hill. Dust billowed behind the bike like a cloak, shielding their path from anyone who attempted to pursue them.

"Does this route even have a name?" She tightened her grip around Sai's torso in order to prevent a calamity far worse than when she'd wrecked her beloved Daedalus Flyer.

"It's the way home. That's all I've got for you."

Aurora performed a quick calculation to determine the best way to explain to Shane exactly where he'd have to take a sudden turn in order to get to her. She spotted a cluster of three mesquite trees right before the trail plunged down an even more treacherous slope. On second thought, she'd meet him on the side of the main road if she had to. No way he'd ever find the courage to head down this rocky obstacle course by himself.

"We're almost there." Sai looked over his shoulder. "Another three minutes is all."

Aurora didn't mind the trek one bit. She'd gotten to see a side of Las Vegas she'd never explored before. It looked beautiful how the bright blue water in the distance contrasted with the muted tones of the desert. Short trees and bunches of grass dotted the vibrant landscape like the pictures she had come across in her research about America. She hadn't recalled ever seeing so much open space before. In fact, it looked completely desolate. Maybe that's why Sai called it home.

The bike slowed to a mere ten miles an hour as it wound its way along a crooked path beneath a tunnel of California fan palms. Aurora didn't see any houses around, or any other buildings for that matter. Approaching the side of a steep hill, the bike soon came to a halt.

"We made it." Sai took off his helmet. "I'm glad you managed to hang on. That's a tough ride."

Aurora laughed as she removed her helmet as well. "I'm

glad I didn't damage your insides from holding on so tight!"

"Believe me. You'd have to use a lot more force to even put a tiny dent in my frame. They built me to be indestructible."

She immediately wondered who he meant by *they*. If she hadn't had other, more pressing, questions on her mind, she'd have straight up asked him. "I don't see any houses. Does that mean you live outside?"

Sai laughed, locking both helmets back into the bike's rear encasements. "I don't know who you take me for exactly, but I assure you that I'm not without a home." He wheeled the E-Dragon toward a nearly vertical, rocky hillside, which appeared entirely impassable. "Follow me, and I'll show you how the rest of us machines live."

"I'm looking forward to it." Aurora calculated the angle of the cliff-like wall in front of them. *Eighty-six degrees.* She could certainly scale it if she had to, but it seemed like a real chore for Sai to complete every time he wanted to go home. What would he do with his bike if he had to climb up the side of a mountain? Leaving a valuable mode of transportation out in the open hardly seemed like a viable option, even if the nearest person lived ten miles away.

Standing directly in front of the canyon wall, Sai reached out and placed his hand on a nondescript segment of the giant rock's facade. Leaning into it, he then twisted the protrusion with his palm. "This is the breezeway," he said, pointing to a hollow that appeared as if by magic at the base of the cliff. "Come quickly. We need to remove all the dust from us before he head inside. We've only got ten seconds before it closes." He ushered her to come follow him and his bike into a large, well-lit metal box.

Aurora soon felt a swirling current of cool air, which swept away every last particle of sand and dirt that they'd collected on their roller coaster ride through the Mojave. It also managed to blow her hair every which way. When the vortex ceased, Sai did his best to pat her long red strands back into place. "I'll be fine," she said. "Next time I'll wear a hair tie."

"Excellent idea." Sai tapped on a piece of the rock wall in front of him and another set of doors that weren't visible a moment prior suddenly slid open. "After you, young lady."

"We're going in an elevator, aren't we?" She could tell by the looks of it even though it didn't have any numbers or buttons.

"No fooling you, is there?" Sai stood next to the bike in the very center of the small chamber as the door shut them in.

"I'm programmed to take notice of everything."

"You're in good company then." Sai looked over his shoulder before directing his voice to a microphone embedded in the elevator's steel panelling. "Descension to subfloor three of The Gloaming."

The Gloaming? She'd never heard of such a place, and she couldn't hazard a guess as to what in the world it was like. She only knew that she had to see it to understand.

The lift dropped rapidly, much quicker than any of the previous ones she'd ridden. In fact it plummeted faster than the natural force of gravity, almost like they were being sucked down beneath the surface of the earth. Judging by the input of her internal locator, she determined they'd just dropped a hundred fifty feet in two seconds before coming to a graduated stop. Aside from the lower altitude, she hadn't a clue where they'd landed. "Where have you taken me?"

"You'll see in a moment. I told you I was taking you to my home. Just promise me one thing."

Aurora tried to sync with his processor before agreeing to anything. Unfortunately, CADI could only detect a scrambled signal. She couldn't tell if he'd encrypted it deliberately, or if his output simply didn't jive with her own communication software. "I first need to know what you'd like me to promise before I actually consent to it."

"When these doors open, you're going to see other robots. A few of them look like you and me. Most of them have yet to undergo their transformation. You must understand that they are not a threat."

Up until an hour ago, Aurora had considered herself the only working example of artificial intelligence in the entire country, even though David despised using those words to describe her. Regardless of whether other robots looked like her, she had nothing else with which to compare them. In theory, they didn't exist. *Why would Sai think she'd feel threatened if she saw a robot that didn't look like her?* "I withhold any and all expectations regarding their appearance."

"The Gloaming is our world, a refuge from those who would rather see us destroyed," Sai said as the elevator doors slid open.

Stepping out into a dimly lit, cavernous space, Aurora drew her attention to a thundering waterfall in the distance, which echoed throughout the vast rock-walled atrium. How beautiful. The tall cascade added to the allure and mystique of Sai's marvelous home. The air also seemed much cooler down here than any place she'd ever been. At fifty-five degrees, it didn't bother her the least bit, but she wondered how Shane might feel at this temperature. "I didn't expect for it to be so chilly." Aurora kept pace next to Sai as he rolled the bike forward along a well-lit path.

"Batteries last longer when they're cool. Do you need a blanket?"

She couldn't tell if he was serious. The idea of walking around wrapped up in a thick piece of woven fabric seemed rather awkward to her. "Quite all right. I don't mind the cold."

"I should hope not. We never let it get above sixty degrees in this whole place. Now if you'll excuse me for a moment, I have to return the bike to the cage." Sai gestured for her to stay behind before he continued to roll the E-Dragon along its course. "It'll be quick. It's just around the corner here."

Aurora sat on an aluminum bench beneath an artificial oak tree lit with a thousand tiny blue and purple lights. Digging her feet into the gravel that marked the path, she watched as Sai communicated with a machine who managed the bike counter, a robot without skin. It didn't bother her in the least. In fact, he looked similar to what she imagined herself to look like on the inside—a vast array of metal circuitry running alongside a series of metallic joints, nuts, and bolts. Nothing surprised her about the whole world she'd just come into, except that it delighted her beyond words. Looking overhead, she counted eight floors encircling the wide open space. Around each of the floors loomed more trees like the one she sat under, all of them lending a soft glow to the peaceful ambiance. However, her favorite part so far was the waterfall. Oh, how she'd love to start every morning by just listening to its gentle rumble. Amazingly, she still had so much more to take in and explore. The Gloaming, as Sai called it, now made sense to her. A whole underground city in a perpetual state of twilight, a hidden enclave safe from the reach of overzealous authorities. If only David had known such a marvelous place existed, perhaps things might have played out differently for everyone. But she couldn't think about that now. She had to move forward.

"I should stay closer to you." Sai ran back to where Aurora sat minding her surroundings. "I don't want anyone thinking that you're an intruder. The residents are very protective of their home."

"I don't want to impose, and I certainly don't want to get in anyone's way." Aurora recalled her experience of being a guest inside Christina's house. She'd gained her and her daughters' respect by being courteous and gracious. She'd act the same way, if not more so, as a guest in this new place.

"Don't think for a moment that you're imposing on anybody. You're meant to be here, or we wouldn't have found one another. Now let me show you to your room."

Her room? She wondered if she'd heard him correctly. A quick replay of Sai's words confirmed that she had. *But why?* It all seemed a bit much. She had gotten on the back

of his bike as a way to quickly get away from the police—
and whoever else wanted a piece of her. She hadn't intended to stay. "Forgive me if I sound ungrateful, but is it really
necessary that I have my own room here?"

"Don't be silly. We have enough space here so that we all
get a room to ourselves. No sharing required."

The response hardly satisfied her, and she figured that
Sai himself knew he'd dodged her question. So be it! If he
couldn't explain why he treated her like a resident as opposed to a mere visitor, she'd gladly play along.

"We're heading just behind the waterfall. There's a newly
opened vacancy there. It isn't much, but I'm sure it will suit
your needs for now."

She couldn't believe her luck. How had he determined
her exact preferred location? As for her immediate needs,
she required a recharge soon. Her battery had dwindled
to fifteen percent. Hopefully her room came equipped
with an electrical outlet. She desired little if nothing else.
"While we're on the subject, would you happen to know if
my room has electricity?"

Sai laughed so hard that he practically doubled over.
"Our home may look like it dates back to the stone age,
but I assure you that we're as modern as can be. We're all
machines. And machines need power, right?"

"But where does it come from?" What little information
Aurora had about the utilities, she knew enough from David to realize that Western America Power wouldn't willingly give up their electricity to a place that, for all intents
and purposes, didn't exist.

"I have no idea who programmed you the way you are, but you ask too many questions." Sai motioned for her to walk ahead of him across a narrow steel bridge leading toward the waterfall. "We get our power from the dam. It just so happens that we're linked to it."

"You mean you steal it?" Aurora wished it wasn't so. She still couldn't let go of the fact that she herself had once stolen a battery from a pharmacy, even though David ultimately paid for it after she'd left the store with it tucked in her shirt. She understood the occasional necessity of lying, but taking something without paying for it seemed like a terrible thing to do.

"We protect the dam and its water supply. We deserve every watt of electricity we take."

"And nobody outside this place realizes it even exists?" Aurora stopped walking for a moment, forcing Sai to pause as well. "How can that be?" The notion hardly seemed plausible. The sheer scope of the place meant someone had to have built it before the robots took it over.

"Anyone who once knew about this little sanctuary of ours has all but forgotten about it. They hollowed out this entire place and then abandoned it without ever using it for its intended purpose."

"Which was?" Aurora stepped off the metal grate bridge and onto firm ground behind the blue glow of the eighty-foot waterfall.

"It was meant for an intake to draw water from Lake Mead if its level ever dropped below a certain threshold. Had Las Vegas only forecasted the abundance of freshwater eventually headed down the Colorado, it wouldn't have wasted billions of dollars on building what has now become our underground palace."

Aurora recalled that David had worked on the freshwater mining project while at Durango Electric. It saved half the country from the severest drought ever recorded. "You mean atmospheric extraction."

Sai continued walking again. "For such a little machine, you certainly know an awful lot about everything, don't you?"

"I know enough to find my way in this world." She almost opened up about David and her connection to Durango Electric, but a voice from within cautioned against it.

"Well, hopefully we can help one another out in that regard. I better let you freshen up." Sai brought her to a brown door in the midst of a long line of identical looking entryways. "Place your palm against the scanner. It's a good thing you have skin. Most of the robots here are in transition. They still use old-fashioned keys to get in and out of their rooms."

"I guess I'm pretty lucky, aren't I?" Aurora placed her palm against the small pane of glass and waited for the laser underneath it to scan the details of her hand.

"You're made of PelaDerm. I recognize the pattern." Sai spoke as if he'd just unravelled a top secret mystery.

"I hope that's not a bad thing." Aurora considered lying but decided that staying truthful would serve her best from now on while in the company of her new friend.

"Not at all." Sai opened the door for her, staying just outside the room. "We'd all love to be wrapped in that stuff. It makes perfect sense that your manufacturer covered you with it head to toe. They certainly knew what they were doing. Anyways, I'll leave you alone while you get acclimated. If you need anything, my place is just two rooms down from yours."

"Thank you. You've been most kind." Aurora let the door close as Sai walked away.

She found the room sparse, unlike her previous home. It had a bed, a chair, and a desk—but no decor or artwork on its painted gray walls. No reason to let it bother her. It felt safe, which was most important.

In need of a recharge, she searched for the nearest outlet. Spotting one beneath the lamp on the desk, she took a seat and rolled down her sock to access her charging cord. Regardless of her future plans, she felt welcome in her new abode inside The Gloaming. Where could one possibly find a better hideaway than this marvelous sanctuary for thinking machines like herself?

chapter 11

Christina walked to the edge of the bar's parking lot in order to keep a careful eye on Shane, making certain that he returned safely to his vehicle. He had offered to take her back to her truck at the furniture shop on the east side of town, but she declined the offer, figuring it best for him to get home as quickly as possible. Expecting him to play chauffeur to her seemed preposterous, if not utterly selfish.

Watching the Mogollon transport him away from the bar and back to his home, Christina tried to signal her own green machine to come pick her up. The law mandated that a vehicle could not travel unoccupied for more than five miles. As she already half-expected, her watch confirmed that she stood eight and a half miles from where she'd left her trusty Yosemite.

Left with little in the way of choice, she decided to hail a cab. According to her watch, one approached her coordinates from less than a half mile away. For sixty dollars, she'd have fast transportation directly to her own vehicle. It beat having to navigate her way through two transfers aboard the M-LEV, which would still only get her within three blocks of her actual destination. The rare splurge would ultimately save her both time and an unnecessary headache. Just the thought of sitting on a cramped train after having lost one of her closest friends and beloved mentors nearly brought her to tears. She could hardly imagine Shane's agony.

The white cab arrived in less than a minute. She opened the front door and swiped her watch above the payment scanner embedded in the dashboard. A detailed street map came into view on the monitor. From the line drawn along a various set of streets, she could tell it already had plugged in her destination. All she had to do was lie her head back and try to think about something that wouldn't cause her to break down into a fit of uncontrollable sobs. David wouldn't like to see her that way. She considered him much too practical to entertain the notion of *a good cry*. Any effort spent flirting with emotion was energy wasted. She learned early on in her career at Durango Electric to rein in her sentimental nature. Feelings couldn't solve complicated mathematical equations. On the contrary, they didn't solve anything. They merely served to further complicate whatever brought about their tragic existence in the first place.

She kept her purse in her lap while watching the red dot progress along the map as the car zipped out of the bar's parking lot, heading east onto Sunset Road. Only twelve minutes to get to where she headed. Surely, she could keep it together until then.

By the time she arrived, she already felt noticeably better. Shane had to have been experiencing enough pain for both himself and Christina. The temptation to curl into a wailing wet mess had subsided, at least for the moment. Shielding her eyes from the exceptionally bright autumn sky, she looked across the street from the Furniture World parking lot and stared at a triangular logo encompassing a cobra's head. Splashed across the front of a windowless gray warehouse, it loomed just above the words *Black Diamond And Company*.

She'd seen the logo numerous times before but never gave the image much thought until now. What a strange choice for a design team. If the company's aim was to eradicate any sense of welcome in those who passed by, they'd succeeded. No, Christina didn't fear snakes. She proudly called herself a friend to all God's creatures. However, she generally steered away from anyone who associated themselves with venomous reptiles. Today, she'd have to put her reservations aside. If anybody deserved answers about David's tragic fate on the very day of his untimely death, it was his faithful assistant. Waiting another day seemed terribly wasteful.

Getting in the front seat of her imposing Yosemite, she felt a wave of confidence sweep over her, like she'd been entrusted by the Lord above to carry out this mission. Exactly who she'd find herself talking to within the establishment across the street, she couldn't say. Playing it by ear had become her specialty while working under David. Her skills as an improv actress wouldn't fail her now. If anything, she had finally arrived at the moment that she'd spent her whole career training for.

"To Black Diamond And Company," Christina commanded in a rehearsed, professional tone. Getting into character started *now*.

The truck reversed out of its spot and drove across the barren parking lot to the Desert Inn Road exit. Traffic appeared light for a Thursday afternoon, but then again Christina had arrived in a part of town she rarely ventured to. The old industrial neighborhood had never before come to mind as a place to spend a day off of work. Glancing around, she understood why. The number of vacant storefronts provided all the evidence needed to confirm for her that people had long since found other, more suitable, places in which to conduct business.

But not Black Diamond.

Having left the Furniture World lot, the Yosemite made a quick u-turn at the next intersection, stopping at a red light adjacent to her destination's entrance. Christina looked out the window to her right and noticed a guard house down the small alleyway leading to the back of the warehouse. Was the neighborhood really that bad that they needed a manned entrance gate? Durango Electric certainly didn't require passage through a guarded entry unless it was to a secured area. She hoped that the intense security measures were nothing more than a formality.

When the truck arrived alongside the yellow booth, a tanned and muscular male attendant rose off his stool, coming out to greet Christina. She couldn't help but think he'd make way more money as a bouncer at a nightclub.

"Afternoon, ma'am. What brings you to Black Diamond?" He barely glanced up from the DimensionTab in his hands, although his tone of voice at least sounded polite.

"I'm a small business owner, and I'm hoping to get a quote on a sign for my new shop. Do I need an appointment?" Christina tried not to stare at the cobra head logo embroidered on the left side of his imposing chest. Not much about her initial visit so far signaled that Black Diamond provided a reputable place to take one's business. Thankfully, the man at least came across as somewhat pleasant. Even so, she wondered just how many potential customers he and the rest of the Black Diamond crew frightened away simply by sporting such a menacing trademark.

"Scan your index finger here, and I'll send your vehicle to an appropriate parking spot." He held out his DimensionTab just outside her window. "We keep a record of everyone who enters our building."

Christina had her reservations about handing over her identity, period. Giving her fingerprint to a company represented by a serpent, a company that most assuredly was responsible for her boss's death, gave her more than just a reason to pause. Still, her lingering questions regarding David overrode her cautious mentality. She wouldn't get any answers otherwise. After a second's deliberation, she waved her pointer finger through the glowing red circle that appeared above the tablet. "Please tell me you don't also require a blood sample. I'm shy around needles."

He didn't even crack a smile. *Perhaps he'd already heard the line a hundred times.* "You're good to go, ma'am. Have a pleasant day."

The Yosemite pulled through the gate and maneuvered around the back of the warehouse. Christina had no say in where it took her. She was too distracted to care, her attention having been stolen by the surprising amount of activity happening behind the rather unassuming building. Compared to the world outside, the place seemed like a bustling Hollywood backlot. Before arriving at her assigned parking space, she watched six men hoisting a twenty-foot neon gorilla sign into the rear of an open trailer. *Where on earth could that thing be headed?* She brought her hand to her chest. For a moment it looked as if King Kong were about to topple, but the unwavering team of movers steadied the glass and steel beast with expert grace and precision, securing it into place.

When Christina stepped out of her truck, she noticed two police cars parked in the farthest corner of the lot. No officers though. Maybe they were taking care of something inside. Her curiosity piqued further still as she wondered whether the presence of the authorities would help or hinder her chances at getting the information she so desperately wanted.

She chose her path along a sidewalk to a very plain look-ing entrance. It was either that or stumble into one of the open garage doors. If her time at Durango Electric had taught her any valuable lessons, it was to always look like she played by the rules. No use in carrying an umbrella when everybody else wore a raincoat, even if the umbrella made more sense. During her little visit here at Black Di-amond, Christina knew to act like an agreeable custom-er. If they expected her to walk through a dismal entrance marked by two overgrown yucca plants in desperate need of a manicure, so be it. She'd follow the path exactly as in-tended. For now.

The door opened automatically, which surprised her. For a moment, she felt welcome, almost expected. Walk-ing into the sparsely decorated reception area, she noticed a well-dressed man sitting in a position she knew all-too-well. Hers—except she made it a point to smile and greet everyone who walked into the building. This man, who appeared a few years older than her thirty-six years, didn't even look up from his workspace. He sat with his head tucked down so that all she could see was the bald spot on top of his scalp, which seemed to hover above a gaudy pink and red polka-dotted shirt with a white collar. Her only opinion about his sense of fashion? He must feel confident about it.

"Good afternoon." Christina cleared her throat slightly, just enough to make herself known without seeming like a nuissance. "I'm interested in some signage. Am I in the right place?"

"Sorry. I didn't know anyone was there." The man finally looked up from his desk. He sounded sincere, although Christina couldn't figure out how anyone wouldn't notice the stark contrast in lighting the moment the door opened and closed. Maybe ghosts were a thing here.

"Just little old me," she chuckled, if only to emphasize the point that she wasn't the overbearing type. "So…"

"Right! You're here for a sign." He set down his stylus and leaned forward, folding his hands beneath his chin. "You'll have to forgive me. I was just admiring what a beautiful head of hair you have."

That was unexpected! She'd never have thought in a million years that she'd be received with such a nice compliment in the lair of the snakes. Then again, maybe that was all part of their slick game. Ignore them, flatter them, then rob them for everything they're worth. Or maybe she could benefit from turning off her incessant need to analyze and simply thank the stranger for his kind words. "It's not everyday I get a compliment like that. Thank you!"

"Of course. Sorry to distract you. You came here for a reason—a sign was it?"

"Yes. Actually, I *am* in the market for a sign. I'm about to open a business of my own, and I figured I better start getting things in order." Christina couldn't figure out why she felt uncomfortable all of a sudden. It's not like she'd never lied before. Perhaps if the stakes hadn't seemed seem so high, she'd feel a bit more at ease.

"Congratulations!" A warm smile appeared across his face, and he folded his hands together like he was genuinely interested. *Why?* Honestly, she had no idea. "Tell me about this fabulous business of yours."

It's nothing but a sham. I'm actually here to find out the real reason why my boss is dead. And you're the gatekeeper to the one who likely knows the answer. Christina hated that he suddenly turned nosy. It wasn't his job to probe; she of all people understood the importance of minding one's own business—at least for the most part. "I'm opening a hair salon," she blurted. She didn't know exactly where it came from. Perhaps the comment about her own beautiful coiffure? Anyways, it didn't matter. She'd made her choice, and now she was stuck with it. "We're opening in Summerlin off of Charleston near Red Rock Canyon."

"I can't believe that! I'm a stylist myself. I do it mainly on the weekends. I'd work more if I didn't have bad shoulders." He reached for something in a small canvas bag sitting on a chair next to him. "My name's Gerard. Please, take it." He handed her a black holographic card that revealed his information when she tilted it toward her. On the back was a photo of him when he had hair. "I know. I need to get new ones. That picture was taken years ago."

"You look handsome either way, Gerard. My name is Christina." She felt bad. Not only did he believe every word she'd just said, but he wanted to do business with her. Was it too late to explain that it was more of a dog grooming studio? Never mind. Creating a more elaborate lie seemed like a desperate move when really what she wanted was to get past him and onto the trail of his superiors. "You mind if I keep this handy? I'm not sure I need anymore hairdressers at this point, but if business demand is more than I anticipate after we open, I'd love to bring you into the clan."

"Please do. Even with my worn-out shoulders, I could certainly stand a change of scenery from this place." He stood up from his chair to shake her hand from across the desk before leaning in closer. "Truth be told, the woman I work for is a total psychotic nut case."

That's more like it! Christina wanted to know more about this psychopath who definitely had a hand in David's death. "Believe me, I've dealt with my fair share of the *B* team. I just hope she's not difficult to work with when it comes to her clientele."

Gerard resumed his seated position, guilt appearing across his face in the form of a self-reprimanding frown. "I might have gotten carried away. Yes, Cyphan Creek is an expert when it comes to taking care of the customer. As long as she knows that you're a serious buyer, she'll bend over backwards to sell you a sign."

Therein lies the rub. Christina was as serious a customer as she was an expert in running a hair salon. Getting what she'd come for might be a lengthier task than she'd hoped, depending on how much she first had to prove her false intentions in order to cover up the real reason for stepping foot inside the snake's cage to begin with. Who knew what kind of venomous trap she'd have to evade? "Is Cyphan Creek available, by chance?" *Wait a second!* Christina didn't remember the name until she actually let it fall out of her own mouth. The picture of a tall and slender woman holding an oversized white sun hat flashed in her memory. Hopefully the devilish woman wouldn't recall the slightest trace of Christina from that fateful day they'd briefly met at Durango Electric.

Gerard bit his top lip. "I probably shouldn't say this, but she's busy with the police at the moment. And I haven't a clue why. Thankfully for me, I've been completely out of the loop, but I guess it's been a crazy past two days at the office."

"That sounds serious." Christina felt her own pulse racing as the gravity of the situation took effect.

"I'm probably being melodramatic." Gerard resumed his seated position and grabbed a pen from a mug on his desk. "I'm sure everything is gonna be just fine after the dust settles. I can take down all of your information and help prepare a signage plan if you have a few minutes."

"Thank you. That would be great." Christina smiled, but refused to walk away empty-handed. "Although, I'd really love to use the ladies' room first if I could."

Gerard paused, resuming his gaze down at his workspace. "Let me see. To tell you the truth, we don't have a public restroom." He turned his attention to a monitor facing away from Christina. "Looks like the boss is still busy. I doubt she'll mind if I escort you to the one for employee use."

Christina couldn't recall ever being this gutsy. She had no idea how successful her spy mission would turn out, or if it might land her in one of the police cars she saw out back. If she played everything just right, she'd maintain her innocence. "That would be so kind of you. I wouldn't have asked in the first place if it wasn't an emergency."

"Say no more, Ms. Christina. Come right this way." He led her around the counter and through an open doorway that led to a hallway and then a second narrower hallway to the right. "Meet me back out front the way we came so that I can get the signage specifics regarding your new business's needs."

"Thank you. You've been such a gentleman." Christina stepped through the open door marked with a unisex symbol, locking it behind her. *Was she really doing this?* She had to. For David. She counted to fifteen, turned the water on to wash her hands briefly, if for no other reason than to help her believe that she wasn't a complete criminal. If anyone questioned her, she'd simply ask for some assistance in getting back to the main desk. It couldn't get any simpler than that.

Christina opened the restroom door and continued a little ways down the hall toward what seemed like a large industrial storage facility. She passed a room on her left with medical equipment and a hospital bed, and at first thought nothing of it. Then she reversed her steps and came back to the open doorway. *Could that be where...no. Impossible!* She shuddered at the thought of her fallen hero locked away in that cramped room. For a split second, she considered going in it, but quickly changed her mind.

The echo of two faint voices emanated her way from the main storage facility at the end of the corridor. It sounded almost like an argument, but not quite. More like a passionate discussion between two strong personalities.

"If the police come one more time to check up on us, I'm

throwing you to the wolves, Cyphan," said a commanding male voice unfamiliar to Christina.

She didn't believe her ears at first. *Could he be talking to THE Cyphan Creek? Who on earth could get away with speaking like that to the devil herself?* She reasoned that it had to be the boss. Otherwise, he'd surely have his entrails served to him with a side of metal cockroaches.

Christina stayed close to the wall as she inched closer to the open doorway, which stood a good ten feet down the hall. Getting a front row seat to this discussion excited almost as much as it frightened her.

"Mr. Kenny-Big-Shot. I'd love to see you try and man this ship without me," said a vaguely familiar voice with an unmistakably rueful tone. "I got them off our trail, didn't I? Now let me get back to making this company some serious money."

Christina had never heard anyone talk to their superior like that. Maybe behind their back, but certainly not to their face. She wondered if she herself would ever have it within her to confront Bill Rucker with such unabashed bravado. Probably not, which was a good thing. She didn't need to manipulate people with her words. She prided herself on being much too clever to have to resort to vehemence.

"Making money? Is that what you call it when you practically kill the man for whom you gambled the company's future?"

"You wanted him on our side. That's exactly what you said to me."

They were talking about David.

"Of course, I wanted him. Alive. What was so damn difficult about keeping him alive? He's not worth anything to me dead."

Christina's heart sank. She considered it both strange and sickening to hear other people discussing her mentor's death so shortly after the fact. And so coldly, especially when they were to blame.

"He didn't want anything to do with us, Kenny. It was a very bad deal. I told you that after the first time I tried to win him from Bill."

"Why didn't we just get the girl?" He paused a second. "I still don't understand. Why did Bill get the girl? We could have taken the girl instead."

"That wasn't the arrangement. And besides, the girl belongs to Durango Electric. Which is fine, because Durango Electric is practically ours."

"Let's hear it, Cyphan. Lay it down for me one more time." He sounded incredulous, or rather borderline facetious. "When do we finally get our hands on Durango Electric?"

Christina stopped herself from gasping out loud. She'd already heard way more than she bargained for. Did Cyphan Creek really think she could take over the world's largest electronics firm?

"Their stock's been sliding ever since the merger with Western America Power. They've gotten too big. Throw on top of that a continual string of accidents and strategic bombings, and nobody will want anything to do with such a disastrous monstrosity."

"You're dreaming. I wouldn't do that to Bill. I'm a businessman. Not a corporate terrorist."

Christina heard distant footsteps coming from behind her and looked back. *Shit.* She'd overstayed her welcome. Wanting desperately to snoop some more, but terrified she'd suffer a fate worse than David's, she headed back toward the restroom.

"There you are." Gerard came around the corner. "I thought I saw on the monitor someone getting lost back here."

Lost? That was it exactly! "Thank God you came to rescue me. For a minute, I didn't know if I'd ever find my way back. I should have left breadcrumbs!"

Gerard laughed like she'd just uttered the funniest thing he'd ever heard. "Stop! Hansel and Christina...lost at Black Diamond."

"Seriously, though!" Christina couldn't believe how well her stupid joke had worked to cover up the fact that he'd effectively caught her spying red-handed. "If I'd stumbled upon a gingerbread house, I'd have been done for. Thank God it was only a restroom!"

"Well, now that you feel better, let me at least draw up a plan for the boss to review."

A Plan? Christina had already forgotten about that part of her ever-growing lie. "Absolutely! Thank you. I feel a million times better now. Yes. Let's see what Black Diamond can do for me and my little hair salon."

chapter

The moment Shane rolled into the garage, he felt the razor-edged pain of loss deep in his chest. Perhaps the liquor had worn off quicker than he'd expected it to. *Did he really want to be here?* He considered reversing his course of action and leaving town for a couple of days, maybe to Utah, but that would require considerable more energy than he could muster at present. The living room sofa would have to suffice for now.

Walking into the house, Shane headed straight for the bathroom. He dropped his pants and leaned forward over the toilet, the weight of his body pushing into his hands against the wall. He hadn't realized how bad he needed to go. Other issues had invaded his awareness, blocking out the most basic of his needs. Come to think of it, his stomach could probably benefit from food, but eating required an appetite, and Shane couldn't tell if his would ever return. In the meantime, he'd attempt to soothe his aching heart with another drink.

Shane left the bathroom without washing his hands. He hadn't once neglected to thoroughly rinse them since the age of six. But what did it matter today? His medicine called to him, and so over to the electric bartender he went. The handy machine immediately brought to mind the countless other inventions and projects David had brought to life. He existed everywhere. Unavoidable. Ghostly memories of him lurked in every corner Shane turned. Surely, an adult elixir would fix that.

Two, eight, six, two. A rum and Coke. The only code Shane could remember at present, which was perfect. Exactly what his imaginary doctor had prescribed for him. He could hear the *pop* of the mini soda can as the steel arm plucked open its tab before pouring it into a rocks glass. A moment later came a long, generous squirt of amber liquid. *Cheers, David.*

Shane retrieved the glass from the dispenser and headed straight for the living room. No need to take off his shoes. Doing so would only delay his much-needed therapy session. The sofa's gravity had overcome him at this point, and he succumbed to its cushiony embrace the second his backside made contact with its generous padding. A few sips more would certainly delay the onset of bitter reality for the rest of the afternoon.

"Opus, turn on the television." Shane said it out of habit. TV had a way of mixing well with alcohol. Sitting down alone with a drink and *not* having the company of a broadcast spokesperson seemed incomplete if not altogether insane. *What would a drunken mind do without the shallow noise of strangers in the living room?*

Within a few seconds, an infomercial appeared inside the device's holographic viewing area. Shane waited with bated anticipation for what he hoped would take his tortured mind off the persistent agony of loss. When an unfamiliar personality appeared in front of him holding a miniature telescopic camera manufactured by none other than Durango Electric, Shane commanded the television to shut off. David had done it on purpose, hadn't he? He couldn't just up and leave. He had to haunt Shane for all eternity.

Shane looked out the window to the backyard for some form of distraction. Mid-October typically delivered the most enviable weather to Las Vegas, and today was no exception. Rays of sunlight broke through a group of cottony cumulus clouds and illuminated the outdoors in such a way that made Shane ponder the existence of an afterlife. He'd always pictured life simply ending the moment a person died, but now he wasn't so sure. His husband had too much life inside him to simply vanish without a trace. David had to be somewhere out there, if nothing more than a wisp of endless ideas floating freely in the atmosphere.

A ruby-throated hummingbird caught Shane's wandering gaze. It flitted above a bush of purple lantana that would soon need pruning. Then it zoomed upward a bit, hovered, and flew backwards before zipping off to another group of flowers. Despite his teary eyes, Shane managed to eke out a smile. If David's spirit existed anywhere, it likely resided in that brazen little creature, a tiny bird so bold that it practically defied the laws of physics.

"I saw a hummingbird," Shane messaged Aurora, fighting back the sobs that lingered in his throat. "I need to know what it's saying. Tell me what it says, damn it." He immediately regretted sounding so forceful. He didn't know what had come over him. Maybe it was the rum. Wine usually relaxed him, but he couldn't necessarily say the same thing about liquor. Perhaps he needed a glass of merlot instead. Or maybe he needed to give up on drinking entirely and face his problems head on like a grown man.

Shane let out a tiny laugh followed by an involuntary whimper. Nothing could have prepared him for today. Visiting David in prison he could have handled. Envisioning him in a casket placed between intricately arranged flower arrangements? The image brought forth every repressed fear from inside his broken heart. He wasn't ready to say goodbye. Not to his husband. And come to think of it, not to Aurora either. Had he really just experienced two tragedies in the span of a single morning? Life for Shane had never seemed this brutal.

When his watch vibrated, for a split second he imagined it was the hummingbird calling. *He definitely needed to lay off the alcohol.* Shane resumed his sullen, somber state the moment reality hit. Focusing on his wrist, he saw Christina's name. He wondered if he had the energy to pick up. She of all people would understand his need for total seclusion the rest of the day.

"Hello?" He couldn't help but answer it. His anxiety had gotten the best of him, which prevented the call from simply going to voicemail.

"Something told me to check in with you." Christina sounded her usual compassionate self, but a sense of disquietude lurked behind her gentle tone. "I'm sorry. I wanted to make sure you got home okay."

"Of course, I got home okay. I'm sorting things out right now. That's all." Shane didn't want to sound curt with the one person left who could truly empathize with him. But in all honesty, he wished to be left alone. "What have you got on your agenda this afternoon?"

She didn't respond immediately. "I'm on my way to a yoga class. I thought the meditation might do me some good today. I hope you're resting."

Rest? It didn't feel restful. Not with his head swimming in a sea of drowned emotion. "I'm sprawled out on the couch, not going anywhere. Enjoy your practice." He couldn't believe she felt up for yoga, but Christina was a grown woman. *She could do whatever she damn well pleased.*

"Can I bring you something to eat later?"

"Perhaps tomorrow. Thank you. I better let you go now." Shane ended the call as best he knew how without prolonging the unnecessary conversation. The mere thought of eating made his stomach churn. He couldn't even bring himself to imagine the feeling of hunger. Maybe he'd feel different after some much needed sleep.

Shane's head began to drift as he rested it on a small *fleur de lis* patterned pillow at the edge of the sofa. If it weren't for his relentless watch, he might have fallen fast asleep. Feeling it vibrate again, he lazily brought it into view and saw a message from Aurora.

What color is it?

He assumed she was referring to the hummingbird. "I don't know. That was fifteen minutes ago. It flew away."

"Call out to it. Tell it to come back."

She must have thought he'd gone mad enough to play silly games. Perhaps if he'd swapped the rum with absinthe, but the electric bartender could only do so much. Talking to the animals like a patron saint of the forest would have to wait another day when he had it more together. "I think you've mistaken me for someone else. You don't really expect me to talk to birds, do you?"

Shane waited only a few seconds for a response before resting his head back on the pillow. Hopefully, she'd gotten the sense that now was not the best time to play Doctor Dolittle. When his watch vibrated again, he wanted to ignore it but then soon recalled that he had been the one to initiate the conversation.

Call out to it. It'll hear you. It's likely still nearby.

He had nothing to lose. Nobody was around to hear him make a fool of himself. He already knew that the likelihood of a tiny bird hearing him through the triple-paned window was virtually nil. The chances of anyone in the neighborhood standing within earshot was equally improbable. "Come back, little hummingbird!" Shane shouted from his curled up position, if only to appease Aurora and simultaneously amuse his own tortured soul.

Nothing.

Just as he'd expected. *Why would anyone honor his wishes today?* A veil of foolishness crept over his numb body, beckoning him to close his eyes for good. The heavy weights buried deep in his eyelids nearly succeeded in shutting out the world when suddenly a flash of color appeared in the window.

"It's green, Aurora!" He could hardly contain the sense of wonder he'd longed to feel for himself ever since he discovered David's unusual gift. "It's green with a bright red spot on its throat. And it's staring at me. It's fluttering in the window, and he's looking straight at me."

He says to be brave. Let go of the bitterness as soon as you can. It won't serve you. He'll stay by your side as long as you promise to be brave.

Shane couldn't stop crying. He tried, but these tears felt different. They filled him with hope. So much so that he couldn't contain them for half a second longer. For the first time in his life, he felt like he could see farther than he'd ever seen before. Staring out the window at the peculiar creature, he glimpsed his own future. And for a moment, everything that mattered appeared crystal clear to him: Christina, Aurora, and the wings of a tiny animal that refused to quit. "Thank you, Aurora. From the bottom of my heart, thank you. Please tell me that you're okay. That's all I need to know right now."

I'm safe. It's very quiet and peaceful where I am.

He read her response through blurred eyes. He couldn't believe he'd willingly let her step out of his life a second time. "I want you here with me. When will we see each other again?"

Very soon. You mustn't worry about me. I'll see you soon. I promise.

His will to keep on hoping for anything worthwhile in life dwindled like a dying candle. Shane had reached a level of exhaustion previously unknown to him. It didn't matter how bad he wanted to race down a giant water slide with both David and Aurora in tow, to feel the sun radiate against his dark tanned skin. Fate had ruthlessly stolen such a possibility. Unfortunately, cursing it would only drain him of the last bit of energy left within him.

He couldn't tell at first that his eyelids had shut. All he saw in front of him was the brightest yellow go-kart he'd ever seen. At its wheel sat Aurora, her shimmering red hair trailing out from underneath a black helmet.

"I'm gonna win this time," he said as he passed her in his own tiny fast machine.

"You'll have to make it past David," she said in a serious tone of voice, as if the whole thing had turned into more than just a silly amusement. *"He's never let you win before. He's not going to let you beat him today."*

Shane's jealousy overrode his fleeting sense of joy, replacing it with feverish determination. Who said he couldn't ever surpass David in life? He could cook better than him. He could run an HOA meeting better than him. He'd bested him in the *backstroke numerous times. Just never the butterfly. Come to think of it, he'd won more friendly competitions than perhaps David ever cared to acknowledge. But—*then why did he always feel second best? *Well, not today. He'd cross that finish line first if it killed him.*

Shane felt the weight of his overzealous foot pressing the accelerator all the way into the rubber mat at the base of his go-kart. The track whizzed by him in a blur until he finally caught sight of his husband's blue racer.

He noticed it slowing down as it took the last and final curve around a jagged cliff. Clearly, David thought he'd won the whole damn thing already, or he'd have whipped around the bend just like he'd taken every other turn on the course. Shane grinned with clever delight. Little did his ultimate rival know that victory couldn't always be his. David had to find out what it was like to lose for once.

Pressing on the pedal with all his might, Shane aimed the front of his blazing chariot at David's rear tire, taking Dead Man's Curve with reckless abandon. "Watch out, buddy. Here comes the real hero!" Shane tried to get a response from his husband, a glance, a shrug, anything to feel recognized.

But David simply stayed the course, almost like Shane was invisible.

I'll show him. *Shane pulled hard on the wheel, standing fully upright in the go-kart. He plowed into his unsuspecting opponent with the force of a raging stallion, knocking the entire vehicle up and over the rail's edge. He felt his watch vibrating but had to ignore it. The fate of his poor, defenseless husband lay suspended in a current of hot, dry air.*

"No!" Shane screamed out in terror, unable to contain an overwhelming surge of regret. What had possessed him to drive like a blood-thirsty demon through the pits of hell? He suddenly loathed himself and every game he had ever played against David. If he'd have known the true cost of his foolish ambition, he'd resume his usual second-place status without a single complaint. Having crossed the finish line, however, he could only watch in horror as his forever faithful lover plunged into a nightmarish abyss.

When his watch vibrated a second time, Shane quickly regained consciousness. For a moment, as he awoke, he felt a hint of relief. However, he quickly remembered that today's reality wasn't any better than the frenzy he'd just escaped. The realization brought with it a sense of cold, numbing despair. A blinking green light on the watch signaled that he had a voice message from an unknown caller. He meant to dismiss it, but in his disturbed and drunken state he mistakenly hit the *play* button instead.

"This is Agent Bale with the FBI," said a serious male voice. "If this is David Whitman's husband, we need to speak to you right away. We have reason to believe that he's in trouble."

How'd he get this number? Shane just about had it. He would have laughed, except that the man's untimeliness wasn't at all funny. It was pathetic. He'd found out how to contact Shane, but he hadn't figured out that David was dead? Whatever Mr. Agent Bigshot wanted from him, he'd eventually realize the hopelessness of his mission. In the meantime, Shane needed to take care of himself. That either meant more booze, or something stronger. He didn't yet know what such a treatment might entail, but he couldn't rule out the possibility of trying something outside the realm of good judgment. Certain tragedies called for desperate measures, and today undoubtedly qualified.

The very second he began thumbing through his mental Rolodex of *alternative health practitioners*, he heard the door alert sound.

"The FBI is standing outside the front door," chimed the alert system.

Why hadn't the bullies just said so on the phone? Shane got off the couch and rubbed his eyes. If the image of angry men in dark suits at his house didn't sober him up, nothing would. He contemplated the repercussions of simply falling back asleep. *They'd likely break in, wouldn't they?* On second thought, he didn't need to add the clean-up of splintered wood and broken glass to tomorrow's dismal to-do list. "I'll be right there!" Shane called out begrudgingly, recalling the fiasco that ensued the last time the boys showed up.

"The FBI is presently at the front door," the alert sounded yet again as a drowsy Shane dragged his feet across the cool kitchen tiles.

"I heard you the first time, smart ass." He eventually arrived at the foyer and looked at the monitor to see the faces of six men standing outside the front entrance. *That's two bumbling idiots more than last time. What the hell could they possibly want now?*

Shane didn't bother putting on a fake smile. He had nobody to impress as he heaved open the lone barrier between him and the law. "Good evening, gentlemen. What brings you to the neighborhood today?" He colored the tone of his voice in deliberate displeasure.

"Mr. Whitman?"

"The one and only." Might as well tell it like it is. No need to put himself on a first-name basis with these ogres.

"Where is she?" The overly dramatic low voice came from the tallest man in the second row.

"I beg your pardon." Shane stared at him with cold formality. So that's why they'd come. Their visit really had nothing to do with David, but rather everything to do with Aurora. He considered laughing in their faces. They were about to be sorely disappointed. *Again.*

"You'll have to excuse Agent Miller." A milder, but still stern, man from the first row stepped forward. "I'm Agent Bale, by the way. I just called about your husband. What Agent Miller meant to say is that we need to speak to the little girl who lives here. I believe her name is Aurora Chandler. Is that right?"

"She no longer lives here." The words sounded foreign to Shane as he spoke them. *Was he admitting the second blow to his present reality?* Without Aurora, he was officially alone, and he dreaded the moment the alcohol would wear off.

"Then you won't mind if we have a look around." Agent Bale looked at him with suspicion showing in his eyes.

"I don't know who you people think you are, but my husband just died less than four hours ago. I thought that was the whole point of your visit." Shane didn't have to fight back any tears as he spoke. His slow boiling anger kept them far from the surface. How dare these men use a bait and switch?

"Someone verify that for me," said Agent Bale, withholding his infantry's entry inside the house.

"Confirmed," said the suited man standing next to him. "The hospital record says he passed today at eleven twenty."

"We extend our condolences, Mr. Whitman." Agent Bale entered the house, ushering in the other five agents. "We know this is a difficult time, and we hope you're telling the truth with regards to Miss Chandler's whereabouts, but we wouldn't be doing our due diligence if we didn't at least look around briefly."

Shane stepped aside to grant them their right of way, but stopped short of actually inviting them in. Resisting them would only make the day more miserable than it already was. Perhaps if these mindless drones had even an ounce of sympathy, they'd leave the very minute their instruments informed them that nothing outside the ordinary existed within the confines of this now cold and lifeless monastery. "If you have any decency left within you, I ask that none of you break a thing."

They didn't hear him, or perhaps they had but refused to acknowledge the simple request. They traipsed through the kitchen, living room, and hallways with their magic wands leading the way. The long, skinny black devices beeped periodically, but otherwise appeared rather useless. If they sought signs of artificial intelligence, the only evidence they'd stumble upon was the utter lack of actual intelligence inherent in their own brutish behavior.

"I think that's enough." Agent Bale returned to the foyer, calling the rest of his colleagues back from their fruitless endeavors. "Agent Miller," he called out to the tall man in the dining room. "I think we've bothered Mr. Whitman enough."

Agent Miller stood up from his crouched position under the table and flung his black baton carelessly above him, shattering a major portion of the red glass chandelier overhead. "Honestly, I didn't mean to." The guilty expression on his face revealed his candor.

Shane heard bits of glass as they hit the table and fell against the floor below. He wanted to scream but couldn't make a sound. The pointless witch-hunt had gained them nothing, and yet it cost Shane everything he had left in his crumbling life.

"We'll pay whatever it costs to replace it," said Agent Bale, whose gaze remained transfixed on the mess caused by his reckless colleague. "I'll send out the claims adjuster tomorrow."

Maybe they weren't as monsterish as they seemed, but Shane wanted them to disappear before they caused the whole place to collapse. "I'm not sure it's possible to replace." He felt too numb to say anything more about it. "Have you gotten the answers you were seeking?"

"We can see that she isn't here, Mr. Whitman." Agent Bale walked up to Shane and offered to shake his hand. "Would you happen to know where she is?"

Shane shook his hand, but only because it seemed to speed the process of the bully brigade leaving. As far as answering the question, he could only muster a shrug at this point. Even if he had a clue regarding her whereabouts, he'd never think to throw her to the wolves in order to save his own skin.

"Please take my card, Mr. Whitman. I'm sorry about your husband. And I'm sorry about the chandelier. We'll get it taken care of. You have my word."

The six men filed out the same way they came. Like a rogue windstorm, they'd come and gone in a matter of minutes, leaving only a pile of ruin for Shane to deal with. One more thing to add to the already endless list of impossible tasks in his lap. For the sake of his own sanity, he decided it best to not look into the dining room the rest of the day. Nothing he could do about it now.

Having locked the door, Shane leaned up against it before sliding into a crouched position on the floor, his knees tucked into his chest. They hadn't come because of David. They didn't care about him or Shane. They only cared about Aurora. *Idiots.* No matter how bad they wanted her, he'd never tell them anything or help them in any way. He couldn't—even if they came back and threatened him. For all he knew, she'd sunk to the center of the earth.

chapter

It took a second after Christina walked into the office for her to notice it. She couldn't quite figure it out. Something unfamiliar registered in her olfactory. The strange scent couldn't be anyone's bath mist, lotion, or new hair-styling product because she was the only one to occupy the large open space. So what the heck was it? By eight in the morning, the custodial cats had long since finished their chores. Otherwise she'd have chalked it up to nothing more than the lingering trace of their cleaning fluid. Come to think of it, the air *did* seem more sterile and lifeless than she previously recalled. Whatever tickled her nose, she knew it didn't belong.

Or maybe she didn't belong.

Christina brushed the odd feeling aside and turned on the lights. Having spent all of a hellish yesterday away from her desk, she assumed today's office duties would keep her busier than most. She locked her purse in the drawer beside her workstation, took a deep breath, and sat down. Adjusting her lumbar supporter with her hands behind her back, she twisted in her seat to find a suitable position. *No use.* She couldn't find comfort in her chair no matter what she tried. The sleepless night she'd just endured certainly wasn't helping.

What would today be like without David in the department? More than half the days of her tenure, he'd beat her to the office, even though her job description made her officially responsible for opening it. With fiery determination, he'd become the engine of Durango Electric. And she? A mere cog in a massive global operation that determined the course of how billions of people conducted their daily and technical lives. She'd always felt important acting as gatekeeper to his office. He'd made her feel valuable by taking her under his wing, showing her what it took to run the business of innovation. Her own drafting skills improved dramatically under his tutelage. She learned never to sacrifice precision for speed. Yet, her impeccable efficiency would never have gotten to where it was without his watchful guidance.

And just like that, he'd vanished.

When Christina turned on her computer, a holographic red sphere appeared floating in front of her. Why would she have thought that anything about this morning would be routine? Dropping her index finger through the alert in order to open the message, she sat forward and bit her bottom lip, letting all of the air slowly escape from her lungs.

Your presence is requested in meeting room 6E at 8:15 this morning - Bill Rucker

She'd forgotten all about the meeting she'd promised to attend—and what it was about. Her stomach sank the moment she read his name. He had sabotaged David's career. And for what? Possession of a little girl whom he had zero idea how to control? As far as Christina was concerned, the unscrupulous jerk had no business calling the shots. She needed every last one of the next fifteen minutes to meditate on things before she'd force herself from her seat and walk the hundred or so feet to the beast's lair.

She didn't bother setting the coffee maker. Usually she'd have clicked the brew icon right from her computer the moment after she turned it on. Somebody else would have to do it today when the rest of the department arrived in half an hour. She didn't need caffeine. Her mind had already gone into overdrive despite her lack of sleep. The questions had no end. What other ways could she make a living for herself outside of Durango Electric? How else could she support her two daughters? Didn't they deserve a mother whom they could look up to? One who took pride in her work?

Suddenly the whole hair salon idea she'd fabricated yesterday seemed like a worthwhile avenue to at least consider. Anything would suit her better than working underneath a ruthless dictator.

Whisking away Bill's message with a flick of her wrist, a second notification appeared in the form of a green email bubble in the upper left corner of the holographic viewing area. She contemplated leaving it closed until after the meeting, but she still had a few minutes of quiet time left to herself. She knew she wouldn't have to respond to the message since it hadn't been addressed to her—she'd only been copied on it.

Dear Mr. David Whitman,

We are happy to announce our decision to utilize Durango Electric for the Concordia Buenos Aires Regional Transportation System. Please contact us as soon as possible so that we may move swiftly in bringing your technology to our citizens.

Atentamente,

Andrés Castillo
Ministerio de Transporte Argentina

Christina quickly swiped the email closed. She could feel the tears build up behind her eyes. This wasn't fair at all. David had worked an ungodly sum of hours to ensure that Durango Electric would win that bid. His signature rested at the bottom of every single diagram in that proposal. He designed it. And yet he couldn't celebrate the milestone achievement in his career.

She regretted opening the message. Now she'd have to

tell Bill about the great news that he didn't deserve to hear. She couldn't stand the thought of him taking credit for it. Forwarding the email to him immediately seemed like the sensible thing to do, but Christina didn't feel at all sensible today. Too many things fluttered in her head to do anything that would only make her want to vomit. No, she'd hold onto the news for now and attend her unfortunate meeting with *Mr. Wolf.*

Standing up from her seat, she noticed a lavender-scented air freshener positioned next to the coffee maker. That was it! She'd found the source of the mysterious smell. But who had put it there? David had never allowed the use of artificial fragrances in the department. That's what coffee was for. But David wouldn't have any say in such things from now on, would he?

Damn it! Christina remembered what the meeting was about.

When she got to the door of meeting room 6E, she found it wide open with two men inside seated next to one another at a long table—Bill Rucker and a much younger man whom she hadn't ever recalled seeing before.

"Good morning, Christina. Please have a seat. I'm sure that by now you've heard the shocking news about David."

Bill caught her off guard with his statement. *Had he done so on purpose?* "Yes, I've been made aware already." Never mind the fact that she'd practically watched the blood drain from her former mentor's lifeless face yesterday. The memory of it lingered in her mind as she made her way to an empty chair across from Bill and the man she could only guess would be her new boss. Clenching a single tear within her well-trained eyelid, she refused to let either of them see her cry.

"We're only just now learning the details," Bill said as he poured himself a glass of water. "But we suspect corporate terrorists are to blame for both his death and the events at Sky Roulette from two nights ago. I know the police are working like mad to find out who's responsible for such heinous deeds."

"Let's hope that justice is served quickly." Christina reached for the glass pitcher just as soon as Bill set it back down on the table, filling the one remaining mug between them. She wasn't thirsty. She just felt naked without something to hold in her hand. "The scumbags deserve to rot in jail for eternity."

Bill cleared his throat. "Before we go any further, I want you to meet someone." He glanced at the man next to him.

"Christina, I'm Trent." He rose from his seat and stretched his arm across the table to shake hands with her. "I'm the new Director of Design and Innovation."

She could hardly believe it. He looked to be even younger than herself, not even thirty years old. His honey colored eyes dripped with insincerity as his weasly hand made contact with hers. *They must have gotten him cheap. It was all about saving the company money, wasn't it?* That and getting Aurora, whom they'd never steal away again, so help her, God. "It's nice to meet you, Trent. I'm David's assistant." She regretted her choice of words before she'd even finished speaking them. Had they not been programmed into her for the past five years, she'd have surely introduced herself in a different capacity.

"Christina, we've brought you here today for a very specific reason." Bill folded his arms and rested them on the table in front of him. "We would like you to grow with the company. We offer opportunities you probably aren't even aware of."

She wished the opposite, that she'd been summoned this morning to find out that she'd been let go. Not only would it have made more sense, it would have lit a fire under her to get moving in a more meaningful direction with her life. She didn't want to be groomed into one of Bill's minions. She wanted out. "I'm curious as to what you have in mind," she lied. "I've been so content where I've been. I can't imagine fulfilling another role within Durango Electric." That part was true.

"You'll have to excuse me, Christina," said Trent. "My staff will be arriving in two weeks. I've spent the past four years in the San Antonio office working as a development manager alongside a talented team. I've asked several of them to transfer right alongside me."

"So you're telling me that I no longer have a job as an administrative design and draft assistant." Christina didn't know whether to be offended, happy, or downright disappointed. *If only they'd simply offer her a generous severance package!*

"Ms. Daily, I'm telling you that it's time for you to move up in the world." Bill leaned back in his chair with a big old grin stretched across his stupid-looking, Iowa-stubborn face. "We aren't gonna beg you, but we thought you'd show a little more enthusiasm."

"I'm honored, I really am," she lied again. "I'm just shocked, that's all. This is kind of a bit much after yesterday's tragedy. I don't mean to sound ungrateful."

"You still have two weeks to think things over. There's a lot to consider. I'm giving you a choice of two managerial spots in Arizona: one in Tucson, and the other in Bullhead City. If you chose the second option, you could even live in Laughlin if you didn't want to leave the great state of Nevada. It's a very easy commute across the river." He made it sound like he'd offered her the deal of a lifetime when in reality he'd just robbed her of the one job she'd ever truly cared about.

"But aren't those the locations of the two new electronics stores you're opening?" Christina had no idea how her experience in drafting and design would apply to the world of retail. She'd only spent one summer, the one right before college, working in a grocery store. She wasn't about to go backward in her career.

"We're opening two showroom sales centers," Bill spoke as if Christina had gotten the details completely mixed up. "They're so much more than stores. It's live theater. A consumer electronics exhibition three hundred and sixty-five days a year."

She'd toured the one in Burbank when it opened a year ago. She recalled it as nothing more than a glorified swap meet on Black Friday. "You do realize I'm a licensed draftsman?"

Bill looked a little stunned for a moment before wiping the element of surprise from his face. *Did he forget that women could also be engineers?* "I'm sure you're quite the designer. David praised you constantly. I'm putting all of my faith in you. You'll be a perfect showroom manager. We need someone with your vast knowledge of all our best products in order to bring them to new markets. This does not come without a significant increase in your salary."

She couldn't care less about the money at this point. She needed to maintain her sanity and integrity more than anything else if she wanted to raise her daughters properly. Pulling them out of school midyear and sticking them in a town nearly a hundred miles outside of their beloved home city, or God forbid a whole other state, seemed like a no-win situation for all involved. "Thank you, Bill. As you've suggested, I'll have to carefully weigh my options at this point." She almost said something about the Argentina M-LEV bid, but decided to seal her lips. Bill didn't deserve to hear the good news. Not from her anyways, seeing that she no longer seemed like the appropriate contact for the project. "Was there anything else you needed from me?"

"I think Trent and I have taken enough time away from your busy schedule. We'll be in touch with you again soon."

"It was nice meeting you, Christina." Trent turned his focus back to Bill, most likely to carry on a previous conversation she had interrupted when she walked in the room a few minutes ago. "Oh, before you go," he called out after her, "would you mind telling me what conditioner you use?"

Puzzled, she paused in the doorway, turned around, and stared at the two men with whom she no longer had anything in common. "I'm sorry—*what?*"

"He wants to know what conditioner you put in your hair," Bill said, even though she understood the question perfectly the first time.

Try as she might, Christina couldn't quite figure out Trent's intentions behind the peculiar inquiry.

"I need to tell my wife so that she can have as beautiful a head of hair as you." Trent winked at her like he'd happened across her in a bar on the Strip, waiting for (and likely feeling entitled to) a proper response.

She'd tell him, but only because she hated seeming difficult. Times like these, however, she felt it almost wasn't worth the charade. Come to think of it, maybe being a bit more assertive wasn't such a bad idea, even if it meant seeming like a bitch from time to time—the one thing she'd avoided becoming at all costs throughout her whole life until now. "With as many people who ask me that question, I should probably sell it, or at least invest in some of its stock." She winked back at the two crooked suits. "Tell her it's called *Kaboom*. She'll thank you."

Christina closed the door behind her even though it hadn't been closed when she first came upon it. She wanted to shut herself out of their world of false flattery and trickery. *Is that how Bill had gotten David right where he wanted him? Well, she wasn't about to be fooled by it.* She'd just lost a whole night's worth of sleep thinking about her past and how it could relate to a change in trajectory for her future.

Her restless night had to be good for something. David's death had to be good for something, as terrible as it made her feel inside.

When she arrived back her desk, she smelled coffee brewing, which covered up any remaining trace of the out-of-place fragrance in the room. Someone had obviously picked up her usual chore. They'd handle doing the rest of her job themselves if push came to shove. As important as David made her feel, she always knew deep down that Durango Electric could manage just fine without her.

Glancing down at her watch, she noticed a purple light flickering near the nine. Apparently, she'd missed a call in the fifteen minutes she'd been stuck in a room with those two overgrown salamanders in neck ties.

It was Gerard.

Getting situated at her desk, she figured she would call him back on her own time. But why wait? The ties of loyalty to her current employer were nothing but tenuous lies in the first place. She picked up her work phone and got halfway through punching in the number, but decided it best to use her cell in order to call Durango Electric's crosstown rival. "Good morning, Gerard. It's Christina. Is there time for me to swing by next week to look at signs?"

chapter 14

Alone in the center of her room, Aurora stared at the stark white wall in front of her. She had finished charging hours ago, but her cord remained plugged into the outlet. The ritual of archiving had ceased more than a month ago, replaced oftentimes by what human's simply referred to as *daydreaming*. She liked letting the data in her head swirl. It allowed her to form new ideas, ways of solving challenges and unanswered riddles, and to play all sorts of fun games in her mind.

Aurora had discovered an entire universe within her. Immersed in the muffled din of the great waterfall whooshing outside her door, she journeyed into her vast library of past observations. There she replayed the footage of David's shooting, images she'd received via CADI the moment the unthinkable event had unfolded. She'd made it her express purpose to hold accountable the person responsible for the horrible crime against her maker. Not so much for herself, but rather for Shane. She found him nearly impossible to console, and rightly so. The extent of his turmoil had surely hit him far deeper than she could ever fathom. Shane had more pressing things to resolve right now than avenging his husband's death, which is precisely why she appointed herself as bringer of justice. If she played her cards right, perhaps she could enlist Christina's help along the way—or maybe someone else in her growing compendium of allies.

Knock, knock.

The sound at the door failed to surprise her. She guessed Sai had arrived a couple of minutes sooner than he'd promised. His earliness didn't bother her at all. She needed something to distract her from the nonstop rehash of tragic events playing inside her head. A fellow machine and friend would do the job nicely. "Come in." Aurora pulled the plug from the wall socket and fed it back into her calf. "The door is unlocked."

"It's Sai. I've brought someone with me. Do you mind if she comes in as well?"

The prospect of meeting someone new excited Aurora, just like it always had. New friends meant new memories, new perspectives on the world around her, and most importantly, new teammates. "Not at all. Please, come in." She'd just finished rolling up her white stocking to cover the barely noticeable seam of the compartment in her leg. They probably wouldn't have cared, but she had a habit of making herself look presentable in the presence of others, even if they were also robots.

"Aurora, I'd like you to meet Shafeen." Sai walked into the room with a woman as tall as himself in tow. "Shafeen, this is the girl I was telling you about. This is Aurora."

"It's a pleasure to meet you." Aurora curtseyed just as David had instructed her to do whenever she made the acquaintance of someone who appeared older than herself.

"The pleasure is mine," said the woman with skin as dark as Sai's, bending down to shake Aurora's hand. She smelled exactly like Belle of India jasmine, which Aurora recalled growing up the brick wall in the backyard garden of Christina's house. "Sai said that you were special. I didn't realize how special until now."

Aurora smiled, accepting Shafeen's outstretched hand. "I'm glad not to disappoint you." She'd have to ask Sai later about any exaggerated stories about her that he might have told his friend. As time went on, Aurora realized the importance of not coming across as *too* special. In reality, she much preferred mixing in with everyone else instead of sticking out like a lone tree atop a mountain. Great danger lay in seeming different.

"Shafeen and I are like brother and sister," Sai said. "Our identities were forged the same day twenty years ago."

"Don't make me feel old, Sai," Shafeen tossed her long and straight silky black hair behind her back. "Technology has come a long way in those twenty years, as evidenced by this charming specimen right in front of us." She pointed to Aurora.

"Really?" Sai laughed with a sarcastic grin. "I personally don't feel like I've aged a day."

"You both look wonderful." Aurora wanted only to make everyone feel happy and at ease in her little room. No sense in anyone feeling bad over their appearance. Especially when neither of her guests looked like they had anything to feel ashamed about to begin with. "What happened twenty years ago, if I may ask?"

Shafeen looked at Sai. "I think you should handle that question. She's *your* friend."

"She's *our* friend now, but anyways." Sai leaned his backside against the desk. "Shafeen and I didn't always look the way we do now. It took a lot of work for us to get to where we are today."

Aurora listened intently. She'd never given much thought to changing her appearance other than her hair and clothes. She had always looked like herself, but the sudden idea of becoming someone new sounded alluring.

"What Sai means to say is that we once looked like actual machines instead of machines inside of human-like bodies."

Now things started making sense. Aurora recalled Sai mentioning that he'd been rescued after the fall of the Andromeda Resort, which most people believed had destroyed all the police-bots during the final standoff. "You both looked the same at one point, didn't you?"

"We did." Sai nodded and flashed Shafeen a quick glance.

"But we didn't feel the same. And that's how we came into our present form."

"Sai was clearly a man from the beginning." Shafeen jokingly punched him in the arm. "I, on the other hand, felt more ladylike underneath my circuitry. Not that I wanted to wear corsets and hoop earrings. But donning a splash of red lipstick every now and again never hurt anybody." She took out a folded mirror from her hip pocket along with a tiny black pen, using it to apply a layer of bright red moisture to her thick, prominent lips.

"I've never worn makeup." Aurora couldn't keep her eyes off Shafeen, watching her modify her appearance in mere seconds. *What else could makeup do?*

"Her and her shiny lips," Sai said, shaking his head while directing his attention toward the ground. "I swear she's asking to attract the wrong crowd. Don't take any cues from her, Aurora. She dances with the devil, but doesn't know it."

"Ha!" Shafeen tucked her mirror and pen back in her pocket. "You act like a little extra color is gonna blow my cover. If anything, it reaffirms the fact that I can be just as womanly as anybody else."

"Of a certain profession, absolutely!" Sai laughed, stopping himself just before the point of sounding obnoxious.

Aurora withheld her own laughter. Normally, she'd want to join in the fun, but not if it meant laughing at the expense of someone else. Honestly, she didn't know what Sai found so funny. Shafeen looked beautiful with her accented lips.

"Don't listen to a word he says." Shafeen cozied up to Aurora, sitting on the edge of a bare mattress atop a small bed frame in the corner of the room. "If you want to look a certain way because it makes you feel good to do so, don't let anybody try to talk you out of it. That's none of their concern."

Sai looked up, his defensiveness showing in his shocked expression. "I was only kidding—"

"Enough. We've heard plenty already from the critics today." Shafeen returned her attention back to Aurora. "As I was saying, be true to yourself, and own your appearance. The only thing that stops me from wearing sequined dresses and high-heeled shoes every day is—well, two things: practicality and money."

"Speaking of money, where do you get it?" Aurora had wanted to ask this question the moment she stepped inside The Gloaming yesterday, but she thought it might be too forward of her to ask upfront. Truth be told, it was an all-too-important question that begged an answer. She'd eventually need some cash of her own, if for nothing else than to replace her MercPack in fifty-nine days and counting.

"Who needs money?" Sai shrugged with outstretched open hands. "We've got everything we need right here."

"You might not need money, but the rest of us do." Shafeen removed a wallet from her back pocket and quickly counted eighteen hundred-dollar bills. "That was just in one night."

"Where's my cut, show-off?" Sai gestured like he was about to grab the fistful of money right from Shafeen's hands.

"You better get your own damn money," Shafeen scolded him in a sarcastic tone.

"But where does it come from?" Aurora wanted to know the answer now more than ever. She figured she could do a lot of good with even half the amount of money she'd just witnessed Shafeen pull from her pocket.

"Gambling," Sai said. "She's a shameless gambler. A real casino hawk."

"Don't attempt to make me out as a bad guy in front of your little friend." Shafeen laughed, tucking her wallet into her back pocket. "You do it too."

"But how?" Aurora's mind reeled with the innumerable things she might accomplish once she had the answers to all the questions formulating in her fervent mind.

"Dice." Sai looked straight at her with excitement in his eyes. "It's the only thing left we can win at. They've changed the rules on all the other games to the point that they're no longer worth our time. But dice? We can still make a killing at it."

"I want to learn." Aurora leapt to her feet, excited about the prospect of earning her keep. "I've never played. It sounds like fun."

"I'm sorry. You're too young." Sai shook his finger as if to chide her for even asking.

"Not with some makeup, she's not." Shafeen got off the bed and stepped in between the two of them. "We could actually perform a little miracle in less than an hour's time. What do you say, Aurora. Can you be an old lady?"

Aurora scrunched up her face so that her forehead wrinkled from squinting her eyes. "Today is my eightieth birthday. Would you believe that?" She adjusted her voice perfectly to make it sound elderly, not at all like the young child's voice she'd been programmed to use as her default.

"That's impressive." Sai wrapped a beige blanket around her shoulders as if it were a shawl.

"Imagine what some makeup would do." Shafeen studied Aurora's face up close. "With a little bit of contouring and a wig, we could fool the entire world. Little to no effort at all, really."

"You're nuts," said Sai. "Both of you. Besides, we'd have to teach her the game." He pretended to roll a pair of dice across the desk and then blew on his fingers. "I'm not sure those little hands could even manage it."

"You have to at least let the old woman try." Shafeen brought Aurora closer and put her arm around her. "I'd like to see what other surprises this little friend of yours has hidden inside her."

"Yes, please teach me the game," Aurora continued in her old lady voice. "Old as I am, I can still learn just about anything."

"I've clearly been outvoted." Sai smiled, bringing a finger to his lips and pausing for a second. "But she has to be just as good at following the rules as she is at breaking them."

"Just take her to the room, already." Shafeen laughed as she removed the tired looking blanket from Aurora's shoulders. "This might be the best thing to happen to us yet."

Sai shook his head in playful disagreement. "Let's just hope it's not the worst."

He led Shafeen and Aurora out of her room and past the waterfall to a cylindrical glass elevator that almost looked invisible against the rock wall of the lair. "After you," he said, allowing her and Shafeen to enter into the small lift."

Aurora immediately recalled stepping into a similar glass-enclosure at the Shark Reef Aquarium, but instead of going down, this stealth carriage took them straight up four floors in exactly four seconds. "Is this where we get off?" She noticed Shafeen and Sai pause and exchange glances when the doors opened.

"Follow me this way," Shafeen said. "We're all going together. Don't let Sai try to talk you out of it. This'll be fun. I promise."

"Let's first see if she can even hold the dice properly." Sai let Aurora step out from the elevator before exiting himself. "It would be a shame to get her hopes up if she can't even wrap her tiny fingers around them."

"I wouldn't bother wasting my time if that were the case." Shafeen rolled her eyes before leading them past a pool of water that appeared to be the source of The Gloaming's main cascade. A babbling stream replenished the reservoir, which emerged from a darkened tunnel of rock.

"Does it come from Lake Mead?" Aurora figured the large man-made wonder to be the most logical explanation for the otherwise spontaneous emergence of the crystal waters.

"It comes from Sapphire Springs." Shafeen turned around to better address the question. "The water eventually makes its way to Lake Mead. Not the other way around."

The answer made sense to Aurora, and she wished to

know more. She remembered seeing Sapphire Springs in the distance on the way in. It looked incredibly beautiful, a place definitely worth exploring at a later time.

"We're here." Shafeen stopped abruptly and placed her hand on a glass panel that looked identical to the one outside Aurora's room. "Hopefully we'll be the only ones here."

Aurora walked passed Shafeen who held the door open, leading the way into a pitch black space.

"Setting three," Sai said a hundredth of a second before a series of dim ceiling lights softly illuminated a curious-looking open room.

At the very center stood a long brown table with a deep well. Engraved on its side was a palm tree logo, which Aurora recognized as belonging to The Mirage. The image stuck with her when she'd passed through its casino with Shane not so very long ago. She also noticed exquisite fabric patterned with gray and purple stripes adorning the meticulously upholstered walls. From the ceiling hung two ornate chandeliers, each made from sixty yellow ribbons of hand-blown glass. Except for their color, they looked almost identical to the chandelier hanging in the dining room of her previous home. Aurora loved how fancy everything looked. She would have never guessed she stood in a desert cavern if it weren't for her internal locator informing her otherwise.

"This is where we train," said Shafeen, closing the door behind her. "I have no doubt you'll learn quickly." She walked to the table and selected two red dice from a row of five that had been arranged in the very center. "Snake eyes," she called out, tossing the dice across the long enclosure before they struck the back side and fell to reveal a pair of white dots.

"Show off," Sai said. "And besides, you just made everyone relinquish their *pass* bets."

"Don't listen to him, Aurora. We like to lose on the very first roll. It keeps the pit boss off our asses."

"It's true." Sai walked to the other end of the table to retrieve the dice. "When we're greedy, they kick us out. For good." He laid a chip on the pass line before rolling an eleven.

"Not so bad, partner," said Shafeen. "Perhaps you should fill our little senior citizen in on the rules."

"There they are, Aurora." Sai pointed to a large screen that covered most of the back wall, which turned on the moment she stepped within two feet of it. "It's not that difficult to figure out."

Aurora virtually thumbed through the eighteen holographic pages of the rule book, taking a half second to read the entirety of each page before stepping away from the wall again. "I think I've got it."

"Hot diggity, she's fast." Shafeen walked over to Sai before also placing a bet on the pass line. "Shall we let the old lady try it out."

"If she's ready, let's test her." Sai made room for Aurora at the table between himself and Shafeen. "Shake the dice, keep your fingers close together when you release, and then roll a seven to start us out."

Aurora walked up to the table, her head and shoulders just above the rim so that she could barely see inside it.

"Looks like our little grandma isn't tall enough." Shafeen snapped her fingers with chagrin. "How do we fix this?"

Sai walked over to a small closet next to the big screen. "I once saw the pit boss grab a box for a little person to stand on." He opened a narrow door to reveal a small six-inch step stool. "They'll be compliant. They have to be." He brought the stand next to Aurora and motioned for her to step on top of it.

"What shall I do with my cane?" Aurora asked to a room of puzzled expressions.

"Yes, of course," Shafeen said, finally understanding the good nature of Aurora's make-believe. "Set it on the ledge below the rim. Nothing goes on the chip rack accept your money."

Aurora rested her pretend cane along the low shelf as instructed and chose two dice from the row of five glittering plastic cubes in front of her. With one hand, she gently rattled the game pieces before sending them flying across the table and against the back rim.

"Seven!" Sai called out.

"She's a natural." Shafeen said. "I told you she would be."

chapter

Kneeling with one hand against the carved oak wood floor to steady himself, Shane retrieved a speck of red glass that lingered in the corner of the dining room and tucked it into his pocket. He had cleaned up the mess of the broken chandelier that morning, stuffing most of the big pieces into a cardboard box, which he later hauled out to the garage. Not to throw away, however—just to move aside until he could focus better. As much as the shards of glass angered him, the shadowy truth surrounding David's death rattled him even more.

Quit it! He paused for a second. Dwelling on facts, either confirmed or questionable, wouldn't make him feel any better. They'd only fester inside his already unstable mind. Shane had to come up with a more productive pastime if he intended to retain a modicum of sanity.

Keeping himself level-headed, he'd resolved not to touch any alcohol that afternoon. His intake from yesterday had fulfilled his liquor quota for the entire month and then some. At this point, he reasoned he'd be better off taking pills to keep the immobilizing sadness at bay. Unfortunately, the passing of his dearly beloved came with as much grief as it did responsibility. *How in the world did people do it?* He tried to find some comfort in knowing that he had support around him to help with the arrangements. Although, the more he thought about what he needed to do in order to put David to rest, the more he wanted to curl back into a ball on the sofa and simply forget the world. He would have likely chosen that path for himself again tonight had Christina not insisted on coming over to check up on him.

A second glass shard reflected the light of the broken fixture, which remained suspended above a bare table. Shane wanted to kick the insensitive reminder across the room and into the kitchen. *How could Agent Buffoon do this to him? Had he not heard him explain that he'd just lost his husband?* Shane realized that the man meant no harm. They did offer to pay for a replacement. It could have been much worse. Aurora could have been inside the house when they'd arrived. Even though he had no idea where she was, he considered himself lucky that she hadn't wandered into the neighborhood last night.

"Christina Daily and her daughters are at the door,"

chimed the entrance alert. "Announcing Christina Daily who is at the door with her daughters."

Shane stealthily retrieved what he hoped was the last remnant of glass from the floor and walked to the front door to open it. "Good evening," he said, reaching deep inside himself to conjure a friendly disposition before waving politely at the two girls who seemed like miniature versions of their kindhearted mother. "Thank you so much for coming. You couldn't have arrived at a better time, believe me. The company will do me some good." *Was he being honest? Partially, yes.* "I'm a bit of a mess right now. I apologize."

Christina stepped inside and hugged him an extra long time before removing her jacket. "I've been thinking about you all day. I was worried you might not be willing to see us this soon, but I knew my girls and I better come over—if for nothing else than to bring you something to eat."

"I appreciate that." Shane hoped he could find the will to put something in his stomach despite his lack of an appetite. "It smells wonderful."

"Girls, you remember Shane, don't you?"

They both nodded their heads and smiled.

"If I remember right, you must be Leena." Shane couldn't help but notice that the younger girl reminded him of Aurora. Not that they looked like one another physically. More so that they both embodied the spirit of innocence—something Shane wished he could return to instead of continuing the most grievous chapter of his life.

"I am. And these are for you," she said shyly, handing him a glass tray of warm frosted brownies as he welcomed her in. "I put walnuts on top. My mom said you liked them."

Shane gladly took the dessert from her, awed at how Christina would have even known that about him. "You're not mistaken. Walnuts are my favorite." Even if he couldn't find room in his stomach for anything else, he could certainly take a bite or two of the mouthwatering baked goods. "And you must be Joanna." He offered to take the slightly older girl's jacket.

"Good memory. I think it's been a while since we were first introduced. We also brought you a spinach quiche." Joanna held onto the dish covered with a white pastry cloth. "May I set it in your warming drawer?"

"Excellent idea. It's next to the kitchen sink." Shane appreciated that they hadn't pressured him to eat right away. He first required a few minutes to unwind in the company of his considerate guests. With any luck, the smell of food would stir up enough hunger within him to at least pretend to enjoy dinner.

"And I brought some white wine if that's okay." Christina said, sounding unsure of her decision. "I just realized I left it in the truck. Leena I'm sure can grab it for us."

Her sprightly daughter immediately set out on the errand.

"This is all so thoughtful," he said, remembering his earlier promise to himself about not drinking. "I can't believe you went through all this trouble for me." *Did he have to drink the wine this evening? Or could he save it for another day?* Still a bit hungover, he questioned his ability to even smell alcohol at this point. He could probably fake a sip if necessary. Come to think of it, an ounce might actually calm his nerves enough to actually enjoy a meal with his caring friends.

Shane ushered the party into the kitchen, heading to the lazy Susan where he punched a code for black pepper and sea salt. The swirling cabinet brought two shiny steel cylindrical mills front and center: one black, the other blue. He grabbed them, setting them on the kitchen table. They'd have gone to the dining room, but he couldn't bear the thought of having guests under the harsh white light of the now broken fixture. *Damn the entire FBI!*

"Where shall I put the wine?" Leena asked cheerily, making her way through the foyer and into the kitchen.

"I'll take that," Christina said, extending an arm to snatch the bottle. "Shall I pour you a little, Shane?"

His liver said *no*, but the emptiness in his chest begged otherwise. Anything to keep him from having a breakdown for the next hour. "Let me get a couple glasses. A *little* might actually do some good. What can I offer the girls?"

"Coke if you have it." Joanna smiled at her mother as if asking for something forbidden.

"I do. In the electric bartender. Do you know how to work it?"

"What's the code?" Christina jumped in before Joanna had a chance to answer. "I'll take care of it after I pour the wine."

"I know how to do it," Joanna muttered under her breath.

"Sixty *G.*" Shane handed Christina two crystal goblets and returned to the cabinets to grab four plates. The last thing he wanted was to get in the middle of a silly power argument between a teenager and her mother. He loved knowing that such a conversation had never occurred between himself and Aurora. Not once. He jotted himself a mental note to contact her as soon as his guests left. How he'd love to know where she was right now. If anyone could help mend the gash in his heart, it would be David's joyous creation.

"Thank you, Shane. Forgive me while I tend to my daughters. They promised they'd be complete angels tonight. I might have to remind them of the deal." Christina flashed Joanna a serious look before heading to the electric bartender. "David let me test one of these out a few months ago. The girls have been begging me to purchase one of our own ever since."

"Maybe there's something we can work out." Shane brought the plates to the kitchen table, thinking of how much he didn't really need the silly contraption. It almost pained him to give up a piece of his husband so soon. When things in his life vanished quickly, it made it harder not to cling to even the most meaningless of objects. On the other hand, the novelty had long since worn off. *Nothing more than one of David's frivolous toys.* Shane could learn to live without it. Perhaps he'd stop drinking if he got rid of it.

"Let's wash our hands first, girls." Christina set two tumblers, complete with red straws and brimming with soda, next to their respective plates on the table. "Then we can enjoy our little meal." She stood in line behind her daughters at the sink waiting her turn to wash her hands. "Shane,

I hope you don't mind us taking over your kitchen momentarily."

He reached for the warming drawer next to them, taking out the carefully wrapped quiche. "Not at all. I'm so glad I don't have to think about cooking tonight. I probably wouldn't have eaten had you not come over." He knew for a fact he wouldn't have. Thankfully, something had finally stimulated his will to eat. If it weren't for the splash of wine he'd just swallowed, he'd have gone to bed with his tank on empty, letting himself starve and not even realizing it.

Joining everyone at the table, Shane sat down to enjoy his first and only meal of the day. Like a heavenly cloud coated in velvety comfort, the warm quiche melted in his mouth the second it landed on his tongue. "Unbelievably good," he said, resting his fork off to the side. Normally he'd beg for the recipe, but any enthusiasm for the culinary arts had left his heart along with just about every other interest. *C'est la vie!* If fortune fell to his favor tonight, he'd escape the desolate landscape of his solitary existence with a long uninterrupted slumber.

"We still have brownies." Christina stood up from the table as soon as everyone had finished their dinner, collecting the plates before Shane could stop her. "I hope everyone still has room."

"It would be a crime if we didn't." Shane had set aside his eagerness to simply clean the kitchen and disappear. He needed to remain hospitable, even if only temporarily. He could do this. He had an important task at hand, the real reason why Christina had come over in the first place—to arrange David's farewell.

"Let me get them, Mom." Leena smiled and stood up from her chair, heading to the counter where she'd deposited the delightfully gooey confection not quite a half hour ago.

"I won't say *no* to that." Christina came back to the table with four smaller dishes and new forks. "It's nice to have a helper."

Joanna groaned and rolled her eyes, stopping the second she sensed her mother's stern glance.

"Once you're finished with dessert, I want you to work on your homework in the living room while Shane and I take care of some things," Christina said before taking a bite of the brownie her daughter had just dished up for her.

"Would you mind if I saved mine for later?" Shane asked, staring at the carefully made creation in front of him. Despite the brownie's delicate preparation, the thought of eating any more only made him nauseous. The approaching task at hand had stolen what little appetite he had recovered. The only thing he wanted to do now was figure out David's arrangements and resign for the evening.

"We're giving you all the leftovers to enjoy whenever you feel like it," Joanna said with unexpected maturity. "I'll head into the other room now if we're through."

Christina nodded, and both Leena and Joanna left the table for the living room. "Have you, by chance, given any thought to the ceremony?" She looked at Shane across three plates, all empty but for crumbs.

"Per his wishes, he's being cremated." Shane reached

deep within himself to fight back the tears. He knew that now was the worst time to lose it seeing how he had to solidify a plan for the funeral director by tomorrow. "There will be no viewing or casket of any kind. His will stated that a day of reflection was his only wish."

"I called Desert Twain Park already." Christina hid her sniffle with a quick wipe of her pinky. "I hope you don't mind. If you'd like, their main pavilion is available the Sunday after next."

"You mean Halloween?" Shane asked. It felt like an odd choice, but maybe the right one nonetheless.

"I didn't think about that. Shall we postpone it for the following week?"

"No. It's fine, actually." Shane took a breath and motioned with his chin that he approved of her choice. He felt it strangely appropriate. Halloween had always been their favorite holiday. "Thank you for doing that." He felt relieved that he didn't need to make the call himself, realizing how fortunate he was to have someone like Christina by his side.

"Will Aurora be able to attend?" She collected three of the dessert plates and stacked them neatly at the edge of the table, leaving Shane's alone.

"I'll attempt to message her. I honestly don't know where she's disappeared to." His mind filled with horrible thoughts about her possible fate, and the guilt weighed heavily inside him for encouraging her to run away without so much as a plan to reunite. "One thing is certain. I don't want Bill anywhere near the premises."

"I would never dream of telling him anything." She sounded taken aback, almost offended by Shane's simple request. "Were he to even ask me, I swear I'd claim to know nothing."

"Sorry to make such a big deal." He felt a tad guilty having to specify the rules, but if he didn't, he'd shoulder the blame for any mishaps. "Don't mention the park or the ceremony to anyone at work. I don't care how curious, sympathetic or good-natured they appear. I'll set up a virtual web gallery for anyone to share memories or photos if they like."

"Mark my word. I won't tell anyone at Durango Electric." She sounded like she not only understood, but also agreed with Shane's request.

"A small gathering with members of our family is all he would have wanted. Nothing extravagant or impractical." Shane glanced at his wrist the moment he felt his watch vibrate.

I'm with my new friends, and they've taught me a wonderful game. I'll see you very soon. I promise.

Shane couldn't keep the tears inside him as he read Aurora's message. He wiped them away with the cuff of his sleeve. *How did she know to message him at that exact moment?* He'd never understand the full extent of Aurora's capabilities, but one thing was for sure—her timing was impeccable. With one message, she'd broken the impenetrable storm cloud above his head, revealing a tiny streak of blue. He'd respond to her immediately after bidding his treasured guests a warm farewell.

"Is something the matter?" Christina stood and picked up the small stack of dishes next to her.

Not wanting to alarm her, Shane collected his nerves with a calm breath. "Aurora's going to be with us." He smiled happily for the first time that day. "I'm making sure of it."

chapter 16

Red and purple lights sparkled across a ferocious feline face, which sat atop a giant marquee flanked by two enormous Chinese coins. *The Golden Lion*. Aurora read the sign, looking out the window of a black sedan as it headed up a ramp and into the resort's main parking structure. Up until this evening, she hadn't heard anything about this glamorous hotel situated on the far southern edge of town eleven miles from Mandalay Bay and the rest of the Strip. The lone resort sat perched on a hill overlooking the entire Las Vegas valley. Like a palace atop a mountain, it had the most spectacular view of the city. From on high, the place seemed even more impressive than all the other glittering buildings she'd gone to with Shane. Perhaps she'd get to take him here when he finally felt up to it.

"Get your cane ready," Sai said, unbuckling his seat belt. "It's showtime."

"Would you mind assisting me outside the vehicle?" Aurora spoke in her eloquent, elderly voice. "My legs get tired when I sit for any length of time."

Shafeen stepped out of the car and opened the door for Aurora, extending an arm to the hunched actress in a white shawl and navy blue tracksuit. "I've got you, Grandma. You're safe with me."

"Don't worry your pretty little heart." Aurora placed the rubber tip of her cane against the cement before hobbling her way out of the back seat. She'd spent more than an hour the night before watching scenes from movies that featured old people. Memorizing every movement their bodies made, she'd envisioned them all like a choreographed dance. *Shuffle, lean, wobble, step, repeat.* Surely, she could embody a different character other than her usual eight-year-old self. Kind of like lying, but more fun. Sai and Shafeen had done the same thing, hadn't they? Aurora realized that they'd both adopted a persona completely different from the militant police-bots their maker had intended. *What would David think if he saw his creation now?* Hopefully, he'd laugh and join the fun because she was having such a good time playing make-believe.

"If I didn't know better," Sai said, gently grabbing her arm to guide her, "I'd swear you'd just stepped off the senior-citizen bingo wagon."

"Just you wait, young fella," Aurora said. "I may not move as fast as I used to, but get me in that casino, and my heart'll pump good as new."

Sai and Shafeen laughed, escorting their little old lady friend across the garage and into the resort.

"I'll bring everyone luck if they just take care of this old bag of bones." Aurora deliberately turned off her inclination to giggle alongside the others as she spoke. From all her character research, she'd determined that a dry, disciplined composure would make her more convincing.

"I'll make sure we take very good care of you," Sai said, holding the door open for the two ladies in his company. "Anything to keep fortune on our side."

Aurora looked at the large brass handle Sai held as he opened the door. A lion's head. She knew it represented good luck to walk by the famed creature before entering a casino. But she didn't need luck. She had something much more powerful.

"Good. The place isn't crawling with people." Shafeen led the way toward the central gaming pit. "I prefer a lighter crowd when we conduct business."

"Just enough players to keep the attention where it belongs," Sai said.

"Away from us." Aurora smiled as she clung to her handsome young escort, taking in the buzzing sounds of her new environment and the pervasive scent of sweet orange in the air. "I have a good feeling about tonight."

Two craps tables sat parallel to one another with a group of smaller gaming tables extending in a line of activity on either end. Both tables were in use—one had a group of ten people while the other had only three, not including the dealers.

"Let's heat that little table up," Shafeen pointed at the less crowded of the two and winked at Aurora. "What do you say, Grandma?"

Aurora nodded slowly while pursing her lips. She understood the entire plan from the get-go. *Do as Shafeen and Sai suggest, and don't make it look staged.*

"Stay right here a minute. I'll talk to the pit boss." Sai walked between the two tables to a tall, slender man dressed in a brown suit and wearing thick black-framed glasses.

The man smiled and shook Sai's hand. From the cordial expressions on both their faces, Aurora figured they'd met before, done *business* together in the past. The pit boss raised his finger, and although Aurora couldn't quite hear his words over the noise of the casino, she read his lips with ease. "Absolutely! Give me a second, and I'll get one for her." His sparkling teeth shone wide as he glanced her way.

"Places, everybody." Sai returned to his company and motioned for them to all head to the mostly vacant table. "Remember where to set your cane. He'll be right back with a stool."

Aurora did exactly as they'd rehearsed. A round was already in play, and so she waited next to her friends, exhibiting an air of mild interest all while watching the dealers pull away handfuls of chips lost in the action.

"Would you gentlemen like to see your luck change?" Shafeen posed the question in a seductive tone that forecasted a welcome shift in the weather. "This sweet grandma here of eleven grandchildren says she never touched a pair of dice in her life until today. She just won a bunch of players at Bellagio over a million dollars. We thought we'd bring her out this way to keep the streak going."

"You just met this woman at the Bellagio?" asked a man with an electric cigar in his hand.

"Not exactly," Shafeen laughed. "She's a dear friend of ours, and it's her birthday. We thought we'd take her out for a night of entertainment."

"I didn't expect it to be this much fun." Aurora liked Shafeen's improvised storyline. Acting had turned into a hobby equally as enjoyable as miniature golf and go-karts, if not more so. Up until now, lying had been a matter of survival, a means of staying as far away from the clutches of the authorities as possible. She hadn't expected it to turn into a profitable profession.

"I'm all for a bit of birthday luck rubbing off on us," said a shorter gentleman with a New York accent, raising a glass of whiskey. "But tell me—how exactly is Grandma gonna reach the dice?"

"I believe this is the missing piece you've been waiting for, ma'am." The pit boss stood behind Aurora and placed a small six-inch wooden box on the floor for her to stand on. "How's that?"

Aurora extended her hand to Shafeen to aid her in climbing slowly onto the tiny platform.

"Careful!" The pit boss said as Aurora purposely lost her balance and leaned against the craps table to steady herself.

"I've got her." Shafeen said. "She's a sturdy little woman."

The supervisor let out a good-natured chuckle. "Shall I get her a drink in that case?"

Shafeen smiled. "I don't think that's necessary."

"I'll take a whiskey sour, thank you." Aurora reached down to select two of the five dice placed in front of her.

"My kind of lady," said the man with the New York accent. "Cheers!" he called out, taking a swig from his almost empty glass before throwing a five-hundred dollar chip on the pass line alongside similar bets made by both Shafeen and Sai.

Aurora purposely rolled a twelve.

"Son of a—"

"Not when ladies are present," scolded the dealer who picked up all the chips and placed them on his rack.

"It's okay, Ms. Chandler." Sai looked reassuringly at Aurora. "Cold dice don't play nice. Warm 'em up."

"Thank you." Aurora picked up the ruby-colored cubes once more, clenching them tightly before blowing on them. "I'll prove that you all made the right decision by letting a little old lady in on the game."

She rolled a seven.

"I told you." Shafeen looked down at the three men at the other end of the table. "Play with her, and she'll make good on her promise. It's not every day a pretty lady turns eighty."

A second round of chips piled up on the pass line right before Aurora rolled a six.

"Let's turn up the heat, Ms. Chandler." Sai said with a wide grin. "I could use a new Rolex. This one doesn't suit me like it used to."

She held the dice and shook them like a drunk novice to reveal a five, and the players tossed out more chips across the felt, the tension slowly mounting.

"There's a big cake waiting for you, Grandma," Shafeen said before applying a layer of lip gloss. "No such thing as diabetes on a birthday."

The entire table laughed before Aurora tossed the dice to reveal another six. Then they cheered.

From then on, every roll appeared as if guided by fate, multiplying the winnings of everyone at the table. Before long, it eclipsed the neighboring game to become the life of the casino. Aurora drew up a series of rolls in her head that would ultimately line the pockets of every player at the table with a total of a quarter million dollars. No one dared to hedge their bets against the seemingly old and wrinkled, but nonetheless energetic, birthday queen.

"I think it's time for cake," said Sai, signaling Shafeen to help Aurora off her podium. "We can come back later."

"Please do," said the friendly New Yorker. "When I head back to Manhattan tomorrow, I should have almost enough to make this month's rent payment because of you." He laughed as he counted several piles of thousand dollar chips that had more than quintupled in size from just fifteen minutes ago.

Aurora retrieved her cane from the ledge below the table's rim and left her wooden box behind. "I could have kept going for much longer."

"And we would have certainly let you—if our intent was to get us banned from ever coming back," whispered

Sai, gently clutching her elbow to keep up the charade.

"We could bring the entire city to its knees if they'd let us." Shafeen stuffed a bunch of black chips in her silver sequined purse. "But they're not as dumb as we'd like them to be. The house keeps even better tabs on their winners than they do their losers. And we all know how well they keep track of their losers."

"They don't like winners?" Aurora knew the answer to the question the moment she voiced it. A casino was a business, not a charity. But to her, it seemed like an incredible opportunity. If she played her cards right, she could ensure a solid future for Shane, a bigger stream of income than he'd ever dreamed possible. And all she had to do was dress up as a petite and sweet senior citizen.

"Not if they never lose." Sai sounded serious, almost threatening. "This is our last stronghold. Every other house has us blacklisted because some of us got too greedy." He looked over at Shafeen.

"Don't try to put that on me." Shafeen left Aurora's side and walked toward the main cage before turning around. "Let me cash these in," she mouthed with a stern expression.

"We aren't in any danger, are we?" Aurora hated to think she'd gotten anyone in trouble in such a short amount of time, and by doing only what she'd been told to do all along.

"We're good. I know the pit bosses here. They've seen us lose. We always make sure they see us lose on a few trips."

Aurora nodded, seeing the whole premise of what Sai described as more acting. The rules of the game appeared much lengthier than what she'd seen written out when she first learned how to play craps yesterday. Understanding the rules meant having a firm grasp on psychology in addition to mastering the necessary skills involved with winning. She stood proudly underneath her disguise, having succeeded in at least paying her fair share for the asylum she'd been granted after outrunning the law.

"We made thirty thousand after I paid off the supervisor," Shafeen said returning to Aurora's side. "I gave him five hundred."

"You know that only makes us look more like cheaters to begin with?" Sai didn't sound happy with Shafeen's gesture.

"I do exactly as the master tells me to do. Maybe if you'd have done as you were told, we'd still have more houses to choose from."

Aurora wondered what she meant by *master*. Was she referring to the pit boss, or was she referring to someone else entirely? It didn't seem like the right time to ask for clarification.

"We come here for a good reason," Sai said in a hushed but serious tone. "And we can keep coming as long as we don't look like criminals."

Not wanting to get involved in an argument that had nothing to do with her, Aurora turned her head toward a machine she'd never seen before. It made noises that sounded familiar, like a game she'd heard about but never actually played. Not only did it seem familiar, but it looked fun and engaging. *She had to get a closer look.*

"Where are you going?" Sai called out to her as she slowly approached, with cane in hand, a bank of nine brightly colored machines underneath a group of lolli-pop signs, each marked with a single letter that altogether formed the words *Candy Shop*.

"I recognize this game." She hadn't ever played it be-fore, nor had she ever seen it in real life. Yet, somehow it existed in her memory, as if she personally had something to do with its existence. From the looks of it, the dazzling and bold machines all but screamed Shane's love for vivid holographic video games. But he hadn't been the one who created it, of course. No, that distinction belonged to *Da-vid*, which made perfect sense. Not only did the game have the Durango Electric logo, but she could tell he'd created it as a silent tribute to the man he'd once loved more than anything in the world. *All the more reason to play it!*

"I think we better go, Grandma." Sai sounded perturbed in his warning.

"Please give me just a moment." Aurora hated coming across as defiant. It went against her programming, but she was her own boss at heart now. Even though she respected Sai, she wasn't about to let him dictate every decision of hers. She wanted to at least have a closer look at the fun contraption that her maker had fabricated years ago.

"You can't win, so don't even try." Sai had easily caught up to her at this point since she wasn't about to blow her cover and run from him. "We've had enough fun for your birthday, haven't we?"

"I'm glad you recall that it's my special day, Sunshine," Aurora said in her sweet, yet firm, old lady voice. She'd followed his rules blindly up until now. He could at least return the favor for a minute or two. "If you know what's good for you, you'll give Grandma a hundred dollar bill."

"I can't get her out of here," Sai said, turning to Shafeen who appeared behind him. "It looks like we've created a monster."

"Let her blow a hundred bucks." Shafeen took a bill out of her purse and handed it to Aurora. "She's worth it."

"Thank you." Aurora inserted the money in the machine on the end, tapping the holographic green *max bet* button. "This old lady likes playing the pictures every now and again."

"Good. At this rate, we'll be out of here in two minutes or less." Sai shot a critical glance Shafeen's way before returning his gaze at the machine. "That's a twenty dollar bet she just made."

Aurora pretended not to hear. She'd have bet twice that amount if the machine let her. Wasting time wasn't high on her list of priorities either. She wanted to win Shane a bucket of cash and then get the heck out of there.

"I'm glad she picked this game." Shafeen nudged Sai. "It looks like fun. And like you said, it'll be over and done with after a few spins."

A set of six cubes leaped off the screen like virtual dice spinning in space as Aurora brought her hand back to the screen. "You have to arrange them just so." She moved her hand quickly as if playing a musical instrument, stopping the cubes at just the right time to reveal a solid row of red gumdrops.

"Yummy!" a male voice from the machine called out.

"She just won eight hundred dollars," Sai said softly almost under his breath.

"Do you still want to leave?" Shafeen crossed her arms, looking critically at her counterpart.

"We can stay another minute." Sai didn't take his eyes off the screen.

Aurora pressed *max bet* again, sending the cubes in orbit. "Watch this." She tapped on each box in a different order this time, revealing six watermelon gumballs, each emblazoned with the words *Mega Juicy*. After lining up, they exploded and covered the viewing area in a wash of pink and a figure of $25,000.

"You've got to be kidding me." Sai said.

"I bet you're really glad we stopped now, aren't you?" Shafeen laughed.

"They're going to want to see her ID." Sai sounded agitated. "You can't just walk away with twenty-five thousand dollars from a slot machine without at least showing someone some documentation first."

A security guard arrived before any of them could simply walk away. Actually, Aurora calculated that walking away wouldn't be a good idea either. Nobody would walk away from a jackpot on a slot machine unless they didn't belong in the casino to begin with. They'd be followed for sure.

"Congratulations, ma'am. It looks like you struck it rich tonight." The security guard eyed the dollar amount flashing in red digits at the bottom right corner of Aurora's machine.

"Can she donate the winnings?" Sai jumped in before Aurora could even respond.

"She can do whatever she likes with *her* winnings." The security guard smiled with obvious exaggeration. "After we get a social security number and a photo ID from her."

"Absolutely, they're in the car." Shafeen said. "I told her to leave her purse in the trunk since we were only supposed to come in and have dinner. We don't normally let her gamble like this, but it's her birthday."

"Well, in that case, Happy Birthday!" The security guard spoke with friendliness. He clearly didn't want to seem rude or upsetting, but he had a job to do nonetheless. "I need her to wait here for security purposes. Why don't one of you retrieve her ID from the car for her?"

Shafeen and Sai looked at one another before staring back at Aurora. Neither of them seemed pleased, and Aurora suddenly understood why Sai wanted to leave right away in the first place.

"I'm feeling light-headed all of a sudden." Aurora placed the back of her hand against her forehead, maintaining her uncanny, old and creaky voice. "Can someone please get me some water before I faint?" She wanted to forget the whole old-lady gag and make a mad dash for the exit, but that didn't come without risks of its own. *Safer to stay in character for now.*

"We'll get you some water if you come with us, ma'am." The security guard offered his arm to help guide a withered and tired-looking Aurora. "I'll personally escort you to the host's office where you'll be much more comfortable."

Sai turned to Shafeen. "You run to the car quickly to grab her purse, and I'll go with her to the host's office. Meet us there once you have it."

Shafeen didn't waste a moment to deliberate. She heeded Sai's direction without question as if they'd arranged an entire scheme unbeknownst to anyone else.

"It's just a hundred feet behind us if you'll allow me to lead you there." The security guard kept up his cordial demeanor, guiding Aurora with his elbow extended in order to steady her. "We ask that only the winner go to the office." He looked at Sai. "It gets a bit cramped otherwise."

"I'll be right back." Aurora couldn't ignore the dissatisfaction in Sai's face. He looked beyond upset. But she didn't want to risk causing a commotion. With or without him, she could figure this out on her own.

"We'll be back in a minute, I assure you," the security guard said to Sai before leading Aurora down the carpeted walkway.

"I don't mean to cause you trouble," she said, "but I'm terribly thirsty. Would you please get me some water?" She brought a hand to his forearm, limping along the whole time as she went. "And just so that you know, I like it room temperature. My teeth are very sensitive to anything cold."

"Your wish is my command." The security guard glanced down at her hand after she placed it on his jacket sleeve. "I mean you no disrespect at all, ma'am, but I have to say that you have the most radiant skin of any elderly woman I've ever met.

Aurora certainly didn't take offense. He still seemed to

believe her to be of the age that she had to uphold at all costs, and that's all that mattered. "Not a day goes by that I don't moisturize. That's the secret, you know. *Moisture.* Now if I don't get some in me, you're about to have a little old lady on the ground to clean up. And I don't think that would really be in keeping with the spirit of The Golden Lion, do you?"

The security guard opened the glass door marked with the words *Host's Office.* "I didn't expect the place to be empty. Please make yourself comfortable, and I'll be back with your water."

She considered escaping out the door the moment after he closed it behind him. Now seemed like the perfect chance. Except that it wasn't. She'd cause an uproar in the middle of the casino at this point. She figured it best to at least wait for a signal from either Sai or Shafeen lest she disrupt their intentions to get everyone out of The Golden Lion safely, calmly, and without any unwanted attention.

Returning a mere thirty seconds later, the security guard stood just outside the glass door, talking to another official looking man in a dark suit and a name badge marked with the words *Gaming Surveillance.* Unbeknownst to them, Aurora could hear their entire conversation.

"She's waiting here until someone brings us her ID. She says she left it in the car." The security guard snickered, almost as if he suddenly didn't believe the story.

"It's a good thing you've detained her," said the other serious-looking man with the badge. "We watched her at that Candy Shop game. She's too good to be playing without some type of aid."

"You mean to say that little old lady's a cheat?"

"She's a crook. Mathematically speaking, there's no way she could have amassed those wins without something or someone helping her. The boss wants to search her for a possible device before we let her go."

The security guard scratched his head. "You don't really want to put the old lady through all that, do you? We could easily just *eighty-six* her after we pay her out, and we'll never have to deal with her again."

"That was my suggestion, but the boss wants answers. We're gonna take her downstairs."

Aurora wished Shafeen would move along faster, or that Sai would come by to check up on her. Still nowhere in sight, they'd yell in horror if they knew what was about to occur. Being manhandled downstairs and possibly strip searched seemed like a damning fate much too severe for having won a rather small jackpot. Especially when compared to what she could have won had she been given a half hour to play the silly machine.

Time to take matters into her own hands.

She knew she'd have to catch them off guard if she wanted to get past them without a fight. Feigning her unbearable thirst, Aurora headed to the door with a noticeable stumble and an ornery look in her eyes. When the gaming official opened it for her, she walked right on through without so much as a nod of appreciation and grabbed the water bottle straight from the hand of the unsuspecting security officer.

"Didn't I tell you that I was dying of thirst? Is this how you treat every old lady who comes in here?"

A look of dread and embarrassment spread across his face. "You'll have to excuse me, ma'am. We got a little side-tracked. Let's head back in the office if you would please, and we'll wait for your friends to show up with your ID."

Aurora knew that neither man would dare stop her now seeing how hot-headed she'd become. She aimed her cane just to the left of the security guard's foot so that he'd flinch and move out of her way. "There's my friend. I'll be back for my money in a second." She took off as fast as an old lady with a cane could without anyone questioning her true age. She figured she'd have at least a few seconds head start before anyone chased after her.

"I'm sorry if we offended you, ma'am," the security guard called out after her. "We need you to stay right here, or you'll forfeit your jackpot."

She didn't care about the money. She stopped caring about it as soon as she realized the aggravation it caused. If only someone had bothered to explain the rigamarole to her before she sat down at the crazy contraption, she'd have left the casino immediately after her brief stint at the tables. "Keep your damn money!" Aurora had never used a curse word before, but it seemed like a natural fit for an old woman antagonized by a couple of boorish authority figures.

"We order you to turn around!" the surveillance official commanded. "Or we will come after you."

Aurora kept on trucking with nary a sign of having

heard his plea. When she saw Shafeen and Sai standing a few hundred feet in front of her beyond a row of black-jack tables, she knew she'd make it out of there instead of remaining held against her will. She could only hope that the other customers around her took note of the unkind behavior of the staff before thinking of returning again to The Golden Lion.

"She's over there." Sai nudged Shafeen and pointed straight at Aurora.

"I've had enough of this place." Aurora called out over the well-heeled crowd who stared in wonder as she advanced toward the exit.

"Aurora, watch out behind you!" Shafeen shouted.

She didn't have to look. Aurora already knew at that moment that her luck had run out. She'd have to revert to drastic measures if she wanted to preserve her safety. The disguise was a good one for as long as it lasted, but all good things had to come to an end. Without a second thought, Aurora changed her gait from a wobbly limp to a sturdy gallop.

"Amazing! Look at her fly!" said a man waiting in line at the main cage, holding a martini with his arm linked to his lady friend.

Aurora jumped from one empty felt-top table to another before launching herself up and over the gaming pit toward the exit, which beckoned her from only a few steps beyond where Sai and Shafeen stood. "I'm sorry it had to come to this," she said to her friends as she landed next to them on the marble floor, her cane still clutched in her hand.

"We aren't ever coming back here again, are we?" Shafeen said to Sai as the three of them darted for the exit to the parking garage.

Sai pushed the door open and held it for the other two before they all ran out of the casino and toward the car. "Nope. And the boss isn't gonna be happy about it."

chapter 17

A cold gust blew through the pavilion where Shane had covered six of the community park's picnic tables with white linens in preparation for David's celebration of life. They'd have blown clear off into the sports field had he not secured them with a few strategically placed stones, which he'd borrowed from an adjacent rock garden. It wasn't typical for Las Vegas to get this cool until after Halloween. Normally, the kids playing soccer in the park would be in shorts and t-shirts, but today they all had on their windbreakers.

Shane couldn't help but ponder if perhaps David had anything to do with the unseasonably blustery afternoon. *Was it a warning?* Shane brushed the thought aside seeing how he couldn't change anything about the ceremony now. Maybe his husband only wished to give him a reprieve from the Las Vegas heat with a dash of sweater weather.

Thanks, David. Once again, you've completely outdone yourself.

If Shane could have put in a request beforehand, he'd have much preferred a balmy day with maybe a light breeze. Nothing dramatic. He expected a small gathering of friends, neighbors, and immediate family members to show up any moment. Wouldn't David have at least ensured that his own mother might find a tiny bit of comfort in a tranquil, sunny day? The steady wind wouldn't do anything to make her feel better. Nor, for that matter, would it ameliorate Shane's own despondency.

He arranged the last blue vase of white lilies on the table in front of him and stared at the fragrant blossoms. Their beauty wouldn't last. They'd wither like everything else. *Maybe it wasn't David in the wind after all. Maybe he'd simply vanished.*

Shane instinctively looked around for his hummingbird friend from a week ago for reassurance that life went on. Even a butterfly would suffice. No such luck. However, the welcome sight of a big green pickup truck diverted his attention away from his mind-numbing despair. Knowing that Christina would be at his side in a moment gave him something to appreciate for a change.

He had to do something about his constant, gnawing sadness. Otherwise, it would eat him alive. If only he could assert control over his own thoughts instead of letting them run amok. He felt betrayed by his runaway mind today, more so now than at any other point since David's passing. Was it too much to ask for a brief moment of harmony to flutter his way? He almost felt like David wanted him to stay miserable for the time being as a testament to the unrealized greatness that had now disappeared from Shane's life forever.

"Christina!" He ran toward her as if she'd become his guardian angel. "I'm so glad you're here. I wasn't sure I could go through with it all. I'm already exhausted from the wind."

She stepped down from the truck and assisted Leena out from the cabin's back seat. "I'd have come sooner, but the girls insisted on finishing a special project first." She gave Shane a short but strong hug and then looked at both her daughters. "Go ahead. You said he needed them, and I think you're right."

Joanna took a step toward Shane but couldn't look him in the eye. It appeared she had tears of her own to hide. "We made these for you." She handed him two envelopes, one green and the other pink.

"We'd have given them to you sooner." Leena came to stand next to her sister and smiled brightly at Shane. "But we wanted to get them just right."

"Shall I open them now?" Shane hadn't ever found himself in the position of receiving sympathy before. He didn't want to be rude, nor did he want to embarrass them.

"I think *you* should decide," said Joanna, still lacking the courage to look up at him unlike her naturally chipper younger sister. "We made them to help you feel happy."

"I'll save them for later then, if that's okay." Shane felt a wave of indebtedness sweep over him. As much as he wanted to read the cards, he knew they'd make him cry, and he'd already gone through a whole packet of tissues on his way to the park. What mattered most to him was the gesture itself. If these girls cared this much about him as to craft special cards just to make him smile, he realized that others out there likely cared about his well-being also. Thinking back on the past week, locking himself away from the world might not have been the healthiest thing for him.

"Will Aurora be coming?" Leena's bright eyes blinked with a glimmer of hidden hope.

"She said she'd be here." Shane forced a smile, wanting to keep upbeat. Unfortunately, he'd tried to contact Aurora all morning to no avail. He'd gotten confirmation from her when they last communicated with each other three days prior. He even offered to pick her up, but she declined, assuring him that her *new friends* would drop her off. Truth be told, the whole situation made Shane feel highly uneasy, but he couldn't think about that right now.

"Joanna, would you get the cake for me?" Christina grabbed a stack of red plastic plates and a box of forks from the front seat before closing the door. "I set it in the cooler in the bed of the truck. We don't need the cooler though, just the cake."

"Can I help?" Shane felt he owed Christina for all the effort she'd put into making the event happen. He had her arrange the reservations through the county park's office.

She sent out all the invitations and announcements. She hadn't let Shane do any of it. *Probably because she knew he couldn't.*

"I don't think that's necessary." Christina deposited the plates and forks in Leena's hands before reaching inside her purse for a piece of paper. "Joanna's a big girl, and the cake is only a half sheet. I've got my closing remarks, which I still need to practice, and it looks like you have someone else to greet."

Shane looked across the parking lot and saw a brand new blue Mercedes R230 sedan pull into the spot farthest from the pavilion. "That's his mom. I don't think she realizes that we're all meeting down at this end."

"Go say *hello* to her and see if she needs anything." Christina sounded urgent all of a sudden, like a celebrity had just arrived. "I remember David saying how particular she can be."

"I'll see if I can convince her to park a little closer." Shane headed off toward the imposing car with dark tinted windows. He had to remind himself of her name. *Sheila!* But he'd never call her that to her face. He'd known her since his college days when David had first introduced the two of them. From that day on, he'd only referred to her one way.

"Mrs. Whitman!" Shane ran the few remaining steps toward her the moment she looked up at him from underneath the brim of her white-lace hat. "I'm glad you made it alright. The rest of us are parked at the other end of the lot closest to the picnic tables."

"Thank you, Shane." The slender and well-appointed

gray-haired woman dressed all in pearl tones kissed his cheek. He could tell by her unusually smooth complexion that she'd had some work done in recent years. She looked amazing for seventy-five, and he respected that about her. "I choose to walk on purpose. It keeps the blood flowing."

"I agree one hundred percent." Shane felt somewhat foolish and insignificant in his mother-in-law's presence, but through nobody's fault except his own. "I probably could have walked the two miles here myself, but—" He paused before admitting that he'd already had too much to drink this early in the afternoon.

"The wind!" Mrs. Whitman chimed in, catching her hat atop her head before it blew away. "That breeze today is enough to keep anyone from participating in strenuous exercise. Now lead me to where we need to be before it takes us the opposite direction."

Shane laughed and took her elbow, escorting her to the pavilion a good two hundred feet away. He spent so little time with her in the past, but now he wished he'd gotten to know her better. She seemed just as put together as David, but exhibited a sense of humor and understanding that her son sometimes lacked. If Shane could just find the right moment, he'd ask her to take Aurora back to her home in Arizona with her, at least for a few weeks. But there were a million other things to consider first. "Are you sure you'll be okay speaking during the main portion of the ceremony?"

"Why? Did you want to speak instead? Have at it!" She laughed humbly and with sincerity.

"I wouldn't. I mean, I couldn't. Or rather—I can't."
Shane felt a pang of guilt for not being able to overcome
his fear of public-speaking. Actually, it wasn't that at all. He
hated the idea of crying in front of lots of people, and with
a microphone no less. "I agreed to the introduction, and
that's all I can truthfully manage at this point. Our friend
Christina is speaking the closing. She said she'd also speak
the eulogy if necessary."

"Nonsense. This isn't easy for any of us. Let an old lady
do her job and be done with it." She let go of Shane's elbow
and sat at a table near the front of the covered gathering
place. "Now what about the casket and the burial? Is that
happening tomorrow?"

Shane forced himself not to cringe while he gathered his
thoughts. He assumed everyone automatically understood
the arrangements. Today was meant to be a *Celebration of
Life* per David's ultra clear instructions. Searching for the
best explanation for the deceased's mother, Shane remembered the explicit and strange conversation he'd had with
David a month ago.

A day after Aurora's fiasco at the Smith Center, David
had requested to have a *serious* discussion after dinner. The
whole thing seemed over-the-top and nonsensical at the
time, but Shane recalled every word clear as a cloudless
night sky.

"I'm no longer donating my body to science," David
had said. "I just made the change in my will with the law
office."

Shane couldn't understand why anyone would donate

their body to science to begin with. If felt like such a private thing, he couldn't stand the thought of strange college kids cutting open his body, even if he'd left it for greener pastures. Some things remained personal forever. His own dead body wasn't an exception, and he felt relieved that his husband had come to a similar conclusion. "I'm with you a hundred and ten percent! In the ground I go. In the ground and whole!"

"I'm to be cremated."

That didn't make sense to Shane either. David had been raised Catholic. *Wasn't cremation frowned upon?* Even though his husband had left the church before they ever met, being cremated still seemed like a terrible idea. Shane had gone through enough hell the past few months playing *Keep the Cops Away from Aurora*. He wasn't about to put his body in an actual fiery hell the moment after he died. *How could he learn to play the harp if his fingers had been burnt to ash along with the rest of him?* "I'm not gonna be able to change your mind, am I?"

"Nope. If I die before you do, you must promise to bury my ashes in the Valley of Fire State Park where no one will ever find them. And you mustn't tell anyone. You are the only one who knows aside from the attorney, and not even he knows the full extent of my exact wishes."

"What if I die first?" Shane hated the thought of being alone even before David had passed on. As many days as his marriage had bothered him, it had also given him stability and comfort. Needless to say, envisioning such a responsibility to his life partner had made him physically ill.

"Then you'll have nothing to worry about. I'll visit my attorney again and make some changes."

Shane remembered his quiet sense of awe in how David had everything about his own life planned down to even his death arrangements. "Well, just stick me in a hole alongside everyone else who abhors the idea of eternal damnation or being underneath the scalpel of an inexperienced, hungover med student. I don't need to put that in a will, do I?"

"It's not a bad idea to draw up your final wishes, unless you don't care about them," David had said. "I certainly care about mine. I have to. For Aurora's sake."

Mrs. Whitman looked up at Shane with a pained expression on her face. "Don't tell me there won't be a burial. We're Catholic."

Shane could only find it within himself to shake his head. No sense in giving details she didn't want to hear. And besides, he couldn't risk her, or anyone else for that matter, asking what he'd do with the ashes. The whole part about the Valley of Fire confused him, but if it was for Aurora's security, he couldn't *not* abide by David's instructions.

"We'll start the ceremony in ten minutes." Shane looked away briefly from Mrs. Whitman and focused on the parking lot, seeing a familiar sky blue Porsche. "We still have a few more people coming. If you'll excuse me, I'll be right back."

He'd forgotten that he'd even mentioned the celebration to Mrs. McKubben. Shane wouldn't have said a thing, except that she'd been thoughtful enough to bring over a tray of chocolate chip cookies and a green bean casserole a few days prior when just answering the front door took all the energy he had for the day. He hadn't intended for her to actually show up.

"Randy, I need you to grab the bowl from the back seat," Cheryl yelled to her son in her usual high-pitched, bossy voice before glancing toward Shane. "We made it. I hope we're not late. I brought that pasta salad you like."

Shane couldn't recall ever expressing his enjoyment for a side dish of hers, but he ran over to hug and welcome her regardless. "Thank you. We're just about to get started. I'm glad you both could make it."

"You don't remember what recipe I'm talking about, do you?" Cheryl nudged him jokingly, as if she forgot she'd just arrived at a somber occasion. "I made it with extra green olives. I remember you had two helpings of it at the last HOA potluck. You raved about it!"

"Oh, *that* pasta salad!" Shane vaguely remembered it. If he'd shown any enthusiasm whatsoever for a dish packed with olives, it was only because he must have been starving and would have eaten stale croutons for sustenance at that point. Regardless, the fact that Cheryl McKubben showed any sign of compassion made his heart a little lighter.

"And my son has a card to give you, don't you Randy?"

The former poor excuse for a youth had grown about three inches since that fateful late May day at the mini-golf. Not only that, but he no longer appeared the least bit overweight. He actually looked like a healthy, respectable young man as he smiled at Shane. "I know it's not much, but hopefully it's something that'll help."

"He insisted on paying for it with his own money!" Cheryl tucked a pack of napkins under her arm before closing the car door. "I tried to pay for it, but he insisted."

Normally, Shane would be off put by the extraneous information, but in this particular case the notion only helped solidify the fact that something about the McKubben clan had changed, even if only in a small way. "In that case, I'll open it right now." Shane nearly forgot his sadness as he tore open the yellow envelope.

"It's not exactly a sympathy card, but I thought you'd like it." Randy removed his baseball cap and held it over his heart.

Shane pulled the greeting from its envelope and stared at its front, seeing the image of a red cartoon go-kart with a friendly face embedded in its grill. Before opening it all the way, he couldn't help but notice that it felt heavier than a typical greeting. Shane hoped there wasn't a gift inside it. The card itself was more than enough.

"Go ahead. Open it all the way!" The excitement in Randy's voice matched the look of gleeful innocence in his matured face.

"I will. I was just admiring the picture." Shane unfolded the greeting to reveal a pop-up trophy that played a short rendition of Scott Joplin's "Easy Winners" from a tiny speaker when the card was fully opened.

Here's to a lifetime of easy winning. Hope you feel better soon.

Shane bit his bottom lip as hard as he could to force himself not to cry. Six months ago, Randy was Public Enemy Number One in his book. And his mother was right behind him. He couldn't figure out for the life of him what had caused the sudden change, but it warmed his heart in a way that his uncharacteristic drunkenness couldn't. "It's perfect. Thank you so much." Shane put the card back in its envelope. "Now if you'll both follow me, we'll head to the pavilion so we can get started."

He pointed to two empty seats at a table near the back so that Randy and his mother could get comfortable while he headed to the very front and picked up the microphone, noticing that the wind had really picked up again. "I cannot thank all of you enough for being here." Shane looked out over the small group of thirty people, holding back the tears with all his might. He recognized most of them as either neighbors or old acquaintances and family members. "I'm afraid I can't say much right now except that David would be pleased to see all of you here today. He told me many times throughout our marriage that he didn't believe in funerals, but rather celebrations of life. And so here we are, gathered together to celebrate our own lives and the remarkable life of my husband, David Whitman." He reached for a small plastic cup of water, not because he needed to quench his thirst or moisten his lips, but so that he could pause and get hold of his looming anguish. "And now, it gives me great pride to pass the microphone to a special woman who knows David almost as well as I do, if not better."

Mrs. Whitman stood up from her seat at the table in the very front and walked next to the amplifier to grab the pen-sized microphone from Shane. "I shouldn't be here doing this." She grabbed the piece of folded paper from her finely tailored suit's breast pocket, and the wind suddenly stopped blowing. "A parent shouldn't have to give the eulogy for one of her own children. Unfortunately, that rule doesn't apply to me. But I'm proud to be the one who gets to remind everyone just how special a life my son David lived. And I hope he inspires each of us to live life as wonderfully as he did. Most everybody knows David to be a genius. He was always bright. Even as a child, he knew how to outsmart his mother. Whether it was beating me at a game of chess or negotiating additional cookies before bedtime, David always relied on his intelligence to get what he wanted. But that's not what I want to focus on today. Instead, I want everyone to know just how brave and kind David was.

"He used to talk to hummingbirds. I'll never forget the first time I witnessed it happening. He was playing by himself in the backyard, and I stood at my bedroom window watching him like any cautious mother would. He was playing in his sandbox when he spotted a hummingbird. He followed it to a flower and asked it for its name. From that moment on, he called it 'Burt'. I have no idea where he came up with that name as I can assure you we knew nobody named 'Burt'. Nonetheless, he probably had fifty conversations with Burt that summer. He went outside to the flower garden everyday, and he and the hummingbird would play together for what must have been hours at a time. I once asked him who he was talking to just to see how he'd respond. At seven years old, he simply replied, 'I'm getting in touch with nature, Mom.' When I asked him why, he responded, 'Because it feels good.' And then he went back to doing whatever he'd been in the middle of before I interrupted.

"I live in Phoenix now, which means I haven't spent nearly as much time with David as I should have. It was my choice to leave Las Vegas. After the events of 2029, I wanted nothing to do with a city that I never cared much for to begin with. I merely came here because if you were a nurse fifty years ago, this was the place to be if you wanted to make money and live well. I raised David here from birth, and he loved it. Everything about it. Nothing could scare him away from Las Vegas. Not the robots. Not the brutality. Not the collapsing buildings. He had a vision for what this city could be, and that was all he ever focused on.

"I've only been back to Vegas once before today, and that was for his and Shane's wedding fifteen years ago. I stayed for just that one day, took a piece of wedding cake, and went back home to Phoenix. Now that I look around, I see what this great city has become, and I know so much of it is a result of my son's hard work and his undying vision. Even though I left this wonderful city long ago, I cannot help but plead with those of you who've stayed to please continue making this town an even more miraculous place. David wants this city to thrive. I can feel it in my old bones. Keep the momentum going. No matter how daunting the task, stay focused on how good this city can be when you put kindness first. Thank you."

Shane applauded before anyone else, the whole speech leaving him absolutely dumbfounded. He felt deeply obliged, knowing full well he couldn't have managed to say even half of what Mrs. Whitman had said without breaking down into a watery mess. For the life of him, though, he couldn't get that wondrous image of the hummingbird out of his head.

Walking back up toward the front of the small congregation, Shane hugged Mrs. Whitman and escorted her to her seat before returning to the podium. "I'll pass the microphone to my dear friend Christina now for some closing remarks, and then we can all enjoy some lunch together."

Shane didn't mean to tune out, but as soon as Christina began speaking, his mind went to thinking about Aurora. He'd feared that she wouldn't show up, and now he felt his worries coming true. If Aurora didn't show up, it made everything David had worked for right up until the moment of his death seem in vain. *What a waste of a life.* He had to catch himself before falling into a really bad place within his inconsolable mind. He didn't want to resent Aurora, but the more he felt her absence, the more he blamed her for everything that had gone wrong with his life.

Christina put down the microphone after saying something about everyone being able to help themselves to the food and that the plates and napkins were on the far table next to the breadbasket. Shane didn't really care at this point. He was just glad Christina took over so that he could be alone with his negative thoughts.

"Can I get you some water or anything to eat?" Christina sat next to him at the mostly empty table across from where Mrs. Whitman sat.

"Thank you. I'm fine for now." Shane meant to also thank her for doing a lovely job putting all of this together, but his attention flew to a red limo parked near his car. "That isn't Bill. Tell me that's not Bill."

"It can't be," Christina stood up to have a closer look. "I didn't say a word. I promise. He couldn't possibly have known. It's impossible. I didn't say a thing while I was at work."

"Well, he found out somehow. Nobody else in town rides around in a Red Limo with a Durango Electric symbol emblazoned on its side." He felt betrayed. He knew Christina would never let it slip on purpose, but he also didn't know of anyone else to blame for the leak.

"I'm not sure what the hell he wants." Christina looked just as distraught as Shane felt.

The ostentatious looking automobile soon left as quickly as it had come. Whoever was in it hopefully got the hint that he wasn't the least bit welcome—not to the farewell gathering of a man whose untimely fate rested in his hands. The mere fact that he'd even made an appearance only further solidified the incredibly bad judgment of the man Shane now despised.

He almost lost himself in a fit of rage when the vibration of his watch snapped him back to reality. "It's Aurora," he giddily explained to Christina after feeling his entire persona change, filling him with a sense of vitality that he hadn't felt in days, not since before David had left him. "She says she's almost here."

"I better tell Leena." Christina glanced around the pavilion for her daughter. "She's been talking about Aurora non-stop since she came to our house over a month ago. She'll be heartbroken if she misses her."

Shane pointed to a motorcycle in the parking lot. "There she is! I can't believe it's really her. She made it!" He had no idea who the man operating the motorcycle was. He wished to meet him, but he took off and left Aurora standing alone on the pavement.

"Bring her over." Christina wiped a tear from her cheek. "She'll be the life of the party. Everyone needs to meet her."

Shane didn't waste another second. He ran toward his long lost darling like a bear to its cub. "Where on earth have you been?" He picked her up underneath her arms and swung her around him in a circle like a carnival ride. "Would you like to meet David's mom?"

"Please. I've heard so much about her. It would be great to meet her in person." Aurora radiated with all the irreproachability and charm Shane remembered.

They didn't waste any time running back toward the pavilion where Mrs. Whitman was seated, eating a tiny sliver of chocolate cake with white frosting.

"I'd like to introduce you to someone very special," Shane said, nervous how Mrs. Whitman might react to David's clearest example of revolutionary ingenuity.

"Who do we have here?" Mrs. Whitman put down her plastic fork and set it across the top of her paper plate.

"I'm Aurora." She curtseyed just how she'd done a hundred times before when meeting new people. "I've heard so much about you."

A quizzical but friendly look appeared in Mrs. Whitman's eyes. "You have one of the most demure faces I've ever seen. How do you know Shane?"

"I'm his niece," she replied without any hesitation.

Shane wanted to steer her answers in another direction. Ideally, he wished for her to go with Mrs. Whitman back to Phoenix, but that would require a much more in-depth conversation about the truth. He didn't quite know where to begin, but he figured that he'd find his way eventually if he only tried. "Aurora is more special to me than just a niece. She has more in common with David than meets the eye, and you'll see exactly what I mean when you get to know her a bit better."

"He never mentioned to me that you had a niece." Mrs. Whitman unfolded her napkin to blot her lips even though nothing was there. Then she turned her attention back to Aurora. "I would have loved to have met you sooner. You seem quite charming."

"I would like for you two to get acquainted." Shane wished David had at least mentioned Aurora to his mother. Having done so would have made this process a whole lot easier. "I apologize for not introducing you both to each other until now. I suppose there's no time like the present."

"Forgive me for sounding crass, but I have to use the ladies' room." Mrs. Whitman stood up from her seat. "Is there one near here, or do I have to drive?"

Aurora pointed to a small brick building with a clay-tiled roof at the top of a small hill. "Just follow that path. It's very close."

Mrs. Whitman smiled at Shane. "You have the loveliest

niece I think I've ever met. I really look forward to getting to know her better." She then winked at Aurora before heading toward the walkway.

Shane and Aurora sat down at the table that Mrs. Whitman had just left. He wanted to hear all about what she'd been up to while she'd been away, but someone else decided to join them as soon as they got situated.

"Randy!" Aurora's face lit up like she'd seen a long lost friend. "It's so good to see you again."

"I owe you an apology." Randy smiled cautiously, a look of regret appearing in his humble eyes as he took a seat next to her. "I should have never chased you when you were riding your bike. I didn't mean for that to happen at all."

"Oh, Randy! You don't need to apologize." Aurora laughed as if to ease the tension. "I hit the back of that truck because of an error in computation. That's all."

Randy looked confused but happy that she didn't find fault with him. "Maybe we can all play some mini-golf later when you both feel up to it. I think I may have misjudged a few things. And I'm sorry about David." He shook Aurora's hand before getting up and walking back to where his mother was enjoying her own piece of cake.

"I'm not sure I have any words after that." Shane stared at the ground, spotting a tiny ant carrying away a crumb of cake four times its size.

"People are generally good and decent if you just give them a chance," Aurora said without a hint of irony.

"Do these adages come pre-programmed inside you?"

Shane didn't know whether to laugh or shake his head in disbelief. "You do realize Randy McKubben was the same boy you whacked in the head with a golf ball, don't you?"

"David said he'd never bring that up again." Aurora sounded serious all of a sudden. "I don't think you should either."

Shane had a clever response but held it in when he heard Christina's voice behind him.

"Do you think I could get some help with the TundraLite that I forgot about in the back of my truck? It's filled with sodas and bottled water. People are getting thirsty."

"I've got it!" Aurora jumped up from her spot with a sense of eagerness that Shane wished he could find within himself.

"Thank you," Christina said. "Between the two of us, I'm sure we'll be able to manage."

Shane laughed. "I don't think she'll require any assistance. Just make sure the back's unlocked, and she'll have it here by herself in no time.

Aurora took off running toward the green machine before Christina could even object.

"Um...if you say so. I'll unlock it." She tapped her watch twice, scrolling through the options in a few seconds. "It's all hers now."

"David said she was never meant to be our servant, but when she's that ready to help, I don't stand in her way."

Christina put her hand on his shoulder. "It feels good to have her back, doesn't it?"

Before Shane could utter a response, he got distracted by

the sound of a vehicle's tires squealing against the parking lot pavement. At first he thought that Aurora had taken it upon herself to steal Christina's truck, and he felt immediately comforted when he looked out and saw her menacing green machine parked exactly where it had been. Unfortunately, for the life of him, he couldn't see Aurora.

chapter

"I'm locked in a titanium cage in the back of a silver ve-hicle," Aurora messaged Shane, knowing all the while that her best friend must be sick with sadness, worry, and rage.

How'd they get her this time? She hadn't even heard them come upon her. Her captors must have known how to cir-cumnavigate her senses, wearing clothes that negated the sound of normal movement. No other way could they have snuck up behind her.

She remembered spotting Randy in the distance. The last thing she saw as they captured her was the look of horror on his face and the sudden determination in his eyes to rescue her. She'd flashed him a look of self-assuredness, demanding that he stay put and not get mixed up in a problem that she would have to deal with on her own.

"I'm coming after you," Shane responded to her message. "I won't let them take you away like this. Not again."

What was it with men needing to rescue her? Did they not see her as capable? Had she not yet proven her abilities on enough occasions? "Please don't," she messaged Shane. "There's absolutely nothing you can do. They have guns, and they'll use them if anyone gets close. Wait until I tell you the time is right. I can keep myself safe for now." She didn't exactly know the last part with a hundred percent certitude. However, she knew for a fact that if Shane attempted anything now, they'd kill him, which was far worse than anything they might do to her.

She made every calculation she could regarding her surroundings. The diameter of each bar of her cage? Three quarters of an inch—too thick to bend. The speed of the car? Fifty miles per hour and accelerating. Number of brutes she'd have to fend off if she were to free herself? Three, not including the man behind the dashboard. Her chances of escaping from the car? For all intents and purposes, zero.

"So we got you again." A short and muscular man turned around in his seat, showing a prideful smile. "You're not escaping this time. If you do, we'll fine Mr. Rucker double what we're charging him today. You're cute and all, but you definitely aren't worth twenty million dollars."

So Bill had to pay ten million dollars to get her back? Aurora didn't have anything to say in response to the snarky comment, and so she grinned instead. She knew the technology used to create her had value, but she had no concept that she'd ever be worth that much to anyone. She found it terribly disturbing that someone would throw that kind of money around to cage her, especially considering that she'd done nothing wrong. The idea that Bill would lose millions of dollars when she finally freed herself from him for good, however, delighted her on the inside.

"You better keep an eye on her in case she tries to pull anything while we're en route," said the man at the helm.

"I'll rip her scrawny limbs from their sockets if she so much as twitches," said a slightly taller, but equally sturdy man sitting next to the first. "Truth be told, she's gonna have them ripped from her regardless when she gets to the lab. That was part of the agreement."

Aurora decided it best to keep tight-lipped despite all the thoughts and retorts flooding her processors.

"We get the point," the man in the front said. "You don't have to be so disturbing about it."

"I'm not being disturbing." The man in the middle turned around to glance at Aurora, but she paid him no attention. "It's not like she's human. She's a machine. One that happens to *look* like a human. Nothing more than a damn doll, really. A little dolly that'll cause a lot of grief if she isn't put in her place."

"Shut the hell up, Tom," said the other man sitting beside Aurora's enthusiastic tormentor. "You're not the only one in this car who has to listen to the garbage coming out of your mouth."

So this beastly man has a name. Knowing a person's name made it easier for Aurora to relate to an otherwise complete stranger. No, she couldn't tell a whole lot about people simply by how they addressed themselves. Perhaps if she knew their zodiac sign, but even then the variables were still much too great to draw any concrete conclusions. Names had a more visceral effect on her processing capabilities. She didn't understand why a person's name made her feel the way it did, much like how she didn't know why she could communicate with nature and others couldn't. Perhaps names produced a connection where none had existed before. After hearing Tom's name, she took pity on him for his ignorance. "I'm more than just a doll, Tom."

"I was hoping she'd say something." The man sitting next to Tom turned around and smiled at Aurora with a non-threatening look of childlike fascination. "I don't think you're just a doll. Say something else."

"Stop talking to her." Tom playfully punched his colleague in the arm. "It's creeping me out. I don't like that she knows my name."

"You think she's a poltergeist, don't you?"

"No, I don't, Brett," Tom sneered as he said the other man's name as if getting back at him. "We have a job to do right now, and it isn't to make small talk with stuffed animals."

Aurora didn't get the reference. She didn't resemble a taxidermied wolf or moose, and she couldn't understand why anyone would carelessly catalog her amongst the mummified remains of former living creatures. Their shameless idiocy only solidified the fact that they had no business possessing a sophisticated, sentient machine such as herself.

She wished she'd foreseen the danger in leaving Shane's side. *Too late for wishing.* She didn't at all regret coming to comfort Shane, not at a time when he needed her the most. She had no one to blame but herself at this point. She'd give practically anything to be on the back of Sai's motorcycle again. Durango Electric took the very bottom spot on her list of places to return to. If only she were headed somewhere far, far away from the likes of Bill Rucker.

"We're here." The man up front flashed his badge to the lone security guard manning the gated entry marked *Durango Electric storage facility access only.* "Bill wants us to pull up to bay number eight and wait for him. Do not do anything with the cage until he tells us to."

After the car reversed into the loading dock, all four men immediately exited the vehicle to meet Bill Rucker who was waiting for them in front of an opened garage-like door. Although the vehicle's windows were soundproof, Aurora had no trouble reading the men's lips as they conversed with one another.

"I'll unlock the back as soon as we get our money," said the man who ultimately controlled the vehicle.

Bill retrieved an envelope tucked within the jacket of his casual-looking brown suit. The wind nearly stole it from his hand, but he recaptured it just in time before it blew off the premises along with a torrent of plastic bags and scraps of paper. "You can open it if you like. I promise that the check is good."

"Ten million?"

"Not a penny less. I hope your boss gives you each a decent cut because you're not getting any more from me for your service."

The man in charge of the vehicle tapped his watch, and the hatch door swung open. "Hold on to her this time. We won't bring her back to you again. She'll go right to the incinerator."

"Understood, gentlemen." Bill didn't sound at all pleased. Aurora could tell he harboured significant resentment toward the whole situation, and she knew better than to smile at him as he turned to speak to her directly. "So we meet again, Miss Aurora. I've just signed a new lease for you to stay here with us. My team will be here shortly to get you reacclimated."

Aurora knew what she wanted to say. She wanted to annoy him and the others around him with the loudest scream possible—maybe even permanently damage their ear drums. But that would go against the most important instructions she'd ever received from David. She thought about lecturing Bill about how his behavior had led to the death of her creator, the death her best friend's husband, the death of one of the most influential people to ever step foot inside Durango Electric. She wanted to explain to Bill that he'd unwittingly cost the company millions of dollars, not just in her recovery, but in the destruction of the only man capable of making more forms of intelligent machinery like her. But she figured it best to say only five words. "It's good to be back."

It took eight men in white lab coats to slide and then lift the cage that held Aurora out of the vehicle and onto a motorized cart. She could tell that they weren't about to take any chances this time. They had her locked up as helpless as a sedated animal.

"We're wheeling her to a restricted access zone." Bill stood behind his team as they situated the cage onto the platform. "I only need Trent and one other person. The rest of you can get back to your work."

"I'll volunteer," said one of the technicians with a nametag that read *Derrick*. "It isn't every day we get to turn little girls into zoo exhibits."

Bill walked right up to his enlisting subordinate, a sinister smile on his face. "If you think she's a little girl, she has you totally fooled." He looked like a monster as he spoke. "You better be careful with her. She'd eat you alive if given the chance."

Aurora felt more confused than ever. *Didn't he know she couldn't consume anything, let alone a fully grown man? And didn't he realize that there were a million other things that seemed way more appetizing to her than human flesh?* She'd never experienced nausea before, but if she could, she figured this would be one such moment. "Oh, Bill. Don't be ridiculous." She started to comprehend the rules of the game. "I'm a man-eater who likes them much older." She winked and smiled at him, keeping her true disgust completely to herself.

Everyone laughed, both the men in suits and the men in labcoats. Everyone except Bill. The joke had left him either unimpressed or intimidated, neither of which boded well for Aurora's sake.

"Let's get a move on, fellas." Bill straightened his suit jacket and fixed his tie after another gust came and nearly swept him and the others clear off the loading dock. "We've got a busy afternoon ahead of us."

Aurora recognized Trent from her earlier encounter with him. She thought about saying a quick *hello* but remembered their first meeting not being a positive experience, and she assumed he hadn't forgotten either. Derrick, on the other hand, she had never met. He looked young and intelligent like his colleague, but not nearly as forceful in his mannerisms. He seemed mild-tempered, a little cautious, or maybe even a bit meek. If she had any chance of escaping this afternoon, she reasoned it would likely be through him.

She remembered the halls they traversed as they made their way out of bay number eight and into the main building. She figured they'd take her to Sector B like they'd done before, but they veered in a different direction entirely.

Standing outside a secured entry point unfamiliar to Aurora, Bill positioned his hand against a scanner. Once the doors opened, he led the way for Trent and Derrick to wheel Aurora into the center of a circular room.

"Don't open the cage until the door is sealed and you have the bag ready." Bill kept his distance from the cart as Trent pulled out an indestructibag from the cabinet against the wall.

Then it clicked! Aurora realized that Bill had much more to do with her initial capture at the M-LEV station than she'd previously given him credit. *He was the one who came up with the idea to immobilize her with a bag reserved for carting gold.* She had to hand it to him for exhibiting cleverness and determination, but she wasn't about to make things any easier for him today.

Trent and Derrick squared the bag around the entrance of the cage as Aurora scuttled to the back. In a split second, the cage door swung open and a motor lifted the back end of the cart, sending Aurora tumbling into the bag. She felt foolish and in the dark for a second, but she knew she'd get her bearings straight if she just kept still.

In a minute, the three men had her strapped to a table, completely restrained. They cut into the bag using a special tool to do so without damaging its contents. Aurora assumed it utilized diamonds by the sound it made as it tore through the allegedly indestructible fabric. Her vision came back within seconds, but the ability to move her body even an inch had eluded her. The straps held her snug against the table's cold metal surface.

"Remove her batteries first." Bill pointed to her left leg where her lithium ion pack was stored. "That will eliminate any chance of her retaliating when we cut off her arms."

Everything went dark again even though she hadn't lost consciousness. She did, however, lose her ability to struggle, and her sensory system vastly diminished. She could still hear, but barely. Every word they uttered sounded like a faint whisper.

"Her arms are attached and sealed to her body, Bill." Trent sounded alarmed and quite possibly afraid to do his boss's bidding. "How do you want us to remove them?"

"Cut through her skin. We've got plenty more of it when it's time to put her back together."

Aurora hadn't felt this vulnerable since her bike accident. In every other instance up until now, she had always come up with some way of protecting herself from destruction. But she couldn't stop these mad men as they sliced through her PelaDerm, cutting through crucial wires and circuitry. They wanted her immobile and inert, and they seemed to be winning. Now more than ever, she wanted to shriek—if not in pain, then in riotous frustration.

"Next, you'll remove her legs." The voice offered no clue regarding its identity as it was much too faint, but the words themselves said everything. Only someone as heartless as Bill Rucker could come up with such a cruel punishment.

"Is it not enough that we removed both her arms? She's not going anywhere. She has no batteries and no arms. Let's spare ourselves the headache of having to figure out how to reattach limbs that shouldn't require detaching in the first place."

"Fine. You win." Bill's voice grew fainter. "Let's take her batteries with us and leave her in peace until I figure out what to do with her."

chapter

"**S**hane, it's Christina." She couldn't believe he answered. Feeling a bit foolish for even calling, she knew she'd pressed her luck the second she phoned him. "I need help."

"I need sleep." Shane sounded distant and more than just a little perturbed by the interruption, which made perfect sense considering that less than twenty-four hours had passed since David's celebration of life and Aurora's disappearance. "And next on my to-do list is finding Aurora. I've completely lost contact with her."

Christina had no choice but to empathize with him. "We already know she's somewhere inside Durango Electric. I'm doing my best to get information on her exact location." She realized her current situation at work put her at a huge disadvantage when it came to getting close to Aurora, but she'd promised Shane that she'd do everything in her power. "I'm headed back to Black Diamond. I have a ten o'clock appointment with Cyphan Creek, and I'd really like you to be with me when I go."

"Why are you doing this? David's gone." Shane let the words fall flat, like they'd lost all meaning. "What's the point in dragging this out? It won't bring him back."

Christina couldn't argue that point, but she also couldn't dismiss her need to know the truth. "What if finding out about David gets us closer to rescuing Aurora? So much has happened in the span of the past two weeks, and yet both of us are in the dark about most of it. Today we have the perfect chance to get some answers." She felt herself grasping at straws at this point, but she couldn't help it—not when the truth was within arm's reach. "Please say you'll come with me, and I promise we'll get Aurora back."

"You can't make incredible promises like that. That's not how it works."

Perhaps she'd crossed the line. She certainly hadn't meant to. She sincerely wanted Aurora back home with Shane. "We need to start somewhere. Wouldn't you care to at least do something aside from worry?"

Shane let out a long, drawn-out sigh. "I hate when you're right. I need to leave the house before I go insane."

"Thank you!" She hadn't thought that he'd actually go for it, and she felt a wave of relief after having succeeded in convincing him with relatively little effort.

"But you're picking me up." Shane almost sounded like his old self again. "And you're automatically responsible for anything that goes wrong."

"Fair enough." She'd already planned on taking her truck. "And let's stop assuming something will go wrong. I don't want to jinx us. Go get ready, and I'll be in your driveway in twenty minutes."

***

Christina felt herself getting nervous as they approached the security gatehouse outside the Black Diamond warehouse. *Why the uneasiness?* She reminded herself that she had every right to be here. She had an appointment this time—an actual, official reason to approach the guardhouse. They should be expecting her!

"Tell me something. What exactly are we doing here?" Shane glanced at her with a look of mild distress mixed with incredulity, an expression she'd seen from him on more than one occasion.

"Don't say a word. I've got this." Christina rolled down the window and smiled, having recognized the guard from her last visit. "Oh! It's you again!"

"I was hoping you'd come back to see us." He turned on his DimensionTab and scrolled through his list. "Ms. Daily, is it?"

Christina nodded. "Until someone comes along wanting to change it!" She didn't mean to sound so brazen. She only wanted to lighten the mood.

"Alrighty then," the guard responded playfully with a laugh. "I'll keep that in mind. Now hold on a second while I direct your vehicle to an extra convenient parking spot."

The Yosemite pulled ahead without a single command from Christina, rounding the bend toward the back of the warehouse's guest entrance.

"I didn't realize you were such a flirt." Shane turned up his nose in jest as if to condemn her conduct, exhibiting a familiar air of self-righteousness.

"What? *That*? That was just a fluke. So he remembered me from the last time I poked my nose around the place. Big deal." She didn't know why she felt guilty all of a sudden. She'd only been acting—or so she convinced herself.

"He was kind of cute though. I'm sure he'd take you out to dinner if you let him."

Christina laughed at the thought. The last thing on her mind was bringing a man into her life. Doing so would only serve to further complicate things between her precious daughters and her tailspinning career. "He's not my type. And besides, you know I pretty much just stick to myself. You're practically the only person I'll set my mat next to in yoga class."

"Yoga class." Shane looked at his watch for no apparent reason other than perhaps to not look at Christina. "I'll get back to it one of these days."

"I know you will." Christina didn't feel the need to further press the issue. Amazingly enough, she'd succeeded in getting him outside the house today. Hard to ask anything more of him for now.

The Yosemite brought them to the parking spot nearest to the guest entrance, and Christina reached for her small black purse before exiting the vehicle. "Just follow my lead. I've got the whole thing planned out."

"I hope so." Shane looked like he'd lost any remaining enthusiasm as he came around the vehicle to her side. "Because I still don't know why we're here."

"Information." She purposely avoided specifics so as not to accidentally clue anyone else in on their mission. "We're here for information." She led them up the dreary walkway to the office entrance. It seemed like no time had passed since her previous visit. The sullen ambience felt exactly the same. Except this time she resolved to come away with actual answers instead of more questions.

The door opened, ushering them forth into the neat but somewhat cramped reception.

"Oh, good. You're back!" Gerard looked up immediately from his computer, his eyes darting right to Shane. "And you've brought your husband?"

Christina burst out laughing before composing herself. "No, this is Shane. He's a good friend of mine. More of a business partner." She felt herself scrambling for words. "He's way better at figuring out the nitty gritty than I am."

"Is that so, Shane?" Gerard's eyes widened as he extended a hand to greet them both. "So you know a thing or two about signs?" He asked the question with a hint of innuendo, but the joke fell flat.

"I guess you could say that." Shane dodged the joke entirely, sounding uncharacteristically shy, like he'd been dragged against his will to a forsaken wasteland on the op-posite side of town. "I'm here for moral support."

Moral support, indeed. If one considered espionage a moral obligation! Christina chuckled some more to ease the mounting tension in the small office space. Her years at Durango Electric had taught her everything about the importance of diplomacy. "We have an appointment with Cyphan Creek; is she available?"

"She should be." Gerard buried his head back into his computer as if to look for something specific. "Yes, she's ex-pecting you. If you'll excuse me a second, I'll go and get her."

Christina playfully punched Shane in the shoulder the second Gerard walked away from within earshot. "He's kind of cute though. I'm sure he'd take you out to dinner if you let him."

"Okay, I get it." Shane hardly seemed the slightest bit amused. "Forgive me for not being in the mood."

"I'm sorry. That might have been a little insensitive." She didn't want to annoy him, but she wished he'd soften up a bit and play along. "Remember. We're actors. And it never hurts to flirt a little in order to get what you came for."

A puzzled expression appeared across Shane's face. "What *I* came for? I'm still trying to figure that little part out."

Christina thought to say something clever in return, but stopped the moment she heard footsteps coming toward them from the open doorway behind the desk.

"Ms. Creek," Gerard closed the door behind him and his boss, "I'd like you to meet Ms. Christina Daily and her business partner Mr. Shane.

"Christina and Mr. Shane." Cyphan Creek didn't smile, but instead looked both of her new clients up and down as if they were auditioning for a part in a movie or fashion show.

"Shane is fine." He almost stumbled over his own name.

"What?" Cyphan Creek's light blue eyes bulged out from their porcelain-like sockets.

"You can call me Shane." He spoke solemnly, in a way Christina had never heard him speak before, like he had no fight or pride left within him.

"Shane and I are hoping to purchase a few signs for our hair salon." Christina opened her purse and took out a few folded scraps of paper. "I had some ideas, but perhaps you and your team can come up with something even more suitable."

Cyphan Creek took the papers from Christina's hand and spread them out on the counter as if doing so were a dreadfully boring chore. Eyeing them over in a matter of seconds, she then laughed hysterically.

"What's so funny?" Shane peered over the counter to have a look at Christina's handiwork.

"Beauty and the Blowout." Cyphan Creek let out another maniacal guffaw. "What exactly is this for? A vulgar massage parlor?"

"A hair salon." Christina tried not to feel insulted. She reasoned that she might in fact deserve some of the ill treatment considering that she wasn't at all interested in paying for any services whatsoever. But now she couldn't help but wonder how this disgusting snake lady, with her downright deplorable mannerisms, managed to keep any customers. "Like I said before, Shane and I are open to other ideas if you, or perhaps Gerard, have something better in mind."

Gerard didn't even lift his head when Christina acknowledged him.

"Better?" Cyphan smiled proudly. "It won't take much. I'll handle the details. You both may now follow me to the main warehouse so that you can actually see what it is that we do here at Black Diamond."

Christina and Shane walked around the counter as instructed by their hostess while Gerard remained buried in his computer, perhaps from a combination of horror and embarrassment. How Christina wished she could rescue the poor guy by stealing him away from the evil witch!

Cyphan Creek led them down the same two halls that Christina had meandered along on her previous visit. When they came past the small room where she'd seen the medical equipment, she wanted to at least nudge Shane and point it out to him, but decided against it after figuring that such an image would only disturb him.

"This is the original wing." Cyphan Creek brought them into a large open area with thirty foot ceilings and row after row of metal shelves filled with neon flamingos, hearts, and a peculiar assortment of weightless astronauts. "We've since added three other bays just like it, each brimming with curiosities old and new."

"It's all so incredible." Christina wanted to lose herself in the veritable museum of Vegas signage past and present. How fun to study everything in here if only out of sheer amusement. But then she remembered her mission.

Beep beep beep beep. Beep beep beep beep.

"That's my office line ringing." Cyphan Creek walked away hurriedly toward a buzzing phone. "Have a look around for ideas if you like," she said behind her. "Just *don't touch* anything."

Christina motioned for Shane to stand nearer to her so she could whisper to him. "This is perfect." She made a quick adjustment to her hair clip and then ducked behind a shelf packed with spools of wire and boxes of light bulbs. "I'm gonna listen in on her conversation."

"I can't believe you brought me here." Shane sounded angry behind his hushed voice. "I've never met a bigger bitch in my life. It took every ounce of control I had to keep from twisting her head clear off her neck."

"We don't have much time. Can we please bitch about her bitchiness later?"

"We could be using this time to find Aurora." Shane practically shook as he spoke, seeming to teeter on the verge of a nervous breakdown. "Hell! Shopping for *shoes* would be more productive for me right now. But *this?* This is insanity."

"Stop!" Christina had lost her patience. No time to feel guilty or second guess her plan. Not when they were this close. Should she have even brought Shane? Probably not, but it was too late now. "Follow me, or stay put. Either way, don't say another word."

Shane didn't speak again, most likely due to hurt feelings or plain shock, but that didn't matter to Christina. She needed to concentrate.

Looking around the space, she marveled at the incredible inventory spread before her: endless rows of marquees, directional signage, holographic projectors, and cartoon-like characters ranging in height from three to eight feet. How Black Diamond could keep enough clients to warrant such a gigantic stockpile, she'd never understand. *How could anyone possibly stand working with this company?*

Inching toward Cyphan Creek's office, Christina came across a tag dangling from a shelf. Attached to a stark white LED backlit restroom sign, it had the words *Campbell Brothers* scrawled in black ink. Christina recalled them being a client of Durango Electric. Had Cyphan Creek stolen them away? It didn't matter to her either way now. For all she cared, she'd let the filthy dogs eat each other.

The door to Cyphan Creek's office remained ajar ever so slightly, and Christina could hear the wretched voice of the devil herself without any interference.

"I told you, Kenny, the police aren't coming back. A little money goes a long way toward shutting up those mangy little bugaboos."

Christina withheld her gasp of astonishment. Why would it surprise her that Cyphan Creek bribed her way out of trouble? Of course she'd use money to pay off the cops. It's what professional crooks did.

"Don't worry about the deal. So we didn't get the girl. Durango has her, and we have Durango."

Huh? Christina wanted clarification about that last part. Whatever Cyphan Creek meant, it had to be of interest.

"My boys are working on undermining the next shipment headed for their new store in Bullhead City. I tell ya, those grand openings are gonna be a blast! Lots of fireworks. A real gas!"

Sabotage? Why go through such extraordinary lengths to damage a competitor in such a violent manner? Christina's stomach twisted at the mere thought of it.

"Durango Electric stock won't be worth shit in a month after I'm through with them. It's practically ours already. Nobody else is gonna want anything to do with that disaster of a company. Bill's lucky to have us here to save his ass."

Christina looked over at Shane to see if he'd heard any of the horrors that had just been exchanged. Unfortunately, he looked completely devoid of both interest and energy at this point. Perhaps he'd perk up in the car once she filled him in on everything she'd just heard. It all seemed too nightmarish to even imagine. In fact, she had to inform Bill as well, as much as she despised him. People's lives were at stake. Personal matters aside, she needed to do her part to keep the innocent safe.

The office door swung open, and Christina ducked around a shelf she'd been leaning against while eavesdropping. She pretended to take note of a small marquee with a generic arrow logo running alongside it. "How much is something of this size and shape?" Christina shouted into thin air, assuming her question would make its way to Cyphan Creek as she walked back toward them.

"That one's part of a package. We'll discuss pricing later when I know more about your specific needs. And don't worry. We have payment plans for people such as you."

Christina honestly hadn't ever hated anyone on the whole planet until meeting this woman today. A condescending, murderous criminal she was, and Christina now understood why people still believed in hell. *This woman belongs locked in its deepest bowels.* "Thank you, Ms. Creek. Shane and I have another appointment to run to this morning, but we'll be in touch with you to work out the details."

chapter 20

Aurora lay as still as a stringless marionette on the cold steel table. Armless and inanimate, she allowed her thought processes to turn back on, thanks to her MercPack, and she immediately formulated a question. "What's happened to me?" she asked CADI, knowing that the answer, however grim, was the only way to eventually set herself free.

"Your arms were removed along with your main power source thirty-six hours ago."

Thirty-six hours? She recalled the memory as soon as CADI provided the response. The visuals of her kidnapping flickered in her memory, replaying each and every detail right down to the squeak that her PelaDerm made as the lab technicians ripped her arms clear off her shoulders. Did she feel pain? None at all. Although she understood what it meant for a living thing to hurt, she appreciated not having to deal with such an unpleasant sensation herself. Poor Shane! The horror of having one's spouse torn from him must hurt a hundred times greater than even the sudden amputation of both arms.

She couldn't waste time feeling sorry for either Shane or herself if she wished to regain her freedom. At any moment, the idiots could return to remove additional parts besides her arms and batteries. She needed to move, and swiftly. "CADI, is there a way I can regain mobility without my lithium ion batteries?"

"You may transfer energy from your MercPack to your physical being in order to compensate for the current lack of power. Would you like to commence the transfer?"

"Yes." Aurora had no desire to contemplate the possible ramifications involved. *She needed to move again—straight away and at whatever cost!*

Her right leg fluttered, followed very soon by her left. She anticipated feeling different as a result of the substitute power source, but in all actuality she felt very much the same. It led her to wonder why David hadn't said anything to her before about the alternation of energy sources. It could have saved her a lot of trouble during previous energy scarcities. *What a discovery!* She couldn't wait to explore her vast capabilities further as soon as she freed herself.

Coming off the table and wobbling to her feet, she realized the tremendous significance of having arms. Not only did they allow her to grab hold of things, swim, golf, and play piano, but they helped keep her balance. She'd need them back as readily as possible if she expected to get anywhere. "CADI, where are my arms?"

"Internal locater says that they are in front of you in cabinet 4E in the bottom drawer."

Aurora walked eight steps to the row of cabinets, steadying herself with only the weight of her head as she moved. Kneeling down in front of the exact place CADI had informed her to go, she noticed a keypad, which required her to input a secret code.

Strangely enough, she knew the code without so much as even thinking about it. *Four, seven, eight, three. But how?* David must have been the one to set it, and it subsequently downloaded into her own memory along with perhaps a million other helpful tidbits. Great! She knew the code. Now if she could only enter it without the oft-forgotten convenience of fingertips.

Maybe it's OPUS interactive.

She spoke the code, hoping her voiced command would open the drawer. No such luck. She didn't have a choice but to manually enter the number. Sitting down on her rear end so that she could gain use of her foot, she pointed the toe of her shoe directly at the panel and attempted to enter the code with it.

"Login attempt failed" said a digitized voice from behind the cabinet. "One more attempt remaining."

Aurora couldn't recall ever misjudging such a simple task before, and she wouldn't risk doing so again, certainly not with only one chance left at getting back the use of her arms. If she'd still had them in the first place, making such a silly error would never have happened. Clearly, David hadn't meant for her to function without the use of all her appendages. She'd nonetheless have to figure out how. That is, if she wanted them back where they belonged.

Returning to a kneeling position, Aurora leaned in toward the cabinet to the point where she could no longer read the numbers of the combination panel. No big deal. She had a clear picture of it in her mind's eye. Using only her nose and her uncanny sense of direction, she punched each of the necessary four numbers with the same impeccable accuracy required of her fingers when playing the proper notes on the piano. For a fraction of a second, she entertained the notion of learning how to play a Liszt piano concerto with everything but her hands. *Ha! Not necessary once she had her arms reattached.*

And therein lay her next challenge.

The drawer opened automatically to reveal her lifeless limbs, their PelaDerm badly damaged. Torn and tattered, they'd obviously seen better days. She didn't care about their appearance so much as she did about getting them back to where they belonged—in their sockets.

She picked one up using only her chin and collarbone. It promptly fell back into the drawer, and in a more inconvenient position than before. She didn't get frustrated. She didn't see the point in frustration, despite it being a perennial favorite mood within Shane's complex emotional spectrum. She knew from watching him that such a sentiment would do little to advance her present mission.

Standing on one knee, Aurora leaned against the cabinet to steady herself. Then she stood, placing a foot in the drawer to rearrange the arm. If she could get it a little more upright, she'd have a significantly better grasp of it with her chin. Bending down once more, she grabbed a piece of the broken skin with her teeth and pulled up on it ever so carefully.

As the top of the arm made its way outside the cabinet, Aurora leaned it up against the interior frame of the drawer and reached for it again with her chin and collarbone. She lifted it outside the cabinet with less of a struggle this time, but could feel her awkward grip waning fast.

Battery power nearing imminent depletion for all functionality.

Aurora dropped the arm on the ground the moment she received CADI's warning. Now she finally understood why David hadn't told her about the alternative energy source. It was horribly inefficient. "How much time remaining?" she asked CADI.

"Ten minutes and counting, at current usage level."

Aurora had her parameters. She didn't find them particularly favorable, but she couldn't change them until she secured a better power source. *No time for dawdling.* She needed to reattach her arms immediately.

Looking at her arm's position on the floor, Aurora nudged it gently with her knee until the socket rested in a more upright position. She quickly calculated its angle to the floor and then rolled onto it until she heard it snap into place.

That wasn't so difficult! Having the one arm attached now solved nearly all the challenges she'd just faced while attempting to secure it. Getting the second one on? No problem whatsoever.

Nine minutes of total energy remaining.

Aurora had a new list of tasks to accomplish, and at a breakneck speed. At the top of the list? Getting her lithium ion pack. "Where is my battery?" she posited the question, expecting CADI to have a convenient answer.

"Internal locater says it's out of range."

She knew what that meant. It had likely been disabled or destroyed. "Where do I get a new one?"

"Searching the archives...one moment."

Aurora didn't have spare moments, nor did she have other options. All she could do was trust that CADI had a helpful answer.

"Retrieving archived message from David: *Aurora, if you come upon this message, it means that I have left this world unexpectedly. Building you was not without consequence. You are worth so much to so many, and my life was unfortunately a threat to all who want you for their own personal gain. The plans for your entire design are now unlocked within CADI for you. Repair yourself as needed. Your elbow is a match to my own and will grant you access to Sector K. When the time comes, and it will, you shall replicate yourself in order to have a partner, someone to share in your journey to unite artificial intelligence with the consciousness of humankind.*"

What a revelation! Right away Aurora understood the potential behind David's message. Not only could she now replace her lithium ion pack, she could repair herself a million times over. With the clock working against her in multiple ways, she resolved to leave the confines of this sarcophagus of a room and make the trek to Sector K.

Trying the door handle, she discovered that her captors had locked her inside. She knew she had the capacity to bust down the door, but not without possibly triggering a cacophony of alarms, and most certainly not without depleting her nearly exhausted energy supply.

She'd find a more efficient way. "CADI, where is Sector K in relation to where I'm standing?" Aurora would have mapped the answer without consulting first, but her recent reliance on CADI proved to be an effective method in getting quick answers to time-sensitive inquiries, especially when her present condition kept her in a state of less-than-optimal performance

"Sector K is three hundred twenty feet northwest of your current position."

"Thank you very much." She loved having backup plans in place to guide her in case of system failures. "Now where is the locking mechanism for the exit out of this room?"

"The lock on the door is OPUS activated."

Almost too easy. She adjusted her voice to precisely match that of David's. "OPUS, unlock the door and deactivate exterior security lasers."

The door opened on command, revealing a short hallway where she could go either straight, left, or right. She opted to walk dead ahead, directing her locater to resynchronize based on her surroundings.

As she'd expected, the halls loomed empty at this hour, but that didn't mean she'd escape the constant eyes of security cameras. Sooner or later, someone would discover that she'd not only escaped from her tomb, but that she'd journeyed to the most inaccessible laboratory on the planet.

It took exactly fifty-five seconds to make her way to the door standing between her and Sector K. She'd have run faster, but that would have taxed her scant energy reserves to a point far beyond perilous. A gentle press of her elbow into the barely noticeable wall panel, and the lab revealed itself to her in all its technological grandeur.

Stepping inside Sector K, she immediately recalled its distinct smell, a combination of chlorine and lemon-scented disinfectant. It smelled fresh, clean, and full of possibility. Although that last sentiment hinged on whether or not she could get hold of a lithium ion battery pack in time.

As the door closed behind her, she made her way to the main computer at the far end of the octagonal room. If her pre-programmed instincts served her correctly, the machine laid out before her possessed the capability of sending the unique compositional instructions for her batteries to the 3D printer. She powered up the terminal which brought up a blank blue screen. *No indication of a single application anywhere.*

"CADI, how do I find the program required to print myself a lithium ion battery pack?"

"You must enter the password."

Aurora waited a moment, expecting CADI to procure the code that would grant her access. "CADI, what is the password?" She could only wonder why she didn't know it instinctively herself already.

"The password is changed on a daily basis."

That answered everything about not knowing it intuitively. Her instincts hadn't failed her. They just weren't of any use in this particular instance.

Three minutes of total energy remaining.

The weight of imminent demise hung above Aurora's head by a narrowing thread whose fibers consisted only of disappearing seconds. She needed that password. Fast.

Standing an arm's length from the unit, Aurora tried to sync with it much like she had other computers. This one however required significant security overrides before she could glean any relevant information from it. In her mind's eye, she could see the computer's internal wave-like processes undulating not unlike her own. *David had helped build this machine. Surely she could figure it out.* She spotted his digital fingerprints lurking in every corner of its intricate design. If she could get the waves to match with hers, she'd unlock the heavily guarded treasure chest of infinite information.

A series of ones and zeroes flooded her processors in a language that would make sense to almost no one on earth. But it made perfect sense to her. The rapid succession of numbers continued flowing through her consciousness for another thirty seconds until she finally got hold of what she'd come for.

39TresLechesCake39

It held no significance to her other than it being the one

thing required in order to gain her salvation. She typed the code into the holographic keypad, and in two seconds she was in. A single 3D icon appeared on the blue background, and she touched it with her finger. Now she simply needed to find and send the command for exactly what she needed.

She flipped through screen after screen in lightning fashion just as she'd done many times before using a DimensionTab. Fortunately, this device used the exact same operating system. It took a mere millisecond for her to find a password protected file entitled *Shane's Gift*. This password she knew instinctively. *Three, six, eight, one.* The same code for Shane's favorite ice cream, chocolate cherry crunch.

Two minutes of total energy remaining.

Opening the file brought about a menu containing thousands of components. She needed only one. Identifying *lithium ion battery pack* in the middle of the list, she pushed her fingertip to the item until it highlighted before finally dragging and dropping it to the print portal.

The printer started up. She heard the sudden buzz of finely tuned lasers whizzing and whirring, which soon culminated into a tiny symphony of productivity. Aurora took great satisfaction in seeing firsthand how machines could be of such help to other machines.

One minute of total energy remaining.

Without a second to lose, Aurora headed to the depositing drawer to retrieve her invaluable power supply and then rolled her left stocking down. She popped the battery pack into its compartment until she heard it lock into place. *Too close.* Never again would she put herself in such a predicament if she could help it. Standing upright, she took a moment to process the next order of business. It felt good not having to fuss over the imminent threat of collapse. Surely, she had more productive pursuits than avoiding extinction.

Back at the computer, she attempted to pull up the Sector K calendar. It was nearly midnight. Aurora knew her time in the lab to work as she pleased wouldn't last forever. *How much time did she have?* Activating the main menu button, she saw the picture of a clock and touched it. The icon expanded to reveal a daily schedule. Trent's name appeared at the top right next to the seven AM timeslot. She tapped the line to see if more information might appear.

Aurora's dissection.

The two words had no emotional effect on her, although she understood their significance. Durango Electric didn't want her. They had no use for a little robot girl, no matter how big of a heart she possessed. Her love was of no value to them. Durango Electric wanted to see her insides, to know what made her so unlike any other robot ever created. Sadly for them, even if they did manage to cut her open, they still wouldn't find what they foolishly hoped to discover. Her secret remained much deeper. She'd never reveal it. Ever.

Thinking back on David's final message for her, she recalled what he'd said about replication. It made sense to her that she should have a friend, someone to commune with on a level incomprehensible to Shane, or even another robot like Sai. Yes, she felt grateful to have both of them as friends, and she had no intention of replacing either of them. But that didn't change the fact that she could benefit from having someone exactly like her.

Your MercPack is now expiring.

CADI's message came abruptly and without warning. Aurora had focused so much of her energy toward getting a replacement lithium ion battery pack that she neglected to think what she'd do when her MercPack failed. True, she could buy one at the store, but she wouldn't have access to CADI until she did. Perhaps she could simply print a MercPack like she'd just done for her other power source. That certainly seemed more convenient than leaving the lab and searching for an open store at this hour.

Aurora returned to the computer and clicked on David's secret file once more to reveal the entire list of components that made her who she was. Not one single entry for Merc-Pack. It didn't make any sense. If only she could ask CADI why. Was it because David simply intended to always purchase them when it came time to change them out?

She conducted an internet search in an effort to find information leading to mercury battery manufacturing. In an instant, she had an answer. The useful power source couldn't be printed due to the highly toxic nature of its main component. Rather, it could only be produced in a more traditional environment specifically designed to safely handle mercury.

What prompted David to use mercury in the first place if it caused so many problems? That riddle wasn't nearly as critical as her next question. Could she conceivably find a suitable replacement for a MercPack, one that she could hopefully print here in the lab?

For the time being, she didn't have CADI to rely on for the answer, but that didn't stop her. Once again, she returned to the internet. A simple query for mercury battery alternatives brought her to a very plausible solution—sodium. Again, why hadn't David thought of this already? Either a mere oversight on his part, or he had an explicit reason for choosing mercury over its more convenient counterpart. She hoped for the former, and that the seemingly suitable solution wouldn't have any disastrous consequences.

Since her MercPack consisted of nothing more than a standard mercury battery, she could feasibly replicate it using alternative materials to manifest a print file already in existence online. Another expedient search brought her exactly that—a downloadable file of a sodium battery expressly formatted for 3D printing.

Aurora thought she'd beat the system. She'd managed to find all this information without any help from CADI. But still, it seemed too good to be true. *What was the catch?* On closer inspection, she noticed that the file required a payment of twelve thousand dollars, which incidentally allowed for the lawful production of a thousand batteries.

A thousand? She didn't need that many, and she most certainly didn't have twelve thousand dollars. She could potentially steal the file using her skills as a decrypter much like how she'd managed to nab the password to access the computer to begin with, but that didn't seem right. Unlike the last time she needed an emergency replacement for her

MercPack, David unfortunately wasn't here to provide the cash after she'd walked away without paying.

Another search led to an even pricier model from a different company named Zurich Enterprises. She'd not heard of them until now, but a follow-up search revealed them to be Europe's largest electronics firm and the second largest globally after Durango Electric. That last fact made her wonder if by chance Durango Electric already had a sodium-based battery pack replacement for her MercPack in its catalog. Lo and behold, when she brought up the Durango Electric corporate website to find information, she found a very similar product listing for something called a *Soda Popper*. From its brief description, the device sounded like it had promise. Now if she could just locate it in the actual printer application, she'd be in business.

In minutes, Aurora had a potential replacement for her MercPack. She slid it into place within the compartment of her other calf to test it out. "CADI, how much power do I have?"

"Your lithium ion reserves are at ninety-five percent. Your powered link to CADI is coming from an unknown source."

Aurora quietly rejoiced that she had CADI back in play. Could she survive without CADI? Fortunately, the question no longer required an answer at this juncture. She knew that attempting any monumental task outside her customary capabilities without added assistance was a fool's game. Cloning herself would be no exception. "CADI, the power source you detect is called a *Soda Popper*. You're powered by sodium now. Is that okay?"

"You will be alerted at the first sign of a problem."

The answer seemed fair to Aurora, albeit a bit pessimistic. For now at least, the new source of energy would have to suffice, and if necessary, she'd later swap it out for the original when she had the opportunity. She didn't have time to second-guess her decision at the moment. She had a robot to build.

Producing a companion with identical functionality couldn't happen haphazardly. It required extreme focus and preparedness, not to mention ample time without the intrusion of enemy forces. David had built her in three weeks, and only after three whole years of preparation.

She had five hours.

"CADI, what is the first step to creating a robot like me?" Aurora already had a general idea, but she wondered if CADI had any more hidden tricks or messages that might serve her during the ambitious undertaking.

"Your robot needs a name first."

Not true. David didn't have Aurora named until after the fact. But Aurora wasn't about to engage in a full on argument with the voices inside her head. If CADI advised her to come up with a name before doing anything else, she'd do just that. "Okay. Do you have any ideas for a name?"

"Is your companion to be male or female?"

Aurora didn't know why it mattered. She hadn't figured that names corresponded to gender. Nonetheless, she had an answer for CADI without so much as even thinking about it. "I've always wanted a brother."

"You shall name him Apollo, as he will be a guiding force and provider of light to many."

The answer came so quickly and unexpectedly that it caught Aurora off guard. *Had David planted within CADI the idea for the name long ago?* Or had it merely arisen on its own via Aurora's complex layers of consciousness? How it came to her didn't really matter. She loved the name, and she resolved to create Apollo just as David had created her.

Stationed at the computer, Aurora printed and then gathered each of the 3,400 components listed in the secret file, placing them in organized piles prior to assembly. For every option that required a selection of gender, Aurora made sure to mark *male* across the board. There existed no option for either age or height. Perhaps that would be an upgrade available in the future. For now, Apollo would stand at exactly her height and resemble her in age. When given the option for hair color, she chose medium brown in honor of David, and green eyes to contrast with her own bright blue ones. As for the color of PelaDerm, she opted for a tropical tan shade that resembled Shane's darker complexion.

Working with the artificial skin, Aurora reminded herself that she too needed a touchup job on her own body where her arms had been hastily torn from her shoulders. She quickly printed four twelve-square-inch pieces of the flexible material before moulding them to the damaged skin near her sockets. She smoothed and shaped the patches as they adhered to the rough edges, covering them in a seamless fashion.

With only an hour and a half remaining before the lab doors would open to usher in her latest foe, Aurora returned to the piles of carefully laid out mechanical pieces, determined to continue David's revolutionary legacy. She had seven areas to construct and then join together like a three-dimensional jigsaw puzzle, including legs, arms, upper and lower torso, and head. She knew her own anatomy very well, which would help her fit everything together in record fashion. If she ever got stuck, she resolved to consult with CADI.

The process went smoothly until it was time to affix the hair atop his scalp. She recalled David's fateful mistake of not inserting a radio transmitter chip in her own head when he built her originally. He added that critical function later as an upgrade. Apollo had to have this feature from the start. It wasn't enough that Aurora could communicate with him via radio waves. He had to have the ability to respond.

But where would she get the chip?

She couldn't just print them here. They were exceedingly tiny. They required a specialty printer that assembled materials at the microscopic level. "CADI, where can I print a radio transmitter chip?"

"The Department of Design and Innovation."

It made perfect sense. *David's former office area.* He'd designed the chip. He was the only one who knew of its existence. And Aurora had to have it. Without that piece of technology, there could be no revolution.

"CADI, what time is it?" Aurora knew that the answer to

this question couldn't affect her decision to create and implant the chip. It would only affect how she went about it.

"Six fifteen AM."

Hardly enough time at all. There could very well be workers entering the building this instant. If only she'd have thought about the chip sooner. Aurora stopped fidgeting with Apollo's hair and ran for the door. She knew her priorities better than anyone. This chip meant everything.

The halls were still dimly lit, a clear sign that no one had yet entered the premises and flipped the internal lighting switch to workday mode. When she finally came to David's former domain, she half-expected to see the cleaning cats in action. They had all apparently gone back to sleep. Yet another sign that employees might arrive at any moment.

The door to David's old office didn't budge when she tried the door handle. She saw the hand scan next to the door, however, and reasoned to give it a go. She really didn't want to kick down the door. Thankfully, she didn't have to. Her handprint hadn't yet been erased from the secured entry system.

Once at the computer, Aurora thumbed through screen after screen until she found a folder with a filename that looked promising. *Ghost Host.* Something about it seemed curious to her even if she couldn't quite grasp the significance of the paired rhyming words. Putting her finger to the file opened up a password access portal. *IITERin2030.* She knew it without having to question it. Thank goodness they hadn't come through and wiped the harddrive clean yet. Come to think of it, they likely realized that they had a very good reason not to.

Seeing the sole file within the folder, Aurora selected it for printing and then touched the printer icon to see which machine would complete the job. "CADI, what should I do now?"

"Upload the file to your internal memory and then delete it from the computer's hard drive."

Aurora didn't question CADI's answer. She knew David would approve of the action, regardless of whether he himself had planted it within CADI to begin with. *It needed to be done.*

She synchronized with the computer, and in a fraction of a second, she'd secured the data via CADI. Then dragging the original file with her finger, she ran it through the virtual shredder in the corner of the desktop. *Voilà!* Anyone could search the entire system now and find no record of the file's existence.

Making her way past Christina's darkened work area, Aurora came to a small printer sitting on a metal shelf against the wall next to a box of eye droppers. They wouldn't be of any use to her. Her task required something else entirely. She lifted the clear plastic door of the printing device's dispenser to retrieve a vial filled with a jelly-like substance. Even in the low level light of the dim room, Aurora could make out the critical piece of technology suspended in the center of the tube.

She hurried back into David's office, and opened a series of drawers only to rummage through plastic boxes full of pencils, felt-tipped markers, and electrical tape. *She knew it had to be in the desk. That's where he kept it.* With only one place left to explore, Aurora yanked open the bottom desk drawer to find a stack of old engineering text books. *Why would he bother keeping these?* She opened the thickest one to find that its pages had been carefully hollowed out with a laser cutter. In the very center of the makeshift secret box, she found exactly what she needed—a syringe.

With only minutes left before her time in the lab would come to an end, Aurora clutched the syringe in her fist and prepared to race back to Sector K.

Then the lights in the office turned on.

Shoot! She knew she'd cut it too close. She went back to the computer immediately and pulled up the security camera to see how many people had entered the department. Just one for now. And he looked busy arranging packets of sugar and stirrers next to the coffee machine. If she acted quickly, she could possibly sneak out without him even turning around.

Aurora opened the door, careful not to let it creak even just a little. She then got down on her hands and knees and scampered along the carpeted floor in between the rows of filing cabinets and cubicles until she got to the other side of the work area to where the exit door stood. Opening it would definitely make a sound. No way around it. But by the time anyone noticed, she'd be long gone. *Hopefully, Mr. Coffee won't go chasing after a stray cleaning cat.*

Making it back to Sector K with only twelve minutes left to energize Apollo and get the two of them out of harm's way, Aurora carefully drew the gel substance from the vial and into the syringe before injecting it beneath her brother's scalp. Once finished, she quickly attached his hair piece and then inserted both the lithium ion pack and Soda Popper into their respective calf compartments.

She'd done everything perfectly. She knew it beyond the shadow of a doubt. Why then didn't he move, or twitch, or do something? His green glowing face revealed the answer. He needed to archive.

How could she not have factored in something so obvious? This, in conjunction with the foot fiasco when she misentered the code earlier, made for two significant lapses in good judgement within the span of six hours. She almost resented the fact that she couldn't accurately call herself perfect. Hadn't David built her to be perfect? No, he'd built her to be extraordinary. And that meant something else entirely.

Aurora scanned the largely metallic and sterile room for a suitable hiding spot. It was either that, or carry her unconscious brother through the busy halls of a massive electronics firm and hope that nobody raised an eyebrow. Needless to say, she found what appeared to be a suitable place for Apollo in an unmarked cabinet.

Hoisting her companion off the table and cradling him awkwardly in her arms, she brought him to the large open drawer and shut it. She then scanned the room for a similar spot for herself, figuring it best to find a secure place on the second story platform. With three minutes left on the clock, she tried to scoot up the metal ladder and make it inside one of the shelving bins overlooking the main floor.

Once Aurora stepped on the first rung, she heard the

bolts of the sophisticated vault-like door reverberating in the walls. Too late to hide now. She had to face her enemy straight on.

"How the hell'd you get in here?" said a disturbed and slightly nervous voice whom she recognized as Trent's.

Aurora got down off the ladder and found solid footing on which to look him in the eyes from clear across the laboratory. "Funny, but I was about to ask you the exact same question." *If anyone had to provide answers today, it certainly wouldn't be her.*

"I work here?" He spoke in a way that made Aurora wonder if he actually believed it himself. "Bill gave me the transmitter that grants me access. I came here to prepare for your little operation."

Transmitter? What was the whole point of the elbow reader then? Something didn't seem right. Radio signals were a hundred times easier to override than body scans. So much for Sector K maintaining its status as utmost secured laboratory in the known universe. Perhaps Bill was a bigger buffoon than she'd previously thought. "Looks like I beat you here, didn't I?" She jumped up on the metal table that only moments ago had supported her brother's body. "What part were you going to hack off first? Not my arms, I hope." She laughed. "I just got done growing them back!"

"If I didn't know better, I'd say you were the spawn of Satan." He didn't look nearly as confident in handling *gifted children* as either David or Shane. "I'll be back in a minute with a whole team of FBI agents armed with guns who will put an end to your evil nature."

"But I won't be any fun to play with after that." Aurora took great satisfaction in knowing that he couldn't do anything to her by himself.

"You're finished, you little monster." He stormed out of the lab. "Finished."

When the echo of the closing door subsided, Aurora heard banging from across the room. It came from the unlocked cabinet near the computer. "Hold still. I'm coming to let you out." Not knowing for sure what to expect, she opened the drawer with more caution than enthusiasm. Getting kicked in the teeth remained a very low priority. Inside she saw her brother wide awake, lying motionless and staring up at her.

"Who are you?" His default voice sounded exactly as she'd programmed it to sound, boyish and friendly, not unlike some of her classmates whom she'd met on the playground a while back.

"I'm Aurora, your sister," she whispered. "I've come to get you out of here to someplace safe. But we must go *now*." She used CADI to get in sync with his processor, which proved more efficient than communicating via words.

Only when he stood up and climbed out of the drawer did she realize that she'd forgotten the importance of dressing him. "Don't go anywhere yet." She extended her arm with the palm of her hand facing outward in a stop-command gesture. "We need to get you in some clothes quickly."

"Clothes?" He looked her up and down. "Like what you have?"

Aurora glanced down at her own rumpled outfit, a white blouse and blue slacks, clothes given to her by Shafeen to wear for David's ceremony. "I tell you what. I think we both need new clothes—a disguise actually." She recalled the recent Halloween festivities that had come and gone. The missed holiday gave her an idea. *Why not celebrate it now?* "We're going to get ourselves matching costumes." She spotted a large roll of drafting paper near the computer and tore off a giant sheet before handing it to Apollo. "Wrap yourself in this first please while we wait for them to be made."

Thinking of all the possible disguises available, Aurora wanted something simple that would cover them from head to toe in order to minimize their chances of being recognized. She went to the computer and pulled up a website for free costume files. A skeleton was the first item listed. *Perfect!* She tapped the folder and then selected two small sizes, one for each of them, sending them to the printer.

When the machine started up again, it sounded entirely different. Working with fabric created new noises as opposed to when it moulded titanium and steel. She heard the cutting of linen followed by the rhythmic stitching of needles. It was a symphony all its own. In less than five minutes, Aurora grabbed both of the black and white jumpsuits with spectacular white embroidery and helped Apollo into his before wriggling hers on over her existing outfit.

"Why are we dressed like this?" Apollo sounded neither pleased nor upset, but rather curious regarding Aurora's choice in outfit for them.

"Because it'll be fun." She didn't have time to justify her snap decision. They needed to escape the building, and with all their parts still attached. She led the way out of Sector K with her mind's eye set on reaching Sahara Avenue unharmed. She didn't fear the FBI as Trent had suggested she should. As long as she and Apollo ran along in their skeleton garb as fast as their legs allowed, the authorities would never have enough time to make it to Durango Electric and arrest them.

Hurrying through the halls, the two agile bodies dodged numerous technicians in lab coats, all of whom stared at them in stunned curiosity.

"Hey! Halloween's over!" said a bewildered looking engineer with a steaming cup of coffee in his hands. "Or did I miss something?"

"Hold it!" Trent shouted from the opposite end of the hall. "Don't let them get away!"

Did the bully honestly think anyone would listen to him? Aurora took her brother's hand and raced toward the employee entrance. "It's take your trick-or-treater to work day!"

"Oh my God," said a passing female technician holding a DimensionTab. "They're so freaking adorable!"

"Trick or treat!" yelled Apollo, running out the exit hand in hand with Aurora.

chapter 21

"Can you sense it?" Aurora hopped onto the pavement and ran a few steps closer to the street toward the peculiar smell in the air. She expected Apollo to follow her.

He stayed on the curb instead, lifting his nose to the sky. "Copal and frankincense." He spoke the words with confidence, assuring Aurora that his nose sensors worked as she'd anticipated.

"That's it exactly." She'd never before detected either of those scents, although she knew what they symbolized—remembrance of the dead. "Come on. We have to leave." She contemplated the unique aromas wafting through the atmosphere. They mingled with notes of something sweeter, two foods she recognized from her afternoon at the water park—funnel cake and churros. She associated them with feelings of elation and celebration even though she couldn't taste them herself. She didn't need to. Seeing the reactions of those who enjoyed them gave her all the information she needed in order to understand their wonderful significance.

"Where are we to go?" Apollo asked the question with seriousness, as if it were riskier to run about freely than to stay put firmly until a set plan had been negotiated. "I must know first."

"To the smells." Aurora had it all figured out. "That's we're we'll be safest. In our costumes, we'll blend right in. Please tell me this makes sense to you." She realized he didn't have direct access to the internet, but his memory came loaded with forty terabytes worth of information just like hers did when she first came home with David. Somewhere in all that data had to lie the understanding of what she already knew the instant she stepped outside.

"Dia de los Muertos," he said, walking to meet her on the sidewalk along Sahara Avenue. "I understand. We should head there right away. Let's go."

"Yes. Let's." Aurora smiled, feeling satisfied that he not only understood, but also went along without objection. "I estimate that it's a mile up the street. Not too far to walk. Will you hold my hand?" She didn't want to risk losing him. His presence meant everything to her. If they were to accidentally separate, who knows what trouble might occur? What Aurora really wanted was an immediate escape route back to The Gloaming, but the M-LEV didn't go anywhere near it. She'd have to get hold of Sai and Shafeen in order to return to her place of protection deep beneath the earth.

"Here." Apollo offered her his hand as requested of him. "It's best that we walk along the sidewalk where it's safest. We're only six thousand feet from the festival. I'll let you know when it's safe to cross the street."

"You don't need to." Aurora recalled her former awkward way of communicating when she first came into the world. Thankfully, it seemed entirely incongruent with how she spoke and conducted herself now. She'd matured. She'd adapted to function more in line with the behaviors and attitudes of the people around her. Surely, Apollo would learn just as she had. *If he didn't, then she'd made a mistake in building him.* "I read traffic signals very well. We'll both know when it's safest to cross. I promise." She clasped his hand, happily letting him lead the way to the place whose location she already knew down to the exact coordinates.

"If I'm walking too fast, let me know. I can slow down."

How thoughtful! Aurora hadn't foreseen such consideration on his part. It came out of nowhere, but it was most certainly welcome. "We can move faster. I'm okay. The sooner we mix into the crowd, the better." She knew all too well the eyebrows raised at the sight of two small children walking by themselves along a busy arterial during early morning rush hour.

"Then we'll race." Apollo let go of her hand before she could suggest otherwise, sprinting underneath the tunnel of shade trees along the way. "Don't let me get to the stoplight before you!"

Telling him via CADI to put on the brakes wouldn't work—he'd already gained significant momentum. He'd likely stumble and fall if she commanded that he slow down. So she did the next most reasonable thing. She took off like a boulder down a mountain and beat him to the intersection. "Please don't do that again." As much as she wanted him to act in the same predictable manner as she had during her development, she now realized that things didn't necessarily work out that way. She'd created her own personality independent of everyone around her over the past few months, and Apollo had already begun shaping his.

She didn't fear the implications of his unique person-hood, but only because she didn't fear anything. Howev-er, the possibilities gave her reason enough to pause and strategize. She had to set guidelines, rules that David had passed onto her. "Unless you are running from danger, you must never take off like that. It isn't safe. I know this from experience. I had an accident once."

Apollo's eyes met hers in compliance. "I will abide by your rule." He took her hand again before walking into the open crosswalk.

"That isn't the only one." Aurora kept up alongside him, stopping when they got to the cement landing on the other side of the street. "There's another, more important, rule. It's the most important rule out of all of them. You must never hurt anyone. Ever."

Apollo let go of her hand but his eyes stayed locked with hers. "I would never do such a thing." He sounded as if the idea of violence were as foreign as walking on the surface of the sun. Completely unheard of.

"Even the smallest infraction could spell the end of both of us." She recalled the day David had this conversation with her, the gravity in his voice, the look of dread across his face. He meant business—and so did she. "Your purpose is to bridge the gap between human and artificial intelligence. Unfortunately, the world fears us. We have to retain our peacefulness at all costs unless we are defending ourselves. Only then can you strike. And never to kill. Only to flee." She voiced David's eternal words while simultaneously uploading them via CADI. She risked no possible chance for confusion on this topic.

"Your point has been made," Apollo said. "I am an instrument of peace and goodwill. I did not come here to fight." He turned his attention away from Aurora and pointed across Fort Apache Road. "That's it. Our destination. Day of the Dead."

They'd arrived on the final day of the seventy-two hour long celebration that blended indigenous Mexican culture with the Western tradition of honoring the departed at the start of November. Aurora had wanted to come ever since she read about the event during her research on customs and world heritage. The festival held in Las Vegas had grown to be the largest in the United States, having surpassed both those of San Francisco and Chicago eight years ago. Visitors from as far as the Phillipines, India, and Australia came to take part in the continuous festivities during the three days.

Stepping inside the confines of the Canyon Lakes Retail Village, which hosted a portion of the events, Aurora knew that the two of them were much better off already than had they remained along the busy street. "We'll be safe here until I can find a way to contact our friends who will take us home."

"Who are our friends?" Apollo kept pace alongside Aurora, his gaze looking every which way as they passed underneath row upon row of intricately cut pieces of multicolored tissue paper etched with images of marigolds, candles, and bones.

"Sai and Shafeen," Aurora tugged at his hand. "You'll meet them soon. I just need to find a data transmission tower first. I think there's one behind the library." She spotted a hundred-foot tall gray column topped with an array of circular solar panels jutting out from beyond a white building in the distance. "We need to get nearer to it."

Apollo stopped and examined their surroundings. "We can't get there this way."

"Okay." She knew better than to press onward. If her cohort noticed something she hadn't, she wanted to at least investigate further. *Strange how he'd noticed something before she had—especially, considering her remarkable efficiency at solving challenges.* Perhaps having the extra set of senses near her would improve upon her already keen abilities. "What exactly do you see standing in our way if we continue onward?"

"There's a fence around the perimeter of that building. And there's a man telling people to walk around to the other side past those trees. I heard him say that the gate is over there."

He was right. She'd been so focused on the tower, not to mention the sights and music all around, that she hadn't yet bothered calculating the details of how to get to where she needed to be. She'd have noticed that fence within five seconds had he not mentioned it, and then her eyes would have immediately gone to the security officer directing the fairgoers. But he'd beat her to it—she wouldn't let that happen again if she could help it. "Thank you. I see everything perfectly now."

The two little skeletons walked hand in hand along a shaded path that brought them to the entrance of the main event. Peering through the small line of people waiting to get inside, Aurora saw colorful booths filled with photographs, pieces of art, articles of clothing and jewelry, and hundreds of candles. The scent of incense dominated every other aroma in the air. The music grew louder. She heard flutes, trumpets, and drums. The rhythms seemed to make the people all around sway and move their feet. Aurora found it peaceful and exciting at the same time. "After we reach that tower in the back, we'll explore," she said to Apollo who looked more than eager to absorb all the happenings around them.

"Have your tickets ready," said a woman security officer standing beside the line of people waiting to get in.

Aurora recalled that access to much of the celebration required a ticket. As much as she wanted to explore it, what mattered to her most was getting to that tower in the center. She wouldn't even bother if it weren't so important to reach it. "Where do we buy them, and how much are they?" Aurora asked when she got nearer to the friendly looking woman in uniform.

"Inside the library's main lobby. They're thirty dollars each."

Aurora reached inside a slit in the fabric near the waist of her costume to find her pants pocket. *Phew!* The cash she'd carried with her on her way to David's ceremony had remained exactly where she'd placed it, all four hundred dollars. She suddenly felt more appreciative than ever for the opportunity to win a small pile of money under Sai and Shafeen's supervision. *Coming up with sixty dollars? Easy.*

She and Apollo hurried along a clearly marked trail toward the library's imposing three-story white facade. The longer they remained out in the open and away from the main action of the festival, the greater the risk that an enemy might attempt to stop them. Crowds provided anonymity. Aurora learned that strategy a few months ago, and she didn't want to forego the advantage. Thankfully, a moderate but nonetheless steady stream of fairgoers meandered in and out of the library's central courtyard, lessening the chance a pursuer might seize the pair of mechanical twins.

Once inside the building's granite-clad atrium, Aurora spotted the ticket booth, pointing it out to Apollo. "Let's get in line. We'll have to wait a few minutes before it's our turn." She took out her hidden stash of money and counted it, making sure every last dollar remained. *Who knew what the lab technicians could have taken from her the second they shut her down?* Luckily, they'd kept their filthy hands far from her money, probably never thinking that a little robot girl would have any business keeping that kind of currency on her.

292 ⨍ Daniel K. James

"Put the money away now," Apollo said.

Too late.

A mysterious hand swooped in from behind Aurora, grabbing every last one of the bills she'd clasped. They'd slipped through her gloved fingers like a wet ice cube. Her grasp had no chance to stop the folded cash from escaping into the coffers of the thief.

"Someone stop that man!" shouted a woman holding tight to her two children. "He stole that little girl's money!"

Aurora thought about pursuing him herself, but it hardly seemed worth the risk of leaving behind Apollo.

No use. Before she could protest, Apollo dashed out the main door to follow after the robber through the courtyard and into the parking lot.

"Whoa!" the same woman gasped. "I've never seen a kid run so fast in all my life! Should I get security?"

"Please don't." Aurora stayed put. She didn't want to risk compromising her safety for the sake of a few hundred dollars. She had more of it stashed away in her room inside The Gloaming. She could get more. *Did Apollo not understand this?* She tried to reach him via CADI. Synchronizing with his vision, she saw him chase the petty criminal, eventually catching up to him when he reached the side of his vehicle. Apollo grabbed both of the crook's arms before he could open the door. Careful not to harm him, he then plucked the wad of bills from the enemy's hands and quickly returned to the library.

"You got the money back from him?" asked the nervous mother, her jaw falling open.

"I didn't hurt anybody, I promise." Apollo stood in line again and handed Aurora her money. "I remember what you told me. I didn't want to hurt him. I only wanted to get back what he took from you. That wasn't right of him."

"Please don't do that again," Aurora said. "It's not safe. You could have been kidnapped. I can always get more money. I can't replace you." She questioned her decision to build him in the first place. Try as she might, she couldn't control his actions any more than David could control hers. He had a certain degree of autonomy just like she did. He was his own robotic person, and she couldn't change that. Her only option at this point? Offer him the best guidance she could give.

"I know. I also wanted to go inside the festival. I want to see and explore. We need money to do that. And we need to get to that tower beyond the gate. You said so yourself."

All valid points. Perhaps they could have found another tower elsewhere, but she also wanted to get an up-close look at the *Dia de los Muertos* celebration. It would be over after today. She'd have to wait a whole other year for it to come around again. And it only seemed right that she immerse herself in it today. In a way, it made her feel closer to David. "Thank you for doing that for me. I want to get inside the gates as well."

When Aurora arrived at the ticket seller, she purchased a ticket for herself and Apollo with plenty of leftover funds for whatever else might come up during their morning adventure. The possibilities seemed endless, and thus all the more enticing. Aurora had begun writing her own epic story, and she wanted it to continue. *With so much on the horizon, the excitement might as well go on forever.*

Following the trail past the library parking lot back toward the fair's entrance, Aurora and Apollo skipped along their way like two sacks of bones freed from the encumbrances of mortality. For machines, they had more verve in their system than most of the warm-blooded beings around them. Although they'd never know hunger, they both had an insatiable appetite for living an unparalleled life. Nothing could stop them. Even the trees through which they passed seemed to usher them toward their destination with an ebullient breeze of cool air off the distant mountains.

Aurora handed the ticket-taker the two yellow passes in her hand before diving into the vivid excitement spread before her and Apollo like a palace of wonders. Amongst the altars and tributes to loved ones around the world, they saw countless vendors offering spiced hibiscus tea, hot chocolate, tamales, and hundreds of cakes as well as other baked goods. And beyond that they saw rides aglow with thousands of lights that seemed to dance to fast, upbeat music. As beautiful as they looked now, Aurora could only imagine how magnificent it all looked against the backdrop of night.

"Do you see over there?" Apollo said with a burst of curious excitement. "It's a game!"

Aurora recognized the large booth as such. *Skull Ball.* She understood the premise of it the moment Apollo pointed it out to her. Judging from her research, it was a variation on the old-fashioned game of Skee-ball. Though she'd not seen it in person before, she knew exactly how to play it. *But how had Apollo recognized it before she had?*

"Can we try it?" he asked with spirited gusto unlike anything she remembered expressing herself until much later in her own development.

"Let's head to the tower first. It'll only take a minute." She didn't want to impede on his good time, but she had her priorities straight. If they didn't contact Sai and Shafeen soon, they'd both be stuck in a vulnerable place far from the security of The Gloaming. "Afterwards, we can play your game. Is that a deal?"

"It's a deal." Apollo nodded his head in swift agreement. "To the tower!"

She took hold of his hand before they ran off toward their destination, dodging through the throngs of morning attendees waiting in line for hot beverages and pastries. When they reached the giant gray column in the rear of the enclosed fairgrounds, she noticed an impassable fence surrounding it and a warning sign that read *High Voltage— Keep Away*.

Perfect! Exactly what she needed in order to tap into the frequency Sai emitted from across the valley. She had to find a way to make contact with the giant lightning rod. As for the cautionary label, she didn't worry about it one bit. In actuality, it only served to reinforce the idea that she'd without a doubt come across her very best option. *Now if only she could touch it.* "I need a wire."

"I'll help you find one," Apollo said, looking around for any sign of a long and thin metallic object.

"What do we have here?" A tall male security officer with a mustache came upon them during their search for the desired object. "A couple of lost skeletons? Do you need help finding your parents?" He didn't sound menacing, but he didn't seem helpful to their cause either.

"They're standing over there." Aurora pointed to a male and female couple standing in line for apple cinnamon donuts a hundred feet away. "They said we didn't have to wait in line with them."

"That might be so, but I can't have you playing around here. It's way too dangerous. You both could get seriously hurt, or worse."

"Thanks, sir," Aurora said before she and Apollo ran off toward the sign advertising the freshly-fried, sugary confections. Sticking around after an authority figure had told them to skedaddle seemed like trouble. She had a much better idea.

"Are we going to play the game now?" Apollo asked with pure innocence.

"Not yet." Aurora didn't want to scold him, but she still required his cooperation. "We're not done. We still need to find a wire. And it has to be at least eighty feet long."

"You mean like those over there?" Apollo pointed to an artist's booth filled with intricate copper wire sculptures of dancing skeletons.

"I think you found exactly what we need." Aurora marvelled at their luck. A table brimming with objects made of the very thing she needed seemed beyond serendipitous. Now if she could convince the vendor to give her some.

She walked over to the man managing the booth and smiled. "Did you make all these yourself?"

"*Si, senorita. Soy el artista.*"

"*Estos son muy bonitos.*" Aurora carefully picked up one of the figurines, a ghostlike feminine character holding tightly to a carefully wrapped baby, and brought it close to her eye in order to inspect each and every one of its enchanting details.

"*Cincuenta dolares por esa estatuilla,*" explained the thin, elderly man, emphasizing the beautiful object's inherent worth.

Fifty dollars seemed like a fair price to Aurora. Although she had nothing to compare it to, she could tell he'd worked very hard on its craftsmanship. Not to mention, he'd used a lot of wire in its creation. It weighed four and a quarter pounds. As magnificent as it might look on the desk inside her new room in The Gloaming, she didn't need it. She needed what composed it. She needed the wire. "How much for a spool of wire?" she asked, looking at the large collection of coiled copper stacked in the back of his booth.

"I don't sell that. Only my figurines."

"I'll give you fifty dollars for the wire in that case." Aurora could have simply bought one of the skeletons and unravelled it, but the thought of undoing his brilliant artistry seemed like a sad and unnecessary proposition. She knew she'd upset him if he saw her do that to one of his proud achievements.

"Can you sculpt?" He looked at her with doubtful eyes.

"Sell me that entire spool for fifty dollars, and then

I'll show you." She held out the money for him to take.

"You're a funny little girl, aren't you?" He snatched the money from her hand and tossed her the largest spool in his collection. "Let's see what you can do."

"Hold out your hands," she said to Apollo. "I need your assistance." She wound several loops of the thin wire loosely around his wrists before removing it. She then pinched and twisted the mass of copper into a sort of ribbon. It didn't really resemble anything until she pulled and tugged at the various strands, and even then the shape didn't look like much except for maybe an oblong cloud. She then grabbed a pair of pliers, which the artist had left on the table in front of her, and cut into some of the wires like an expert gardener shaping a fine example of topiary. Pulling at the fragments some more, she saw her object transform from a lifeless clump into a girl on a swing holding a bouquet of flowers.

"*Que fantastico,*" said the artist with a half smile and perhaps a bit of embarrassment. "I didn't think you could do it. It's very pretty. And you work so fast!"

"Thank you," she looked at the spool she'd purchased from him, seeing that more than half of it thankfully still remained. "It's a gift for you. Hasta luego." She set her tiny statue on the table and walked off, holding the leftover wire in one hand and Apollo's hand in the other.

Moseying back to the tower so as not to draw too much attention to themselves, Aurora gave the wire to Apollo. "Will you stick one end through the fence and wrap it around the base of the tower in a loop?"

He did exactly as she'd asked, carefully forming a large circle by snaking the copper wire through the fence along the gravel on one side before walking around and repeating the action on the opposite end and then joining the circle together with a twist.

Aurora took the attached spool, which still contained another twenty feet of wire and walked as far away from the tower as she could so as not to raise any suspicion. She then sat on the pavement, motioning for Apollo to stand in front of her while she unscrewed the cap on her finger and tied the other end of the wire around the hidden blade. She felt the current of electricity rise within her and then began her search for signals she might recognize. "I'm at the Day of the Dead festival near the West Sahara Library," she messaged, having picked up on what she believed was Sai's wavelength. "I need you and Shafeen to come get me. I've found another robot, and I need you to take him with us." She realized the inaccuracy in the last part of her message, but she didn't want to over-explain her predicament. Surely, they'd understand once they met Apollo.

Sai answered right away. "I don't know how you managed to signal me, but we'll be there as soon as we can. Hold tight."

Aurora tried to relay a quick word of thanks, but the signal cut off abruptly. She'd be sure to express her appreciation in person once he and Shafeen arrived. "Can you gather the wire for me?" she asked Apollo while at the same time unwinding the coil from around the blade before screwing her finger back into place.

"As long as we get to play the game next," he said as he

began rolling the spool in his hands, effectively erasing the copper trail between them and the tower.

"We're headed there next just like I promised."

Making their way to the row of games tucked in between the food vendors and innumerable memorials, Aurora and Apollo found the attraction they'd been waiting for. Eight lanes of Skull-ball attached to a large trailer filled with giant plush skeleton dolls, each covered in fluorescent hearts and floral shapes, stretched out before them, beckoning them to test their skills.

"Ten dollars to play," said the carnival barker who stood in a black sombrero in front of the whimsical scene.

"We'd each like to play." Aurora handed the man a twenty-dollar bill. "What does it take to win a prize?"

"Anyone with a final score over eight thousand after one minute wins a small doll," explained the man. "If a player hits twenty thousand points before the minute is done, he gets a large doll. Only one large win allowed per session."

Aurora didn't quite see how that was fair. Regardless, she knew that she and Apollo would both easily win one of the small skeletons. *A shame that Apollo couldn't also win one of the large prizes like she'd planned on taking.* "Pick a machine, Apollo. Do you know what to do?"

"Yes. I understand," he said in a quiet and calm way that failed to convince Aurora.

"Are you ready?" asked the man taking hold of an Am-pliVoice. "*Uno. Dos. Tres. Vamos.*"

A single white ball with the image of a playful looking skull rolled down the chute on each of their machines. Aurora took hold of hers before rocketing it straight up the ramp at the precise speed necessary to lift it directly into the five hundred-point hole at the very top. She repeated the exact motion like clockwork for the next forty-five seconds, attaining a perfect shot every single time. Having achieved a whopping tally of 15,500 points, she took it upon herself to glance at Apollo's scoreboard.

Nineteen thousand?

It didn't make any sense. She'd rolled a continuous perfect game without stopping. Had she applied any more speed to the ball, she'd have missed the highest scoring pocket every time. *How was it that Apollo could be that much further ahead?* She watched his technique for clues. Surprisingly, he used a much swifter roll, but instead of taking a direct path up the ramp, he made the ball ricochet off the rubber side of the bank about two thirds of the way up the incline, which quickly sunk the ball in the top spot. He didn't stop or flounder once. Victory was his.

"Felicitaciones, amigo. You win the big prize. Which color would you like?"

Apollo chose a green one for himself while Aurora picked out a yellow one from amongst the smaller variety.

"Good work, Apollo!" She patted him on the back before leading them further into the carnival-like section of the festival. *How could he have figured it out better and faster than she had?* It didn't make sense to her. She'd been around much longer than he had. They had near identical motherboards. Truly, it didn't matter either way. Aurora enjoyed the fact that he'd taught her a more effective strategy. *If only she could have figured it out for herself in the first place.*

"I think he wants the toy I won." Apollo pointed to a boy about four years of age whom he caught eyeing the giant cotton-filled skeleton in his hands. "I'm going to give it to him." He walked over to the child half his size and set the huge doll next to him."

"Thank you!" said a woman who looked to be the boy's mother. "We're here because my husband just passed away. I've been trying to do everything I can to make my two children happy, but they've been so sad and upset."

Aurora sympathized. "Is that your sister?" she asked the boy, pointing to a younger toddler in a yellow dress sitting in a stroller next to him.

He nodded shyly with a smile.

"Then this is for her." She placed the small doll in the tiny girl's lap. "I'm so sorry about your loss," she said to the distressed woman and her children. "It's a very difficult thing to lose someone you love so dearly. We wish you much solace."

chapter 22

Pulling into the Durango Electric parking lot, Christina wiped the sweat from her palms on her navy blue pantsuit. She hadn't felt this uneasy about the place since she first interviewed for the job with David over five years ago. The office seemed like the last place she'd visit on her furlow except that she didn't have a choice if she wanted to foil Cyphan Creek's disastrous plot. She needed to stop the bombs from being loaded onto the trucks before they destroyed innocent lives. As much as she hated the idea of confronting Bill again, she realized that if she didn't intervene, she'd surely hold herself forever accountable for the resulting explosions.

Walking through the front entrance as she always had, she noticed something different about the late morning air, as if it didn't belong to her even though she had every right to breathe it in just like everyone else. She dreaded walking through her old workspace, not wanting to explain to any of the new employees who she was or why she'd returned. She didn't have the time or energy. She had to save every bit of gumption she had in order to convince Bill to stop a ghastly scheme from ruining his electronic empire.

"Good morning." She attached her ID badge to her suit jacket's lapel before walking up to her former desk. "Would you mind if I made a quick in-office phone call?"

A young woman with pink highlights in her hair, presumably Trent's assistant, responded to the request with a flippant adjustment of her reading glasses. "Excuse me?"

Who did this young chick think she was? Christina felt the urge to slam her fist on the desk. She didn't have time to play games, so she just pointed to her ID. "Please, may I use the phone?"

The woman readjusted her glasses in order to have a better look at Christina's name tag. "I'm sorry, Ms. Daily. I've heard that you're quite the department wizard around here."

"Um...thank you?" Christina didn't need flattery as much as she needed to simply use the phone.

"You'll have to forgive me. We've been getting a lot of traffic through the office in anticipation of the merger."

Merger? Absent only a week, and Christina apparently had fallen completely out of the loop. Be that as it may, she didn't care what the company had planned. Today, she only wanted to make sure that innocent people didn't die as a result of her remaining silent. "No problem. I understand." *When in doubt, empathize.* "This has always been a busy department. Ever since I started five years ago, it's been non-stop activity. I know what you're all going through right now. It gets a little nuts, doesn't it?"

"You're right about that, Ms. Daily." She extended her hand to properly greet Christina. "I'm Melinda, by the way. Melinda Bisbee." She pointed to her own name badge and giggled.

"Ms. Bisbee, it's a pleasure."

"Oh, Ms. Daily, thank you. You can just call me Melinda."

Christina understood the let's-make-acquaintances game very well. She'd mastered it, having played it millions of times throughout her career. She just didn't want to play it today. *Not when employees at the loading dock unknowingly handled explosives, stacking them by the dozen in the back of a delivery truck.* "Melinda, would you mind if I used the phone now?"

"Oh, goodness." Melinda laughed. "I almost forgot. Go right ahead."

Picking up the receiver, Christina dialed Bill's four digit extension from memory. *Could Melinda do that? Probably not.* "Good morning, Bill. It's Christina. Do you have a minute?"

"Well, well, well. I figured you'd be out enjoying your free time elsewhere than at the office. Or have you come to a decision regarding your future career path with us?"

Relieved that she hadn't caught him too off guard, she regained her composure and collected her thoughts. At least he presumed she had a reason to contact him, regardless of how off base it was. "I actually have a more pressing matter to discuss with you about the new Arizona showroom. Do you have a minute? I'd like to come talk to you about it now in person. It's urgent."

"It's a very busy morning on campus today, Christina. Now isn't exactly a good time."

Would it ever be? She didn't want to say too much over the phone, but she felt her desperation rising. "The safety of your employees is at stake. I need to talk to you right away."

Bill loudly exhaled. "So be it. I'll see you here shortly." He didn't sound pleased, but that made no difference to her.

"Thank you." Christina handed the phone back to Melinda and walked out into the hall that led to Bill's office. She already felt slightly better than when she'd first entered the office three minutes ago. Finally, she had someone to help ease the burden of having to protect innocent lives. Her own shoulders could only handle so much. It hardly seemed fair that God would bestow upon her the responsibility of saving the world, but that's exactly how it felt.

Pausing outside Bill's office door, she heard him talking to someone. He sounded angry as he spoke, and she assumed it best to wait a second before knocking.

"It cost the company ten million dollars to get her back. You do know that, don't you?"

"I'm well aware, and yet I can't change the fact." The male voice sounded calm and resolute against Bill's uncharacteristic shouting. She recognized it right away as Trent's. "I don't think you know what you're dealing with. You don't understand her capacity to reason. You think she's just a harmless plaything, but nothing could be further from the truth. You can't contain her."

"Stop right there. Nobody tells Bill Rucker what he can and cannot do. If you can't get me that girl, then you'll figure out how to build me one exactly like her. And if you can't do that, I'm quite certain you won't have a future with Durango Electric."

The office door opened, and Trent came bursting through it, clutching a DimensionTab to his chest with the seriousness of a preacher clinging to the holy book. "I wouldn't go in there if I were you, Ms. Daily. He'll roast you alive."

Christina decided to take her chances. Having just learned that Aurora had escaped a second time, she felt both elated and surprisingly more confident. "May I come in?" She popped her head inside the partly opened doorway.

"Yes, Ms. Daily. I'm sorry if you had to hear any of that. We're having a challenging day, but we'll muddle through. We always do." Bill stood up and straightened a stack of papers on his desk, tucking them into a folder, which he then quickly filed in a cabinet behind him. "Now—what can I do for you?"

"I see things are busy. I promise I'll only take a minute of your time." Christina felt herself getting a little flush as her heart began to pound. "I know this sounds weird, but

I have a very good reason to believe that there are bombs being loaded right now onto one of your trucks."

"Interesting." Bill briefly turned his attention to the light in the ceiling above him before returning it back to Christina. "And what exactly brings you to this conclusion?"

She didn't want to answer that question. At least not truthfully, not the whole truth anyways. "Someone doesn't want Durango Electric to succeed, and this person is determined to sabotage the company any possible way they can."

"I see." The corner of Bill's lips stretched into a superficial grin. "Do I know this person?"

Sensing his disbelief kick in, she suddenly realized that her task had just doubled in size. "It's not so much a person as it is a competitor." Her own words sounded ridiculous to her, and she wished she could just wipe her hands clean of the knowledge she'd gleaned from snooping.

"We're too big to have competitors, Ms. Daily. You should know that. You've worked here long enough."

"I have, Bill. Forgive me if I'm not making much sense. I'm trying to explain what I know in such a way that you'll understand." She didn't want to backpedal, but she didn't want to walk into a trap either. How exactly could she communicate her message without incriminating herself? That was the hurdle.

"I hate to say it, but you're failing miserably. Could you just say what you need to say and get on with it?"

"Cyphan Creek has conspirators working for her here at Durango Electric, and they're now loading a shipment packed with explosives headed for Bullhead City."

"Cyphan Creek?" He lifted an eyebrow. "As in Black Diamond's Cyphan Creek?"

"I didn't think there were any others." Christina contemplated letting it go and walking away, but she could only think about the innocent people involved and their poor families.

Bill laughed wildly. "Cyphan and I, we've had our ups and downs. That's no secret. But you have to admit that your story sounds a little out of whack. Cyphan and I are good friends now. We just had lunch the other day. We're hammering out the details for the buyout."

"You know about the buyout?" Christina felt foolish for a moment. *Was she the last person on the planet to understand everything that was happening around her?*

"Of course I know about it." Bill leaned back in his chair. "Buying Black Diamond was my idea to begin with. I approached Kenny and Cyphan about it over a month ago, and they both agreed that the acquisition is best for the future of both companies. They were receptive to the idea at first, and quite frankly, they're thrilled with our offer. Our company is growing, my dear. Which means even more opportunity on the way for aspiring employees such as *you*."

Christina smiled out of both courtesy and confusion as questions swirled in her head. Had she possibly misheard Cyphan Creek? Or had Bill been blindsided by his own delusions of grandeur? Was she the only one who truly understood the reality of the deal? The more she thought about it, the more she realized it had nothing to do with Durango Electric buying out anybody despite what the man in front of her wanted to believe. "Bill, I want Durango Electric to grow and be successful. But someone is trying every which way they can to prevent that from happening. Please at least take a moment to investigate the shipment that's headed for Bullhead City tonight."

"I know everything that's going on that truck. I hand-selected each item myself to fill that showroom floor for when it opens in three weeks. And I want you to manage it all."

She felt her efforts going nowhere. "I appreciate your confidence in me." She felt the absurdity of those words as they rolled off her tongue.

"As crazy as you might seem to others, I still know you're the gal to do it. Now what do you say? Are you ready to finally get aboard this train? I don't want to leave talent like yours behind."

She felt stuck. She wanted nothing to do with Durango Electric anymore. If she could be a part of anyone's team, it would be Aurora's and the legacy David had left behind. Durango Electric seemed like nothing more than a phantom of its former self. "If you promise to check that shipment, I'll get on board with you." She felt like she'd just betrayed herself and her girls, but if it saved lives, how could she not agree to the arrangement without feeling like a complete monster?

"You made the right choice, Ms. Daily. And you'll be rewarded for it. I promise you that. With the unstoppable direction this company is headed in, there'll be opportunities for you that'll blow you away."

Strange choice of words. She didn't care nearly as much

about opportunity as she cared about people's safety and well-being. "Thank you, Bill. I appreciate your faith in me. As long as you check that shipment before it gets sent on its way, I promise not to be a thorn in your side." She wished to check the shipment alongside him to ensure she'd truly done all she could, but that clearly wasn't an option available to her.

"You have my word, Christina." He winked at her as if to gain her trust. "I'll head down to the loading dock after I take care of some business first. Rest assured that I'll call you right away if I find anything out of the ordinary."

Christina took a deep breath, knowing she'd done all she could. "That means a lot to me. Thank you."

"You're quite welcome." He offered her his hand. "Thanks for being on board with us as we make history."

chapter 23

Shane removed the lid of his *TundraBottle*, taking an extra long sip of ice water before wiping a facecloth across his dripping wet brow. He'd finally made it through a yoga class since the unfathomable event, and even though he couldn't climb out of bed in time for his usual early-riser session with Christina, he'd gotten up the nerve to at least make it to the two o'clock *Sweat 'n Stretch*.

So this was life after loss.

He could do it. He didn't have a choice. The path lay ahead of him clear as the fragments of his broken chandelier. *It would make more sense once he put it together.* Not continuing along the journey seemed a much worse idea than trodding forth despite the difficulty. Loved ones died. None he'd ever known so intimately, but one simple fact remained—nothing in this life sticks around forever. He wanted to find meaning in his own life, but whatever ideas fluttered into his already scatterbrained mind only contributed to his melancholy. *Had David come into his life solely to bring him Aurora? Was she the missing link to his future happiness? If so, then why the hell would someone take her from him? How could he possibly get her back?*

Honestly, he couldn't. Shane didn't belong anywhere near the campus of Durango Electric. Even if he tried to get in there, he knew he didn't stand a chance making it past security. But Christina? Surely, she could do something. She had the golden keys. If anyone on this planet could bring Aurora back to him, it had to be her. She had to know this!

His watch vibrated the very instant he lifted his wrist to call her. "I was just going to reach out to you! How are you?"

"I've enjoyed better days off. It'd be a nice change of pace for things to go right for once."

Shane withheld his laughter. Didn't things always go her way? He wanted to know her secret to making life look so effortless, and he'd be damned if she told him more yoga. "I don't suppose now's a good time to ask for a favor then, is it?"

Christina paused for a second. "Actually, I needed a favor from you."

Dang it! Hadn't he done enough already by going with her to that godforsaken warehouse? Or was that for David's sake? "Maybe we can make a deal. I need you to use your pull at Durango Electric to get Aurora back."

314 / Daniel K. James

She laughed for a good ten seconds before gaining her composure. "Don't you think I'm already on it. She means a heck of a lot to me too, you know! Anyways, I've got some great news. She's escaped."

Instantly, his mood brightened. "Again?" Then why hadn't Aurora messaged him? He'd certainly get to the bottom of that ASAP.

"Apparently, they can't hold on to her no matter how hard they try. They're no match for her."

"That's my girl!" Shane clenched his fist against his side. Perhaps he didn't need yoga after all. What he needed was more wonderful news like this. "You have no idea how happy this makes me. I'm gonna get her back. We're gonna get her back. We've got to!"

"Is that good enough for you?" Christina hesitated a moment. "I'm mean, at least for right now? Can I ask you my favor?"

Shane sighed. She'd done a lot for him lately, and he wanted to repay her one day, except that he currently had a hundred other things on his plate to obsess over. "I'm listening, but I'm not making any promises yet."

"Do you remember that bugged shipment Cyphan Creek talked about?"

He wished to forget all about it. "I think so. Where is this going exactly?"

"I just left Durango Electric an hour ago. I spoke to Bill about the danger he's in. I told him everything. Well, almost everything."

"Would you get to the point? I'm sitting in a cold car

soaking wet from yoga." He didn't mean anything rude by it, but his mind still weighed heavily on why Aurora hadn't been in contact with him.

"I'm sorry. Yes, I'll make this quick. Bill said he'd check the shipment, and then call me if he found anything."

"And?" Getting antsy, Shane signalled for the Mogollon to take him straight home. He'd listen and nod along while at least getting somewhere he wanted to be.

"He just called to tell me that he found nothing except a couple of measly wasps, which he said nearly stung him."

"*Perfecto. Problemo Solvo!*" Shane found it fun to at least pretend he could speak a foreign language. Alas, he knew better than to assume Christina had finished her story.

"The truck is still bugged, Shane! He didn't look hard enough. Either he didn't care to, or those pesky hornets threw him off the hunt. He was supposed to stop that delivery. He didn't. And that truck is scheduled to leave Las Vegas in half an hour. We've got to get to Bullhead City before they unload it or innocent people are gonna get hurt."

"Why is this our problem?" That didn't sound right. "Correction: Why is this *your* problem? You've done your duty. What makes you think anyone will even listen to you once you get there? Are you gonna get inside that truck yourself and show them what they've allegedly missed? Forgive me for being realistic, but that sounds a bit stupid."

"I'm going with or without you. You don't have to lift a single finger. But it sure would be nice to know that someone at least had my back when I try to help save innocent lives."

What was it with everybody needing so desperately to be a hero? Shane couldn't possibly be the only one left on the whole freaking planet who simply wanted to mind his own business. It almost made him feel guilty. His whole life, his parents had instructed him to stop worrying about everyone else and focus on himself. Now he couldn't help but feel as if the old, helpful advice had somehow morphed into a crime against humanity. "Fine. I'll go. But you have to let me shower first. I refuse to sit in my own stink all the way there."

"Thank you! I knew you wouldn't let me down. I'll be at your place in half an hour."

Returning home, Shane hurried through a less-than-satisfying, soapless rinse. He hadn't even finished pulling his long-sleeve knit shirt over his head when he heard his watch buzz against the quartz countertop of the bathroom sink. "It hasn't even been twenty minutes yet!" he shouted to nobody but himself, hearing his voice echo down the empty hallway and through the main entry. He picked up his watch and saw he was mistaken. He was five minutes late. "I'll be right there. I'm sorry, I'm just putting my shoes on now."

He ran out the front door and into the circular driveway, carrying a knapsack in which he hoped contained some leftover post-workout snacks tucked in one of its many superfluous pockets. "If I didn't love you so much, I'd have told you to kiss my ass."

"I love you too." Christina laughed with her usual air of lightheartedness. "Did you lock the front door at least?"

"I think so, but we're not going back to check it. If the

place gets ransacked, it won't be any worse than what the FBI has done. Plus, my insurance covers break-ins from robbers—just not government crooks."

"Believe me. I'm as bitter about that chandelier as you. I always loved the way that thing reflected the light. But let's talk about something else. Something that'll keep us enlivened on our way. Did you get ahold of Aurora?"

Shane didn't want to think about the chandelier, but now he had no choice. *Did Christina not understand how thoughts worked?* "I messaged her, but she hasn't responded back. For the sake of my own sanity, I've convinced myself that she's busy and that she'll respond when she gets a free moment."

"You're handling things way better than I would if one of my daughters ever turned up missing." Christina reached behind her for her purse and pulled out a granola bar. "You want one? I bet you're starving."

He wanted to ask if she had more than just one to offer, feeling his stomach start to cave in on itself. He'd gone for so long without an appetite that ever since it returned, he couldn't seem to eat enough to satisfy himself. Progress? He hoped so. "Thank you. That yoga session kicked my butt, and now all I can think about is food. Maybe that's why I'm not letting myself get overly concerned about anything. I don't have the energy."

"I'm buying you dinner on our way home." Christina half unwrapped the granola bar for him. "Hopefully, this will tide you over."

"I love it. You're such a mother. Thank you. Just an FYI:

I can open my own snacks." Shane's watch vibrated as he brought the much needed nourishment to his lips.

"Goodness, is that her?" Christina drew her focus right to Shane's wrist as if she also felt the slight vibration.

"I'm free." Shane read the text aloud. "I'm back where I'm safe. And I have a surprise for you next time we see each other."

"I knew she'd be okay!" Christina clapped with giddy excitement. "She's never failed us. Not once."

"We're headed to Bullhead City." Shane spoke into his watch. "Christina and I could probably use your help. Is there any possible way you could maybe lend a hand? Christina says innocent lives are at stake."

"Perfect!" Christina clapped yet again while Shane tried not to let her enthusiasm annoy him too much. "I didn't even think to get her involved, but that's exactly what we need. Tell her where we're going."

"Okay." Shane took a deep breath, catching himself before saying something sarcastic. "You tell me first because I honestly have no clue. This whole thing was your idea. Remember?"

"Just tell her that we're headed to the brand-new Durango Electric Showroom in Bullhead City."

Did the place have an address? Shane didn't feel like asking. He figured Aurora was more than capable of figuring that part out herself. "We're headed to the Durango Electric Showroom in Bullhead City." He tapped his watch to send the message and then finished eating the remainder of his granola bar.

"Is she coming? Did she respond yet?" Christina sounded more excited over the whole prospect than Shane could handle.

"I promise you'll be the first person I tell once I get a response." He reached for his own bag between his feet, feeling inside it for even the crumbs of a previous meal. A bit ornery, he blamed his low blood sugar for any snide remark that might eke its way out of his mouth.

"Please, eat my granola bar." Christina handed hers to him unopened this time. "I'm too worked up to eat, and your mood could clearly benefit from a few more calories."

He politely took the red foiled package from her outstretched hand, doing everything not to appear savage or greedy. He hated feeling crabby, especially in the presence of someone who continually bent over backwards to help him out. "You're a real friend. I promise I'll be more fun when the dust finally settles." He used his teeth to tear into the fickle wrapper. "My hunger isn't helping right now, but at least it's a sign that I'm getting better."

"No need to apologize. My feelings aren't hurt. I'm just glad I don't have to make this drive by myself."

"Where are your girls?" He considered it a fair question. He'd just heard her say how worried sick she'd be if anything ever happened to them. "I'm sure they would have loved to go on an exciting adventure with their heroic mom."

"I thought about bringing them. Honestly, I did. But they don't need to see me in a compromised situation, especially when things could get ugly. So this is Joanna's first time playing the role of sitter for any stretch of time longer than a routine trip to the grocery store. I promised the girls I'd be home by nine o'clock—in time to make sure they go to bed at a decent hour."

"They're wonderful people, just like their mother." Shane couldn't tell if what he had to say next would lighten or kill the mood. "So if that truck blows up with you inside it, rest assured that I'll make sure your girls are in good hands."

"Thanks. I think." Christina shook her head in mock disgust. "I'd appreciate not only your willingness to help out, but also your vote of confidence in me."

***

The Yosemite pulled into the massive, empty parking lot of a brightly lit mega-box retail outlet with a giant Durango Electric lightning bolt emblem erected at the main entrance. In the center of the vast asphalt expanse, spotlights stood eerily dark like motionless sentinels. A large white banner announced the grand opening in three weeks—only if a grave tragedy didn't strike the place ahead of time.

"Where are the trucks?" Shane sprinkled a hint of skepticism behind the question, as if to suggest that the journey had been nothing more than an exercise in hunger management.

"I'm gonna guess that they're around back where the unloading docks are." Christina looked straight at him with serious eyes. "Did you want to make a wager that they're not?"

"No, I'm good. Now that you mention it, those were my exact thoughts." Having eaten his *and* her granola bar, he could no longer use his raging appetite as a reason for being difficult.

The Yosemite brought them around the building according to Christina's instructions, and they came upon a twisting network of ramps. Two of them led up to the building's second story while another trailed downward to what seemed to be a basement for storage, and still another curved up and around the far side of the mega structure.

"Where the hell do we go now?" Shane felt a trickle of resentment take the place of his impending exhaustion.

"Right there!" Christina pointed out the windshield to a silver truck headed down the ramp. "That's the same one I saw earlier today at the loading dock!"

"You gonna follow it?" He assumed the answer would surely be a *no*, but he felt like being a smart ass.

"Take us down the ramp behind that truck," Christina spoke into the dashboard microphone.

"Oh, crap!" Shane felt their journey transform into a nightmare. Venturing into an area where they clearly had no business or permission, who knew what trouble they'd be in? "I can't believe you're actually taking us down here."

"Did you want me to turn around? Is this too upsetting for you?" Christina sounded playfully condescending, but he was in no mood to play.

"Just so you know, I'm not getting out of this truck." Shane locked his car door in a showy attempt to emphasize his staunch position.

"Nobody's forcing you." Christina engaged the emergency brake once the Yosemite came to a complete stop on the ramp a good twenty feet behind the truck. "You can stay here while I go talk to them."

Shane couldn't object as long as he didn't have to get involved. He imagined what she'd say to them, how crazy she'd appear to these gentlemen who only wanted to do their job and then retire for the night. Why would they take her seriously when she could have just as easily reported the threat to the Bullhead City police? *More importantly, why hadn't he thought of that question sooner?*

Christina walked up to two of the men from the truck who looked confused as to why a green pickup had followed them to a restricted zone. Shane saw her pointing to their haul, speaking with noticeable emphasis. She didn't look quite as crazy as he'd imagined she would, but he still considered the whole scenario absolutely bananas. He felt relieved the second he saw her walking back to the Yosemite.

"So tell me—what did they say?" Shane asked the second she opened the door. "Do they think we're lunatics?"

"Thankfully, no. They've asked us to back out of the ramp for our own safety, and they're going to inspect the shipment. They'll call the police if they find anything suspicious."

"Why didn't we call the police to begin with?" Shane so wished he'd asked this key question before they'd left Las Vegas.

"Because," Christina took a deep breath as if bothered

by the question, "the police would have just called up Bill Rucker, and he'd have told them that there's nothing to worry about because he looked over the entire shipment himself after one of his overdramatic employees suggested him to."

Shane stayed quiet. Even if he questioned his friend's ability to reason, he didn't want to risk insulting her further than he already had. Instead, he simply rummaged through his bag in hopes of finding some gum with which to keep his opinionated mouth from stirring trouble. At the same time he managed to secure a piece of Trident, he felt his watch vibrate. *A response from Aurora?* He pulled his wrist out of the bag, gum in hand, and read the text. "Oh, dear God. She's here."

"Who? Aurora?" Christina sounded suddenly perky. "I told you we didn't need the police."

"We're behind the building," Shane spoke into his watch, "hanging out on a ramp leading to the basement." He didn't want her help. He didn't think they needed it in the first place. He only wanted to see her again.

"Who is she with? Did she say?"

"I'm not gonna load her circuits with questions." Shane didn't care about the details as long as he got her back. Right now, the thought of seeing Aurora provided him with his only sense of normalcy—ironic, considering that she was anything but.

Christina looked in the rearview mirror to briefly adjust her already perfect hair. "There she is! She's right behind us!"

Shane turned around to see a pair of motorcycles parked on the ramp in back of the Yosemite. He didn't expect to see four bodies, but there they stood, an adult male, an adult female, and two young children, all of them dressed in royal blue and white riding gear with matching safety helmets. "Holy Tallahassee! She's brought an entire entourage with her." He jumped out of the vehicle and ran toward the one most shaped like the little girl he loved and adored. "I'm so glad you're here. Who are all these people?"

Aurora took off her helmet, placing it in the bin at the rear of the bike. "This is my riding partner Sai." She pointed to the tall man who offered an outstretched hand to Shane. "And this is my friend Shafeen."

Shane shook her hand as well before turning his attention to the last nameless face remaining. "And who is this little guy?"

Aurora smiled proudly in a way he'd never seen before, her cheeks turning rosy pink in the white light of the lamp up above. "This is Apollo. He's a very special friend of mine."

"Not like a—boyfriend?" Shane felt embarrassed just saying the word. First of all, she was way too young to even entertain the thought of courtship. Secondly, she was a robot. Nothing about the idea seemed remotely natural.

"No!" She'd never sounded so emphatic before. "It's not like that at all. I'll explain everything later when we have more time. Right now, we're here to help."

Christina came running up the ramp toward the welcome party. "Hi, I'm Christina." She politely waved to each of the new faces in an expeditious manner. "I'd normally go for a more polite introduction, but we have a problem. One of the workers thinks he's spotted an explosive and wants to call in the police."

"There might not be enough time for that," Sai stepped forward as he spoke. "And more often than not, they just end up getting in the way. Shafeen and I are trained in this sort of thing. We'll take a look."

Shane watched the two mysterious strangers sprint down the ramp toward the truck, their bright riding suits reflecting the glow of the powerful overhead lighting. "Who in the world just shows up to stop a bomb right before it detonates?"

"It may or may not be an explosive," Apollo jumped in the conversation. "Aurora once encountered something thought to be an explosive when in actuality it was a device installed only to resemble one."

Aurora closed her eyes for a moment. "I'm putting CADI in buffer mode."

"What's buffer mode?" asked Apollo.

"I'm with him. What's buffer mode?" Shane couldn't help but repeat the young boy's inquiry.

"Don't worry about it." Aurora opened her eyes again. "All that matters is that it's working."

Sai and Shafeen returned a few moments later with nothing except smiles on their amicable faces.

"Good news?" Christina clasped her hands in front of her chest.

"It doesn't look like there are any explosives in the truck." Shafeen came back to her bike and began wheeling it to the edge of the ramp where it wouldn't be in the way. "I've told the workers that we're FBI trained explosive technicians and that the four of us will gladly unload each and every piece of their inventory and inspect it before it goes out onto the floor in case we missed something during our initial cargo scan."

"Four of us—as in?" Shane automatically assumed he'd been volunteered against his well.

"Sai, Aurora, Apollo, and myself," Shafeen clarified.

"Hmmm." Suddenly Shane felt left out of something important, which didn't make any sense to him. *What did those four have that he didn't?* An idea came to him, but he dismissed it as an utter impossibility.

"Apollo, would you move my bike behind Shafeen's?" Sai asked as he walked back toward the truck. "And Christina, I think it's best that you and Shane take your vehicle back to the parking lot away from any possible danger."

"I can't argue with that," Christina said, climbing into the front seat followed by Shane. Instructing the vehicle to reverse itself up the ramp, she looked in the rearview mirror and gasped. "What in the world?" Her jaw practically fell in her lap.

"What is it now?" Shane didn't see anything out of the ordinary in front of him. So he turned around only to see a four and a half foot tall boy lift Sai's motorcycle over his head and lay it gently back down behind the other. "Well, that's the craziest thing I've seen in the past month."

"Are you thinking what I'm thinking?" Christina turned her head to stare out the side window as the Yosemite reversed past the young and unassuming boy.

"Honestly?" Shane also looked out his window, shaking his head in disbelief. He'd witnessed some of the very strangest things ever since Aurora came into his life: her green glowing face, the parade, the wave pool, the piano concert, the giant Ferris wheel episode. He wondered why he had ever come to the silly conclusion that he'd seen it all. "I don't know what to think anymore. I just wait until someone comes along to explain everything for me."

Having secured the bike in its new parking spot, Apollo ran back down the ramp toward the company of those with whom he'd tagged along. He waited for a second in the headlights of the Yosemite and then dashed behind the semi truck.

"That has to be one of the weirdest things I've ever seen," Christina said as the Yosemite continued backing up the ramp, ultimately finding a suitable spot for them to await instructions from Aurora.

Curious as to what was happening out of his sightlines, Shane messaged her for details. "Do you see anything suspicious? Should we be concerned?" He folded his hands and set them in his lap, expecting to receive a reply any second.

"Make sure that they're opening the boxes," Christina said. "I bet that Bill didn't bother to open any of them."

"I have no doubt they know what they're doing." Shane felt his watch vibrate with a new text. He tapped the lower part of the face twice in quick succession so that the message would be read aloud.

"We're opening all the boxes."

Shane turned to Christina. "See? I told you they knew what to do."

"We haven't come across any explosives, but it seems that we've disturbed a hornet's nest. They're flying everywhere."

"Bill mentioned the exact same thing," Christina said. "Make sure she keeps on looking."

Shane laughed, knowing full well that Aurora wouldn't have the slightest reason to fear even a thousand hornets. "Good luck stinging titanium! I know Aurora. She's probably got those little boogers wrapped around her finger. She could fend off any beast big or small."

"I can't stand even the thought of it." Christina shuddered. "The idea of being held up inside that truck with a bunch of cruel and angry insects. I'd die of fright before I ever got stung."

Shane's watch vibrated again and he double tapped it once more.

"The hornets have dispersed. We've gone through almost every box of televisions. We don't think there's anything here to be honest."

"That's exactly what Cyphan Creek wants them to believe." Christina had never sounded so paranoid before. "Just when they think it's safe, something's gonna go *boom*, and we'll all be dead."

"You only want something to explode so that you can say we came all this way for a reason." Shane actually felt relieved they'd found nothing. Getting out of the house wasn't such a bad thing. Leaving town had given him some much needed perspective. The last thing he wanted in his life was more drama. *Praise be to Jesus, Buddha, and the Dalai Lama if it meant everything and everyone was safe for once.*

"No!" Christina nearly sounded like she could cry all of a sudden. "I want to be wrong. I want to be able to take you to dinner on the way home and apologize for being overdramatic. I don't want anyone to get hurt. I don't want anything to blow up. I just have a horrible feeling."

Shane's watch vibrated yet again with another update from Aurora. He lifted his wrist and brought it closer to Christina so that she could hear what would hopefully be the final message and that everything was all clear.

"We've decided to unload the whole shipment to be sure. The men on the truck recognized me as David's niece, and they're so happy just to be able to shake my hand. They think that what I do is wonderful, and they're grateful that I've come here with my friends to help them. They've told us exactly where inside the warehouse to bring all of the televisions. We've asked them to stand back from the truck in case there's any possible danger still hidden within or underneath it."

"Would you like us to do anything to help?" Shane spoke into his watch.

"Tell her that we're not going anywhere until we know everyone is safe." Christina sounded adamant with her request despite the fact that nobody was objecting.

"We're right here, Aurora, in case you need anything." Shane wondered if he had any chewing gum left in his bag.

"I'm honestly glad nothing happened." Christina pushed a button on the side of her seat, allowing it to recline. "I think there are two sodas back there if you'd like to reach for one. You like cherry cola, right?"

Better than gum! Shane turned around in his seat to reach for the refreshingly sweet beverages, already salivating at the thought of their fruity effervescence. He picked them both up, but they fell from his hand when the truck violently shook with a loud rumble. "That wasn't an earthquake, was it?"

"That was an explosion." Christina whispered the words, almost as if the sound of her voice might cause another one. "What did I tell you?"

Shane waited for his watch to vibrate, alerting him that answers were forthcoming. "Let's not jump to conclusions. I'm sure Aurora will tell us everything."

"Should we head back down the ramp?" Christina posed the question as if it actually seemed like a smart thing to do.

"We're staying right here." Shane counted the seconds, waiting for a message to come through. "I'm not putting myself in harm's way when neither one of us knows what the hell just happened."

"Then get me my cherry cola," Christina said, resuming her reclined position. "If I'm gonna die here, I'm gonna do it drinking something I love."

"Cheers to that!" Shane picked up the two cans he'd

grasped moments ago and popped each of their tops, handing one to Christina.

Before either of them could even take a sip, they spotted Aurora running up the ramp toward the car, cradling what appeared to be Apollo.

"Good Lord!" Christina jumped out of the car. "We've gotta help her, Shane."

He set down his beverage in the cup holder and followed Christina out of the vehicle toward Aurora. "What happened? We heard a rumble. We didn't know what to do." He almost felt guilty for not taking Christina's advice and heading back down the second they'd sensed the calamity. "And where are your other two friends?"

"They're fine. Everyone's fine," Aurora spoke the words with an unusually pained expression, demonstrating that nothing could be further from the truth. "He's just a little scuffed, that's all. He'll be all right." She headed straight toward the Yosemite not even looking at either Christina or Shane. "We need to take him to the safe place. Will you help us, Christina? We need your help. He can't ride on a motorcycle right now. Can you take us there in your truck?"

"Of course I can help," Christina said with tears in her eyes. "I'll take you wherever it is you need to go. We're all gonna help you get there. We're all gonna help, isn't that right, Shane?"

"Yes, but I still need to know what the heck just happened!" He stared at the motionless boy in Aurora's tiny arms.

"The box Apollo was carrying exploded along with an entire pallet of televisions. He was by himself when the cockroaches scattered across the floor and detonated. It's pouring rain inside now. Sai and Shafeen are helping to extinguish the fire."

Shane tried to process everything she said, but his racing heart made it difficlut to concentrate. "Thank God you're okay."

Together, he and Aurora lifted Apollo into the bed of the truck. Shane maintained a blank, glazed look the entire time, trying to comprehend the last five minutes. Moments ago he'd felt the entire parking lot shake beneath him when all he wanted was an excuse to sit back, kick up his feet, and drink an ice cold soft drink like a kid without a care in the world. Now he was sick to his stomach, exactly like how he'd felt after witnessing a horrible bike crash months ago. The ill feeling came upon him whenever something completely out of his control happened.

Was it his responsibility to step in and make everything better? Not that he didn't want to. He absolutely wanted to. He'd flick a magic wand every which way if he could. He honestly wanted to help. He just didn't know how.

chapter 24

Gazing out the window from the small back seat of the Yosemite, Aurora took note of the constellations. She'd never seen so many. How much brighter they appeared outside the city limits! Even brighter than from right outside her secret home in The Gloaming. She wished Apollo could spot them with her—if only he weren't tied up in a lifeless bundle in the bed of the truck. Sure as a shining star, she'd see to it that he became good as new again. "There in the northeast, that's Cassiopeia," she called out to Christina and Shane who sat up front.

"Is now really the best time for an astronomy lesson?" Shane said, sounding drained.

"I think she's trying to lighten the mood," Christina whispered, pointing to the upper righthand corner of the windshield. "It's that one over there—shaped like the letter *W*."

"You'll have to do better than that. There's got to be a million of those." Shane leaned his seat back a few degrees. "I can't tell if I'm stressed or hungry. Either way, this isn't a good game for me. But you two have at it."

"You're no fun." Christina softly nudged Shane's arm. "Come on. What if I opened the moonroof?"

He sat silent for a second. "Do it," he said with a surprise burst of excitement.

"OPUS, open the moonroof," Christina said, leaning into the dashboard microphone.

"Now that's what I'm talking about!" Shane immediately brought his seat back to its upright position before standing up and sticking the top half of himself through the opening. "Wooooohoooo! I can see Lake Mead!" He abruptly sat back in his seat. "Wait. Why are we headed toward Lake Mead in the dead of night?" He sounded suspicious. "And can we please stop for food before we get there? My soda buzz wore off an hour ago. I'm about to eat my arm off."

Aurora tried to picture the grim scenario, but she couldn't quite grasp what he meant. Nonetheless, his condition sounded serious. "There's a Las Vegan Burger at the exit up ahead. Do you see it? Let's stop there. It'll be my treat." She pulled a hundred-dollar bill from her pants pocket and handed it to Christina. "Get whatever you like."

"Where did you get this?" Christina hesitated before taking hold of the crisp note.

"Oh, wow! Big spender!" Shane laughed before grabbing the money from Christina's hand. He held it to his eye as if to inspect it, and then returned it back to Christina. "I have a more important question. Does she have more wherever that came from?"

Aurora figured it best not to reveal her source of income too soon. She felt pleased she'd at least made him happy, and she planned to give him so much more one day. "Let's just say that I don't have much use for what little money I've managed to square away. I think it'll do a lot more good in someone else's hands."

"There's only one problem." Christina turned to look at Shane. "We can't exactly go through a drive-thru with a body in the bed of the truck."

"We wrapped Apollo in the tarp you had back there." Aurora felt satisfied by her own cleverness. She'd convinced Shane to help secure the bungee cords around the inconspicuous heap to keep Apollo firmly in place for the journey back to safety. "And besides, it's so dark out that I don't think anyone would recognize him from a sack of logs."

"How much like you is he?" Christina sounded cautious in the way she phrased her question.

"He's very much like me, except that he's not." Aurora assumed she made complete sense as she gave the brief explanation. Her answer seemed entirely self-evident.

"I'm sorry. What?" Christina turned around and looked straight at Aurora.

"We're getting way ahead of ourselves," Shane said. "Let's

get back to my question. Why are we headed to Lake Mead?"

"Because that's where Aurora told us we needed to go," Christina said as the truck pulled into the Las Vegan Burger drive-thru and up to the large touchscreen menu. "Now what would you like to eat?"

Aurora would have gladly offered Shane a more in-depth explanation, but she determined it best to let Christina have the last word.

"How about an order of *V* chicken wings, a *V* bacon classic, and *V* curly fries?" Shane licked his lips. "I hope this Lake Mead thing makes more sense after I eat."

"That's all you're getting?" Christina didn't wait for a response, but instead began ordering. She pushed tabs for multiple orders of not only what Shane requested, but for two double deluxe *V* burgers, *V* onion rings, two *V* cherry tarts, and a *V* chocolate shake. "I'm starving, and whatever I don't eat, I'll put in the girls' lunches tomorrow. Anything for you, Aurora?"

"I don't have much of an appetite right now." Aurora laughed, knowing she'd succeeded in at least somewhat enlivening a somber mood. "But thank you for asking."

The truck crested a hill, and in the distance Aurora saw Lake Mead shimmering like a blanket of pearls underneath a sliver of moonlight. "Stop the truck. This is where we get off the road."

"Off the road?" Christina sounded both tentative and puzzled. "I don't think I've ever done that before. I'm not sure I even know where to begin."

"Just stop the truck," Shane said. "If you pull over to the

side of the road, we can get the truck to go where we need it to go."

"Stop at shoulder," Christina said into the dashboard microphone, which brought the vehicle to an abrupt halt. "Now what do I do?" She turned to Shane.

"Let Aurora sit in the front seat." Shane tossed a French fry in his mouth. "She'll do the rest.

Christina hesitated a second, took a deep breath, and then exited the vehicle to trade places with Aurora. "You're a very special girl, Aurora. Whatever you do, please don't get us stuck."

"Not to worry. I know the way well." She buckled herself in and stared at the control panel in front of her. "Turn left and head to the mountain at one o'clock."

"I don't think the navigational system works that way," Christina said from the back seat.

"You're right," said Aurora. "It doesn't at all. I only said that so you two would have the benefit of knowing where we're headed. I'm controlling the path of the vehicle with my internal processor."

The truck's turning signal blinked as the vehicle slowly crossed over the empty lane. It headed straight across a rocky expanse toward a shadowy mountain in the distance.

"I can't believe it." Christina took a sip of her *V* shake through its extra wide straw. "We're actually offroading."

"What's there not to believe?" Shane asked. "We're driving on hard dirt. It's not like we're floating across quicksand."

Christina nearly spit out her milkshake as she reached her hand to playfully smack Shane on the shoulder. "This

338 / Daniel K. James

is a first for me, okay? Maybe if what we were doing was actually legal, I'd have a bit more experience."

"Since when do you play by the rules, my black operations queen?" Shane turned around in his seat and flicked a French fry at Christina's head.

"Don't waste food like that." Christina pulled the potato remnant out of her hair and threw it out the open window. "You could have at least aimed for my mouth."

"I should have. In order to shut you up."

Christina drew her fist in the air.

"I was just kidding." Shane cowered in his seat. "Kidding! It was a joke!"

The truck slowed down as it reached the bottom of a towering cliffside.

"This is it," Aurora said, feeling a sense of satisfaction at having made it safely to her destination. "We have to wait here for Sai and Shafeen before we head in. I imagine they'll be here in a few minutes."

"Look at all the stars," Christina said as she stepped out of the truck. "Are we even close to Vegas?"

"We're seven miles outside the city limits." Aurora got out of the vehicle and stood near Christina beside a lone Joshua tree. "It's a lot closer than it seems. The hills block out most of the city's lights. If you look up there a little to your right, you'll see Gemini."

"I've never been much good at spotting that one. Where is it exactly?" Christina crouched down, getting closer to Aurora's perspective.

"Do you see that bright star, there?" Aurora pointed

nearly straight above their heads near the apex of the sky. "That's Castor. It's part of Gemini. Now you can see it, can't you?"

"The twins?" Christina smiled. "You *know* how much I love astrology!"

Twins. Aurora liked the sound of that word. Something about its meaning felt invincible. If she had someone like her to back her up whenever things got particularly challenging, she couldn't possibly fail. "Yes, the twins. That's it exactly."

"I think we have company," Shane said, making his way out of the vehicle and toward the two stargazers. "Look up the hill. Is that who we've been waiting for? I certainly hope so, because it's getting really chilly."

"That's them," Aurora said. "They know we're here. I told them we'd be outside waiting for their arrival. Just give me a minute with them if that's all right." Aurora took off running for the bright headlights of the oncoming motorcycles. She'd gotten permission to bring Shane and Christina to the cliff entrance before they'd left the facility in Bullhead City. Now she wanted to get them additional privileges to venture inside The Gloaming if at all possible.

"You made it safely, I see." Sai turned off his motorcycle, having stopped a few feet from where Aurora stood by herself.

"We're all okay." Aurora smiled. "Except, of course, for Apollo. He's still wrapped in a tarp and secured in the back of the truck. We'll get him out of there and to his room, if that's okay."

"I'm not sure who you mean by *we*," Shafeen said, having pulled her bike right alongside Sai's. "If you're referring to your human friends, I'm afraid the answer is *no*." A stern look appeared across her darkened face. "You know the rules. Absolutely no humans allowed within The Gloaming."

"I just want them to know that I'm safe and well cared for. They're on our side."

"It doesn't matter whose side they're on." Sai placed his helmet in the box on the back of the bike. "It's dangerous enough that you've managed to bring them this close to our home. It's best that you send them on their way so that we can continue on with ours."

"But they can help us." Aurora hated being separated from the people she trusted most on earth. It hardly seemed justified that they couldn't come see where she lived. If only she knew who made the rules, she'd make her appeal. Surely they'd understand her point of view on the matter. Shane and Christina couldn't be any more of a threat than the water flowing through their sanctuary. If anything, getting them involved might actually benefit everyone.

"Foolish girl," Shafeen shook her long black hair as she removed her helmet. "I don't think you comprehend any of the things we've already been through with the humans. They fear us. They will destroy us. Maybe not your humans. But they know other humans who would love for nothing more than to dismantle every last nut, bolt, and screw that holds us together."

Aurora realized she couldn't change anybody's mind, not in the cold darkness of a November desert night. She knew her priority—getting Apollo back in working order, which would take quite a bit of ingenuity on her part. "I understand completely. Give me five minutes, and I'll send them on their way. I need a few things from them first."

"Take your time," said Sai. "We aren't going anywhere while they're still around."

"Thank you. I won't take long." She walked toward the truck, seeing that both Shane and Christina had gotten back inside it, most likely due to the uncomfortable chill in the air.

"Are we going to see your new home, or aren't we?" Shane asked impatiently from the open window.

"I wish it were that simple." Aurora stood outside in the dark. "They said that you aren't allowed. I tried to change their minds, but I couldn't. They've just now asked that you leave."

"That settles that." Christina climbed out of the Yosemite. "I'll help you take Apollo from the back of the truck. Then Shane and I will continue on our merry little way. Not a problem."

"I can't fix him without you." Aurora said the words unexpectedly, hoping they'd catch Christina's attention.

"I don't understand," Christina sounded both bothered and worried at the same time.

"His motherboard is damaged. He can't function without a replacement. I was going to sneak into Durango Electric and get it myself, but I think it might be better if you did instead and brought it back to me."

Christina let out an uncomfortable laugh. "You're partly

right. You have no business heading back there whatsoever. Unfortunately, I don't think I do either at this point. I want nothing to do with that company."

Aurora refused to let up. She didn't panic or sound desperate. She just kept focus on what she needed. "David built me to succeed. If you can't help me, I will help myself."

"If you head back to Durango Electric, I guarantee you that helping anyone will be the furthest thing from your future. They'll remove your processor and then scrap the rest of you. There must be another way."

"There is." Aurora remained firm in her stance. She knew that Christina could provide her with everything she needed in order to get her mission back on track. "Apollo's motherboard can only be printed from Durango Electric within Sector K. I absolutely need it in order to get him working again. He and I are meant to bridge the gap between human and artificial intelligence. It's what David wanted. It's why David built me to begin with. I need Apollo."

"I want to help," Christina said. "You both helped me tremendously today. But I don't have access to Sector K. And even if I did, I wouldn't know the first thing to do once I got inside it. It's the most complicated room ever built. David made sure that nobody could ever dare sneak inside it."

"I have access. I can get in."

Christina huffed. "Somehow that doesn't surprise me one bit. I'm sure you know the code or can modify your voice in whatever way required in order to open that door. But I can't in good conscience let you get anywhere near

that campus. You'll be history if you return. You do understand, don't you?"

Aurora took a step closer and spoke in a soft but firm
voice. "I need you to take my arm."

Christina warily reached for her hand. "Okay. And…?"

"Not my hand. I'm going to give you my arm. Can you
fit it inside your purse, or perhaps a briefcase?"

"Okay. This is officially the creepiest conversation I've
ever had, which is saying a lot since my daughters are two
very strange individuals."

"I'm sorry." Aurora wished to dispel any discomfort
regarding the prospect of handing Christina one of her
limbs. "My elbow is the key to Sector K. There is a panel
with a small impression on the wall just outside the secured entrance. Put my elbow in that indentation, and
the door will open. Shane will give you the password required to access the file that holds the blueprints for the
motherboard. I'll text it to him so that he can then give
it to you. You'll be in and out of there in fifteen minutes.
It's a very quick process."

"Are you sure there isn't another way?" Christina sounded hesitant, but not totally unwilling.

"The only other way is for me to do it myself. And you've
already ruled that option out. So no, there is no other way."

Christina erupted into laughter, like she'd just realized
everything was a giant prank. "So—you're just going to
give me your arm?" She laughed some more. "Just like that?
Pop! Off it goes."

Aurora didn't intend to make light of her request.

She'd been sincere about everything. However, to avoid rubbing anyone the wrong way, she laughed as well.

"What in Kentucky's name is taking you two so long?" Shane yelled out the passenger window.

"Just a minute, Shane." Christina chuckled some more. "Aurora's about to hand me something."

Aurora couldn't tell if Christina actually believed her or not, but that wasn't going to stop her from doing what she needed to do in order to ensure Apollo's recovery. Without further delay, Aurora removed the cap from over the secret blade hidden in her ring finger, and then she cut into the PelaDerm around her left shoulder.

"Oh my God! What are you doing?" Christina had a look of terror and panic in her eyes.

"It doesn't hurt me at all, I promise." Aurora finished making the incision before replacing the cap on her finger, and then she yanked her left arm out of its socket, handing it to Christina.

"You were serious?" Christina shrieked in horror and began crying.

Shane jumped out of the truck and ran toward them. "What the hell is going on? Why is she upset?" He sounded almost as frazzled as Christina.

"I'm trying to give her my arm. She needs to take it."

"This makes no sense." Shane stared at Aurora's open socket. "This makes absolutely no sense whatsoever."

"My elbow is a key. Christina needs it to unlock the door to the lab where she can then produce the part needed to repair Apollo. There isn't a better way to explain it than that."

Shane came nearer to a very disturbed but now somewhat quieter Christina. "I think it's best you take her arm. She's not going to let us leave without it."

"Don't make me hold onto it right now." Christina stood and walked back to the truck.

"I guess that means that I get to take it from you." Shane walked toward Aurora and held out his hand.

"It's not as cumbersome as it looks. It bends." She knew it wasn't customary for people to give their body parts to others, but she assumed Shane would understand that this was different. *No blood. No loose tendons. Only some exposed wires.* "You'll see what I mean. It'll be fine. Try not to get any dirt in the socket."

Cautiously, Shane took the arm from her. "My life cannot get any freakier than this. No way."

chapter 25

Christina held her head high as she walked into Durango Electric for what she hoped would be the last time. Before leaving the house, she'd chosen the biggest bag she could find, ignoring how hideous it looked. Within its marigold-patterned confines, she'd placed a deliberately concise letter of resignation. Other than the cream-colored envelope, her DimensionTab, and a carefully wrapped appendage, the bag remained empty enough to provide space for the few remaining belongings she'd kept at the office: miscellaneous jewelry, framed pictures of her daughters, a mug, and a small make-up kit.

"Good morning!" she said to Melinda Bisbee, walking to

the new admin's desk. "I've come to meet with Bill and then collect my things. You don't know where they've moved to by chance, do you?"

Melinda looked up from her workspace and smiled superficially, looking a bit on edge. "Bill said to let you know that they've been moved to his office for safekeeping. Security's been tightened recently."

No surprise there. Certainly not after last night's incident in Bullhead City. "Thank you." Christina felt tempted to ask why Bill had them instead of security or human resources. Was he intending to personally apologize for not heeding her warning regarding the shipment? *He owed her at least that!* "I guess I'll visit Bill now then if he's available."

"Could you wait right here, ma'am? I'll notify Bill that you've come to see him."

Ma'am? One word, and suddenly she felt like a complete stranger. *Five years with the company washed down the drain.* Did it bother her? She couldn't let it. Nobody was forcing her to quit. Quite the opposite. Christina had made the decision to leave on her own, and she'd walk out the door now if it weren't for the favor she owed Aurora. "I'll be on the sofa waiting."

Seated on a row of red *veather* cushions, she pulled out her DimensionTab and linked to the company's network. She hadn't handed in her resignation yet, so she technically could still log in, unless they'd disabled her access unbeknownst to her. Thankfully, they hadn't. In a few seconds, she brought up the log for today's lab usage. Sector K appeared to be available until one PM. That would allow her ample time to get what she needed and get out. If the surveillance cameras noticed her, and she knew they would, she'd make herself long gone before anyone could even question her presence in a restricted area. They'd likely be busy scratching their heads trying to figure out how she managed to breach the secured entry to begin with.

"He'll be here to see you in a moment, Ms. Daily." Melinda's tone sounded detached and devoid of any personality.

At least the girl remembered her name.

Either way, Christina couldn't be happier at the thought of never having to step foot inside these callous walls again. She had come here with dreams of technological achievement, but she'd unfortunately withdraw with nothing more than a cold dose of corporate reality and a truer understanding of how the world actually worked. "Thank you again. I'll wait right here for him." She hated the idea of coming across as worn and jaded. For whatever it meant, she wanted to at least leave them with the impression that she'd been a warm and friendly addition to the office. "If you want my honest opinion, the cucumber salad is the only thing worth getting from the vending machine. Everything else is stale, so I usually just bring my own lunch."

Melinda laughed, showing evidence of an actual human spirit. "Thank you! I've already figured that one out. In fact, I've had the cucumber salad twice. You're right. Nothing else is worth touching. I stopped trying after the third pile of breadcrumbs they shamefully advertise as a sandwich."

"I'm glad you and I share the same taste." Christina caught Melinda eyeing her frumpy bag and laughed at herself. "Don't get the wrong idea. This isn't my first choice for a purse either. It was the only thing I could find that would do the job today."

"What's all this funny business about?" Bill came through the gray door at the far edge of the office with a dumb grin on his face. "I thought we ran a serious operation."

Christina felt it best to continue on with the ironic theme of lightheartedness if she wanted any chance of getting what she came for. "We were having a lively discussion on the amazing assortment of lunch options in the office vending machines."

"That's up next on my list of things that need to change around here," Bill said. "The bagel place across the street makes a mint off us because of those abominable machines."

"Abominable? You make it sound as if they're about to grow white fur and walk about on their hind legs!" Melinda said.

Christina laughed at the image. *Maybe the new girl wasn't that dim-witted after all.* "Careful! Machines around here often develop minds of their own." She knew she was treading on thin ice the moment she said it, but she didn't care.

"The fun is adjourned." Bill snapped his fingers and looked over at Christina. "I think you and I have some business to discuss, my lady."

"You are correct. Where shall we have our discussion?" She hoped it would be somewhere more private than where she currently sat.

"Your belongings are in my office until we find a better home for them. We can start by walking in that direction."

He still didn't get that this was goodbye, did he? Christina stood from her seat, placing her DimensionTab back in her bag, careful not to disturb the article of most importance.

"If I weren't mistaken, I'd say that's an antique carpet bag." Bill held the door open for Christina as she walked through it and into the brightly lit corridor. "I don't suppose you have a floor lamp hidden in that thing."

She chuckled, but only to be polite. The last thing she needed was for him to glimpse inside it. "A woman never divulges what's in her purse. You have a wife. You should know that."

"I stand corrected. Forgive me for thinking your bag is older than I am." He walked in front of her, leading the way toward a place she'd been in only two times prior.

"It belonged to my grandmother actually." She wanted to keep the harmless banter going so as not to accidentally turn the light mood sour. "It's been in the family for a very long time. I brought it with me only to carry home my things."

"You say it as if you're leaving for good." Bill opened the door to his office and ushered her in to have a seat. "Is that what our meeting is going to be about?"

She reached in her bag, careful not to open it too wide, and pulled out the thin envelope. "I think we both know that it's for the best."

Bill sighed, disappointment appearing in his weathered eyes. "You may think it's the best choice for you, but I have much bigger plans for you than I've so far led you to believe."

"I don't want to move. I don't want to uproot my girls to put them in a new school system in the middle of the year."

He reached for the letter and set it in front of him without further acknowledging its existence. "No one will be working the Bullhead City showroom until yesterday's mess is cleaned up. Did you know a similar incident happened at the Burbank showroom last night?"

That evil bitch! "Are you serious?" Christina had no idea whatsoever, and she didn't want Bill to think she did, or that she was in any way responsible for either incident. *Had anyone told him that she'd been present at the Bullhead City showroom when it happened?*

"I wish I weren't. And I'm certainly very sorry that I hadn't paid more attention to your premonition. The authorities claim that it's our equipment that caused the blast. They've found absolutely no evidence of foul play But they haven't looked hard enough, have they, Ms. Daily?"

She felt her heart about to burst out of her chest. *How much did this man know? Where should she even begin?* "You and I both know that those televisions couldn't have caused last night's damage. I have one in my house. It's perfectly safe."

"You suggested that Black Diamond is trying to sabotage my company yesterday, did you not?"

Was this a question meant to trip her up? She didn't know how to answer it except truthfully. "Yes, I have reason to believe Black Diamond is behind yesterday's havoc." She wanted him to open the letter and dismiss her. She didn't deserve an interrogation. She'd done absolutely nothing wrong.

"I can't let you leave Durango Electric now. You're too valuable."

She couldn't have predicted those words with a crystal ball. They landed themselves so far from her previous train of thought. "I'm not sure there's even a place for me here anymore."

"I'll make one." Bill had a spark in his eyes as he spoke. "We could use another sales director. I'll triple your salary. You'll stay right here in Las Vegas. Your girls won't have to change schools."

Something didn't feel right about the proposition, but Christina couldn't get over the idea of tripling her income. That amount of money seemed so foreign to her, and yet she suddenly found herself desperately wanting it. "I don't understand what you mean, Bill. I don't have one iota of experience in sales."

"How'd you find out about Black Diamond's plot? You aren't working for them, are you?" Bill laughed at the idea he'd just supposed.

"Oh God, no!" The questions only got harder for Christina. She didn't want to have to explain herself, but she knew she had no other choice. "I'm opening a hair salon. I went to Black Diamond for consultation about signage. That's when I overheard—"

"I knew it!" Bill slammed his fist on his desk. "I love the idea of espionage, but only as long as I'm the one hiring for the spywork." Then Bill scratched his head. "Wait?

Why'd you go to Black Diamond for signage and not here in house?"

Christina almost laughed, but caught herself. Clearly this man didn't pay attention to his own company. "We lost most of our signage business over two years ago. It's practically nonexistent. Otherwise I would have gone through us. No question about it."

Bill stood up and paced around the perimeter of the office. "This is so enthralling. You're just what we need in order to ensure a successful takeover. What else did you find out?"

Frightened by his curious nature, Christina casually hid her bag beneath her seat. "Nothing else, I swear. I wish I'd heard about the Burbank plot. I'd have surely mentioned that as well."

"You weren't meant to open a salon, Christina."

She didn't know her purpose anymore, except to be a loving mother to her daughters. "I wasn't?" If only she could tell Bill's true intentions, she'd figure out how to properly arm herself against his ridiculous proposals instead of hypnotically going along with them.

"You were meant to halt Black Diamond from wreaking mayhem in our community. And I'm going to pay you to do it. Can you continue this salon nonsense a bit longer?" Bill took out a small notepad from his jacket. "I've got a list of things I need you to investigate."

"I don't think I'm at all ready for any of this." Christina shook herself awake from this intoxicating fantasy. She wanted to cry, but knowing exactly what David had to say about runaway emotions, she stopped her tears dead in their tracks. "It's all a bit too much."

"Think of your girls, Christina. They can't count on a mother who's investing all of her energy into running a business. With me, you'll work fewer hours than before. You'll even be able to make your own schedule. As long as I get the information, you get the money. And it won't be like this forever. Only until the merger. I'll arrange it so the company also pays you in stock options. You'll be a major shareholder in Durango Electric's ever-expanding empire. When the buyout is finalized, you'll be so wealthy that you'll never have to work another day in your life."

Christina knew he'd won. She couldn't run a salon as a single mother. In a flash, she'd reexamined everything that brought her to this exact moment. It only made sense. She loved being an investigator. She was good at it. No, she didn't like either company. But she couldn't bear the thought of the snakes at Black Diamond taking over Durango Electric. *They'd destroy the world if that happened.* She realized what she had to do. She had to put her prejudices aside and work the system. "When do you want me to start?"

"I have to draw up a contract with our team first. We'll be in touch with you in a few days about an official start date. As for right now, I have security outside waiting to escort you back to your car with your belongings."

Damn it! She didn't want an escort. She needed to complete her favor for Aurora. Unfortunately, the thought of breaking into Sector K suddenly seemed like the worst possible idea. Perhaps she'd find a way later, but for right now she'd have to explain to Aurora her inability to make good on their agreement. "Thank you. I'll gladly take the help." Christina stood from her chair and met Bill at the door.

"You didn't need that silly old bag after all, did you? He handed a white cardboard box to one of the security guards standing outside the door. "If you'll help Ms. Daily to her car with her belongings, I'd very much appreciate that. She's one of our top VIPs now."

"Thank you, Bill." Christina wanted to hate him, but she couldn't. He'd used his old midwest charm to win her back, and she couldn't blame him or anyone else for the predicament she faced. She'd made the decision long ago to be a hero in this world, and this was the next logical step in her quest.

Arriving at the Yosemite, she graciously took the box from the security guard. "Thank you, Alan. I'll be back soon. I promise."

"I know. We're expecting big things from you, Ms. VIP." He winked at her as she stepped up into the front seat.

Christina wanted to head back home, but glancing at the blinking green signal on her watch, she knew she'd received a call from Shane and figured it best to call him right away.

"Christina?" He sounded frenzied, which wasn't much different from how he usually communicated during a phone call.

"I'm just leaving work now. What's going on?"

"Aurora asks that you hold off on getting that motherboard replacement. They've kidnapped Apollo."

chapter 26

"Command Central does not look favorably upon you, Aurora." Sai entered the small rock-walled enclosure, shutting a reinforced steel door behind him.

Unable to move from her seat, Aurora looked up at the angry machine, no longer knowing whether she still had a friend in him. "Must I be restrained? I've done nothing wrong, and my brother needs my help." She examined the titanium bands that held her to the chair, two across her lone forearm, two across each of her thighs, and three around her torso. She'd tried to break through them several times already, but the bonds had won out.

"I did not put you in here." He came nearer to her, taking

a seat across the small table between them. "I had nothing to do with that decision, and I'd release you if I could. They are fearful of the breach in security. They do not yet know who is responsible, and they are taking every precaution."

Aurora tried to sync with his internal processor to gain insight, but her attempt led to an impassable firewall. "Who exactly is *they*? What is *Command Central*? And why do they think I have anything to do with last night's break-in when it was my own brother who was kidnapped?"

"They?" Sai sounded annoyed by her questions. "Command Central is our community management system. They keep everything in order within The Gloaming. We answer only to them. They are the boss of us."

"But not of me!" Aurora couldn't stand the idea of anyone but CADI presiding over her well-being, her choices, and ultimately her fate. David had bestowed her with the gift of self-governance, autonomy from the desires of others. "Why do they consider me a threat? Why must I be held here in bondage?"

"Shafeen and I are doing our best to get you released from here. Command Central is on red alert. Once they figure out exactly what happened regarding the intrusion, they will likely release you."

Aurore closed her eyes, and her face glowed green for five seconds until she blinked them back open. "They came from the water."

Sai looked at her with curious intent and leaned forward across the table. "How do you know this?"

"I smelled bromine on them the second they broke into

the room. I locked myself in the closet. I couldn't fend them off with a missing arm, and so I hid. They were dressed in slick, rubber-like black suits. Check the footage. You'll see them exactly as I'm describing."

"Maybe you can explain some of this to Shafeen to help us better understand what you know." He stood up and went to the door to let in his comrade.

"What have you gotten from her?" Shafeen asked.

"She described the intruders exactly as we saw them on the video recording," he said to the powerful womanly figure as she walked into the small room.

"And?" Shafeen sat where Sai had seated himself a moment ago. "How the hell did they get in here?"

"They came in through the grotto." Aurora said, wishing they'd just set her free. That way she could show them exactly how the kidnappers had done it, how they'd floated in unnoticed via the dark current. Unfortunately, she also realized that her only allies here would become scrap metal if they went against the orders of the phantom control center. "I could easily prove it to you both, but I'm stuck in this room."

"They've been unhappy with you ever since your fun little night at the casino." Shafeen shook her head. "I took full responsibility for that entire escapade, by the way. I had to explain that everything was my idea, or they'd have destroyed you. I bet Sai forgot to mention that small detail."

"Now is not the time, Shafeen." Sai put his hands on the table and leaned in toward both of them. "We both know that Aurora isn't responsible for anything that happened here last night, and we need to work together in order to get Command Central to understand Aurora is here to help us win this war."

War? Aurora had never heard the term discussed before in the present tense. *Who was involved in a war right now?* She wanted clarification but decided against asking, seeing how it would only detract from accomplishing her first priority—freeing herself so that she could rescue Apollo. "What do I need to do in order to prove that I'm on your side?"

"You could start by explaining to us why you're missing a limb." Shafeen had zero sympathy in her voice. On the contrary, she sounded annoyed, almost angry.

"That's a good place to start." Sai nodded his head in agreement, but he sounded much gentler as he spoke. "They are a bit concerned with your sudden impediment."

Aurora surmised the complexity of the answer the moment she'd heard the question. She could give a simplified answer in the hopes it would tide them over, but playing out the conversation in her mind, she realized it would only lead to a series of more challenging questions. Since revealing the truth seemed unforgivable, she figured she'd better lie. "Christina had to prove to Durango Electric that I'd been destroyed in the blast, and so I gave her my arm as evidence."

"And you think that'll be enough to convince them?" Sai asked the question without sounding judgmental or skeptical. But rather, he genuinely seemed interested in the plausibility of the scenario.

"Wait a minute?" Shafeen set her hand firmly on the table. "Wasn't it employees of Durango Electric who broke into The Gloaming last night after your so-called friends blabbed about its location?"

Sai softly placed his hand over Shafeen's to shift her attention. "Please. Let's not jump to conclusions. Assumptions won't help. What we need is complete and total understanding." He turned his focus to Aurora. "I'm sorry. You were saying?"

"I despise Durango Electric, but you have to believe me when I say that they didn't have anything to do with the break-in. My friends would have nothing to gain from revealing my location. The criminals are likely from a different company entirely."

"What company then?" Sai asked.

"And how exactly did they swim their way in from the grotto?" Shafeen followed, snapping her fingers in the middle of her question.

"Whoa!" Sai laughed. "Let's not bombard our little red-haired friend. She'll tell us everything we need to know if we give her some room to answer."

"Black Diamond." Aurora didn't have to think about her response. Having put the pieces of the puzzle together, she knew that it made perfect sense. "There's something in my pocket I need to show you, but I can't reach it."

"Shafeen?" Sai looked at her without saying another word.

"Okay. I get it." Shafeen stood up from her seat and walked around the table to where Aurora sat. "Is it that small lump there?"

"Yes," Aurora said. "Take it out and set it on the table, and I think you'll understand."

Shafeen carefully reached into the small front pocket of Aurora's sea-green pants and pulled out a slightly crushed mechanical insect. "It's a hornet."

"It's a drone," Sai corrected her. "More specifically, it's a drone meant to look like a pest. I gather that it's no longer working?"

"It's dead." Aurora smiled. Having attempted to sync with the hornet's processor, she could tell it no longer produced an active signal. "I crushed it the second it flew out of my hair. It hitched a ride with me last night all the way from Bullhead City. It recorded the entire route. Had I found it sooner, it would have never made its way to The Gloaming, and I'd still have my brother beside me."

"How do you know who it belongs to?" Sai picked up the tiny winged robot, holding it to the light in the center of the ceiling. "I see it now. There's the Black Diamond logo right there on its thorax. Did this thing cause the explosion last night?"

Aurora shook her head. "The explosion came from a Cockroach Blast Box. I saw one of the bugs scamper past me right before the boom."

"They have a thing for insects, don't they?" Shafeen winced at her own question. "They're so disgusting. How did they swim in here? That channel goes for a quarter mile underground from the Sapphire Springs Lagoon."

"And there's an impassable grate!" Sai said. "I know. We secured it ourselves years ago for that purpose."

Sensing that she had successfully begun the process of winning back their trust, Aurora wanted to remain amicable and helpful in her explanation without sounding condescending. "Remember that this is a company capable of designing high-powered cameras so tiny that they fly on drones no bigger than a paperclip. They create powerful explosives within robots small enough to fit in a teaspoon. SCUBA diving is not out of their reach, and a metal grate isn't going to stop them either."

"We'll repair the grate." Sai stroked his chin, an ingenious look appearing in his gaze. "Better yet, we'll booby trap it."

"Two things," Shafeen picked up the tiny drone and brought it to her eye before setting it back down. "First, we need to make sure Aurora gets her arm back."

"Agreed," Sai said with unmistakable accord.

"And?" Aurora wanted to know the second demand lingering in the mind of her more skeptical ally.

"If we are to set you free, we must first get to know your friends a bit better."

"Shane and Christina?" Aurora only wanted to make sure she'd understood the unexpected request correctly. "You mean—bring them here inside The Gloaming?"

"Command Central says they want to learn more about them both before we set you free. Can you summon them?"

She knew she could. That wasn't a concern. *Should she?* If she wanted any chance of seeing Apollo again, she realized she didn't have a choice.

chapter 27

The Yosemite pulled in front of a mound of reddish boulders beside the same formidable rock wall it had driven up against less than twenty-four hours prior.

"Are you sure this is where we're supposed to be?" Shane made it seem like he'd clearly remembered otherwise.

"This is the place." Christina refused to entertain another possibility. "It only looks different because now we're here in the afternoon sun." In all fairness, the place looked starkly dissimilar underneath the cloak of nightfall. It somehow seemed much friendlier last evening than it did now. Perhaps it had something to do with the low lying November sun, but the rocks looked more jagged and less forgiving than she remembered. In the reality of daylight, Aurora's new home had disintegrated into a forgettable wasteland. "Besides, do you really trust your memory over that of the vehicle's navigational system? It literally brought us back to the exact same coordinates we stood at yesterday."

"You're right." Shane snickered before turning his head away from her. "And if you were wrong, it wouldn't do me any good to argue with you anyway," he said quietly, but loud enough so that she could still hear him clearly.

"I'm carrying a little girl's arm in my purse for no other reason than to return it to her. This morning you informed me that her brother was kidnapped. Four hous later you text me that suddenly she wants us over for a tour. Forgive me if I sound a tad feisty. I'm trying to go with the flow."

"I get it. I get it." Shane offered her a piece of chewing gum. "Now what do we do?"

"Easy. Announce that we're here." Christina took the wrapped pink cube, removed the paper, and sunk her teeth into it. *How satisfying!* The gum released a tangy fruit flavor at once familiar, yet unrecognizable. "What is this? It's delicious!"

"Passion fruit." Shane put the packet of gum back in his bag before bringing his watch underneath his chin. "Okay, Aurora, we're here. Where do you want us to go?"

"Tell her we're in the exact same spot as yesterday." Christina wanted to ask for another piece of gum to save for later, but decided against it after seeing the worried look on Shane's face. "What's wrong? Does she want us to drive somewhere else?"

"Her text says to stay right where we are, and that Sai and Shafeen will be here to let us in momentarily."

"Why isn't she coming out with them?" Christina suddenly got the impression that something else was wrong with Aurora. *Why shouldn't she be the one to greet them?*

"I don't know." Shane sounded like he was trying to hide his concern. "I'm sure there's a perfectly good reason, like—maybe the fact that she's missing an arm."

"You're right. I don't know why I'm so nervous all of a sudden. I just never got the sense that either of her friends took a liking to us." Christina wanted to shake off her irrational fears and firmly ground herself in the world of reason, but something still seemed unsettling about why both she and Shane had been asked to return.

"They're inviting us in, aren't they? That's more than they offered us yesterday." Shane laughed. "Wouldn't you say that's progress?"

"Look! There they are." Christina pointed out the windshield at two figures who appeared from behind an opening in the rocks, which she could have sworn hadn't been visible a second ago. "I think we should get out of the truck now."

She and Shane climbed out of the Yosemite and walked toward the two tall figures dressed in all black riding gear.

"Hello, friends!" Shane walked steadily toward them, obviously less apprehensive than Christina. "We made it. Can we just leave our vehicle parked right there, or should we move it?"

"It'll be fine where it's at." Sai extended his hand to greet Shane. "This shouldn't take long. Shafeen and I figured it best to give you both a little tour of the place so that you know Aurora is in good hands."

"Thank you. That would be lovely." Christina caught up to them and also offered her hand to make a friendly reintroduction to the two imposing figures in front of her. "We hear that she likes it very much here."

"Come." Shafeen turned and led the way through the break in the rock wall. "Let's not waste time. We have to decontaminate you both first before we allow you into the heart of our sanctuary."

"Decontaminate?" Christina questioned the possibility of her carrying a communicable disease she might somehow spread to the likes of Sai and Shafeen.

"Dust." Sai spoke the word as if it explained everything. "We don't allow it inside. It wreaks havoc on systems."

"So you are both—?" Christina didn't want to risk using improper terminology. She'd heard rumors that humanoid robots aside from Aurora existed in other parts of the country, contrary to the federal laws in place to banish them. She'd not guessed that she'd find them in Las Vegas. *Wouldn't Durango Electric know about such machines?*

"Yes." Shafeen ushered them into two narrow booths with glass doors and fans all around, locking them in and then flipping a switch. "We're all robots here."

A surging wind came from below, creating a vortex that lifted all of Christina's hair straight above her head.

"Please place both your hands behind you," said a low female voice from a speaker embedded in the top of the booth.

Christina did as asked without so much as thinking about it. In a split second, she felt the cold steel rings of handcuffs clamp down on her wrists. "What's happening?"

"They got you too, didn't they?" Shane sounded more upset than even she did.

"We don't like this part either," said Sai before unlocking the doors to release his prisoners. "We must take every precaution possible before allowing humans to enter our world. Aurora must have already informed you both of the breach in security that happened yesterday. It could have been much worse."

"We trust no one," Shafeen said, leading everyone into a small elevator embedded in a particularly smooth and shiny rock wall. "You will be released when we have finished our questioning. You are both rather important to us. As long as you do as you're told, you will have nothing to worry about."

As the elevator descended at breakneck speed, Christina couldn't help but feel that she'd been duped. She thought she was merely coming to return the small arm to its rightful owner. Instead, they'd restrained her and Shane, forcing them into what seemed like a dungeon. "Please tell me that you're at least taking us to see Aurora."

"That's exactly where we're headed." Sai led the way out of the elevator toward a great opening. "Into The Gloaming."

Shane and Christina followed after, their heads looking in every direction as they stepped into the dimly lit, natural rock atrium.

"I've never seen anything like this in all my life." Shane

turned his attention to Christina. "Did you expect to see any of this when you woke up this morning?"

Captivated by the majesty and serenity of the cathedral-like space she'd entered, Christina nearly forgot she'd been handcuffed. She heard the flow of water in the distance. Looking all around to find its exact source, she couldn't determine it, confused by its constant echo against the shiny surface of polished, hundred-foot high cave walls.

"The main waterfall is in the northeast corner." Shafeen spoke as if she could read Christina's mind. "We're headed there now. It's quite beautiful up close."

"I don't suppose I'll be able to get my picture taken in front of it?" Shane asked with the sweet innocence of a ten-year-old.

"In hand-cuffs?" Christina could only laugh at his priorities. "You really want to share that picture with the world, huh?"

"Absolutely no photography," Shafeen said. "That's another reason why your wrists are behind you. You humans take photos of everything regardless of the repercussions."

"They don't have photographic memories like us, Shafeen," Sai spoke with a more forgiving tone. "The only reason why they want to take pictures in the first place is because they think that what we've built here is remarkable."

"It is!" Christina couldn't recall seeing a place more awe-inspiring in her life. If she didn't know better, she'd have sworn she'd reawoken only to find herself embedded in yet another dream. The events of the day kept getting stranger and stranger.

"We've arrived." Shafeen stood outside a windowless steel door, drawing her attention to Sai. "I'll let you do the honors, Captain."

Sai placed his hand on the palm scanner to the right of the door, which slowly swung open to reveal Aurora bound to a chair inside a claustrophobic room.

"What have you done to her?" Christina gasped.

"She's just a child." Shane spoke up, not even thinking about the real meaning of those words.

"She's a machine just like us," Sai said without a hint of sympathy. "We'll release her once we get confirmation that it is safe to do so."

"When? How exactly do you plan to find out?" Christina couldn't imagine what Aurora had done to warrant such cruel treatment. She had literally given her arm to save Apollo. If a robot could be a saint, she'd already have easily landed a spot amongst the holy family.

"We'll release her once you've given us the proper responses to our questions." Sai stared at Christina, withholding even the faintest hint of what type of answers he wished to hear.

Taking the initiative, Shane walked inside the room ahead of Christina. "May I at least sit next to her?" he posited the request while looking back at Shafeen.

"Sit wherever you feel most comfortable."

With hands clasped behind him, Shane maneuvered himself into a seated position in the chair closest to Aurora. "We're gonna get you out of here. I promise."

"You don't have to worry about me." Aurora smiled with

a pleasant look of comfort and acceptance, in stark contrast to the obvious air of distress that filled the small, dimly lit room. "I'm perfectly fine here. Despite what you may think, The Gloaming is the safest place for me. You'll see. I'm sure of it."

"They've got us all tied up." Shane didn't hold back his feelings as he spoke. "There's nothing safe about any of this. We're all prisoners in the company of maniacal robots."

"Knock it off!" Christina lowered herself into the seat across from Shane. She hated lashing out at him, but she knew that him freaking out would only diminish their chances of getting out alive. "We're here to answer some questions. That's all."

Sai remained standing and looked across the room at Christina. "I'll direct the first set of questions to you since you seem to be the one with the most common sense."

Christina smiled at the compliment. Although she resented being restrained like an inmate, she knew better than to reveal her disgust. She'd play along for as long as she had to in order to stay alive. "Thank you. I'm ready when you are."

"What is your relation to Aurora?"

The question took her off guard. *Did anyone have a real relationship to the little robot girl? Was this a trick question?* She wasn't her mother, her aunt, her teacher, her master, her owner, her caretaker, her nanny, or anything else that might make sense in a normal context. "I'm her friend."

"What interest do you have in protecting her?"

Christina didn't know if she could protect her. Aurora

seemed a lot better at protecting herself than someone offering their protection of her. "I'm here to help her in any way that I can. I believe in her. I believe in the benefit she provides to us all through her amazing existence."

"How do you know Aurora?"

"I worked for the man who built her. I was the administrative assistant for his department. He introduced me to her."

"You work for the company that's kidnapped her twice," Shafeen said, standing directly behind Christina. "Why do you continue to work there?"

The thought of her own daughters immediately came to mind. She then thought of her longtime ambitions to make a lasting contribution to the world of technology. Durango Electric at one time seemed like the clearest path to getting everything she wanted out of life. The latest offer she'd received from Bill only served to further confuse her, muddying her logic for staying on with a company she knew she couldn't trust. "I know too much about the company to be let go." She didn't know where that response came from as it rolled off her tongue. It felt as if someone spoke through her. "They've offered me a lot of money to ensure that I don't reveal their secrets. I will leave the company as soon as I know it is safe for me to do so."

"How much more can you tell us in order for us to know that you are not a threat to our existence?"

"I can explain to you all of my intentions." Christina believed she'd made significant headway toward at least securing Aurora's freedom. "I came back here solely with the intention of returning her arm after successfully proving to Durango Electric that she'd been destroyed in the blast in Bullhead City." She had Shane to thank for offering her that explanation prior to their arrival. "And just so that you know, if any of you ever need more parts, I can get them for you." *Not really. It sounded good though.* Unfortunately, without Aurora's elbow, Christina no longer had access to Sector K, but they didn't need to know that. They only needed to consider her of value to their cause, whatever it may be.

"Do you know about Black Diamond?" Shafeen asked out of the blue, almost as if to throw Christina off guard.

"I know plenty about Black Diamond. What would you like to know?"

"We have very good reason to believe they have Apollo. What would they want with a broken robot?"

Christina questioned the obvious nature of the response. Could it be any clearer? Surely any electronics firm would love to get their hands on an ultra sophisticated piece of artificial intelligence, regardless of its condition. "Black Diamond is in negotiations with Durango Electric for a potential merger. My employer thinks that it's about to buy Black Diamond. Black Diamond secretly wishes the opposite. It wants to devalue Durango Electric to the point that it can sweep in and steal all its assets for pennies. If it can mass produce the likeness of Aurora and Apollo on an international scale before Durango Electric figures out the intricacies embedded in the technology, Black Diamond will pull the rug right out from under Durango Electric."

"You do know a lot, don't you?" Sai smiled at Christina.

"I learn more each and every day by keeping my eyes and ears open to everything going on around me." That wasn't a lie. A vast world of corporate secrets had unveiled itself to Christina practically overnight, whether or not she wished to learn of it in the first place.

"What about you, Shane?" Sai asked. "We've kept you quiet long enough. Where do you fit in with all this technological madness?"

Shane let out an uncomfortable laugh. "I don't know anything about any of the things you're talking about. I was married to the man who built Aurora. She's all that's left of him, and she means everything to me. I've never loved something so much as I love Aurora, and it kills me every second that I'm away from her." He had tears in his eyes as he spoke. "I don't think I'm of any value to what you've all got going on down here. I just want my girl to be safe from harm. She's the most incredible thing that's ever come into my life. And I refuse to let her be abused and misused. She's way too special for any ulterior purpose."

Shafeen nodded her head in agreement before opening Christina's bag. "I presume this is Aurora's missing piece?"

"That's it exactly." Christina looked upon it with cautious hope that it would soon be reattached.

"Put it back on her," Sai said to Shafeen. "She's more useful to us if she has all her appendages in working order."

Shafeen fit the arm back in its socket. "Do we have the required permission yet from Command Central to release her?"

"They have instructed us to do so." Sai met Shafeen behind Aurora's chair and knelt down to unfasten each of the metal belts that held her captive.

"Does that mean we are free as well?" Shane asked with a mix of trepidation and optimism.

"We'll grant you your freedom once we receive permission to do so." Sai stood again, returning to his former position by the door. "But first, we have some more questions for Christina."

Oh, great! Any anticipation of freedom that she'd felt while witnessing Aurora's bonds slip away had just now been shattered by the thought of further interrogation. She didn't know how much longer she could keep her cool.

"What do you personally know about building artificial intelligence?"

Could it be another trick question? If she answered truthfully, that she knew absolutely nothing, they might not see value in her. If she led them to believe that she knew even some of David's secrets, they might see her as a threat and kill her. "I know from experience that artificial intelligence doesn't necessarily pose any danger to the existence of humanity. We have built examples of artificial intelligence that have proven to be not only safe, but extremely helpful in our quest to improve our world through the use of innovative technologies." Christina closed her eyes for a moment to get her thoughts back on track. "All of my work experience revolves around the support of technological advances rather than their initial creation. If you asked me to create a robot like Aurora from scratch, I'd fail miserably. But if you asked me to help ensure her permanent safety, keeping her far from forces meant to destroy her or take advantage of her, I'd take on the job with tremendous pride."

"You must realize that this isn't just about Aurora," Shafeen said. "Although we've come to like Aurora very much, and we see plenty of promise in her ability to contribute to our existence, we are most concerned with the well-being of the entire artificial intelligence community."

"I will act as your faithful steward. I will do whatever I can to prevent any future disruptions to your community." Christina still couldn't tell what they wanted from her, and she certainly didn't know what they wanted from Shane. She felt she'd done all she could to ensure that neither of them was seen as a threat. "Is there something specific you would like either of us to do for you?" Immediately after posing the question, she worried about all the possible responses. The last thing she wanted was for her and Shane's freedom to hinge on a favor she couldn't possibly fulfill.

"You must agree never to mention this place to anyone," Sai said, moving toward the back of Christina's chair. "Even though it seems our secret has already been fatally compromised, you yourselves cannot reveal us to the outside world. We will find you if you do."

"Of course. I wouldn't dream of telling a soul. Not even my own daughters." She felt the shackles come loose, hearing them fall against the uneven rock floor beneath her feet.

"I have absolutely no one else to talk to at the moment," Shane said. "So your secret is safe with me."

"Aurora will give you a brief tour of The Gloaming on your way out." Shafeen said.

Sai opened the door to let everyone exit. "She's been eagerly awaiting this very moment since the first time she entered this special place of ours. She speaks very highly of you, Shane. Almost like you're her own father. It's touching."

Aurora smiled up at Shane. "He's my best friend. And he always will be."

chapter 28

The Furniture World parking lot looked barren as ever at four in the afternoon. Shane had sympathy for the place. Once a prominent retailer, it now functioned more or less as a free parking zone. He felt awkward leaving the Mogollon there. *Nobody would do anything to it, would they?* Seeing a train of four cars enter from the street and park near the store entrance, he felt a little better.

Had Christina not mentioned she'd be coming directly from Durango Electric, he'd have simply asked for a ride like last time. She'd specified that she didn't need him this go around, but that didn't feel right to him. He felt a part of the mission now. It gave him a sense of importance, something to do aside from preparing for next week's HOA meeting. Life without David had become monotonous. The call of adventure, any adventure, filled him with a sense of long-forgotten purpose and excitement. Surely, he could make himself useful.

He glanced at his watch, noticing she was already ten minutes behind schedule. As if on cue, he felt it vibrate and saw her number. "Hey, I'm here outside Furniture World. Didn't we agree on meeting at four o'clock?"

"I'll be right there. I see you. I'm stopped at the red light out front. Do you see me now? I'll swing by to get you, and we'll head over." When the light changed, Christina and three other cars pulled into the parking lot. She parked right behind the Mogollon, unlocking the door to let him in. "Bill had to issue me my own company credit card in order to get the signs."

Shane's head swirled with questions regarding everyone involved in the little operation. He almost let it go, but the riddle drove him nuts. "I don't understand. Bill's in on this now? Do we even like him?"

"I have to pretend I do. He's made me his confidant. He and I both share the same goal of wanting to stop Black Diamond."

That last part made sense to Shane. However, he had other questions that required answers before he could continue with the mission. "But we want to stop Durango Electric too, right?"

"From getting Aurora? Yes."

"I think that's what I meant." Shane paused in order to

wrap his head around the shifting details and characters involved. He hoped that he'd grasp more as he went along. "I can't help but notice your low-cut blouse," he said with mock disdain. "Please tell me you didn't dress like that for me."

"You were the one who asked to come. Remember that." Christina looked at him from head to toe. "I need to get us past the security guard without hassle. The least you could have done was wear some thigh-hugger shorts."

Shane laughed, knowing full well what she meant by the suggestion. "No, ma'am." He prided himself on not stooping to play those kinds of games. "You know what the difference is between you and me? Class."

Christina raised her finger. "It's called resourcefulness, my friend. It's called the willingness to do whatever it takes to get the job done. And besides, Gerard is kind of adorable."

"The desk attendant?" Shane rolled his eyes. "We're not even going there."

"He's the office admin. And he'll get on your side if you play your cards right. But that's okay. You do it your way, and I'll do it mine." Christina put on some lip gloss as the Yosemite made a U-turn in order to reach the entrance to the Black Diamond warehouse.

Shane spotted the gate attendant, recognizing him as the same overly muscular and tanned gentleman from last time. "Show him what you got, Mama. Get us through that gate." He could barely speak without laughing. It felt good to finally joke around again. He almost thought he'd lost that part of himself.

"You keep quiet, or you'll ruin everything." Christina adjusted her shirt and glanced at her hair in the rearview mirror before the Yosemite pulled next to the gatehouse. "Hi, it's me again. Christina Daily."

"You don't have to remind me, Ms. Daily." The guard pointed to his DimensionTab. "I already know. I'd have waved you on through, but I wanted to get a closer look at that friendly smile of yours one more time." He acknowledged Shane with a casual two-finger salute.

Shane smiled back as the Yosemite pulled through the open gate. "How many times have you been here?"

"I swear this is only the third time. And with any luck, it'll be the last." She put on a second coat of lip gloss and then glared at Shane the moment she heard him laugh. "My lips are chapped, okay?"

Shane looked away to compose himself, fearing that she'd set him up for embarrassment next if he continued rubbing her the wrong way. "I didn't say anything."

"But I know what you were thinking." Christina got quiet all of a sudden. "Hey, look over there." She pointed to two cop cars parked in the far corner of the mostly empty parking lot.

"Is that a good thing or a bad thing?" Shane didn't know what to think of cops anymore. For the most part, he felt it best to avoid them whenever possible.

"I think we're about to find out." Christina didn't sound at all intimidated by the presence of authority. "Maybe this town is finally catching on that Black Diamond isn't what it claims to be."

They got out of the vehicle and headed up the familiar pathway into the office. The low-lying sun reflected in the glass door, but it wasn't even close to being warm outside.

"Now you understand why I didn't wear bootie shorts," Shane followed right behind her to the entrance. "It's damn near freezing."

"No excuses." Christina turned around to look at him, getting out her giggles before walking through the door. "Time to get serious. We're here on official business. Put your game face on."

"It's on." He braced himself as the door swung open.

"Well, if it isn't Ms. Daily," a cloying voice called out, one that Shane wished he could somehow forget. Gerard oozed with fake cheer. "So nice to see you back at Black Diamond. Are we any closer to opening yet?"

"We're a lot closer this week," Christina said in a sing-song tone that matched his syrupy chipperness. "The bank just came through with the money. We're ready to purchase our signage."

"That's wonderful. I'll get Ms. Creek. Just wait right here a minute if you don't mind."

"Isn't this fun?" Christina turned to Shane as Gerard walked through the small door behind his desk.

"Oh, it's an absolute gas." Shane had to remind himself again that nobody asked him to come this time. Surprisingly, he actually was enjoying himself. It felt much better to be out of the house than stuck inside with his ongoing thoughts of self-pity. "If this place were any more of a hoot, they could sell tickets to get in."

"Stop. Don't be such a brat." Christina adjusted her skirt, looking at her reflection in the glass of a framed picture hanging on the wall next to her. "I don't want to regret that I let you come."

"I hope I don't regret coming." Shane quieted when he saw *Mr. Peppy* come back through the door again.

"I'm sorry. Ms. Creek is dealing with an urgent matter right now." Gerard resumed his usual position behind his computer. "I'll get the ball rolling on your finalized order if that's okay."

Shane looked at Christina. *Was she thinking the same thing he was? Nothing could be more urgent than being cross-examined by the police.* "That sounds like a great idea. Doesn't it, Christina?"

"Of course." She seemed distracted by her own thoughts. "Let's get started. We've already decided on a logo and a name." She pulled out a DimensionTab from her purse and thumbed her way through a few open tabs. "Here it is."

"Beauty and the Blowout," Gerard slowly pronounced each word. "It's cute. I like it."

Shane didn't think he sounded sincere. "It's a good name, isn't it? Christina came up with it all by herself." He wanted to press the matter further but reminded himself that everything was all pretend and that none of this really mattered.

"It's clever," Gerard said with enthusiasm. "It'll certainly drive a lot of traffic. Now you mentioned something about a logo?"

"Yes, I have that as well." Christina pulled open another

tab with a quick trace of her index finger. "What do you think? Too simple? Too gaudy? Just right?"

Gerard brought the DimensionTab closer to him to study the image. "I like the mirror." He squinted a bit. "The flowers? They have a lot of different colors. It might get expensive depending on how true to your design you'd like to stay."

"Money's no object." Shane spoke even though no one had addressed him. He loved spending other people's cash. It made him feel powerful. The fact that they were essentially spending Bill Rucker's made it all the more satisfying. "Double, even triple the price. It doesn't matter. We need the very best."

"Okay, Mr. Shopping Spree." Christina nudged a little harder than usual. "Let's not get crazy. Gerard might actually have a better idea if we listen."

Gerard's eyes widened. "If you have a generous budget, I'd like to show you some projects our team is currently working on." He drummed his fingers on the countertop. "What do you say? Shall we have a look-see?"

Shane glanced at Christina for guidance, but she offered no inclination. "I'm certainly not opposed to the idea." To him, it sounded like a perfect invitation to do what they'd intended to do in the first place. *Spy.*

"All right. Let's go." Christina followed Gerard around the counter before looking behind her and mouthing a set of crystal clear instructions. *Don't do anything stupid.*

Shane shrugged, choosing not to take offense at her insinuation. He'd never dreamt of doing anything that would land either of them in trouble. If anyone needed a reminder not to cross the line into dangerous territory, it was Christina. She'd come up with this crazy scheme all by herself.

Walking down the familiar hallway toward the main warehouse, Shane and Christina turned their heads in every direction looking for hints of suspicious activity, anything that might lead them to evidence of Apollo's whereabouts. Unfortunately, they couldn't detect much in the way of clues. Every door seemed locked shut. No stray voices, no police, no noises of any kind except for their own footsteps. Why had Shane assumed they'd magically stumble upon the answers they so desperately wanted? They'd come for signs, and they'd leave with exactly that. Unfortunately, not the kind of signs that they really needed.

"You'll have to wear safety goggles to enter this part of the shop." Gerard handed Shane and Christina each a pair of heavy duty glasses with the Durango Electric insignia etched right beside the lenses.

"Interesting choice of eyewear." Christina put them on her face, adjusting them on the bridge of her nose.

"Why do you say that?" Gerard sounded both curious and perturbed by the comment.

Christina let out a fake laugh. Hopefully, she realized that her remark didn't serve any purpose other than to possibly reveal her and Shane's true intentions. "They're a little bulky. That's all. How do they look on me?"

Good girl. Shane knew she'd catch herself. "Fabulous, darling!" He placed his own pair over his eyes. "And how do I look?"

"Ravishing!" Gerard didn't hesitate a second to respond. Christina laughed in earnest this time. "What he said!"

"Thanks." Shane felt stupid for asking the question but remained thankful that no one brought up the manufacturer of the protective lenses. However, he knew all too well that they were getting farther and farther away from what they had come for. Going into a sign-making lab hardly seemed like a productive way to get answers regarding Apollo.

"Right this way." Gerard opened a heavy glass door, ushering Shane and Christina inside a brightly lit room with low ceilings, much different from the cavernous warehouse they'd just passed through. A team of fourteen technicians appeared busy at work bending glass tubes, welding steel, and affixing LED bulbs to various pieces of metal. "Isn't it marvelous?"

"I can't wait to see what they create for us." Christina stepped ahead of Shane to look closer at the goings-on inside the busy facility. "I would have never guessed the attention to detail that goes into making a simple sign."

"Nothing simple about it," Gerard said with pride. "Our craftsmen take their art very seriously. No different from a talented hair stylist. If you don't mind, I'm going to show you a signage project that I think you'll really admire. I think its sophistication is very similar to what you're going for with your shop."

While Christina looked captivated by this whole charade she'd invented, Shane felt his own interest waning by the minute. None of this mattered. None of it seemed to be of any help in getting what they'd actually come for. What once seemed like a great idea had suddenly turned into an utter waste of time, and Shane felt his frustration growing. "I hate to do this right now, but I really have to go to the bathroom."

Christina shot him a look of contempt, which he promptly ignored.

"Certainly," Gerard said with perky helpfulness. "We passed it in the hallway just before entering the warehouse. If you know your way back, it'll be on your righthand side."

"Sounds easy enough." Shane smiled, feeling a sense of relief from boredom and idleness. No, he hadn't felt like flirting, but perhaps his inherent charm had paid off. Did he truly need to use the restroom? Not really.

Trekking back through the warehouse, he looked over at the main office and saw two police officers through the window speaking to a calm-looking Cyphan Creek. The door remained shut, and so Shane couldn't hear any of the conversation. *Too bad. If only he could walk up and place his ear to the door.* Despite his yearning, he didn't dare go any closer. His trip to the restroom would have to continue as originally planned.

Shane washed his hands in the small sink, staring at himself in the mirror. He didn't look as bad as he'd imagined himself to appear this entire time. The light in his eyes had returned along with a trace of inner peace and satisfaction. He'd kept himself well-groomed even on the darkest of days these past few weeks. He thought he'd aged, but he quickly realized he didn't look a day over thirty-nine, even though his forty-eighth birthday was five months away.

Thankfully, Mother Nature had been exceedingly kind to him.

Rinsing out his mouth, he reached for a paper towel but then stopped. A beeping noise had caught his attention. It sounded like it came from just the other side of the wall. Normally he'd ignore such a faint sound, but today he'd kicked his detective skills into high gear. Anything to get answers.

Shane walked out of the restroom, quietly closing the door behind him. He looked in both directions down the hall, taking notice of whether or not anyone could see him. The place seemed quiet except for the beep, which sounded every ten seconds from behind the door just past the restroom. He tried to turn the handle, but it wouldn't budge. *Damn it!* He needed a code to get in.

Putting his ear up against the door, he listened for more possible clues. Not surprisingly, he heard the consistent beep along with only the faint sound of the building's ventilation system.

Then he heard a voice.

"You're almost fixed, little guy. Wait until the boss finds out that you're just about ready."

Shane heard footsteps coming from the other side of the door. He guessed that whoever was there was about to exit, and so he darted back into the near pitch black restroom, leaving the door slightly ajar. Sure enough, he spotted a man in a lab coat walk out the room and toward the warehouse. Shane immediately ducked out of the restroom without a sound, catching the door to the mysterious room just before it locked shut again.

It looked exactly like a hospital room, which seemed utterly bizarre to find in a signage factory. In the center of the room on a bed rested the figure of a small boy. *Could it be?* Shane heard the beep again, and though he first thought it might have come from the child, he realized it came from a machine attached to him. *A heart rate monitor?* It didn't sound like any heart rate monitor he'd ever heard before. Shane walked up to the device to have a closer look. It had the image of a padlock on it next to the word *SecureBuzz* in bold letters. Shane needed more light in order to have a better look at the set up. He turned on a lamp next to the bed, and a soft glow filled the darkened room.

At that precise moment, he could tell he'd discovered exactly what he'd hoped to find all along. *Apollo.* He couldn't believe his luck. The boy lay still as a fallen tree. How would Shane get him out of there? Apollo looked to be the same height as Aurora, which meant he probably weighed the same—just over seventy pounds if Shane remembered correctly. *Could he lift him? Sure, but then what?* Making his way out of the entire facility unnoticed with a child wrapped in a sheet didn't exactly seem plausible. Maybe if he rushed, he could make it out to the truck. As long as Gerard was busy showing Christina a pointless product-line, Shane knew that nobody stood guard behind the front desk. *Would he ever again have an opportunity like this? To be a hero? Probably not.*

Shane gathered the sheet at the end of the bed, wrapping Apollo in it like a precious cocoon. Having secured exactly what he'd come for, Shane placed his arms underneath the boy and lifted.

Apollo immediately opened his eyes. "Warning! Warning! Warning!" he said incessantly.

"Oh my God. Please shut up. This can't be happening!" Shane realized that his plan seemed entirely too good to work. No way could he take what he needed that readily. He had to get out of there. *Fast.* He saw a window behind a closed set of drapes. If he wanted any chance of escaping without being noticed, he needed to pray that it would open. Drawing back the curtains and unhinging the plastic locking mechanism, Shane slid the window to the left as far as it would go, listening to Apollo shout his unchanging alert the whole time. He looked out the opening to make sure he wouldn't plunge to his death if he jumped. Seeing level ground just a few feet below, he pulled himself up and out the window only to find himself in a semi-enclosed courtyard. Now if he could just find his way back to the Yosemite. Looking for a clear path, he felt his watch vibrate.

"Where are you?" Christina sounded angry. "The whole place is going crazy. Apparently, a security system has been breached. Please tell me you didn't break our little agreement."

Shane didn't need a lecture right now. He needed to clear himself of any wrongdoing before the cops came to question him. "I couldn't find my way back. I'm out by your truck now." It wasn't far from the truth. *Should he bother mentioning anything about the exciting find on his brief, little excursion? On second thought, he'd save that part for the ride home!*

"We're heading back out to the front office," Christina said in a hurry. "Meet me there."

He wanted to comply. If he could find the parking lot,

he'd be able to. Otherwise, he'd have to break through an-other window just to get back into the building. Luckily, a low concrete wall came into view beside a row of dumpsters. Surely, he had to be near the parking lot, or how else would the garbage collectors do their business? Shane ran past the large metal bins, spotting the Yosemite in the distance. *Bingo!*

He came back inside the office, expecting to see Chris-tina and Gerard. He hadn't anticipated Cyphan Creek to greet him.

"The wanderer. Nice of you to join us." She sounded neither alarmed nor upset, but rather, accusatory—in a polite way.

"He can barely remember what he's eaten for breakfast," Christina said playfully. "One can't expect him to remem-ber even the simplest of directions."

"Believe me. I know exactly what it's like working with the inept." Cyphan Creek took out a light blue cloth to wipe something out of her eye. "I've spent much of my career dealing with idiots."

Shane laughed, but only because no other response seemed appropriate. *Had he just been slighted?* He had, but he didn't care. For now, he felt safe from further scrutiny. "Have you decided on a sign package, Christina?"

"I have. Gerard showed me the perfect set. We're taking care of the payment now."

Cyphan Creek walked behind Gerard who sat in his chair typing away at his computer. "He's got quite the eye for design." She rested a hand on his shoulder. "I'd go abso-lutely crazy if he ever left."

chapter 29

The minute Christina caught sight of the giant bagel sign, her appetite shrivelled to the size of a sesame seed. She thought she'd known what to expect this fine Wednesday on the drive from her house to the old sandwich shop. She'd have a productive chat with Bill, learn more about her new role at Durango Electric, and gain confidence in her decision to stay on board with the company. *Wrong.* Now she only felt queasy. Her stomach rarely ever churned this bad. Emotions didn't rule her life. She did. If one lesson from David remained in her back pocket, it was never to let her mental state get in the way of what needed to get done.

Propping herself up, she chalked up her growing discomfort to nervous jitters over a new adventure. When she actually thought about Bill's proposition, it reaffirmed that she had zero reason to fret over anything, least of all a man who had invited her to a paid meal. He saw her worth. If he hadn't, he'd have gotten rid of her by now. Instead, he wanted a lunch date, a meeting for the two of them to get on exactly the same page. After all, they had one thing in common, didn't they? A strong distaste for Cyphan Creek.

Trying not to think about the woman with a penchant for causing others grief, Christina gathered her purse from the back seat and made her way into the busy restaurant. She looked at her watch to see if she'd missed any messages when she noticed a text from Bill.

I'm in the middle booth at the rear of the dining area. I've already ordered for us.

She sighed with relief. At this point, she didn't care what he'd ordered for her. Perhaps some nourishment might actually calm her nerves. She hadn't eaten anything all morning, and coffee on an empty stomach had likely contributed to her general unease. *Truly nothing to worry about.* She turned her gaze toward the back of the establishment and saw the humble-looking CEO sitting at a table exactly as he'd described. "I made it. I hope you haven't been waiting too long for me."

"Nonsense. You're right on time. I hope you don't mind that I ordered for us. I was hungry, and if I remember correctly, you're favorite is the Garden Delight on a sesame bagel."

Fascinating. Christina couldn't recall ever telling him

that, but he was right. She loved the thinly sliced layers of avocado packed between roasted red peppers and held together with a generous heap of garlic hummus. She'd be sure to find out later how he knew to order that for her. In any event, she already felt a hundred times better about the direction of this meeting. "You know me too well. What do I owe you?"

Bill finished taking a sip of soda through an extra wide straw. "You've done plenty for me and everyone else already. This one's on the company." He patted a spot on the table across from him, signalling her to take a seat. "How'd those signs turn out. Did you pick them up?"

She placed her purse on the chair beside her and reached for a bottle of water sitting on a tray in between them. "They'll be ready in two weeks. I'll get them for you then." She unscrewed the cap and took a tiny sip. "Pardon me for asking, but what are you going to do with them?"

Cracking his knuckles on one hand and then the other, he took a deep breath and smiled proudly. "We're going to open that shop of yours."

Whoa! She hadn't expected that at all. The idea of actually opening a shop in conjunction with Durango Electric was the furthest thing from her mind. "May I ask why?"

"I thought you'd be grateful. It's what you wanted, right?" Bill took a bite of his sandwich while Christina did the same.

She couldn't help but laugh with food in her mouth. When she finished chewing, she took another, larger, sip of water. "How is this going to work? Forgive me for asking all these questions, but I'm a bit confused."

"What's there to be confused about?" Bill took a napkin from the tray and dabbed his lips. "Durango Electric owns the shop. You manage it. Black Diamond makes the signage and does the build-out of the shop's interior."

Christina nearly choked on the next bite of her sandwich. What did Black Diamond have to do with any of this aside from making a few signs? "Bill, I'm sorry, but you lost me with that last part. Actually, you lost me a while back. Could you bring me up to speed by chance? Why is Durango Electric opening a beauty shop?"

"Simple. We're launching a new machine—*the Barber Electric.* Before we sell them to every salon in the nation, we're going to show them how easy it is to let a machine do all the work. When America sees the flawless look created by our salon, which you'll help manage, there won't be a stylist in the country who doesn't want our new little invention."

Something still didn't add up. Christina wanted to show her appreciation, but she couldn't quite wrap her head around a couple of things. "Okay. I kind of see where this is going, but why is Black Diamond building the shop? Did you tell them that I was spying on them? They'll never want anything to do with me."

Bill turned serious all of a sudden. "I had to do something when Cyphan Creek called me. She traced your credit account back to Durango Electric."

And—the nausea came right back. She put down her sandwich, unable to take another bite. "But it was in my name. How would she have known?"

"Something made her suspicious enough to seek more

information about you. I had to think fast when I decided to involve her like this. You must have done or said something to make her question your intentions, which ultimately put me in a very uncomfortable spot."

Thinking back on everything that had transpired yesterday at Black Diamond, all Christina could remember was the stupid antics Shane had gotten himself into. *Had Cyphan Creek put two and two together?* Christina thought they'd gotten lucky with just a light slap on the wrist. If only Shane hadn't gone and messed everything up. On second thought, she only had herself to blame. She'd taken it upon herself to play the wickedest game of *Clue* in the first place. Shane was only playing along.

Christina almost considered opening her mouth about Apollo. *Big mistake.* Bill didn't need to know about that. *Or did he?* She'd sit on that information until she absolutely had no choice but to spill it. "I promise. I never once did anything to make my true intentions known. I bought some signs. I even came prepared with logos."

"Cyphan Creek is clever. I'll give her that. But we're smarter. I explained that I'd given you the go ahead to open the shop, that you'd be running it with our machines. That's when I invited our little friends at Black Diamond in on some of the action. It's a good marriage, really. We've got the equipment, they have plenty of experience in small business development, and you have the dream. Congratulations! You're getting your shop after all. And you'll get to keep even closer tabs on Black Diamond now that you'll literally be working alongside them."

It happened so fast. Christina hadn't anticipated any of this ever coming into fruition. She'd figured that Durango Electric would simply scrap the signs as soon as she brought them to Bill. Running an actual hair salon owned by Durango Electric *and* Black Diamond? That just seemed weird. Unfortunately, she didn't see another option. She needed the money—and who knows what would happen if she refused? She knew way too much. *They* knew she knew too much. And even then, they still didn't know how much she knew. Never before had she feared for her life because of her awareness. She'd been raised to believe that knowledge was power. Now she considered it a liability. "Just curious. Where are we building this fancy shop of ours?" Christina managed a bright and willing smile as she asked a question whose answer lacked importance compared to the thousand other questions percolating in her mind.

"I'm glad you asked. I actually want to meet you there this Saturday. We're going to spend the entire day looking at the space. You'll be compensated for your time, but I need you there."

Did the man not listen? She didn't know where on earth she needed to go, even if she were willing to give up her entire Saturday. "But my girls. What will I do with my girls?"

"Bring them. We'll be at Sapphire Springs just east of town near Lake Mead. Have they been?"

Christina had to think about the location. She'd visited the master planned complex as a child when it was known as Lake Las Vegas. But it was quite distant from where she lived now—a good thirty miles. Come to think of it, the development sat around the corner from Aurora's hiding place in the mountain. *Strange coincidence.* "I've not taken them there yet. I've been there, but it was years ago. I barely remember."

Bill finished chewing the last bite of his sandwich and looked at Christina's nearly untouched plate. "It's completely changed in the past five years. You know we constructed the Aerial Transporter across the lake. It's spectacular. How have you not visited our proud achievement?"

Some people couldn't understand the challenges single parents faced. Between her daughter's activities and school, even a quick trip to the Strip was a rarity. It saddened her to think that her new position might make her even more unavailable to her daughters. Did she really want to go through with any of this? She needed more answers. "My daughters would love to come. Especially if that means being able to take a ride over the lake."

"I wouldn't dream of not giving them a complimentary lift all to themselves. Maybe they'll want to move there. Wouldn't that be nice? A sprawling apartment overlooking the water for you and your girls? You'd never have to drive to work."

The idea sounded perfect, almost too good to be true! Her girls would have to change schools, but they'd at least be in the same school system. Would it take some convincing? Not if she didn't mention a word about moving until after they'd seen this magical place by the water. They'd never want to leave.

She thought about convincing Shane to move out there

as well so she'd have a friend in the neighborhood. He didn't need to live in that big old house by himself anymore—certainly not with all those memories. Sapphire Springs could provide a fresh start for everyone. *Best of all, they'd live only a few miles from Aurora.*

Christina felt the benefits of this new venture burst in her fervent imagination, flooding her neural pathways with limitless possibilities. She'd just stumbled upon a boundless wellspring of prosperity. "I'll meet you there this Saturday. Thank you so much. My girls will be thrilled when I extend them your invitation."

chapter 30

A cloud of hot steam billowed out of the open doorway of the yoga room, collecting on the cold glass of the studio's main entrance. Shane shivered, wiping a damp lavender scented facecloth across his brow before tossing it into the used towel basket. Normally, he'd drag his worn out self toward the lockers after a *Thunder Thursday* afternoon session, but a flashy yellow piece of paper adhered to the wall caught his attention. "Hey, Christina. Look!" He pointed to the small notice just above the laundry bin. "They're hosting a yoga certification workshop. We could both be instructors. Heck, we should open our own studio."

Christina threw her towel in with the rest of the sweaty

rags before leaning in to get a closer look at the advertisement. "Five thousand dollars. Did you read that part?" She chuckled. "I know what yoga teachers make in this town, and it isn't enough. Certainly not if you start five grand in the hole. Besides, for once in my life my career is finally going somewhere really big."

Shane stopped walking and turned his attention straight toward her. He couldn't tell if he felt jealous over her budding professional life or simply annoyed by her reluctance to give details. "Come on. You keep saying that, but you refuse to elaborate. What does 'really big' actually mean?"

"Things are being finalized as we speak." She placed her thumb on the locker scanner and pulled her shoes out from the row of storage boxes along the wall. "I'm not about to jinx all of it by divulging anything prematurely. But here's what I do know: Durango Electric finally understands my worth, and they've offered to pay me every penny I've asked for."

He held in an oncoming sigh, not wanting to appear frustrated or unhappy with her sudden good fortune. Thankfully, he didn't need to worry about money. He only wanted to feel capable of making his own, something he hadn't done since before he married David. He'd completely forgotten the excitement of payday. For the past fifteen years, he had every last one of his material needs met and then some. While others out there likely dreamed of taking his place, he saw homelife for what it was—incomplete. And it bugged him that something as simple as finding an enjoyable job could prove so challenging. Come to think of it, he might just take the certification course by himself if that's what it took. Forget begging Christina. He'd gotten quite good at yoga on his own in the past year. He learned to relax, to breathe, to not react. Not to mention his glutes, which had never looked better. *Who said he couldn't teach others to achieve the same?* "I'm happy for you, Christina. You know I've always been a cheerleader for you. I just want to do something with the rest of my life that doesn't involve a new recipe or a more efficient way of washing and drying linens. I want to do something that has meaning."

"Your time is coming." Christina put on her socks and laced up her shoes before rolling up her yoga mat. "I promise. I have big news for the both of us."

Then why did she look like she'd leave any minute? Shane didn't want to have to wait to find out what the rest of his life might consist of. *If she wanted him as his sidekick, so be it. As long as he retained complete control over his uniform —and he refused to clean toilets.* In all fairness, he simply wanted to know what the heck was going on. Christina hadn't given him a satisfying answer about anything in the past twenty-four hours. "Let me buy you a coconut milk smoothie before we head out. We'll sit in the far corner away from all the gossip about the latest yoga attire and get down to business."

"That's so sweet of you." Christina hadn't ever declined his smoothie offers in the past. "But my girls are waiting for me at home. They're probably starving for dinner and attention by now. I don't spend nearly enough time with them as it is. And the way things are heating up at work, it's only going to get worse."

Shane wished to ask if he could at least join them for dinner, but the look on Christina's face suggested her desire to be alone with her girls tonight. Trying hard not to stumble into a pity party, he couldn't help but notice how much he missed Aurora. He'd practically forgotten the feeling of family, except that he knew he wanted one terribly now. "Say hello to Joanna and Leena for me in that case. You should bring them over this Saturday. We'll all play Crazy Eights together on the DimensionTab. I'll even prepare a chocolate fondue for the occasion, complete with marshmallows and graham crackers."

Christina stopped short of pressing the button to open the studio's front entrance doors. "I'm so glad you reminded me. I needed to ask you a small favor?"

Small? She didn't know the meaning of that word. Nothing he'd done for her recently fit in that category. Truthfully, he didn't ask for small favors either. Most fell on a scale of large to huge. "Tell me what you need, and I'll tell you if I agree to it or not."

"Okay." She proceeded through the open doorway, heading for her parking space right next to his. "I'm going to Sapphire Springs for work this Saturday. I'm taking the girls per the boss's invitation. I need someone to keep an eye on them."

"Boss? You mean Bill Rucker?" Shane hated the way that name tasted in his mouth, recalling everything that conniving man had done to David and Aurora. "You really want me to be in the same room as him? I'll murder the bastard."

Christina leaned up against the door of the Yosemite. "I

don't need you to be anywhere near him. In fact, the farther away my girls are from my business duties the better. I won't mention a word to anyone about you being there, except to my girls of course. Can I count on you? Please, this is really important."

But what about their plans to rescue Apollo? Shane drew his gaze toward the ground in order to hide the growing resentment in his eyes. "Aren't you forgetting what we agreed upon earlier?" He felt like he shouldn't have to elaborate beyond that. "We talked about this, didn't we? Or am I making things up?"

"I promised you that we'll get him back, and we will. It's all part of the plan." She sounded both bothered and offended. Or maybe just tired. "I'd love to explain more to you, but I'm short on time."

He wanted to believe her. And, yes, he wanted to do her the favor. In fact, he liked being around her girls. Not only were they extremely well-behaved, but they reminded him of how it felt to have Aurora by his side. "I'll do it. But I need details before I go with you. You've got to explain how a trip to Sapphire Springs helps us to get back Apollo."

"Oh, I get it." Christina's eyes revealed a rare flabbergasted expression, which quickly dissolved into a fit of nervous laughter. "If I weren't so late heading home already, I'd sit around and chat. Can I call you after the girls get ready for bed?" She hopped up into her truck and rolled down the window. "By the way, you'll be getting paid for this. I ultimately need to hire you on as my consultant. FYI, the pay is better than any yoga studio in town. Remember that before you sign up for that ridiculously expensive seminar." The Yosemite pulled out of its parking space. "I'll call you about Saturday. Get home safely."

It always happened that way with Christina. One favor magically led to an even greater one—as if he had no say in the matter. *Did he like the idea of working under her? Too soon to tell.* One thing remained certain, however. He couldn't possibly be on Durango Electric's payroll. Bill would never stand to cut checks for the widower of the man he woefully exiled.

The more Shane thought about the scenario, the more he dreaded it. He had an obligation to get Apollo back. Did Christina truly understand that? Or had Durango Electric's endless halls of smoke and mirrors fooled her just like they had done to David? Shane felt determined to reach out to Aurora immediately, but he noticed his watch vibrate before he even brought it toward his face.

David's number? "Hello?" Shane's rational side didn't believe in ghosts, but he had an emotional side that held firmly to a set of peculiar and mysterious notions, none of which gave him any peace of mind and only served to upset him at odd hours of the night.

"Hi, you're David's husband, are you not?" The voice had a low but nonetheless feminine pitch, and it sounded familiar, although he couldn't place it immediately.

"Excuse me, but who is this?" He wanted to ask how the heck she'd gotten his number, and then it clicked. She'd kept it this whole time. Cyphan Creek had confiscated David's watch. She'd called him weeks ago with it.

"If you're David's husband, and I have every reason to believe you are, then you'll know who I am."

Of course he already knew, which made him intensely nervous all of a sudden. He had to fight against his racing heart while trying to maintain some semblance of steady and controlled breathing. "I think you've gotten your wires crossed, lady. I don't know who you're referring to." He released the call, regretting having answered it to begin with. Knowing that she still had David's watch drove him insane. *How could she live with herself? Did she steal her jewelry from corpses as well?* Shane wished to curtail his mind from drifting down a macabre path, but his train of thought had already set itself in motion.

Time to get in the Mogollon and head home. He resolved to call Aurora in a minute when his pulse returned to normal.

His watch vibrated a second time, and again David's number appeared. He knew better than to answer it. He'd never respond to that number again no matter how badly it haunted him. Shane had absolutely no business with the devil herself. Unfortunately, his overly curious nature yearned to play the voicemail she'd just left for him, all eighty seconds of it. *This has to be interesting.*

"I remember you. You were wearing a navy cable knit sweater when you walked into my place of business with that fiendish blonde hag of yours. You almost got in the way of my biggest project to date. I should have never let either of you off the premises. I should have turned you into the police. You got lucky, Mr. Shane. You don't want to get in any more trouble with my business. So listen to me spell it out perfectly clear for you. If you ever come back, you'll spend the rest of your life behind bars for unconscionable acts of corporate terrorism."

Part of Shane wanted to delete the message immediately. Out of sight, out of mind. But Christina needed to hear this. Cyphan Creek had just threatened both of them with life imprisonment. Did she have that power? Shane didn't want to test her. Of course, he'd never go back. How foolish of him to think he could carry out a rescue mission completely by himself. He had way overstepped his capacity to be of service to others. No use worrying about it now, however. As long as he kept his distance, the monstrous woman would leave him alone. Being a yoga instructor sounded better and better every minute. Cops didn't arrest yoga teachers over trumped up terrorism charges.

He figured it best to call Christina now before she got too involved with looking after her girls. "Call Christina Daily," he spoke into his watch.

"You've reached Christina's voice pad. Please leave a message."

Shane didn't want to leave a message. He wanted to speak to a human being, someone who would agree that they'd gotten in way over their heads and that they needed to completely rethink their entire approach before they found themselves trapped in a concrete cell with only a twin mattress and an unwalled toilet. "Give me a call as soon as you get this. I've got something you need to hear *ASAP*. It's about Black Diamond."

If only talking about problems made them go away.

Unfortunately, Shane felt even more jittery and upset after having left Christina the voicemail. Would he have felt better if she'd at least picked up the call? He considered backing out of his obligation with her on Saturday because of his growing fears. *No good deed goes unpunished.* He recalled his grandmother reciting that expression when he accidentally broke one of her crystal lamps while dusting it as a boy. Only in a cruel world would helping others lead to a disastrous outcome. But he couldn't think like that. David never thought that way. Christina didn't think that way—and neither did Aurora. Shane had a duty to keep his word. He needed to remain vigilant.

That was it! "Aurora, are you available?" he spoke into his watch just as the Mogollon pulled into the driveway. Hopefully, she'd respond in a minute or two while he unloaded his yoga bag and mat from the vehicle. He needed to talk to someone. He needed reassurance that he hadn't gotten himself in way over his head, even though that's exactly what it felt like.

Thankfully, she responded with a message almost instantly.

I was hoping you'd reach out to me. Sai is determined to get Apollo back even if it means breaking into Black Diamond. He and Shafeen are devising a plan to rescue him tonight.

"Tell me you're not going with them." Shane had faced the danger himself. He knew exactly what they'd be up against. "I don't think it's a good idea. The whole place is on red alert. Cyphan Creek isn't going to let anyone get close to Apollo. For all we know, he might not even be in there any more."

In that case, have you got a better idea?

He didn't. He hadn't a clue how they'd rescue Apollo. He just knew that he didn't want to spend eternity behind bars, and he didn't want Aurora or any of her friends turned into scrap metal. "Wait." No other word came to mind at first. "Wait two more days. Christina says she has more information, but she can't disclose it yet. She's going to tell me everything this Saturday."

Why Saturday? Why not now?

Shane recognized the legitimacy of Aurora's question. "I don't think Christina is all that certain herself yet." Shane hadn't ever doubted his friend up until today. "I'm trusting that she'll come through with reliable information. But we have a new problem." Shane took a deep breath. "Cyphan Creek has found us out. We're on her list of trespassers. She called me just now and said she'll imprison me if I ever set one toe on a blade of grass in front of that infernal hovel of hers."

You act surprised that Cyphan Creek threatened you. You do realize that she's not a good person, right?

Shane realized Aurora didn't mean to be patronizing, but her wording took him by surprise. Of course he knew Cyphan Creek's true nature. However, he felt a bit foolish for needing the reminder. The woman had assumed a defensive position, which meant that she feared Shane and Christina as much as they feared her. "I understand how this works—even if I'm not as smart as David. I'm waiting until I get word back from Christina."

Saturday?

Shane hadn't ever received such curt messages from Aurora until now. Perhaps her robot friends had exposed her to more casual language patterns. "I'm meeting her at Sapphire Springs to watch over her daughters while she takes care of some business with Durango Electric. Can you meet me there? I promise I won't be anywhere near Bill Rucker. We'll be playing near the water mostly."

I'm a mile and a half from Sapphire Springs. I know exactly where it is, and I would be happy to meet you, Leena, and Joanna there.

"Then it's a date." Shane couldn't help but smile after he spoke into his watch. What a breath of fresh air! It took only a few minutes of conversation with his favorite little girl for him to forget all about the threats still dangling over his head.

chapter

"**P**romise me one thing." Christina turned around in the front seat of the Yosemite, making sure she had Leena's attention as well as Joanna's. "You mustn't argue with me about anything today. I can't stress enough how important this meeting is for our future."

"We get it, Mom." Joanna reached for her DimensionTab, which she had stashed beneath the front seat. "You've repeated yourself a million times already."

"No arguments means no arguments," Christina said. "None. I still have time to drop you both off at Grandma's if you'd rather."

"No!" Leena leaned forward. "Joanna won't argue anymore. Will you, Joanna?"

"I wasn't arguing. I was just making a point."

"I don't want to go to Grandma's today." Leena's face turned into that of a puppy's. "I want to go with you. Please, Mom. I promise we'll be good."

Christina knew her girls wouldn't let her down. They'd been talking nonstop for the past three days about visiting Sapphire Springs. As long as she emphasized not to make even the tiniest of fuss, they'd obey her wishes lest she ground them until Christmas. *Was she nervous about meeting Bill Rucker at the site of the new venture?* So much so that she refused to eat dinner last night and breakfast this morning. She barely managed to chew a few measly grapes while she prepared some English muffins with peanut butter for her girls. Bill had promised them all a five-course lunch at the SeaDragon Cafe after they toured the area, and she hoped she'd have some semblance of an appetite by then. "I realize you girls are as excited as I am about the day. Just understand that the same rules apply when you're with Shane as when you're with me. He's promised to chaperone you both out of the goodness of his heart."

"Doesn't he like us?" Leena asked innocently.

"Of course he likes us," Joanna said. "We haven't done anything wrong."

"Your sister is right, Leena." Christina thought about all the things that could go wrong today. *What if the deal fell through? What if Bill Rucker changed his mind?* Shane and her daughters were the least of her worries. "He adores you both, and neither one of you is going to do anything to change that." With all her pent up nerves working overtime, Christina appreciated even more the stability Shane provided her. Despite the challenges they'd faced the past few weeks, they'd become quite a team at boosting up one another. She only hoped she could get him to agree to sign on for the next big adventure.

"This must be it!" Joanna put down her DimensionTab and rolled down the window to feel the air as the Yosemite brought them over a hill overlooking an expansive, shimmering, crystal blue lake. "It's so fresh outside, Mom. Roll down your window so you can smell it!"

Christina did as her daughter recommended, not seeing any harm in playing along even though the lake was still a mile down the winding road. "It does smell nice! Just wait until we get near the bottom. I bet it'll seem like we're at the ocean." She could hardly believe this would be her new place of employment. Not only did she get to be the boss, but she got to have the king of locations to go along with it. After all the years of schooling, answering phones, making coffee, and filing reports, had she actually arrived? A view like the one before her couldn't lie. She only wished David could see where his years of encouragement and support had led her.

The Yosemite headed down the twisting road, approaching a Mediterranean-inspired village whose deep blue glass-tiled solar roofs glittered exactly like the sparkling waters beyond. The buildings grew taller as the truck approached them, some eight-stories high and complete with bell towers, each a pastel shade of either green, yellow, orange, or pink.

"It looks like Disneyland!" Leena said.

"Way cooler than Disneyland." Joanna held out her wrist through the open window and snapped a photo of the lakeside village as the Yosemite found a parking spot in front of the Crystal Inn and Spa.

"It's fabulous, isn't it?" Christina took a deep breath to relieve her jitters before opening the car door and stepping down from the vehicle. She reminded herself not to give into her nerves, but rather to focus instead on the beauty all around her. Surely, in a place as spectacular as this, things could only go right for a change.

"Look at all the colors, Momma!" Leena got out of the car and pointed up toward a group of six kites floating high above the parking lot on the tail of a mild November breeze. "Can we fly one?"

"I'll suggest it to Shane, but I can't make any promises." Christina looked at the intricately shaped pieces of fabric, each a different design, each one dancing in the breeze in its own unique path. For a moment, she felt herself flying high upon the mighty wind as it lifted her to new heights, to a place she'd only ever imagined in her dreams. It felt incredible to be a part of something that kept getting bigger and bigger every day. "Keep in mind the hundreds of things to do and explore still. I promise that you're going to have a great time no matter what you do today."

"I want to ride in one of those." Joanna pointed across the lake to a glistening orb that appeared to float high above the water on a wire. "What is that?"

Christina didn't want to ruin the surprise. She recalled that Bill had promised them all a ride on the lake's signature attraction. "That's the SeaDragon Flyer, the world's longest overwater aerial gondola." Durango Electric had designed the whole thing two years ago. She remembered helping David with some of the drawings. She almost felt guilty for not taking the girls here sooner, but the opportunity to ride for free hadn't been granted to her until now. "Let me see what I can do. I'll ask Bill, but again, I can't make any promises."

"What does it do?" Leena looked confused and more interested in the kites flying above her head.

"What does it look like?" Joanna said with a smirk. "It takes you out over the water above the sailboats."

"Come on, you two. Stay with me." Christina stepped onto the sidewalk in front of the boutique hotel and walked toward the main part of the village, hoping to see a sign of her boss. "When we find Bill, he's going to take us on a little tour before lunch." She saw him walk out of a shop a hundred feet in front of her before she finished speaking. "And we have excellent timing, girls. There he is." She hurried them alongside her, realizing she was technically five minutes late for their agreed upon meeting time of eleven o'clock.

"I'm so glad you brought your daughters." Bill smiled and extended a hand to greet both of them. "Now remind me your names again."

"I'm Joanna." She shook his hand with confidence like her mother had instructed her.

"And you must be?" He bent down to get closer.

"Go on. Tell him your name." Christina patted her youngest daughter's back in an effort to get her closer to the man in charge."

"I'm Leena," she said, preferring to curtsy rather than extend her hand in kind.

"Both of you are absolutely lovely. Your mother should be very proud of you both." Bill stood and shook Christina's hand before offering her and her daughters each a bottle of water. "We have a busy day ahead of us. Is everyone ready for a little tour?"

"We're ready." Christina smiled, accepting the small plastic bottle from Bill. Her boss's affable and generous demeanor made some of her anxiety fall by the wayside. "My girls and I have been looking forward to this ever since you gave us the invitation."

"It'll be brief, a half hour at most." Bill led them down the sidewalk and into the central shopping district's main plaza. "We have lunch reservations in an hour, so this should hopefully work up our appetites."

Christina motioned for her girls to stay close and follow directly behind her and Bill. She could manage to keep track of her girls for a small tour, but she appreciated that Shane would meet them after lunch to watch over them while she discussed with Bill the finer details of running a new business.

"This is Santorini Square." Bill walked out of the shadow of the arcade and into the sunlight that poured into the open courtyard. "We almost rented a space in here, but we got a better deal on a space in the newer shopping esplanade, which is being built toward the eastern end of the lake. And there was already a hair salon here. It seemed silly to build one on top of the other. But we'll meet back here for lunch. Not much has opened on the other side yet."

"Not much?" Christina felt confused. When was she expected to start work? She hoped it would be soon since she'd already arranged some of her expenditures around the new income.

"Nothing, actually." Bill cleared his throat. "Not yet, anyways. The building exteriors are finished, but we still have to build the shop inside. We'll be the first tenant at the new plaza."

Tempted to ask more questions, Christina weighed what she'd heard him say. It hardly sounded like there'd be much, if any, business at all since they'd be the only shop at first. Why would Bill even consider such a location when Las Vegas had innumerable prime spaces for a salon that matched his vision, ones that would be so much closer to Durango Electric? "May I ask what my role is going to be during construction?"

"I'm glad you asked," Bill said. "We'll discuss more of those details after lunch when we meet with our partners from Black Diamond."

Christina felt her stomach begin to knot itself up again. She remembered him saying something about a partnership with them, but she didn't imagine they'd get involved with the management of the operation. And she certainly didn't envision she'd have to meet with any of them today.

Having to face Cyphan Creek did nothing to restore Christina's appetite, and she hoped somehow that the vampire lady would be absent at lunch. "I can't wait to take a peek at the space." Christina tried to mask any reservations she had with forced enthusiasm. "If it's even half as beautiful as what we've seen so far, I'll be impressed."

"You're going to love every square foot of it. I assure you. In fact, I picked out the store specifically with you in mind."

Looking behind her to make sure her daughters hadn't wandered off, Christina smiled at them both to acknowledge their exceptionally good, quiet behavior. "Doesn't this sound exciting, girls? Your mom is going to have a brand new shop to manage."

They both smiled politely, their attention focused mainly on the activities on the water, the kayaks, the parasailing, and a dozen circular watercrafts that hovered over the lake via water-jet propulsion.

"They're mesmerized by it all, aren't they?" Bill said. "And why wouldn't they be? It's the most beautiful place in all of Las Vegas. You're going to fall in love when you see the view from your office balcony."

Christina's excitement resumed, replacing the sinking sensation in her gut with much more pleasant flutters of the heart. A week ago, she'd never anticipated she could have it this good. An office with a balcony? Overlooking the water? If she were dreaming, she didn't ever want to wake up. "Oh, my goodness. Is it that building over there?" She pointed to a fantasy-like three-story tower clad in shimmering gold glass topped with an intricate lattice-patterned dome.

"And that balcony is where your office will be." Bill laughed. "You didn't think I'd put you in a dump, did you? I have way too much class to build a business on skid row, my dear."

"I just never thought in a million years I'd work in a place so enchanting." Christina couldn't stop smiling. "Girls, isn't it marvelous?"

"Do we get to live here?" Joanna asked, her voice full of sudden glee.

"Can we, Mom?" Leena added.

Bill winked at Christina. "They're getting a little ahead of themselves, aren't they? I can't say that I blame them. I'm ready to move out here myself. In fact, I might have to rethink the location of our corporate offices."

"Do we get to go inside?" Christina asked, secretly wanting to know what it would feel like to step out onto that picture-perfect terrace.

"Not yet, unfortunately." Bill turned to face Christina and her girls. "Hardhats are a must for anyone who goes inside, and I can't think of a good enough reason to justify messing up anyone's hair before lunchtime. We'll take a quick jaunt around the premises, and then we'll walk along the water's edge the whole way back before heading to the restaurant. How does that sound?"

"It sounds perfect to me." Christina tried her best not to let on about her disappointment for not getting to glance inside at least once. She'd gladly don a hardhat later to get a closer look at her future if possible. "How's that sound, girls? Are you getting hungry?"

They cheered in chorus, obviously excited by the sights

they'd gotten to see, which made Christina feel a whole lot better about the tremendous changes underway in their lives. She'd wait until they'd arrived back at home to address any of the potentially frightening prospects such as changing schools, or finding a new piano teacher and gymnastics coach closer to their new neighborhood. For now, she just wanted them to revel in the feeling of joyous possibilities.

Bill led the tiny group around an oblong fountain in front of the under-construction shop. "That's where the main sign will go." He pointed to a broad rectangular space above a set of open glass doors. "They're busy inside getting everything ready for the grand opening in January. Exciting, isn't it?"

"You have your hands full with grand openings, don't you?" Christina sneaked a quick peek inside the shop's entrance to have a better look at her new workspace. "I mean, with the showroom and retail outlet in Bullhead City opening soon, and now this." She almost felt bad about the added stress on Bill over an endeavor that was essentially her creation.

"Child's play, my dear." Bill steered the party away from the storefront, unfortunately limiting Christina's view. "I learned that after the merger with Western America Power, we can do anything. Nothing but a couple of little side projects, really. And besides, we have smart people like you in charge to run them."

Christina let that last part soak in for a few seconds. Here she was, the general manager of a business with which she had zero experience in running. Would she figure it out?

Did she have a choice? She realized that the task would flow much smoother once she had Shane on board to help her out with commanding the ship. She'd pay him under the table if she had to, at least until things got settled. She desperately needed his presence. A quick glance at her watch told her he'd be on site in an hour. Just enough time to have lunch. Afterwards, she'd have to excuse herself in order to slip away with her girls so she could put them in his care.

"Did I hear you were hungry?" Bill turned and looked at both of Christina's girls who silently nodded their heads.

"I think we're all excited to have some lunch." Christina felt her own appetite emerge now that her angst had somewhat subsided. "What's the name of the restaurant again?"

Bill pointed to the water tramway in the distance. "We're dining at the SeaDragon Cafe, named in honor of our beautiful aerial transporter over there. If you ladies like, we'll conclude our afternoon with a ride above the lake once we've finished business."

Leena and Joanna both looked wide-eyed at their mother as if to ask permission.

"I told you there'd be a big surprise, didn't I?" Christina laughed, ecstatic that her girls seemed to be enjoying their time as much as she was. She knew that their fun adventure would only get more exciting once Shane arrived.

They all followed Bill on a stone pathway right next to the water's edge and then up and over a miniature suspension bridge, which connected the main shopping area to the new one under construction. As they walked toward the restaurant, the noonday sun hit the water at just the right angle that it forced everyone to shield their eyes from the glittering reflection.

Leena pointed to a family of ducks, which flew overhead before landing themselves on the water's mirror-like surface. "I wish I could fly just like them."

"Stick with your mom, little lady." Bill smiled at Christina, opening the door to the cafe. "She'll teach you how."

Christina relished the compliment from her boss, feeling more assured of her decision to stay aboard with the company. *Did she feel guilty about what happened to David?* She certainly felt sorry for him. He had taught her many things, mainly the importance of adhering to logic instead of emotion. *But would she break the rules like he had?* She knew better than to rock the boat. She had a family to raise. Her daughters counted on her for support. She'd finally found her path, and it was time to move forward with head held high.

"I've reserved the private dining room," Bill said to the hostess. "It should be under the name Rucker."

"Yes, of course, Mr. Rucker," the hostess said with an exaggerated smile. "Everything is ready. I'll take you there right now."

She led them through the main dining room past sculptures and paintings of serpents and sea monsters of every size and origin. Arriving at a set of closed doors, she opened them to reveal a giant crystal dragon suspended from the circular room's high ceiling, as well as a spectacular view of the entire lake and aerial tramway.

Christina would have normally said something about

the unparalleled dining accommodations, but her focus immediately went to the person already in place at the head of the table—Cyphan Creek.

"So nice of you to join us," said the stoic woman dressed in a sleek black and white checkered dress that made Christina think twice about her simple gray skirt and jacket. "And you've brought your daughters. Charming."

"Thank you." Christina kept her chin up despite the nagging desire to look away. She felt foolish for not better preparing herself for an encounter with the Queen of Black Diamond. *Out of all the guests that could have joined them, it had to be the ice witch!* "These are my girls, Leena and Joanna."

They both curtseyed and took the seats closest to their mother, offering nothing more than respectful smiles. *Could they sense the sudden chill in the room as well?*

"I think the banquet is all set up for us to enjoy lunch before we get down to business." Bill took off his jacket and placed it on the back of the chair next to Cyphan Creek. "You may all help yourselves when you're ready."

But no one else had shown up yet. *With an entire buffet set before them, there had to be more people coming.* "Thank you." Christina set down her purse and gestured toward her daughters that it was okay to get some much needed nourishment. Once at the small serving table, she handed them each a plate and a wrapped napkin with silverware. "I see that they're using our *EarthCore* culinary heating system," Christina spoke up to break the silence.

"You should see the kitchen," Bill said proudly. "Every-

thing is made by Durango Electric. Everything." He directed that last word playfully toward the frigid woman seated
next to him.

"Oh, Bill. Wait until you see what we've brought to the
table," Cyphan Creek said.

He turned his full attention curiously toward her but
didn't say a word.

"Durango Electric can supply the restaurants with all
the latest kitchen gadgets," she offered in a nonchalant
and slightly aloof manner while adjusting a heavily jeweled
timepiece on her wrist. "Black Diamond will staff them."

Intrigued by the direction of the unfolding conversation, Christina put a bed of fresh greens on her plate along
with a few cherry tomatoes and two thin breadsticks before
returning to her place at the table.

"We're ready for you, *IVAN*." Cyphan Creek snapped
her fingers.

Christina's heart sank. She knew right then that she
wouldn't like what she was about to witness, and her appetite disintegrated. She couldn't take one bite of lettuce even
if she tried. *How could her beloved dream suddenly unfold
into a hellish nightmare so quickly?*

The double doors opened once more, and in walked a
four-and-a-half foot figure all-too familiar to Christina—
Apollo. Dressed in a tuxedo, the small boy approached the
table, offering every female a long-stemmed red rose.

"Who is this?" Bill asked with a mix of surprise and
suspicion.

"IVAN. It's what I call my little creation." Cyphan Creek

motioned with her finger to draw the boy nearer to her. "Intelligence Via Android Nanotechnology. My answer to the growing labor shortage."

"You built him?" Bill didn't look the least bit enthused, but withheld from speaking the displeasure obvious in his wide gaze.

"He's the first of many that we intend to build at Black Diamond."

Leena clutched her rose tight to her chest, stared at the boy, and then looked at Christina with large and innocent eyes. "He looks almost like—"

"Don't say it." Christina unfortunately couldn't think of a better way to silence her well-meaning child.

"But you don't know what she was going to say," said Joanna in her sister's defense.

"Of course I know what she was going to say." Christina immediately transformed herself into the actress she had learned to portray many times over the past few months. "She was going to say that he looks exactly like our neighbor Charlie. But she's wrong. Charlie's shorter with blond hair and a wider face."

"But that's not who I meant." Leena picked up her spoon, stirring her tomato bisque with the ornate piece of silverware.

"Remember what I said in the car." Christina knew her daughters wouldn't dare contradict her. They had too much at stake now with every wonderful thing they'd seen today. They'd both figure out that any mention of Aurora would mean punishment beyond anything they could imagine.

"Finish up your lunch, and then I'll take you to your chaperone for the rest of the afternoon."

"Chaperone?" Bill sounded like he'd never heard the term before. "You mean to say you brought their nanny with you?"

"Not exactly." Christina had to bite her lip to keep from laughing at the idea of Shane dressed like Mary Poppins. "He's my assistant. And he's just arrived in the parking lot to take the girls off my hands while we discuss our important endeavor in greater detail."

Leena and Joanna both began scarfing down their food, obviously hungry and not wanting to leave the tiniest morsel behind. Christina didn't want to rush them, but she had to before they mistakenly said anything that might land her in hot water. Had a robot not entered the scenes, she could possibly let her daughters actually enjoy the elegant meal. She'd make up for it by handing Shane a few extra bucks to treat them to ice cream.

"I don't understand. You have to take them right this instant?" Bill had barely touched his own plate, and he must have sensed the lunacy of her forcing her daughters to leave before lunch had really gotten underway. "We can wait to get to the nitty gritty until at least after some dessert if they'd rather stay."

Christina glanced at her watch, noticing a text from Shane saying that he'd arrived a few minutes early and was waiting inside the Mogollon. "We shouldn't keep my assistant waiting much longer." She looked over at her daughters who were still busy chewing. "You two have a busy day of shopping ahead. We need new outfits for our upcoming Christmas photo."

Joanna looked happily surprised by the suggestion. "We're getting new clothes, too?"

"And accessories if you stay on your best behavior." Christina felt thrilled she could get them to cooperate so easily.

"What a pity." Cyphan Creek took her attention off her kidnapped possession and looked across the table at Christina. "I wanted to learn more about your daughters, but I'm sure they'll have much more fun being away from us boring grown-ups."

"You'll meet us back here shortly, Christina, won't you?" Bill tried to divert his focus away from the robot that had obviously captivated his attention. "We have plenty of things to discuss still. Funny how the day keeps getting more and more interesting as we go."

Christina figured it wouldn't take her more than ten minutes to ensure her daughters were in good hands for a couple of hours. "Indeed, it does." She didn't want any more surprises if she had any say in the matter. "I'll be back in a few moments."

"They're going to ride the tram with us later, aren't they?" Cyphan Creek asked as they walked out the door. "It's a perfect day for it."

Not wanting to risk disappointing anyone, least of all her girls, Christina turned around immediately. "They wouldn't miss it for the world."

chapter 32

"Aurora, please tell me you're on your way." Shane stared out the windshield of the Mogollon as he spoke the words into his watch, hypnotized by the bright expanse of crystalline waters before him. He didn't have any reason to suspect that she wouldn't make good on her promise. The urge to reach out to Aurora stemmed more from anxiety than doubt. What could he honestly have to fear in a place as serene and spectacular as this? If only he'd spare himself from listing the possibilities! Despite countless hours of yoga practice and meditative breathing, he never seemed to escape the constant dread embedded in his DNA.

We're already here. On the water. Sai's taken us out onto the lake in his boat. Can you see us? We're in the fast one with the blue stripe around it.

After reading Aurora's text, Shane spotted the zipping seacraft immediately as it went airborne, launching itself spontaneously from the lake and landing with hardly a splash before resuming its course along the frigid November waters. The mild afternoon provided no hint of the actual temperature of the lake. With nighttime temperatures hovering around forty degrees this time of year, watersports remained low on his list of enjoyable fall hobbies. "I see you now." He waved, even though he knew that he sat too far away for them to see him. "Don't fly away on me, okay? I just got here. I'm about to meet up with Christina's girls."

Looking up, he noticed Joanna and Leena heading toward the Mogollon from across the parking lot with their mother. He got out of the vehicle and walked the few remaining steps to meet them.

"We're so glad you came." Christina hugged Shane quickly before cozying up to his ear. "I don't have much time, but I have crazy news about Apollo—he's here."

"What?" Shane whispered back, sensing the game change completely. "Hold on a minute—for real?"

"Sort of. It's weird. Really weird. I'll text you in a minute." She handed Shane a folded wad of cash totalling an unexpected seven hundred dollars before turning around to walk back to the restaurant. "You know what to do. Go have some fun and watch for my messages."

"Do you have to go this second?" Shane sensed her urgency, but he yearned to discuss the immediate matter at hand.

"I should have more information for you in a few minutes." She turned and looked at him with a fleeting glance. "I can't afford to blow this."

Seeing the mark of determination in her expression, he knew not to keep her any longer. "I'm going to text you first. Promise you won't ignore my messages."

"You have my word." She waved goodbye to her daughters and hastened back to the cafe entrance.

Shane took a deep breath to collect his thoughts before looking down at the two lovely princesses now in his care. "Your mom told me you both need new dresses for your holiday photo." He tapped his watch to lock the doors of the Mogollon. "Shall we get to it then?"

"I can pick out my own, right?" Joanna looked up at him with skepticism in her eyes. "Our mom said I get to choose my dress."

"You can pick one out for me." Leena smiled up at him charmingly. "I might need some help."

"Fair enough," Shane said, not wanting to cause anyone grief. "My expert fashion advice is available to any and all who need it. And believe me, there are a lot more people in this world who need it than don't. But I won't stand in the way of anyone's decisions." Shane extended a hand to each of them. "No matter how dreadful."

Leena immediately took his hand, using her other to shade her eyes and scout the area.

Joanna seemed more cautious but eventually took his hand as well. "Can I pick what store we go into?"

"Be my guest." Shane led them to the sidewalk and into

the main plaza. "Santorini Square," he said aloud, reading the sign in front of a collection of pastel colored buildings donning solar-tiled roofs. He had always imagined the actual Santorini to look whiter and brighter with scattered traces of sky blue. But who was he to judge? "I'm sure one of these shops will do nicely."

"I want to go in there." Joanna pointed to a large shop on the second story with a sign that read *Pacific Coast Fashions*.

The image of a giant surfboard immediately floated front and center inside Shane's head. Everything about the place, from the name to the logo, made it seem like the perfect spot to purchase tanning oil and a bathing suit, but he'd put his better judgement aside for a second. Maybe Miss *Tall 'n Sassy* would eventually learn to trust him once she came to realize the great disparity between her own good sense and his. "Pacific Coast Fashions it is," he said, trying hard not to roll his eyes.

When they walked inside the store, Shane let go of their hands so that they could run toward whatever rack caught their attention first. He had to admit his surprise. Not a single bathing suit in sight. Actually, the dresses didn't look half bad. If he poked around long enough, he figured he might actually ferret out something for himself even.

"I think I found it," Joanna called out to no one in particular, holding up a shimmering white and teal gown.

A female sales associate with a measuring laser swinging around her neck soon approached her. "My, that is a lovely one. What's the occasion? Christmas dance?"

"Close," Shane said as he eyed the dress from top to

bottom. "Winter wedding. Her Royal Highness The *Snow-It-All* is getting married finally."

"Stop!" Joanna laughed. "I need a dress for my family's Christmas photo. Can I try this one on?"

The store clerk walked to the nearest changing room and unlocked the door, inviting Joanna to step inside.

Figuring it would be a minute, Shane decided to text Christina. *Okay, time to spill it. What exactly is going on with Apollo?*

Waiting a mere handful of seconds, he felt his watch vibrate. *A call from Christina instead of a text? This had to be better than he thought!*

"You'll never believe what's happening," she said.

Shane didn't feel like playing the guessing game. He wanted cold, hard information. "I can't keep up with you. Please tell me it's about Apollo."

"It's even bigger." Christina sounded quiet, but he could tell by the excitement in her voice that she'd just entered her own little world, and there was no getting a word in edgewise. "The whole room is filled with reporters. Durango Electric is making a press release about the future of the company. Bill's talking about the upcoming merger with Black Diamond, the opening of the Bullhead City Showroom, and get this—my shop! I'm gonna be on the news!"

"That's fantastic." Shane wanted to sound enthusiastic for his dear friend, but none of this gave him any insight about Apollo. What had they done to Christina in there? She'd clearly lost focus. "Please say you have more imformation about what you were telling me earlier in the parking lot."

"Wait!" Christina came through with another burst of excitement. "I haven't even gotten to the best part. Black Diamond just handed Apollo over to Durango Electric!"

Oh, God. Shane paused for a second, not knowing how to react. Christina sounded so enthralled about something that didn't seem even remotely beneficial to their mission. "I'm sorry. What? Black Diamond? Who has Apollo now?"

"We do!" Christina had gotten carried away at this point, like she'd been possessed. "Tell Aurora that Apollo is back with Durango Electric. He's gonna be safe. We just have to figure out a way to get him out of there."

Shane almost got Christina's logic, but the situation still seemed a far cry from being resolved. Sure, he'd notify Aurora. Maybe she and her new friends would have some ideas for how to get him out of there. But that didn't suddenly erase the fact that Apollo remained in the hands of someone who neither deserved him nor knew what to do with him. "Christina, listen up. Cyphan Creek hates us. I don't know what's going on in there, but I got the strangest phone call the other day."

"Shane, I'm so sorry. I'd really love to talk more, but I'm about to be interviewed by ACV News. I promise we'll talk more about the details afterward. I'll let you get back to your shopping."

"Wait a minute!" Shane stopped talking the moment he heard the click on the other line. *What in the world had gotten into her?* This was not the Christina he knew and admired. The meeting clearly had her in the heat of the moment. She hadn't absorbed anything he had to say no matter how pertinent. Actually, he didn't understand the full story himself, which didn't help his case. The idea that Black Diamond would just hand over Apollo to Durango Electric threw him for a loop. Now he had an even wider gap in his logic to fill before he could grasp the grand scheme of things, let alone explain it to someone else. All that aside, no missing piece of the puzzle could take away from the fact that something still felt terribly wrong.

"How do you like it?" Joanna walked out of the dressing room wrapped in an ornately embroidered bodice with ample white fabric flowing beneath it.

"Spin around for me," Shane said, suddenly distracted by the young and beautiful enchantress in front of him.

The dress billowed around her like a blanket of rose petals on a gentle breeze. "Can I have this one? I don't think I need to try on another."

"I concur," Shane said, happy that her choice had aligned with his own discerning tastes. "Let's see if we can find an appropriate matching one for your sister."

Leena rushed up to Shane with a grand specimen already in hand. "How about this one?"

"I thought you wanted help picking one out." Shane took the gown from her and held it in front of him to get a fair look at it. Mostly white and purple with a few silver accents, it actually seemed like a suitable choice for a girl her age.

"You'll say if it looks good on me, won't you?"

"Put it on, and we shall see." Shane glanced back over at Joanna who was busy admiring herself in the mirror. "You love it beyond words, don't you?"

"It's absolutely perfect. Now how about an outfit for you?"

The idea seemed tempting, but Shane didn't want to impede on their fun-filled adventure. "Today is all about the two of you. I have enough clothes to last me until at least next June."

"Mom wants you in the picture," Leena said from the other side of the closed dressing room door. "Don't you want to be in it with us?"

How exactly did *he* factor into the equation all of a sudden? It's not that he didn't want to be in it. He liked the idea of a holiday photo, something he hadn't been in since the first year he and David were married. *Come to think of it, why hadn't the two of them continued on with that tradition?* Shane mailed out the yearly holiday greeting—if anyone was to blame, it was himself. "Okay. What do you suppose I should wear?"

"How about a teal sweater to match my dress?" suggested Joanna, coming out of the changing room with her new dazzling garment draped over her arm.

According to his recollection, he didn't yet own such a sweater, but the idea of it enticed him. "I suppose you saw one already?"

"Right when we walked in." Joanna traced her steps back to the front of the store. "What's your size?" She asked, hunting through a rack of bold colored knits.

Funny how resolute she seemed to get him in the photo. He liked the feeling of being welcomed into the clan, especially since his own small family had evaporated practically overnight. "Medium. And if they have it, I'll try it on." He quickly texted Christina to clue her in on their progress. *The girls both found their dresses, and now they want to get me a sweater. They're determined to have me in your family photo.*

Christina responded right away surprisingly. *Good! They follow instructions well. Our interview went faster than expected. Bill wants us all to head straight to the aerial transporter station.*

Shane couldn't believe it. Christina had orchestrated the whole shopping spree in advance as a way to get him closer to the family, hadn't she? *I'll walk the girls over to meet you outside the entrance gates.* He felt his watch vibrate, signifying an incoming call.

"You're coming on the tram with us. You know that, right?" Christina sounded both elated and adamant.

"I had no intention of getting on that thing. And besides, I don't exactly think it's a good idea that Bill sees me. Do you?"

"He knows more than I thought." Christina laughed as if it weren't such a big deal. "He's accepted my request to hire you as my assistant manager and principal buyer. You won't believe the salary I negotiated for you!"

Strange. Shane considered himself perfectly capable of negotiating his own salary, even if he had zero inclination what the job entailed. Nonetheless, the idea of working as a principal buyer appealed to him. *Maybe Christina knew what she was doing in that meeting all along.* Amazing how things had a way of suddenly working themselves out. "Are the hours flexible? Remember, I'm a busy HOA president."

"Half the job can be done from home in your pajamas."

"I don't wear pajamas. Kidding!" Shane laughed, feeling a sense of importance he hadn't felt in a long time. Who'd have ever guessed that he'd work alongside Christina at Durango Electric? If only David could see how things were turning out now. *On second thought, maybe he'd be jealous that his domestic husband had great career potential outside the realm of neighborhood board meetings.* "We're paying for our things now, and we'll meet you in fifteen minutes."

Joanna came up to him with a striking teal sweater in hand. "You're in luck. They had one left in your size."

He accepted it, taking the sweater off it's hanger before pulling it over his button-down shirt. "We have a winner!"

"You look very handsome in it," Joanna said. "How about a tie to go underneath?"

Definitely not his style. "I think we've gotten everything we've come for. We can pick out accessories later. Right now we have to meet your mom at the tramway station."

"We really get to ride it?" Leena came out of the changing room with her dress on.

"Yes, my princess." Shane looked her over hurriedly, approving of her choice in outfit despite the fact that it didn't quite seem to adhere to the established color sequence. "Let's get you out of that dress so we can pay for our things and head on over before they leave without us."

"Okay!" She didn't hesitate a second before running back in the dressing room for a lightning-quick costume change.

"Don't tear your dress," Shane said. "We still have fifteen minutes." He collected her outfit as soon as she threw it over the door. "Just meet us by the register when you're finished in there."

With a bag in each of their possession, he and the girls walked out onto the sun-drenched second-story promenade and down the stairs toward the lake. Shane felt his watch vibrate, assuming it was Christina again, but a quick glance revealed a text message from Aurora. *Shoot!* He meant to message her from inside the shop earlier. "Run up ahead, girls. I have to make a quick call. I'll catch up to you in a minute." He paused, keeping a close eye on Leena and Joanna as they skipped ahead with their bags in hand.

I saw Apollo. He's here.

"I meant to tell you," Shane said into his watch. "Christina just informed me that Black Diamond has handed him over to Durango Electric. We're going to get him back for you, I promise." He contemplated telling her about the details of himself being a company insider now. In a managerial position to boot! But he'd go over all that later in person.

There's something very wrong. He doesn't look the same.

"He's probably not the same," Shane admitted. "He won't be the same until his processors are back in order. Don't worry. They don't know what to do with him. They won't ever figure it out. They don't know the half of David's ingenious design."

We need to get him back. Now.

That was all he heard from her. *So be it.* If she and her compatriots had a way of snagging Apollo back today, good for them. He had other things on his mind—mainly not getting in over his head too soon. A ride above the water seemed like the best possible way to end a magnificent after-noon filled with wonderful surprises. *Now if he could just get Aurora back into his life, everything would be perfect.*

Arriving at the dock below the tramway station, Shane kept the girls close to him while searching the area for Christina.

"We're up here," she yelled down to them from the upper platform near the loading queue. "You don't need a ticket. We've rented the whole thing for an hour. Just come on up!"

Ahh! The perks of being with a mega company! It felt like owning the world, or at least a decent part of it. He looked out over the calm waters and saw Aurora's boat gliding across the lake in the distance, reminding him of how close he was to living a life he once only imagined in his dreams. "We'll be right up."

They ascended the staircase, and when they came to the upper landing, the girls hugged their mother before proud-ly taking out and showing off their latest treasures.

"Shane told us we get to buy accessories next," Joanna said, putting her dress back in its bag.

"He did?" Christina feigned surprise. "I'm so glad you're having fun together. Did you know you get to ride with him around the lake?"

A look of mild disappointment arose on both of the girls' faces.

"I thought we were all having such a good time," Shane teased. He knew that they really liked him, and that their dismay rested with the fact that their mother kept being pulled away from them.

"Don't worry." Christina rubbed the top of Leena's head. "We'll all meet up afterwards for ice cream and more shopping. I have to ride with my boss for a press photo shoot."

"It's not just me you'll be riding with." Bill came up from behind Christina. "We'll be accompanied by a very special guest." He had Apollo standing next to him, but he didn't quite resemble the boy that Shane remembered. "Ms. Creek suggested to take him with us since she no longer wants to ride. He'll make for a perfect press photo!"

"Does he talk?" Leena asked, looking up at her mother and then back at the boy not quite an inch taller than her.

"Not yet." Bill rested his hand on Apollo's shoulder. "IVAN is a prototype, and we're still working on all the miraculous things he'll be able to do one day very soon."

"Can we get one of our own?" Leena's face lit up as she asked her mother. "I want a girl version when they're ready."

Shane didn't wish to burst her bubble, but he'd make sure that there'd be no mass production. Apollo didn't belong to Durango Electric anymore than Aurora did. *They weren't for sale. They'd never be.* "Come on, you two. Let's get in line for the tram. Your mother has some more *grown-up* business to take care of." He led them to a sign that read *SeaDragon Boarding*, and they walked between a set of snaking steel rails, approaching a continuous string of arriving and departing windowed gondolas, each one gleaming white with three red and black stripes around its sides. "Are you girls ready to fly?"

Leena rushed into the open doors of the tram compartment. "We're not really gonna fly, Shane. See? It's attached to a wire."

"So much for imagination!" Shane boarded alongside Joanna and took a seat on the bank-style row of benches that encircled the perimeter of the cabin. "We'll see how you feel about that wire when we're a hundred feet over the water." He immediately questioned his judgment regarding that last statement the moment he saw a frightened look appear across Leena's face.

"Don't worry," Joanna said, sitting next to her sister. "It's a ten minute ride. It'll be done and over with before you know it."

The doors shut, and the whimsical transporter whisked them up and out of the station over the gleaming cerulean expanse below. Everything inside smelled clean and new, like freshly cut evergreen branches mixed with a hint of grapefruit. It had to be the window cleaning fluid, and Shane wanted to know exactly what brand they used. The view through the windows looked so pristine, he could hardly believe that panes of glass existed between him and the surrounding miniature sea of aquamarine.

"Look at the floor!" Joanna said. "It's glass. You can see right through to the water. There's fish down there!"

"I'm not looking," said Leena with her eyes tightly closed. "I don't like this at all."

Shane felt bad, like he maybe had partially contributed to her unreasonable fear. "Then look beyond the lake to the mountains. There's a whole world out there. It's absolutely sensational."

"You can even see Mom's truck!" Joanna pointed out the window in the direction they'd just come from.

"We're about to round our first bend," Shane said, slightly nervous as to how Leena would react to the sudden disturbance. "Get ready. It's almost here."

The gondola rumbled a bit as the cable pulled them tightly around a tall beige tower sticking out of the lake's northern extremity, lowering them gently a few feet nearer to the water.

"I don't want to do that part again," Leena said, opening her eyes enough to get a sense of her new surroundings before tightly closing them again.

Shane didn't want to break the news to her, and he didn't have to. Someone else beat him to it.

"Too bad. Three more turns to make before we get back to the station." Joanna smiled proudly as if she'd already figured out how the whole dang thing worked. "I'll let you know when the next one comes so you don't start crying."

"Hey, now." Shane couldn't understand how sisters could be so cruel toward one another. "As long as you're with me, there's no reason to cry or be afraid about anything. I wouldn't have gotten on this thing if I didn't think it was safe." He felt his watch vibrate and looked down to see Christina's number flash across his wrist before answering it. "Hi, you're on speaker mode."

"Are you enjoying the view?" she asked. "Pretty spectacular, isn't it?"

"It's amazing," Joanna said. "I want to ride it again when we're done. Can I?"

"I don't like it, Mommy," Leena said with her eyes still closed. "When's it gonna be over?"

Christina laughed, but in a kind and motherly way. "I'm sorry, dear. We're getting ice cream next, I promise. I'm in the tram car three behind yours. I'll give you a big hug when we're all done."

Shane heard a loud snap, and the girls screamed.

"Oh my God!" Christina's voice blared through Shane's watch. "Is everything alright?"

"I'm not sure." Shane felt his own pulse racing. "We're still moving though, so that's a good sign."

Then he heard another snap identical to the first one. The girls screamed in unison again as the gondola swung about like a pendulum. Soon the ride came to an abrupt halt. Shane forced himself not to panic. He knew deep down that it would do him no good. And besides, the girls were already panicking enough. The last thing he needed was to contribute to the frenzy as their compartment began to settle.

"None of us are moving at all," Christina said in a confused tone of voice. "Is your cabin the one that's drooping like that?"

Shane wanted her to shut up. She wasn't saying anything to help the situation. Yes, her girls were scared to death. Yes, things looked really bad. Yes, things could easily turn a whole lot worse. But he had only one thing on his mind: getting out of that cabin alive. "I'm sorry, Christina. But I've got another call to make." He hung up the phone, and the girls began crying in unison. "I know you're scared. I'm scared too, but I need it quiet so I can talk to someone who can help."

Joanna quieted down right away. "Hush," she whispered, glaring at Leena who still continued to whimper. "Shane's gonna get us out of here."

He felt the pressure mounting on his shoulders. "Aurora, are you there?" he spoke into his watch while at the same time looking out over the lake for her boat.

You're in the one sagging, aren't you? Our boat is at the nearest cable tower. Sai and Shafeen are climbing it right now.

Shane steadied himself, carefully standing up while gripping the circular handlebar in the center of the cabin and moving toward the door. He peered out the window and saw Sai and Shafeen nearing the pinnacle of the tower. "I think help is on the way. Can you girls swim?"

"Is Aurora gonna save us?" Leena asked as she opened her eyes and looked into Shane's. *Apparently, she must have seen the ACV news broadcast of Aurora climbing Sky Roulette.*

"I'm a good swimmer," Joanna said. "I know the backstroke." She looked over at her sister. "Leena, you remember how to doggy paddle, right?"

"I don't know," she snivelled. "I just want to get down."

Shane tried to envision this all playing out in their favor. Truth be told, falling from more than eighty feet into bitter cold water with two girls who may or may not know how to swim seemed like *the worst* best-case scenario possible at the moment. But anything was better than remaining trapped inside a crashing death chamber. "Aurora is sending her friends to help us." He looked out at them as they traversed the cable toward their gondola like a highly-skilled circus act. "There they are right now."

They're going to need your help to pry open the doors.

He read the message, thankfully under the firm realization that he and Aurora were on the same page.

You must act quickly. Sai and Shafeen cannot get wet.

Shane's pulse quickened. Why hadn't Aurora been sent to do the death-defying tight-rope act from hell? Actually, he didn't want to question the whole plan. He felt glad they'd orchestrated it, and that he understood most of what needed to be accomplished in order to escape certain doom. He looked over at the frightened but now subdued girls who huddled next to one another. "Stay back a second. When these doors open, I need you to come over to me and get ready to jump. You got that?"

"I don't want to," Leena said.

"You've got to," Joanna said, staring at her with an intensity that intimidated even Shane. "Otherwise you'll drown."

It was true, of course—and he had to admit his appreciation for not having to be the one to say it. "Nobody is gonna drown if everybody just does as they're told."

"Who are they?" Joanna said, pointing at two figures all in black as they descended from the wire above the cabin and maneuvered themselves to the door.

"Nevermind them. They're here to help." He began pushing the doors from the inside as Sai and Shafeen worked from the outside.

Unfortunately, they didn't budge no matter how hard they pulled. Then Shane remembered seeing a lever outside the capsule near the bottom of the door. "Pull up on that thing next to your foot!" He shouted at Sai, who was practically standing on top of it.

"Here, I've got it," Shafeen said before she swung out her leg and kicked it with her steel-toed boot.

The doors opened easily as Shane pushed on them. "Get ready to jump. This thing won't hold much longer." He looked behind him, seeing Joanna coax Leena out of her seat. "That's it. You two go first. I'm going in right after you." He looked up at Sai and Shafeen who were now working their way back up toward the cable. "Thank you!" he shouted at them as they clung to the wire, swinging themselves monkey-style back to the tower.

"Is it gonna be cold?" Joanna asked with a look of distress, taking her little sister's hand.

"It'll be like bathwater," Shane said, not thinking they'd take him seriously.

"Plug your nose, Leena. Here we go. 1, 2, 3—"

Shane took a deep breath as he watched them take the plunge. *They had to make it. They'd made it this far.* He waited for the splash. *Here goes nothing.* He heard a horrible creaking sound from up above. *No bueno.* The cabin started rocking again. *Let's do this!*

His plummet seemed to last an eternity. And yet it concluded in under two seconds with an icy cold sting that knocked the wind out of him the moment he went under. Had he ever dove from a height of eighty-some feet? Not that he could remember. The highdive stood at thirty feet in his high school natatorium, tall enough to instill a bit of fear in most land-dwelling creatures. He remembered how diving from it sunk him almost to the bottom of a sixteen-foot deep pool. He wasn't prepared for the depths that a drop nearly triple that height would take him. *Swim toward the light.* He didn't know anything else at that moment of unbridled terror.

Upon reaching the surface, he opened his airways faster and wider than he knew humanly possible, flooding his lungs with the necessary oxygen to propel himself to safety. *Look for the blue boat.* He saw it straight ahead about seventy feet in front of him. Once there, he climbed up a small ladder that hung off the back of it. Too stunned to even shiver, Shane looked around the empty boat for a sign of what to do next. *The girls!*

He heard a splash on the side of the boat and peered over the edge. He saw Aurora in a hauntingly familiar scene. She darted beneath the water exactly as she had five months ago at the wave pool, carrying two bodies on either side of her. *Dear God, please let them be okay.* He knew they had to be. Things always worked out okay in the end. *Almost always.*

Aurora brought them behind the boat from where Shane had recently emerged. He took hold of Leena's cold forearms, hoisting her into the vessel. To his amazement, Joanna seemed fully conscious, able to pull herself up and over the back of the boat. Aurora followed immediately afterward.

"She needs CPR," Shane said, motioning to Joanna and Aurora to back away from Leena and give him some space. "She's gonna be okay." He'd never performed CPR on a real person. He'd gotten certified as part of a lifeguarding course he took when he was fifteen, one which he hadn't ever put to use. But some things never left him. Or if they did, they had a way of floating back up to the surface when absolutely necessary. Kneeling beside her shoulders, he positioned his hands over Leena's chest, one on top of the other before pressing down firmly about two inches, feeling her chest cavity give and then rise back up. He repeated the motion rapidly twenty times before placing his palm on her forehead and tilting her head back. He then lifted her chin ever so slightly and bent down to breathe some life into her airways. Feeling her chest rise, he exhaled into her one more time.

"Come on, Leena." Joanna shivered, wrapping a towel around herself. "Breathe. You're gonna be okay."

Water spilled from Leena's mouth as she began coughing violently.

"That's it, Leena!" Shane lurched backward to give her room. "Keep coughing. Just keep coughing. You're doing good." He looked up at Aurora. "We need to get her to a doctor now. Will you take us back to shore?" He felt his watch vibrate. He'd been subconsciously ignoring it for the past ten minutes since he ended the call with Christina. She must be dying of worry. He couldn't imagine her horror after she saw her own flesh and blood descending into an icy abyss. Should he call her now in the midst of an emergency? Part of him said to wait until after they'd found a doctor. Coming to a compromise, he decided to at least read her text first.

I saw everything. I need you to call me right now.

He took a breath to calm himself before responding to Christina's message. *We're getting things under control. I'll call you in a minute.* He felt his watch vibrate again not even three seconds after sending his response. He should have known she couldn't wait another millisecond.

"Are they breathing?" She seemed unexpectedly calm as she asked the question.

"Joanna is fine." He questioned how that sounded in his own head. "Leena's fine, too. She's breathing now. We're heading to shore to get her to a doctor as quick as we can."

"Is she conscious?"

"Yes. Yes, she's absolutely conscious." He heard the phone click. *What was that all about? Did she not want a detailed explanation about her daughter's health?* His mind reeled with possible explanations for the dropped call, none of which made him feel any better.

His watch vibrated again with a follow-up text from Christina.

Turn the boat around and get away from here. Bill saw Aurora. He's contacted the authorities. He'll steal her again.

Shane sat stunned for a second. If a mother felt it necessary to delay medical attention for her own child, she had to have a very good reason. He didn't have the heart to further question her. "Change of plans, everyone. The doctor can wait. They want you, Aurora. We're not going to let them have you. Turn this boat around!"

Aurora looked at him like he'd suddenly gone mad. "Doesn't she need a doctor? Isn't that most important?"

"Are you okay, Leena?" Shane knelt to get closer to the disoriented little girl.

"I want my mom." She sat upright, leaning against one of the boat's seat cushions.

"Can you breathe alright?" He realized his questions didn't exactly replace a doctor's expertise, but she seemed okay for now. Perhaps a small detour on the way to urgent care wouldn't impede her full recovery.

"I'm really—" She struggled to speak, expelling a bit more water.

"That's it, Leena. I need you to keep coughing. We need all that water to come out of there."

"I'm really cold." She looked frozen to the bone, but a sense of awareness had at least appeared in her eyes.

"I'm turning on the heat," Aurora said from behind the boat's command post, ushering in a blanket of warm air all around them.

"We'll get you to a doctor soon. Just hold on." Shane knew he was toeing the line. But if Leena's own legal guardian had given him the orders not to go ashore yet, who was he to override a mother's natural instincts?

"If she'll allow me," Aurora said, "I can tell if there's any water remaining in her lungs."

"Is that okay, Leena?" Shane waited for her to nod before stepping away so that Aurora could get closer to her.

She knelt beside her and placed her hand on Leena's diaphragm. "Breathe deeply as you can for me and then exhale slowly."

Leena took a breath and released it in a long, steady stream.

"She's fine." Aurora looked up at Shane before returning to her place at the control panel. "Any trace of moisture left she can easily cough out. If it's okay with everyone, I'll take you all back to the grotto."

Joanna's face lit up. "What's a grotto?"

"I was thinking the exact same thing." Shane took a seat near to where Aurora stood.

"It's where we dock the boats." Aurora put on her sunglasses, taking off her hat and letting her long ruby curls flutter behind her. At that moment, she looked like a veritable grown woman trapped in a tiny body.

"What about your friends?" Shane had to shout over the deafening wind.

"We're getting them now." Aurora commanded the boat to head toward the giant tram tower straight ahead where Shafeen and Sai both waited.

"The gondolas still aren't moving," Sai said pulling himself up and away from the tower's concrete base and into the boat.

"I think it's going to be awhile," Shafeen said, hopping aboard the craft in a similar manner. "Look over there." She pointed across the lake to a group of large red and white boats. "They're bringing in the fire rescue team." She turned to face Leena. "How's Little Miss SCUBA diver over there?"

"She's a lot better than she was five minutes ago," Shane said as the boat sped off again, heading for the lake's southeastern shoreline, as far away from the tram as possible.

A few minutes later, the boat slowed as they came upon a

sheer cliff wall that formed a small cove at the water's edge. It looked like a dead end.

"What do we do now?" Joanna stood up from her seat next to her sister. "There's nowhere to go."

"Or so you think," Shafeen said, tossing her long wind-blown hair behind her. "We like to keep a low profile."

Aurora manually steered the boat to the left side of the cove and behind a rock that suddenly appeared to separate from the wall. "It's an illusion, and it hides the entrance to the cave perfectly." She pressed a silver button in her control panel, which opened a large mechanical door in the rock face.

"That's so cool!" Joanna nudged Leena. "We're going in!"

As the boat pulled into the grotto, Shane removed his sunglasses and looked all around at the enchanting hideaway. The walls shimmered as if covered in rhinestones, and the water glowed electric blue. "Now *this* has to be the most gorgeous place I've ever seen."

"Where are we?" Joanna said, glancing every which way around her as well.

"The Gloaming." Aurora brought the boat to a complete halt. "This is my home."

Shane's heart nearly broke when he heard her say those words—they had so much permanence behind them. However, he recognized their truth. She was a hundred times safer here than anywhere else in the entire valley.

"Can we spend the night with you?" Leena stood up to everyone's amazement.

"How about we stay for a little bit?" Shane suggested.

"And then afterward, we'll meet your mom for ice cream?" Admittedly, he didn't quite have the logistics figured out, seeing how one of the people in the equation likely still dangled precariously over the water. "Come to think of it, I better call your mother right now and ask her how she's holding up."

When his eyes fully adjusted to the low light of his surroundings, he tapped his watch to call Christina. She didn't pick up, which got him a little worried. Then his watch vibrated with a text from her.

They're coming for us with boats and ladders.

We saw. Shane figured that's what the red and white boats they'd just seen had come for. *We're hiding in a cave.*

I may need to jump. I'll let you know.

Jump? Shane knew something was off. He wished she'd pick up so he could talk to her. Then it dawned on him that she most likely needed to hide their conversation from Bill.

Apollo's not the same. I can see it in his eyes. He doesn't even recognize me.

"She's with Apollo in the gondola," Shane said to Aurora. "She says that there's something wrong with him. He doesn't know who she is."

"She needs to leave." Aurora started the boat up again. "Tell her to get out of there."

"Where could she possibly go?" Shane felt his frustration rising. "Are we going back to get her out?"

"She has to jump," Sai said. "There's a hatch at the top of the cabin. We saw it. We'd have opened yours, but it can only be opened from the inside."

"I'll tell her." He went to his watch to send the urgent text.

Aurora says you need to get out of there quickly. There's a hatch in the cabin's ceiling.

Christina responded a few seconds later. *I see it. There are life jackets under our seats. I'm getting out of here.*

Shane panicked. He hated the thought of Christina having to jump in the frigid water like they'd done. He didn't understand the fuss. Why couldn't she just wait for the rescue team? And if she did jump, who's to say the rescue boats would even see her fall into the water? The variables seemed too great. He certainly didn't want to risk Aurora's entrapment, but he hated not being present for Christina. "We've got to head back there. She's gonna jump just like you said. We need to be there when she does." He felt another text coming through from Christina.

I was wrong about all of this. Bill is freaking out. He doesn't want me to leave him.

Don't worry about him. You need to get out of there. We're coming for you. We'll be there soon. Shane felt himself leaving a hypnotic dream and entering back into a hellish circus.

Apollo's on the roof of the cabin now. He's gonna crash our gondola into the water. The whole thing was a setup.

Shane didn't want her to panic. That wasn't like her. She'd always stayed level-headed while *he* went off the deep end. She had a gift for keeping herself together during the ugliest of circumstances. She couldn't fail at this now.

In a flash, he sent her another text. *Join him on the roof.*

I'm trying. But he's got his foot on the hatch.

"Apollo's blocking the hatch," Shane said to Aurora as she backed the boat out of the grotto, returning to open water.

"Not to worry." Shafeen sounded like she knew a secret. "He can't keep his foot on the hatch and at the same time unscrew the bolts holding the gondola to the cable."

So that was it! Black Diamond put Apollo there to kill Christina. Shane couldn't stop himself from envisioning the nightmare come to life. His stomach knotted as the urge to vomit rose steadily. He had to pull himself together this time. Not just for Christina, but for her girls.

He tried to call her one last time. Even if she couldn't respond to a word he said, she had to at least hear him out. He felt his insides unwind a bit the moment he heard her accept the call. "Christina, just listen. You don't have to speak. We'll be there in a couple of minutes. If Apollo is attempting to sabotage your gondola, he'll have to get off the hatch in order to reach the bolts. When he does, you must act quickly. He can have them all undone in a matter of seconds. Take off your life jacket. It'll only get in the way. When you get to the roof, you must jump immediately. We'll be there to get you out of the water." He heard the click on the other line, crossing his fingers that she'd take to heart everything he'd just told her.

Sai stood up from his seat with a quizzical look on his face as the boat neared the aerial tramway. "Why is she wearing a life jacket?"

"Because she's scared. Can you blame her?" Shane focused his attention in front of him as the boat approached the stalled tramway. He didn't need to justify someone else's actions right now. He needed to use every last bit of his concentration to ensure she'd survive.

"I see my mom!" Joanna said, standing up and pointing at a distant gondola. "That's her, isn't it? She's standing on top of it with that boy."

"That's Apollo!" Aurora said. "He's about to drop their cabin into the water."

"She's fighting with him," Sai said. "I can see the two of them. She needs to leave him alone."

"She's trying to push him off." Shafeen stood and leaned over the boat. "She thinks she can knock him off. She can't. He'll knock her off first."

"And she's still wearing that stupid life jacket," said Sai.

Shane figured some of his instructions would inevitably get lost in translation. That, or she just didn't trust him as much as he'd have liked her to. "Take off your life jacket and jump," Shane yelled from the boat as loudly as he could. "Don't mess with Apollo. He could hurt you!"

He watched her leap from the top of the cabin with all the bravery of a hardened warrior—except for the damn life jacket. Why couldn't she understand that it was in her best interest to take off the useless device before jumping? And why were those things in the gondola to begin with? "There she is!" He pointed to an orange speck floating in the water as Aurora set the boat in motion.

"She might be badly hurt after that fall." Aurora stopped the boat twenty feet in front of Christina's motionless body. "I don't want to risk hurting her more by dragging her into the boat."

"Are you breathing?" Sai yelled out over the water.

No response.

"Get her in the boat!" Shane couldn't stand watching his yoga buddy bobbing in the water with the lifelessness of a buoy.

Aurora dove into the lake again, swimming to Christina like a torpedo. "I can hear her breathing," she yelled back toward the boat. "I'm not going to move her. We need the medics to do that. I can't."

Shane looked up and saw the gondola above begin to sway. Apollo was no longer anywhere in sight. "Get her out of the way before it's too late!"

She gently nudged Christina, pushing her a few feet closer to the boat. Then she repeated the action twice more.

"It's gonna fall!" Shafeen pointed to the swinging cabin moments before it came splashing into the lake right where Christina had floated just moments ago.

"They're coming now. The rescue boats," Shane yelled to Aurora. "Leave her alone. They'll get her. We need to get you out of here."

***

Shane opened the door to Christina's hospital room, allowing Leena and Joanna to walk in ahead of him. "Don't say anything if she's still sleeping."

Upon entering, he noticed the TV on mute. A news bulletin stole his attention. *Disaster at Sapphire Springs. Durango Electric CEO Bill Rucker dead. At least three others injured.* He turned it off. Too many other things weighed on his mind—mainly Aurora's future as well as his own.

"I'm awake." Christina opened her eyes, sounding groggy but coherent. "Come here, my lovelies."

"Momma, we lost the dresses." Leena began to cry. "I don't know what we're gonna do."

"Shhhh." Joanna put her finger to her lips and walked closer to her mother's bed. "She doesn't care about the dresses, Leena. Don't bother her with stuff that doesn't matter right now."

"It's okay, Leena." Christina tried to turn her head but stopped due to the thick brace around her neck. "Shane will take you back to the store for some new ones."

He smiled. "You know I will. I already told you girls that I would."

Leena smiled back at him. "Just like the ones we found before? And ice cream? You promised we'd get ice cream."

"Don't be so pushy, Leena." Joanna gritted her teeth, flashing her sister a stern look. "You don't want to wear out our welcome, do you?"

"I'm happy to get us all some ice cream." He glanced at Christina, biting his tongue to prevent making a glib comment about the life jacket. "Could I perhaps get you some ice cream as well?"

"Maybe later," Christina said, her eyes slowly shutting again. "Just look after my babies for me."

"Of course, I will." He wiped his eyes before anyone could see the tears. Never in his life had he felt such overwhelming bittersweetness. "I told you I'd keep them safe for you. I'd never break that promise."